THE CHRISTMAS LOVE LETTERS

Sue Moorcroft writes award-winning contemporary fiction of life and love. *A Summer to Remember* won the Goldsboro Books Contemporary Romantic Novel award, *The Little Village Christmas* and *A Christmas Gift* were *Sunday Times* bestsellers and *The Christmas Promise* went to #1 in the Kindle chart. She also writes short stories, serials, articles, columns, courses and writing 'how to'. She is the current president of the Romantic Novelist's Association.

An army child, Sue was born in Germany then lived in Cyprus, Malta and the UK and still loves to travel. Her other loves include writing (the best job in the world), reading, watching Formula 1 on TV, hanging out with friends, dancing, yoga, wine and chocolate.

If you're interested in being part of #TeamSueMoorcroft you can find more information at www.suemoorcroft. com by clicking on 'Street Team'. If you prefer to sign up to receive news of Sue and her books, go to www. suemoorcroft.com and click on 'Newsletter'. You can follow @SueMoorcroft on Twitter, @suemoorcroftauthor on Instagram, or Facebook.com/sue.moorcroft.3 and Facebook.com/SueMoorcroftAuthor.

Also by Sue Moorcroft:

The Christmas Promise
Just For the Holidays
The Little Village Christmas
One Summer in Italy
A Christmas Gift
A Summer to Remember
Let it Snow
Summer on a Sunny Island
Christmas Wishes
Under the Italian Sun
A Home in the Sun
Under the Mistletoe
Summer at the French Café
A White Christmas on Winter Street
An Italian Island Summer

Sue Moorcroft

The Christmas Love Letters

Published by AVON
A division of HarperCollins*Publishers* Ltd
1 London Bridge Street
London SE1 9GF

www.harpercollins.co.uk

HarperCollins*Publishers*
Macken House, 39/40 Mayor Street Upper,
Dublin 1, D01 C9W8
Ireland

A Paperback Original 2023
1
First published in Great Britain by HarperCollins*Publishers* 2023

A catalogue copy of this book is available from the British Library.

ISBN: 978-0-00-863676-0

Typeset in Sabon LT Std by
Palimpsest Book Production Limited, Falkirk, Stirlingshire

Printed and bound in UK using 100% Renewable Electricity
at CPI Group (UK) Ltd

This book is produced from independently certified FSC™ paper
to ensure responsible forest management.

For more information visit: www.harpercollins.co.uk/green

Acknowledgements

The Christmas Love Letters would not have come into being without Anne Millen, who passed a batch of real love letters into my hands at Swanwick Writers' Summer School. Those hand-written letters tell the story of a real love and long-kept secrets, which inspired this book and created much of the backstory. I changed names – though I kept many of the locations – but I hope I've captured something of the spirit of that decades-long affair, without sugar-coating. I so enjoyed filling in blanks via my imagination.

Thanks also to:

Lucy Moorcroft and Angie Torley for help on private dialling and burner phones, and Lucy for introducing me to DS Adi Sharpe from Northamptonshire Police's Missing Persons. Adi provided untold help in constructing Adey Austen's disappearance. Any inaccuracies are mine and not his. I still feel guilty that we both earned parking fines because I kept him talking too long. That my character and he are both named Adrian and known by such similar short forms was a touch embarrassing, but Adi wasn't offended.

Paul Matthews for advice on the teaching profession – and leaving it.

Trevor Moorcroft for continuing to undertake much of my research, finding me the right material to read or watch, and generally saving me a lot of time.

Ashley Panter for adding another pair of eyes to the proof reading.

Daniela Teale for talking through a plot point with me when I got stuck.

Nurses David and Julia Roberts for helping with the facts around Adey's broken lower leg. I consult David and Julia on the injuries and ailments of all my characters and they're always generous with their time and knowledge.

Mark West, for the work-in-progress chats at the Trading Post, and for being my long-time beta reader, despite his commitments to his family, his writing career and his day job.

Pia Fenton/Christina Courtenay and Myra Kersner/Maggie Sullivan for the Sunday-evening WhatsApp calls and their unfailing authorly support, for asking, 'How's the writing going?' and actually wanting to know.

Team Sue Moorcroft for not only sharing my posts and spreading the word about my books but contributing character and place names on request. You are the best!

Book bloggers, reviewers and all my social media friends for unending support.

Juliet Pickering, my amazing agent, who's such a joy to work with, as is true of all the fabulous team at Blake Friedmann Literary Agency.

Helen Huthwaite and the fantastic Avon team for publishing my books with enthusiasm and skill, and always being friendly and approachable. This is my fifteenth book with Avon, a situation I once could only have dreamed of.

My publishers around the world. It's a joy for me to reach readers in so many languages.

And, most of all, my wonderful readers. Thanks for reading my books, writing positive reviews and sending me charming messages. You make it possible for me to have the best job in the world. I hope you enjoy *The Christmas Love Letters*.

For writers of love letters.
You leave something of yourself on every page.

Prologue

My dearest, darling Ruthie,

I'm hoping you receive this by 22nd Dec. before your Xmas visit to your sis and family in Nelson's Bar. They sound like good sorts (<u>but</u> could <u>never</u> love you as much as I do). Perhaps your family might sense you need a break before returning to work in Jan. and will take care of you. (Are you <u>sure</u> you should go back that soon??)

I enclose card and present, but it's <u>nothing</u> in comparison to what you've given me. I want you to know that that beautiful, special, wonderful gift is happy and much, much loved.

Are you recovering, darling? I can't bear it that while I was on Remembrance Day parade you were alone in hospital! You say you've come to terms with things but part of me knows I should've stayed away from the wonderful civvy female who came to work 'under me' (ho ho ho)

1

at the barracks. The other part is thankful that you've transformed my life.

I wish we could be together!! I miss you all the time.

I hope we can find a way to meet in the New Year so I can see for myself how you are.

I love you, Ruthie. God bless you and keep you safe.

All my love, Nigel xxxxxxxxxxxxxxxxxxxx

My dearest, darling Nigel,

'It's a Heartache', Bonnie Tyler sings to me, whenever I switch on the radio. She's right.

I know your 'gift' is in the best of hands and will get a better life than I could have given her. Knowing she's well and happy is the only way I can cope with the loss.

I love you and miss you.

Yours always, with love from a frosty, snowy Nelson's Bar,

Ruthie xxxxx

Chapter One

The present day

As the early November wind blew Maddy Cracey along the cliff path from High Cottage that Friday morning it was hard for her not to think of her fair-haired, grey-eyed husband, with his naughty grin and capricious ways. Eyes drawn to the tossing sea, for the millionth time she sent out her thoughts to him: *Adey, where are you? What happened that night?* Adey Austen had done a vanishing act one snowy December night nearly seven years ago, and since then, Maddy's life had been defined by a secret and a lie.

The secret? Maddy hadn't told Adey she was pregnant. Pulling up her collar against the chill, she ticked the reasons off in her mind. He'd been thrown for a loop by their financial mess. The pregnancy wasn't planned and, the last time she'd raised the subject he'd declared himself unready for kids. And maybe it had been pregnancy hormones making her distrustful, but a suspicion that he might have suggested abortion had nagged at her. Now that Lyla was a laughing, lively six-year-old and the centre of Maddy's world, she felt guilty for ever having thought that of him. But she did wonder if he'd somehow sensed the new responsibility looming.

The lie, she thought, as she turned off the cliff path towards home, might more accurately be called 'other people's expectations'. The village had thought her frozen with fear at her husband's disappearance. In fact, as she'd stood watching police dogs comb the cliff path while a helicopter quartered the wintry sea, Maddy had been furious.

Fun and feckless Adey, harm himself? She didn't believe it.

Blowing off the cliff in a blizzard when Adey had known the dangers of the cliff path all his life? Possible, but not probable.

Adey leaving Maddy to face their debts and disaster alone . . . ? Yes. *That* felt right. They'd been together since senior school and only one of them had ever grown up – Maddy.

But her heart softened as she remembered their happy times. The parties they'd thrown only to slow dance with each other all night. The holidays in Spain or Greece when they'd read on the beach or splashed in the sea. Adey, the child of miserly parents, had rebelled against his upbringing by actively enjoying spending money on fun, and – to be fair – on Maddy, showering her with jewellery and nice clothes.

Had she been responsible for the transformation from loving husband to trapped man? It had been her idea to buy run-down High Cottage, led by her vision of their happy, jolly life together continuing, but with a great view over the sea. But High Cottage had proved a money pit.

Adey had wanted to sell. Maddy had thought they just needed to work hard and economise. That had been the turning point, when every discussion turned into an argument and Maddy refused to let Adey cuddle her into changing her views. Adey had said it felt like being a kid again, when all his suggestions regarding anything non-essential had been met with a flat 'no'.

Since Adey had gone missing, Maddy had not only made High Cottage habitable but herself solvent by renting it out while she and Lyla lived with Maddy's sight-impaired great-aunt Ruthie. Ruthie had always shown Maddy the love that Maddy's mum Linda seemed incapable of, and now Maddy cared for Ruthie along with Lyla.

Nelson's Bar, high on a headland that seemed to have erupted from the salt marshes and into the pounding surf, was first to greet the freezing ocean air that blasted in from the North Sea. A fresh gust of wind shoved Maddy, and she staggered, sending a loud, 'Hey!' back at the buffeting wind.

'First sign of madness, cackling to yourself,' returned a male voice, Norfolk rolling through every vowel. 'Eh, Mad Crazy?'

Maddy held back her wind-ravaged hair to glare at the owner of the voice – Harris Soley, lifelong friend of Adey, lifelong thorn in Maddy's side. 'Don't call me that.'

He only laughed, his unkempt hair standing straight above his head.

Bloody Harris. As well as having been Adey's best mate, last year he'd dumped Maddy's best friend Heloise, after being an item for a few months. Maddy's hackles rose every time she saw him, and she saw him a lot, as they both lived in the same dot on the Norfolk map.

In turning her back on Harris, she turned her back on the sea, marching along the final few yards of Marshview Road before turning in to Droody Road at the gabled stone building that was the Duke of Bronte pub then left into Jubilee Crescent. There, cottages peeped over box hedging while frozen and ragged leaves carpeted the pavement, and Maddy saw a much more welcome villager heading in her direction. She called out, 'Hi, Della.' Ruthie's friend Della was nearly always willing to visit Ruthie when Maddy needed to go out for more than a short period.

Della beamed, huddling into a green cocoon of a coat, iron grey hair blowing. 'We'll get another bad winter, I reckon. Coldest spot in Norfolk, Nelson's Bar, so high and exposed.'

Maddy shivered as the freezing wind blew down her neck. 'Our weather is a bit crazy.'

'I'm off home for hot coffee,' Della declared, and Maddy continued towards her own well-loved home. Red brick with aged diamond-pane windows, The Hollies sat back in a garden that was something else Maddy looked after. Passing under the canopy porch, she stepped gladly into the flagstone hall beneath beamed ceilings. 'I'm back, Ruthie. There wasn't much wrong with the tumble dryer at High Cottage. The tenants Garth and Leanna had managed to get a zip caught. I yanked it out with pliers.' After pulling off her coat, she removed her big butterfly hair clasp to smooth her long, brown hair after its encounter with the wind, rewound it and then crammed the clasp back on. Not getting haircuts had begun as an economy but now she liked her thick mane. She spent so much time in practical jeans and warm jumpers that switching around between buns, plaits and twists provided an ornamental touch.

The door to the front room stood ajar and she strode through it, her mind already on filling the woodstove and making hot drinks. 'I met that shitbag Harris—' She halted. A dark, stubbled man had risen politely from an armchair. 'Hello?' she said questioningly, her gaze flying to where Ruthie sat, thick glasses winking in the light from the lamp. Grey hair curled around her face and the years had softened her short body so that it was hard to tell which folds were her favourite oversized cardigans and which were Ruthie. Apart from vision troubles, she wore her eighty years lightly.

'This is Rafferty,' Ruthie said stiffly, and without her usual smile. 'He says I worked with his father.'

Ruthie sounded so odd that Maddy crossed the room to take her hands. 'Do you know him? Was it a good idea to let him in? You could have told Alexa to ring me; I would have come straight back.' She turned to frown at the man, whose own brow was creased in concern. 'As you've probably gathered, Ruthie's sight-impaired. I'm Maddy, her niece and carer.' She didn't always bother to add the 'great' to their relationship.

The man cleared his throat. 'I'm not here to cause anxiety, but I'd love to talk to Ms Willson. I'm trying to trace someone. It's quite important to my family.'

Maddy studied him and his blue eyes – more striking than her own boring mouse brown – met her gaze steadily. She turned to Ruthie. Was it Maddy's imagination, or did she look pale? 'Could you have known his father?'

Ruthie gave an odd laugh. 'I don't know yet, do I? He hasn't had time to tell me much about him except he was in the army. I knew lots of army personnel.' Ruthie touched trembling fingers to her forehead. 'I think I'd better hear what he's here for, dear.'

Maddy's protective instincts noted the tremor, but the mention of the army was reassuring. Ruthie had been a civilian with the Ministry of Defence in a role that had required her to sign the Official Secrets Act. Originally attached to the Aldershot Garrison in Hampshire, she'd eventually returned to Nelson's Bar and passed her final working years providing support services to the MOD in Norfolk. Maddy had been nine when Ruthie had come home. Grandpa Herbert had just died and Grandma Elsie, Ruthie's sister, had been adrift and Ruthie was a rock to cling to. Maddy had clung to her herself.

She bit her lip, juggling responsibilities. Ruthie was capable mentally, but her failing sight made her vulnerable. 'I have to go up to The Green to meet the school minibus soon. Shall I ask Mr Rafferty to come back another time?'

'It's Raff,' he put in. 'I have my driving licence if you want ID. I was a deputy head teacher at Martingdale Road Academy in Northamptonshire until the end of the summer term so I'm pretty respectable.'

Maddy swivelled her head to study him more thoroughly. He didn't *look* that respectable. His tatty jeans were a similar grey to his thick hoodie, his dark hair needed cutting and his stubble needed the attention of a beard trimmer. 'You're a teacher?' she asked, thinking that, if so, teachers weren't so clean cut as when she'd been a student.

'Was. Now I'm a self-employed writer.' His gaze became rueful as it fell on Ruthie. 'I shouldn't have just turned up. Sorry. I moved to Norfolk a few months ago and as I'm still familiarising myself with the area, I was driving nearby. I thought I'd call in, but I should have written first.'

'It's OK, dear.' Ruthie fumbled with a box of tissues

on the table beside her, then blew her nose. Everything she might want was on that table, which Maddy had painted white so whatever rested on it stood out. Voice-responsive TV remote and phone – both also having big buttons. Tissues. Murray mints. Water. Inhalers. A magnifier with its own light. An Alexa that would play her audiobooks or music – and, now Maddy had worked out the app, operate her phone.

Maddy lowered her defences. 'If you want to chat, Ruthie, I'll ask Heloise to pick Lyla up.' She stepped out into the kitchen, filling the kettle one-handed, her phone to her ear. Until a year ago, there had been neither mobile signal nor broadband in the village, but a campaign had resulted in the acquisition of both for Nelson's Bar and other nearby rural 'not spots'.

'Hey,' she said, when she heard her friend's voice. 'Any chance you can get Lyla for me when you meet Jude and Blake from the bus? Someone's come to talk to Ruthie, and I could use a child-free hour . . . Oh, thanks, that's brilliant.' Heloise had no children of her own, but now utilised her nursery nurse training as a childminder. For variety, she pet-sat, too, or spruced up vintage clothing in which to dress her tall frame. Having inherited from her parents, including a cottage in Traders Place, Heloise's work-life balance was firmly in favour of 'life'.

Maddy took orders for hot drinks, made them and carried them in, putting a mug on her aunt's table first. 'Your tea's on the table, Ruthie.' She turned to Raff. 'And here's your coffee. So,' she said, when she'd taken the remaining mug and seated herself on the sofa. 'What makes you think Ruthie might know your dad?'

Under the weight of two pairs of eyes, he propped his elbows on his knees, and fixed an intent gaze on Ruthie.

'I believe you worked together in Keogh Barracks when Dad was a sergeant in the RAOC.'

'What's RAOC?' Maddy's tongue stumbled over the unfamiliar abbreviation.

'Royal Army Ordnance Corps,' Ruthie answered absently. Her gaze was fixed on Raff, though Maddy knew most of her central sight was a blur. Then, in a tiny, squeaky voice, she blurted out, 'Nigel died in 2000, didn't he?'

'Nigel?' Maddy queried, puzzled by the sudden change in direction.

But Raff ignored Maddy and answered Ruthie. 'I'm afraid so. You knew?'

Ruthie nodded. 'We'd stopped writing by then, because we had mobile phones. His calls . . . just stopped.' And she burst into tears.

Shocked, Maddy scrambled up to dump her mug on the floor and kneel beside her aunt's chair. 'Who's Nigel?' She shot a glare at Raff, who was looking surprised at Ruthie's tears . . . but not exactly shocked.

Ruthie cried harder. Then her breathing hitched. She gulped and coughed, a cough that was punctuated by a wheeze. Her hand lifted to her chest.

Alarmed, but familiar with these attacks, Maddy reached for the inhaler and pressed the red device into her aunt's hand. 'Here's your puffer.' She watched Ruthie take it, then close her eyes and sink back in the chair as her breathing strained.

Maddy, watching intently to ensure that things were getting no worse, said, crisply, 'Ruthie has asthma.'

He sounded dismayed. 'I'm sorry.'

Then Maddy felt guilty, because Ruthie's asthma wasn't his fault, and he hadn't been rude or insensitive. Before she could say so, Ruthie gave a combined sigh and whimper. 'What happened?'

Raff answered sombrely. 'It was a heart attack.'

Ruthie's fingers curled and uncurled, a fresh tear tracking down her face. 'Cigarettes and chips,' she murmured. 'I used to tell him it was unhealthy, but it was how many people lived.' She reached out a fumbling hand for tissues to blow her nose in.

'I'm afraid so,' Raff agreed ruefully.

Ruthie sniffed. 'So. You're Rafferty Edmonds?'

'I am.' His gaze held concern, but also fascination.

Maddy glanced across at Raff, troubled, but concentrating her practical mind on priorities and ignoring the questions that were flying about her astonished brain. 'I think Ruthie should rest now.'

But Ruthie ignored her. 'How did you know about me?' she whispered. Then she began to cough, a series of staccato barks with short pauses to crow for air, wheeze, and cough again.

Evidently, Ruthie wasn't going to stop talking while Raff was there. Taking matters into her own hands, Maddy snatched her phone from her pocket, opened a new contact and thrust the handset at him. 'Please put your number in so I can contact you another time. I don't want to have to get her on her nebuliser.'

Raff did as he was asked before passing back the phone. 'I'm sorry that my turning up has caused this upset,' he said quietly to Ruthie, as he rose. 'I had rehearsed how I was going to tell my story, but . . . well, you guessed so much.'

Maddy's priority was to ease Ruthie past her asthma attack, so she readily accepted the regrets on her aunt's behalf. 'Of course,' she said. Then seeing that Ruthie was regarding Raff with the same kind of fascination with which he'd been watching her, she added, 'She'll be all right after a rest from talking.'

Without removing his gaze from Ruthie, Raff began to move towards the door. 'Get well soon,' he said with a smile. A brief nod to Maddy, then he crossed the hall, opened the front door and was gone.

Despite huge curiosity about the until now unknown Nigel, it was Ruthie's story to tell or not, and Maddy kept her attention on Ruthie's wellbeing. 'How about lying on your bed for a bit?'

Wearily, Ruthie nodded. 'OK.' She heaved her short frame upright, pausing as if getting her bearings, then made for the downstairs bedroom with shower room that had once been the dining room. With Maddy hovering to check whether she needed help, she sank onto the bed, then rolled onto her back, closed her eyes and tilted her face away.

Softly, Maddy fetched the tissues to slip onto the bedside table. She had a feeling her aunt might need them. Then she returned to the front room and, although she rarely sat and did nothing during the day, sank down onto a comfy red armchair and gazed absently around at the familiar mirror over the mantel, the well-worn rug and the basket of Lyla's toys – a hazard for Ruthie if left strewn about the floor. Beside the basket, three books and a plush blue pony sat on the top of a princess castle they'd made from cardboard boxes at half term.

But now Maddy's mind was far from turrets and crenellations. How could she not have known about a man called Nigel who had been in her aunt's life right up until the year 2000? She calculated quickly. Maddy would have been sixteen, which was about the time her mum began talking about leaving for Spain with a boyfriend when Maddy reached eighteen. She knew she'd leant on Ruthie, who'd even helped in a tentative attempt to develop a relationship with Derek Cracey, the father who'd left when Maddy was a baby – though he'd proved good for no more than occasional emails.

And throughout all that, Ruthie had been grieving? Maddy shouldn't have been too wrapped up in her own life to notice something as big as that.

Outside, one of the holly bushes that gave the house its name had dressed in scarlet berries and was tapping at the window as if to draw attention to its finery. In a few weeks, Maddy and Lyla would make a Christmas wreath from the whippiest twigs and Ruthie, a past member of the village crafting group, was bound to keep them company at the kitchen table as they worked.

Ruthie was always there for them.

Unsettled, Maddy rose to gather the tea and coffee mugs and dump them beside the kitchen sink before calling Heloise. 'Is there any chance you could drop Lyla off?' she asked. 'Ruthie's had an asthma attack, and I don't want to leave her alone.' Luckily, they had the kind of friendship that went back to childhood and involved the easy asking of favours.

'No sweat,' Heloise replied cheerfully. 'The boys' dad has just fetched them home, so I'll have Lyla back with you in ten.'

Maddy's heart lifted at the prospect of seeing her bright, chatty little daughter, and had hardly begun thinking about supper when Heloise and Lyla bundled through the door, the latter ditching her school bag on the hall floor. Maddy held her arms wide. 'Hello, gorgeous! Did you have a good time with Heloise, Jude and Blake?'

Lyla flung her arms around Maddy's neck. 'Yes, but tomorrow Miss Edge is going to tell my class our parts in the Christmas play. I want to be an angel, but she said not to be disappointed if I'm not. That means I'm not, right?'

Maddy hugged the tiny, hot body, uncaring that it involved a face full of fair hair that smelled of biscuits and orange juice. 'Poor Miss Edge has to find parts for everyone.' She grinned at Heloise over Lyla's shoulder. 'Coffee?'

Heloise was finger-combing order into her bob cut over her pleasant, pretty face. Her parka was covered with embroidery and so were the jeans showing beneath. 'Always.'

Maddy extricated herself from Lyla's embrace, retrieved her lunchbox and book bag from the floor and hung up her coat. 'That means Lyla gets TV for half an hour,' she said, winking at her daughter.

'Yay,' Lyla called happily, making aeroplane arms as she raced for the sofa. 'Where's Grauntie Ruthie?'

'Lying down. She got a bit out of puff.' Maddy hoped that by the time Ruthie emerged, she would be recovered.

Heloise followed Maddy into the kitchen. 'Has Ruthie been letting someone's cat sit on her lap again?'

Maddy rolled her eyes at this reminder of a past trigger to Ruthie's respiratory issues. 'No. This guy turned up, interested in his family history. His dad's dead and Ruthie once worked with him. It might have been better if he'd contacted her first to make an appointment.' Not a lie, but Maddy suspected she hadn't heard the whole truth yet, and that Ruthie might not wish details leaking out into the tiny, gossipy community of Nelson's Bar. Immediately realising that there was little in the picture she'd painted to prompt Ruthie's asthma attack, she blushed.

But Heloise had obviously missed the weakness in the explanation, as a sly grin split her face. 'Was the guy hot, by any chance? You've gone all pink.'

Glad to take the heat, Maddy laughed. 'I suppose, but a lot of hair and stubble.' Her turn to grin. 'More your type.'

Perhaps prompted by the reference to her preferences in men, Heloise said, 'I hear Harris has been made redundant.'

Maddy's hands carried out the automatic movements of spooning coffee, trying not to be too glad that Heloise's thing with Harris had ended last year, though Heloise had been quiet and sad. 'I saw him early this afternoon but didn't think to wonder why he wasn't at work. I suppose I ought to feel some sympathy for him, for once.' Her own redundancy had contributed to her and Adey's financial problems, causing – according to Adey – his letting the insurance premium go unpaid. And then High Cottage had been flooded . . . If she closed her eyes, she could still see the water from an unsoldered pipe gushing down the stairs, and through ceilings and light fittings. Within an hour, Adey had been gone and Maddy's life was upside down.

Heloise agreed. Then, perhaps remembering Maddy's bad memories attached to redundancy, diplomatically changed the subject to whether Heloise should have blonde highlights in her fair hair.

Later, after Heloise had left, then supper, reading, clearing up, play time, bath time and story time, Maddy quietly pulled Lyla's bedroom door to and then padded downstairs.

She'd worn her best happy-mum face for Lyla, but now the little girl was half-asleep and curled up with her blue pony, Maddy's parental responsibilities should be at an end till morning.

Caring responsibilities, however, were not.

She entered the front room where Ruthie gazed silently at the colourful TV screen, where André Rieu conducted his orchestra with snaking arms and shaking ringlets. She'd been quiet over dinner, and had only picked at her food. 'How are you feeling?' Maddy asked, flopping into an armchair.

Ruthie used voice control to turn off the TV, then gave Maddy a wan version of her usual smile. 'I'd like to tell you about Nigel now.'

Maddy hesitated, wondering whether Ruthie needed more time to get over this afternoon's attack. The older she got, the more her asthma seemed to knock the stuffing out of her. 'You've had a tricky day. We can talk any time.'

Rather than accept the opportunity to postpone the conversation, Ruthie plunged in. 'I'll be open with you, dear. I began an affair with Nigel in the early Seventies. We got on well at work because I was the best at deciphering his loopy handwriting and we both liked gardens. Not that I had one, in my flat.' Her smile flickered. 'I'd left the village and spread my wings, but women didn't get paid as much as men, so I couldn't afford a house.'

Maddy had assumed there had been a fling, but knew this wasn't the time to explore it, nor questions of equality at work, so she waited while Ruthie stared at the flames licking at the glass of the woodstove and seemed to gather her thoughts. At last, her voice thin, she said, 'I want you to understand why I intend to see Rafferty again – and why his visit threw me for a loop.' A long breath, then: 'You see, Maddy, I had a baby. A little girl. Nigel and Sindy couldn't have children together, so I let them adopt her. They'd already adopted a boy, who must be Raff. He'll be able to bring me news of my daughter. Since Nigel died, I've known nothing.'

A log shifted in the stove. A car rumbled down Jubilee Crescent, its lights briefly illuminating the curtain. Stunned, Maddy just stared at her beloved aunt, whose lined face had puckered, almost as if expecting a slap. A *baby*? Ruthie? The same Ruthie who'd showered love on Maddy and Lyla had *given a baby away*? 'I had no idea,' she whispered.

Ruthie's laugh was mirthless. 'I made sure that none of the family did.' Sunk in her chair, she looked tiny and exhausted. 'Please will you get in touch and ask Raff to come back? After the weekend, when Lyla's at school. Would it hurt your feelings if I saved the rest of the story till then?'

Numbly, Maddy said, 'Yes, of course I'll contact him, and I'm not hurt. It's up to you what you tell me and when.' She smiled reassuringly, automatically. Then, moving gently, went to Ruthie's chair and gathered her in her arms, feeling the soft shoulders quivering, breathing in the love and goodness that emanated from Ruthie as clearly as did the scent of her soap.

Today, Ruthie had been on a gruelling journey to the past, and it was Maddy's role to do everything she could to make the next steps as easy as possible.

Chapter Two

On Saturday morning, Raff was jerked from his writing by a phone call, forced to transport himself from his imaginary world to the tiny house he rented in the village of Docking, where he worked in the downstairs living space, kitchen at one end, table and sofas at the other. Once an outbuilding, the house came with a concrete yard where he parked his car.

When he answered the call, a woman's voice said, 'This is Maddy Cracey. Is there any chance I could see you alone?' There was the muffled rattling of wind in the microphone, then she added, 'Please.'

He pushed aside his laptop, a vision of Maddy filling his imagination – a mane of hair shoved into a clasp that would hardly take it and big brown eyes, glinting with gold. Vivacious. Voluptuous. He considered saying, 'You bet. Take me to dinner and I'm yours.' But then he remembered yesterday's visit to Ruthie Willson's house when Maddy had treated him with caution, if not downright suspicion. He answered with a friendly, 'I assume this concerns your great-aunt.'

'She asked me to call,' she replied quickly, with the air of one intent on cutting off potential objections. He imagined her lips curving up, though yesterday her mouth had mostly been a straight, uncompromising line, as she'd presented herself as her great-aunt's protector.

However, years of dealing with teenagers had taught him not to accept glib, reassuring remarks at face value. He probed, 'She asked you to see me without her?'

Silence. Then, 'No,' she answered frankly. 'I can't do much about it if you won't see me before you talk to her again, but I'd appreciate the opportunity to check we're on the same page about a couple of things. I'm responsible for my great-aunt—' he wondered if she'd popped the 'great' in there to remind him of Ruthie's age '—and that was a nasty asthma attack yesterday.'

Then her voice became muffled. 'Yes, I'll watch you on the slide after this call.' Presumably she was talking to her daughter, and he wondered whether her little girl looked like her. Her voice returned at full volume. 'How local are you? I'd offer to come to you, but I don't want to be too far from Ruthie. She's quite—' She paused, as if searching for the right phrase. 'She's unsettled. It's an imposition, but how about Nelson's Bar this evening, to talk about your next step with Ruthie? On Saturdays, one of her friends usually spends the evening with her while I go to the Duke of Bronte with my friend. That's the village pub,' she added.

Another visit to the small village appealed. It was only six miles from Docking but off the beaten track, through a stand of pine trees. Nelson's Bar had given him a Brigadoon feeling – otherworldly, if not actually magical, with cutesy cottages and not much else except – apparently – one pub. One of those cottages, at the top of the steep

21

road into the village, had even been round, like a cookie jar. Maddy might be relaxed, in her local, and Raff could discover more about her and, crucially, Ruthie. 'Next step' sounded positive, and he devoutly wished to avoid further asthma attacks. 'Sure,' he answered. 'What time?'

As if she hadn't expected such immediate co-operation, she pounced on it. 'Any time between eight-thirty and ten. I'll be in the old bar, off the lounge. Thanks.' And she ended the call.

Raff resettled his laptop and stared at the words marching across the screen in neat Times New Roman font that felt too conservative for the content. He wrote fantasy. Maybe he should choose a font with 'gothic' or 'bold' in the name. It would suit his hero, Adeckor, a tousle-maned warrior at his king's right hand, a 'huscarl' or member of the royal bodyguard, a shifter who could transform himself into an ebony black centaur – half-man, half-horse. Adeckor was at the heart of a kingdom's politics and wars, and Raff enjoyed getting beneath his skin and thinking as Adeckor thought.

But instead of reimmersing himself, he jumped up, pulled on a thick fleece, then set out on foot down a drive barely wide enough to admit a car, hurrying against the chill of the morning. Wood smoke scented the air; an occasional brick bungalow spoiled the prettiness of Docking's flint cottages and long brick walls. When he'd visited the village shop a couple of days ago, the Christmas lights had been going up. Soon, the cottages would be decorated too, adding to Docking's prettiness. Since he split from his wife, Antonella, he'd been spending Christmases here with Ffion and Chloe, but this year he'd be a resident. A skein of geese made a V in the sky, while smaller birds squabbled in the hedges. At the village hall, a chalkboard advised him that the pizza van would be there that evening and the Christmas fair was scheduled for December the 2nd, then he turned right at the church, its square tower soaring between the trees.

Ffion's modest stone terraced house was in Church Place, bought fourteen years earlier when a job had brought her to Norfolk and Chloe, her daughter, was two. Although Ffion had had two long-term relationships – neither of them with Chloe's dad – she hadn't gone for live-in lovers. Currently, she was single and worked from home.

A quick knock, then he let himself through the salmon pink door. 'Me, Ffion,' he called.

Her voice floated down the passage. 'I'm in the kitchen.'

At the end of the narrow hall, he found his sister at the table, peeling carrots onto a fold of newspaper, a pan of water at her elbow. It was expedient for her to keep her freezer stocked for the days when fatigue made everyday tasks hard. 'Chloe get off to Harrow OK?' he asked, unzipping his fleece. His teenage niece was an enthusiastic member of a street dance crew and was currently at the UK Street Dance Championships. He washed his hands, picked up the sharp knife and took a chair at an angle to Ffion's, ready to slice as she peeled.

She flashed him a smile, though her narrow face was, as always, pale and drawn. 'I took her to pick up the bus in King's Lynn last night. Heats start this morning and she's dancing in solos and in crew. She's best when she has something to focus on. Less time to worry about me.' Her smile became pensive.

Raff didn't have to ask what she meant – the spectre of Ffion's upcoming mitral heart valve surgery in February cast a dark shadow over them all. His fingers would deform if he crossed them any harder for a good result, and Chloe was deeply anxious. Hoping to distract Ffion, he said, 'I would have thought you'd have been pestering me since I went to see Ruthie Willson.'

Ffion's hands dropped to the table, a half-peeled carrot rolling to the floor. 'Oh. Crap. Chloe's not sure now.'

He froze. 'You made the decision. We agreed that I'd make the first contact on my own to spy out the land.'

'But I didn't realise you meant *this* Friday. I thought you meant next. Chloe got all weepy and said she's not sure about meeting Ruthie anymore.'

'Fucksake, Ffi,' he groaned, appalled. 'We *agreed*.'

'Yes, but I didn't realise— Oh, dear,' Ffion said faintly. 'How much have you told her?'

He stared at her. 'Not much, as it goes. Unfortunately, she had an asthma attack when I explained who I was. Her great-niece, Maddy, who cares for her, asked me to come back another time and wants to meet me tonight to talk before I get near her great-aunt again.'

Ffion sank back in her seat, emotions chasing one another across her face – apprehension, dismay, curiosity . . . excitement. Apprehension again. 'So, what did happen?'

'She'd worked out that Dad had died,' he said. 'Although the letters you have ended in the mid-Nineties, apparently they were in touch till the end via mobile phones. When the calls stopped . . .' He tailed off and picked up the carrot she'd dropped to the floor and began to peel it. 'Should I meet Maddy this evening? Or drop it?' If it was the latter, would Maddy Cracey be relieved? Or cross that he'd disrupted her great-aunt's peace for nothing? He suspected the latter.

'I don't know. I should have called you the instant Chloe changed her mind.' She coughed. Her heart condition often made her breathless, just as Ruthie's asthma did, ironically. If anything, she looked paler than when he'd come in.

He said, 'Don't get upset. We could talk about something else, like the birthday meal I'm taking you and Chloe out for. November 10th is less than a week away so we should book somewhere.'

'We're looking forward to it,' she said absently, fiddling with carrot peelings, sweeping them into heaps with the side of her hand, her mind evidently far from her upcoming forty-sixth birthday. 'I'm trying to decide what Chloe wants, because she's taking my illness so hard. She's only sixteen.' She wiped the corner of her eye on her sleeve.

He made his voice gentle. 'We've got every reason to hope for a successful outcome from your surgery.' Then, although the notion of things going badly for Ffion chilled him to his bones, because they'd learnt not to avoid the hard conversations in the fifteen months since the rheumatic fever that had affected Ffion's heart, he added, 'You know that whatever happens I'll be there for Chloe.'

Wearily, Ffion parcelled up the peelings in the newspaper and returned to the more immediate problem. 'I suppose you should go ahead with meeting the niece and hearing what she has to say.' She emitted a long, weary sigh. 'What's she like?'

'Ruthie?' he clarified, as he'd been absorbing the knowledge that he'd have been disappointed if Ffion had asked him to pull the plug on this evening. 'She's small, like you and Chloe; an ordinary woman of about eighty. Sight-impaired, hence the niece caring for her. Her mind's still active and she seems pleasant. She cried over Dad.'

'Oh.' Ffion's voice wavered.

Raff put his arm around her. 'Forget Chloe for a

moment. What would *you* like to do about Ruthie? It concerns you more than anyone.'

Ffion gazed at the newspaper bundle as if reading one of the fast-dampening columns of print. 'It's just odd, after living the life I was given, to think about crossing into a sort of parallel one,' she said at length. 'The life I never had, because I was adopted.'

Though an adoptee himself, he'd never had such hard choices to make, so he picked his words carefully. 'When you accepted the job in Norfolk and moved to Docking, you knew the address on the top of the letters, and that it was possible she still lived in this area. I thought that at least part of the reason you accepted the job was with a view to interacting with her one day.'

Ffion looked troubled. 'But I've never done so, have I? And I've lived here for fourteen years.'

Raff sat back. While Ffion had been ill, he'd taken on the role of her support staff, seeing what had to be done and doing it and eventually moving to her village. But when there was only confusion and indecision, with he and Ffion getting their wires crossed and Chloe changing her – admittedly changeable – mind, he felt helpless.

The only set idea Ffion had voiced in the last minutes was that he should meet Maddy tonight.

He'd do that.

In the dark evening, Raff drove through the pinewoods, their long trunks making them look like Christmas trees on stilts, up the appropriately named Long Climb to Nelson's Bar. His sat nav took him straight through the village, past the kind of lampposts Mary Poppins might like to dance around and roofs that looked like frosty hills and valleys, to the Duke of Bronte, a stone pub at the very end of the headland. There he found a lower storey larger than the upper and the whole pub smothered with fairy lights. An illuminated, laughing Santa was mid-stride above a window, a bulging sack on his back. It was seven weeks to Christmas and the Duke of Bronte obviously didn't intend being left behind.

There weren't many cars in the car park, but he supposed the village homes lay within walking distance. Locking his car, he took a moment to check out the cliff edge to admire a silver sliver of moon in a jet black sky, the night so still and clear that it was hard to recall yesterday's blusteriness. Below, the surf broke with a measured *sigh . . . shush*, comforting in its timelessness.

He glanced at his watch. Fifteen minutes to nine – comfortably within the time window Maddy had suggested. For a last moment, he huddled into his coat, breathing the icy, briny air, then turned and headed towards the brightly illuminated pub. It was busy, he saw through the run of windows, and difficult to date from its style. The floor was tile and the wooden bar counter a golden wood. The walls were pale green, punctuated by lights with frosted glass shades. People gathered around wooden tables, at long grey velour bench seats or at the bar, and a Christmas tree stood under a sign reading: *Don't forget to book your festive meal!* and decorated with a red Christmas cracker. A fire danced behind a brass guard. He pulled open the heavy oak door marked *Lounge*, assaulted simultaneously by a babble of conversation and a welcome warmth. He hung up his coat, presuming this tiny, almost isolated village to have such a low crime rate that it would be there when he returned, and tucked his car keys into his jeans pocket.

Many of the chatting, relaxed-looking patrons glanced

up, but he spotted no Maddy Cracey and no area that might answer the description of 'the old bar'.

He made for where the optics glittered on one wall, staff working briskly between them and the beer pumps, and found a space between two men leaning elbows on the polished counter beside their pints. A young woman in black jeans and polo shirt served a customer. She looked barely old enough. Just a few months ago, she might have been studying prose, poetry and drama with a teacher just like himself.

Someone beside him spoke. 'All right then?' His Norfolk accent was not unlike a broad Northamptonshire one.

Raff glanced around and saw a man of about his own age with a lank mop of dark hair and a beard was giving him an affable nod over his pint. 'Evening.' Raff nodded back.

'New villager?' The man sipped his beer then folded his bottom lip over his moustache to suck up the froth.

Raff smiled. 'No, just meeting someone. Seems a nice village, though.'

'Everyone loves Nelson's Bar,' the man affirmed. He stuck out a hand. 'I'm Harris Soley.'

Raff gave his name in return just as the young server arrived and, as if he'd introduced himself to her too, she said, 'Can I get you something, Raff?'

'Heineken Zero, please.' He grinned, amused by that level of friendliness.

Harris laughed. 'What's the point of that, then? Alcohol-free beer?'

Good-naturedly, Raff laughed back. 'That's between me and the breathalyser.'

'Good on you,' Harris replied, taking several gulps from his presumably alcohol-laden pint. 'Who you meeting?'

Raff paid for his drink with a tap of his debit card. 'She said she'd be in the old bar. It's off this room, is it?'

Harris burst into loud guffaws. 'You're *not* here for Mad Crazy or Hell's Bells? You on a date with one of them?' Without waiting for an answer, he tugged Raff's sleeve to draw him a couple of paces to the right. 'See through that gap there, beside the post? That's the old bar, that sort of alcove.'

Startled by Harris knowing who he was seeking, Raff saw a modest space enclosing two tables. One was empty. At the other, Maddy Cracey sat with a fairer woman. Maddy was smiling. Raff had noticed her hair yesterday when it was shoved messily on top of her head, but tonight, part upswept and the rest hanging in a glossy river over one shoulder, it made him catch his breath. In make-up and a slinky blue top, she was hot.

He glanced at Harris. 'Mad Crazy and Hell's Bells?' he repeated.

Harris laughed. 'Madeline Cracey and Heloise Bellingham, if you prefer.' He took a slug of beer and wiped his mouth. ''Course, Mad Crazy married Adey Austen so she's Maddy Austen really, but nobody much called her it, even when Adey was around.'

Although part of his brain noted that Harris's final words suggested Maddy was separated, divorced or widowed, Raff was mainly busy reacting to Harris's sneering tone. Had it been one of Raff's past students, he would have instigated a calm conversation, aiming to build trust and understanding so they could discuss unkindness and its impact on others.

But Raff was no longer a teacher. And Harris was a grown man. Raff gave a conspiratorial laugh. 'And you're Harris Soley. Bet they called you Arsehole, eh?'

Harris's smirks were quickly replaced with a scowl. He put down his pint. 'You know about her husband Adey, I s'pose? He was my best mate. Went for a walk one dark night and ent never been seen again. Straight up. I reckon he jumped off the cliffs to get away from Mad Crazy.'

Raff recoiled from the spiteful, outrageous claim, but refused to give Harris the satisfaction of displaying curiosity. Instead, he glanced over to where Maddy chatted happily to her friend, hair shining in the lights of the bar, her generous mouth parted as she tipped back her head and laughed. 'I wouldn't jump off a cliff to get away from her.'

As Raff stepped away, he caught sight of himself in the mirrored wall behind the bar. He hadn't found time for a haircut since finishing teaching at Martingdale and he hadn't shaved for days. He'd been so busy since moving to Norfolk. His first publisher had been a small independent and Raff had sold them completed novels. But now his agent Elinor had got him a great deal with a big publisher he had to write fresh material, and to the deadlines on his shiny new contract. But maybe he was looking a little too much like the hero of his novel, Adeckor.

And, hell, he shared a look with Harris Soley.

It was probably why Harris had struck up a conversation, thinking Raff a kindred spirit of the dishevelled kind. He fished in his pocket, found the elastic he sometimes used to hold back his hair when hiking along the Norfolk lanes, and secured it at the back. He retrieved his non-beer then rounded the corner to the old bar.

It was obvious when Maddy spotted him, because her smile faded.

He made sure his greeting was friendly. 'Hi. Here as promised.' He glanced at her companion and smiled. 'I'm Raff.'

The fair woman looked interested. 'I'm Heloise. Cool man-bun.' Then she gave Maddy the kind of meaningful look that spoke of arrangements already in place, and added, 'Just popping over to chat to my friend Clancy.' In a moment, she'd picked up her drink and entered the main lounge.

Maddy glanced up at Raff. 'Thanks for coming. You want to sit down?' Her Norfolk accent was slight, just an attractive lilt. Gold threaded through her silky-straight brown hair and flecked her wide eyes. Her skin was smooth and natural rather than the full-on effect his ex-wife Antonella wore.

'Thanks.' Raff seated himself on a brown leather stool. As she had a full glass there was no point offering to buy her a drink, so he got straight to the point. 'You have something you'd like to say?'

Relief flitted across her face. Perhaps she appreciated the direct approach. 'A couple of things,' she murmured. A vertical crease appeared between her eyebrows as if she'd tucked away her thoughts there. 'As Ruthie's carer, her welfare's my concern.'

He nodded, aware of the assessing light in her luminous brown eyes.

She hesitated. 'I appreciate why you want to talk to her, and she wants to talk too, but her breathing suffers when she's upset.'

'I'm very sorry about yesterday,' he put in honestly. Because of the letters from Ruthie to his dad that Ffion had let him read, he'd almost felt as if he'd known Ruthie before they'd met, and it had been a worrying moment. 'I'd planned a gentler lead-in.' He deliberately didn't share what he'd been leading to. Ffion's story was too delicate.

Her eyebrows quirked. 'I'm sure. But I need to pre-empt

31

problems if I can.' She tilted her head. 'It would be helpful to know whether the rest of the news you have for her is bad, or good.'

He considered. 'Good, I hope.'

Maddy contemplated him. 'I hope this isn't insulting,' she said slowly, 'but as I don't know exactly what you're here for, I must say it. Ruthie's not rich. The Hollies sounds a grand address, but you've seen it. It's just a brick cottage that needs new windows and carpets. We get by, that's all.'

Irritation prickled up his spine. 'It *is* insulting. I've left teaching, but I'm far from destitute,' he answered evenly. Then he paused. He couldn't really blame her for questioning his motives. To him, it had seemed an effective yet cautious approach to turn up at the address he held before involving Ffion. To Maddy, it had been inconsiderate and suspicious. He summoned a smile and tacked on, 'I'm not after a handout.'

A short, narrow-eyed silence. Then Maddy smiled, suddenly and disarmingly. 'If Ruthie gets emotional, I don't want my daughter Lyla to see it. Would you like to come for lunch when she's at school? How about Monday?'

Taken aback that he'd apparently somehow lurched past the gatekeeper, it took an instant to answer. 'Um . . . great. Thank you.'

Again, the tuck appeared between Maddy's eyebrows. 'Ruthie's symptoms have settled, but can I trust you to be sympathetic to her condition? No badgering.'

'Naturally,' he replied flatly, irritated by the word 'badgering'.

Her expression softened. 'Sorry. Ruthie hadn't had a bad attack for ages and when I get scared, I get prickly. She's been wonderful to me, and if your dad once meant something to her, then I shouldn't be on bad terms with you.'

He might be a sucker for a pretty face, but he found himself quick to offer the reassurance she seemed to seek. 'He definitely meant something to her.'

She picked up her drink and swilled the ice. 'Do I need to know anything foodwise? Are you veggie? Any allergies?'

At this sudden swerve towards hospitable courtesy, he returned his best smile. 'Whatever you'd usually have will be great.'

Solemnly she added, 'It will include cake. Ruthie's very keen.'

He laughed. 'I'm with her on that.' He wouldn't be shocked to learn that cake was in Maddy's life, too. Her curves spoke of enjoying an occasional treat and living an energetic enough life to keep herself looking good.

She finished her drink. 'Noon on Monday then, unless I message you to say Ruthie's not up to it?'

He rose as she did. They said goodbye, and Maddy made for where Heloise had joined a couple in the lounge.

Her passage attracted the attention of Harris Soley. 'Oy, Mad Crazy, you found your old man yet?'

Maddy glared back at him without slowing, somehow swerving to avoid the twinkling Christmas tree. 'Bet you think I threw him off the headland, don't you? You better watch out, eh, Harris? Might be you, next.'

A couple of people tittered at Maddy's fighting response, more exchanged startled looks, and one shook her head disapprovingly. Raff found himself grinning. He finished his drink, then wandered back past the bar himself. Harris, pint in hand, switched his gaze from Maddy to Raff. 'And how was Mad Crazy tonight?' he demanded with a snigger.

Much more inclined to align himself with Maddy than with the unpleasant Harris Soley, Raff adopted a smitten smile. 'Mad-crazy beautiful. I can see why you're obsessed with her.' Then he winked at Harris's dropped jaw and grabbed his coat, enjoying having had the last word.

It was only when he got outside that he realised he'd committed himself to meeting Ruthie again, even though Ffion had only sanctioned tonight's meeting.

He paused, rubbing his stubbly jaw.

The sound of the waves reached him through the cold air, and he wondered if his dad had ever been here before him, to this charming village with its intriguing characters. Had there been clandestine visits to The Hollies? Had he found some happiness here?

He found himself hoping that he had. Nigel had been a great dad to Raff and Ffion, filling weekends with walks or visits to the park, trips to the cinema and help with homework. He'd spent a lot of time in the garden, and Raff remembered hanging out with him there, Nigel digging and Raff collecting worms. If there had been a lack of warmth between Nigel and their mum Sindy, he'd never let it affect how the children were loved.

Though Nigel's connection to Ruthie had begun when he'd served in the army, he'd left when Raff was six. Though he'd given up the khaki, he apparently hadn't given up Ruthie. Raff remembered his shock when Ffion had first shared the letters with him, and he realised Dad had survived his frosty marriage by loving someone else. Raff had gone through patches of resentment for Mum's sake. But finally, he and Ffion had agreed that Dad hadn't been the kind to have an affair unless something enormous was missing from his life.

34

So, Raff wanted to know the rest of his dad and Ruthie's story, and he was pretty sure Ruthie wanted news of their daughter, even if that daughter, Ffion, stayed away.

He'd go ahead.

Chapter Three

In honour of their lunch guest, on Monday Ruthie wore a deep blue woollen dress and fleecy leggings, rather than her usual winter cardigans. Maddy hadn't made quite as much effort, though her red jumper was a favourite and she'd bothered to weave a French plait in her hair. Home-made vegetable soup simmered in the kitchen and the woodstove warmed the front room.

It was an understatement to say Maddy had been shocked to learn of her aunt's secret baby. She was both curious and nervous about hearing the whole story and was pondering this hitherto unknown branch of the family tree: If the baby arrived in the Seventies, Ruthie would have been in her late twenties or early thirties. The 'baby' must now be in her forties or early fifties, so Maddy, at thirty-nine, wasn't too much younger. Maddy's grandmother Elsie – the older sister by eight years – had had Maddy's mum Linda at twenty, meaning Elsie had become a grandmother only a handful of years after Ruthie had become a mum.

Ruthie, unaware of Maddy's computations, pottered

about the kitchen, where the lights were bright, surfaces dark and equipment white, to help her find things, and chattered about what Lyla might like for Christmas rather than married lovers, hush-hush babies or their expected guest.

Until the doorbell rang. Then she jumped as if Maddy had prodded her with a pin. 'Oh! Is that him?'

Maddy gave her diminutive aunt a reassuring hug, the cushiony shape familiar in her arms. 'Are you still up for it?'

Ruthie looked indignant. 'Yes, I've had my puffer. Just let the man in. You're quicker on your feet than I am.'

Grinning, Maddy hurried across the small, flagstoned hall. When she passed the red-carpeted stairs that rose to the upper storey and opened the door, she found a clean-shaven man, hair falling in a wing above his eyes, a bunch of yellow chrysanthemums in his hands and a bag over his shoulder. For an instant, she wondered why a cover model had come to the door.

Then dark eyebrows flipped enquiringly above vivid blue eyes. 'Hello, Maddy,' Raff Edmonds' voice said.

Oh! On a rush of embarrassment, Maddy realised who it was, shorn of his scruffy hair and stubble. 'Sorry, Raff, come in.' She pulled the door wider, cheeks scalding.

He grinned as he stepped indoors, perhaps guessing that his appearance had caught her wrong-footed, ducking as if not sure the doorway would be tall enough for him.

Then Ruthie materialised from the kitchen with an uncertain smile and Raff presented her with the yellow chrysanthemums and asked how she was. To Ruthie's unreliable eyes, his tall, straight figure probably didn't look any different than when they'd met on Friday.

To Maddy, it was as if he'd gone on a TV makeover

show. Without the grunge look, he appeared younger, friendlier, more approachable . . . and gorgeous. Heloise had said he was, after he'd left on Saturday evening, but she liked long hair and beards, hence her fling with Harris Soley. What Maddy had noticed about Raff Edmonds had been his eyes, blue as the sea on a sunny day.

Suddenly realising that Ruthie and Raff were gazing at her, Maddy shook herself from her thoughts and took Raff's coat. Normally, she'd have sunk into the background while Ruthie and her visitor talked before the fire. Today, though, she planned to be present for Ruthie's conversation with this man who'd shown up a few short days ago and made her cry herself into an asthma attack.

'Do you mind eating straight away? The soup's ready. I don't know about you, but I'm starving.' Maddy ushered them to the kitchen table. Raff hung his bag over the back of his chair, while Maddy took bread rolls from the oven, filling the kitchen with delicious smells.

Raff chatted to Ruthie about having to scrape frost from his car before setting out from the village of Docking.

Maddy carried steaming bowls of vegetable soup to the table and joined in. 'But you come from Northamptonshire, Raff?'

'It's where my last job was. I was brought up in Scotland. You've always lived in the village?' Courteously, he passed the rolls, so Ruthie and Maddy could take theirs first.

'Always,' she agreed. 'When I had Lyla and Ruthie needed help, we joined forces.'

'Maddy's a wonder,' Ruthie chimed in. 'She looks after me and Lyla, the household, the garden and my paperwork. She's a very twinkly star.'

Maddy cringed. Anyone could cook, shop, garden and

pay bills. She glanced enquiringly at Raff. 'There isn't much sign of a Scots accent.'

'Och, noo,' he said in a ferociously fake accent before dropping into his usual tones. 'Mum and Dad retained their Englishness.'

At the mention of Raff's parents Maddy shot a look at Ruthie, but she was gazing into her soup bowl, expression unreadable.

They continued with polite chitchat as they ate. After clearing the soup bowls, Maddy arranged chocolate brownies on a plate. Ruthie took an audible breath and pushed to her feet, one hand on the tabletop. It was a characteristic she'd developed as her sight failed, trailing her fingers over furniture to mark her route. 'Shall we take our cake and coffee into the front room? I think it's time I heard what Raff has to say.' Evidently, she'd waited as long as she could.

Raff rose too, his expression a strange mixture of eagerness and apprehension.

Maddy's stomach turned over, but she reminded herself that whatever Raff was here for, it was Ruthie's concern. Maddy's was a support role. But worry made her throat tight when she murmured, 'Of course.'

When they were settled, Raff having transported cake and Maddy the drinks, Ruthie blinked through the thick glasses that helped a bit, but not enough. 'How much do you know?' she asked directly.

Raff drew forward on the edge of his seat. His voice was deep and soft. 'I know you and Dad had a long affair, and that although my sister Ffion and I are both adopted, Ffion was Dad's natural daughter. And yours.'

'Oh,' Maddy heard herself say softly. She'd guessed it must be this, had heard of people adopting their own children for various reasons, but it was still a shock to hear it confirmed. Automatically, she checked Ruthie, but saw nothing in her face or body language to suggest she was going to give way to distress this time.

Slowly, Ruthie picked up her coffee in a trembling hand. She sipped, sighed, then smiled reminiscently. 'As you know, we worked together – that was in the early Seventies. I was a civilian; he was in the army. I was single, but he was married, which I knew from the start.' She gave a short laugh. 'My big sister Elsie, Maddy's grandmother, she liked women and men to be neatly paired up, like shoes. She stayed in the village with her husband Herbert, and their Linda, Maddy's mum, was a teenager. Elsie used to get on to me for living the single life. You'd think Hampshire was Timbuktu, to hear her go on.'

Maddy ate a bite of brownie, pausing to lick chocolate from her fingertips. For an instant, she thought Raff watched her, but when she looked his eyes were on Ruthie.

He smiled, relaxing back in his chair. 'Dad liked the army.' His tone gave no hint of judging Ruthie or feeling resentful towards her having an affair with his married father. 'He used to talk about how he'd come up through the ranks.'

'He went in at seventeen.' Ruthie nodded. 'We were in our mid-thirties when I knew him in Keogh Barracks.' A smile tugged at her lips. 'In our office, there was a system for Wednesday afternoons. You either had the half-day off, or you covered while others did, so every third week it was just the two of us covering the phones and everything.' A shadow crossed her face. 'I had trouble with a corporal in the office, because of being homely.' She lifted her hand and touched her face, the dear, ordinary face Maddy loved so much.

'You're not homely,' she protested. 'Was this corporal a hunk or something?'

Ruthie laughed. 'He was not, but that never stopped him making remarks. Then one day, Nigel snapped at him, "Learn some respect or I'll teach you some!" Everyone in the office was shocked. The corporal stopped his nasty ways. I got such a crush on Nigel, but I never let it show.' She glanced at Raff. 'Are you certain you want to hear all of it?' She sounded apprehensive.

'If you'll tell me,' he answered quietly. 'My parents had an unusual relationship and I'd like to know the background.'

Ruthie sank into the cushions of her armchair as if someone had let some of her air out. It took her a moment to go on. 'One day, I was chatting to another typist about visiting Virginia Water Gardens and how to get there on public transport. Later, I happened to be alone with Nigel and he suddenly said he wanted to go to Virginia Water too, so why didn't he give me a lift. I shouldn't have accepted.' Her gaze became even less focused than usual, as if straining to see the past. 'But he was such a nice man, and I thought if he was going anyway, what was the point of me bothering with buses and trains? So, we went together, our next Wednesday afternoon off. He was out of uniform, and I thought he looked smart with his short back and sides. Most civilian men had long hair in the Seventies.'

Maddy could see that the woodstove needed stoking, but it seemed important not to break the spell, so she nibbled her brownie and sipped her coffee and listened.

'The sun shone,' Ruthie went on quietly, 'and the flowers were beautiful. When Nigel talked about gardens, his face lit up. He knew lots about them. Then, when I asked if his wife – Sindy – liked gardening, too, it was like the sun went in. He said no, so I asked was that why she didn't mind him being out with me.' She paused to put her coffee mug on the table, checking it was firmly seated before releasing its handle. 'He said, "I suppose it's fair that you ask." Then he told me about how they'd got married because he'd got her pregnant while they were tipsy. Both families were big churchgoers.' Suddenly, fiercely, as if they'd disputed her memories, she added, 'People talk about the Swinging Sixties and Sexy Seventies, but those names are deceiving. You were "in trouble" in those circumstances. A woman couldn't afford to bring up a kid alone and her dad didn't see why he should pay to bring up "another man's mistake". So, people got married to avoid the stigma and shame, and to have the father's name on the birth certificate.'

Raff stirred in his chair.

Ruthie obviously caught the rustling, as she turned to him. 'Probably you already know, everything went wrong with that pregnancy. A growth was discovered on Sindy's womb. They had to terminate, and then give her a hysterectomy.' She paused, eyes more than usually clouded. 'The reason for their marriage was gone but they were stuck with each other. Divorces didn't happen in families like theirs. You've no idea how people judged. When Nigel's cousin left his wife, Nigel's parents told the cousin he was a disgrace and never spoke to him again.'

'What you describe is more or less why I was adopted,' Raff observed softly.

'Well yes, dear, I know.' Ruthie gave him a tiny smile. 'Your dad and me, we went through a period of not seeing each other, and your adoption happened then. Your birth mum was an unmarried mother – a teenager. She got kidney failure and died. Her parents said they didn't

42

feel able to look after you.' She sighed. 'Sadly, in those days people cared more about gossip than about the illegitimate grandchild.'

'I knew those grandparents,' he murmured. 'They were more like family friends, though. Mum and Dad's parents were ones I treated as my real grandparents.'

'It's good your blood relatives made some effort,' Ruthie said, though her tone suggested she didn't think much of the kind of effort they made. Absently, she picked at the brownie. 'That day in Virginia Water Gardens, Nigel said he knew it was wrong, but he had feelings for me. And I said I'd fallen for him. Then we were kissing, and it felt so right.' A coy smile touched her lips. 'Wednesday afternoons were quite different after that.'

They sat in silence. The fire behind the glass in the stove shifted and settled. Maddy, who'd listened with a feeling of unreality, finally felt she could get up and add more wood. As she resumed her seat, she stole a glance at Raff, wondering how it felt to hear about his dad's passion. And infidelity.

He was frowning. At length he said, 'Dad was a religious man. He must have loved you a lot to break his moral code.'

Maddy thought that made him a massive hypocrite, but Ruthie just looked troubled. 'I was always on his conscience. I tried a few times to end things. He'd say that I'd given him the happiest times of his life. Then it would all start up again. We didn't seem to be able to help ourselves. We wrote to each other all the time – notes we left on each other's desks, and through the post, as well. The mail was very quick in those days. He could post me a letter early Friday evening and I'd get it on Monday morning, before I went to work.'

Maddy tried to picture it. 'Hadn't you been together at work all day on the Friday? What else would he have to say?'

'Whatever was in his heart,' Ruthie replied, patiently, as if Maddy had asked a silly question. 'At work we talked about forms in triplicate and inventories he needed typing straight away – unless we both happened to be in the stock cupboard at the same time. Then we . . . shared a moment.'

After a small silence to digest this confession, Raff ventured, 'Your relationship went on for most of the rest of Dad's life, didn't it?'

'Apart from the times we tried to keep apart, as I mentioned.' Ruthie hesitated. 'How do you know so much, dear?'

Chapter Four

It was time for Raff to introduce his family's side of the story. He picked up his bag, which he'd brought in from the kitchen. He hesitated, scratching his chin, which felt odd without stubble. It had been worth taking time away from his keyboard to smarten himself up just to see Maddy's face when she answered the door and had trouble recognising him.

He dipped in his bag and rested his hand on the sheaf of thin, aged paper inside. Cautiously, he began, 'Ffion's my adoptive sister. We're only a year apart. That's how the adoptions worked out. And now I'm going to stop using the term "adoptive" because we consider ourselves brother and sister, just like any family.'

Raff paused, looking from Ruthie to Maddy, checking that he wasn't stressing the elderly lady out again. Then he continued. 'When Dad died, Ffion and I helped Mum dispose of his things. Mum was shocked to be left alone in her mid-fifties, even if Dad had spent most of his time in his garden.'

Ruthie nodded. 'He liked azaleas and rhododendrons.

We bought some together once and he planted them. Said they always reminded him of me.'

'Oh, Ruthie,' Maddy breathed. 'I had no idea about any of this.' She sounded desolate, as if she'd failed her aunt.

Ruthie shifted awkwardly. 'If you have an affair with a married man, you don't usually babble on about it.'

Raff had to smother a smile at this pragmatism. 'When Ffion cleared out Dad's shed, she found . . . something.' His throat tightened at the memory of how shocked he'd been when Ffion had finally told him. He removed his hand from inside his bag to pick up his cooling coffee and take an easing sip. 'Something she kept to herself till Mum died a couple of years ago.'

Awkwardly, Ruthie whispered, 'I'm sorry to know that your mum passed. Despite everything.'

'Thanks,' he said gruffly. 'She gave Ffion and me a lot of love, even if not showing much towards . . . others.' He meant his dad. Ruthie, above everyone in the world, knew how chilly Nigel's marriage had been. He cleared his throat. 'Mum and Dad weren't great together, but, individually, they were wonderful.'

Ruthie answered in a tiny thread of a voice. 'I knew she'd be a good mum.'

Unable to look at her for fear of getting emotional at the thousands of memories he had of his mum, he continued, 'What Ffion found was proof that Dad was her birth dad, information she kept to herself till Mum died, in case she was hurt.' He brought out the thick bundle of paper, more than two decades' worth of clandestine love in neat handwriting on flimsy writing paper, blue, cream or white, faded like old confetti. 'These are your letters to Dad.'

46

Ruthie let out a horrified squawk. 'My letters? You've not read them?'

'Quite a few,' he admitted, feeling his cheeks heat up at confessing to reading the closely written pages of deep love and abiding affection. 'Sorry. I know it's private correspondence, but it illuminated things we'd never understood. When Ffion finally shared them with me, I was surprised but unsurprised.' If he'd been wearing a collar, he'd have loosened it. He cleared his throat again. 'It was unexpectedly comforting to know Dad had had someone. He was a good bloke, and we accept he had human needs. Mum and Dad, they treated each other so politely. We couldn't imagine that they ever . . . fulfilled those needs together.'

'Oh, my days,' said Ruthie faintly, pressing her hand to her forehead and flushing a deep, embarrassed red.

Slowly, Raff slipped the letters back inside his bag. When he and Ffion had discussed whether they should offer them back, they'd never reached a conclusion. Now he knew Ruthie's poor vision wouldn't allow her to read them, he decided to keep hold of this part of Dad for now.

Then Ruthie sat up, wiped her eyes on the cuff of her dress, and begged, 'Please tell me about your sister.' The yearning in her voice made his chest constrict.

He smiled at the small woman, the recipient of his dad's bottled-up passion. 'I will. But first can we talk a bit more about after you and Dad got together? How Ffion . . . happened?'

Maddy interrupted. 'Ruthie, I think you need another drink and to take your inhaler.' She sent Raff a meaningful look, her dark eyebrows cradling that little crease between them. 'She gets breathless when she talks a lot.'

Ruthie cut in. 'But I don't want Raff to leave yet.'

Maddy managed to smile at her aunt at the same time as subjecting her to a searching look. 'I know. There's some of your favourite tropical Lucozade in the fridge. That'll give you a bit of a lift.'

A smile bloomed on the old lady's face, and she groped for Maddy's hand. 'Thank you for looking after me, dear.'

For an instant, Maddy looked as if she might cry, then she whisked into the kitchen with a muttered, 'Won't be a minute.'

While Ruthie felt for her inhaler, Raff waited, understanding that he wasn't meant to restart the conversation until Ruthie had taken a break. He looked around the low-ceilinged room. The brick fireplace and wooden beams were timeless, but the green patterned carpet had seen better days. Flames danced behind the woodstove's sooty glass pane, and he watched them as he listened to the whooshing of Ruthie's inhaler, knowing from the many children he'd taught that some people didn't like spectators.

Then Maddy reappeared with a glass of Lucozade for her aunt and more coffee for him and herself. Her plait swung forward as she passed his mug to him, and she gave a practised flick of her head to prevent it from dipping into the coffee. He said, 'Thanks,' and she half-smiled.

After sipping the Lucozade, Ruthie returned to her story. 'In 1973, Nigel got posted to Scotland,' she said. 'Service personnel have to go where they're sent.' Her voice dropped, the tone becoming flatter. 'Sindy was expected to go with him, of course. Nigel told me how trapped he felt. Divorce would have been a proper mess, what with his family and the church, *and* the army all

48

disapproving, even if the law had begun making it easier by then. Nigel came up with schemes for me to move up there. I would have had to leave the MOD and be a long way from everything and everyone I knew though. And still on the sidelines.' She gave a mirthless laugh. Slowly, she leant back, feeling for her glass of Lucozade and lifting it waveringly to her lips, taking several sips, before returning it to its place on the table.

For the first time, Maddy voiced an opinion on something other than Ruthie's state of health. 'All this seems so out of character for you.'

Forlornly, Ruthie nodded. 'When he was posted to Scotland I cried for a week, and I did begin to wonder about following him. But then Elsie visited me. My sister, Maddy's grandmother,' she broke off to remind Raff. 'One of Nigel's letters landed on the doormat, and she said it looked like a man's writing and asked was I seeing someone. I must have blushed like fire, because she said, "Oh, Ruthie, you're not messing about with someone you shouldn't, are you?" When I confessed, she called it tawdry.' She turned pleading eyes on Raff, her lip trembling. 'But it was love. Nigel had my heart,' she quavered. Desolation swept her face. 'After he'd gone, his CO – commanding officer – had me in for a quiet word. He said he knew what had been going on and he'd had Nigel posted because he couldn't condone it. It had either been that, or I'd have had to find another job. I was mortified.'

Maddy gave an outraged gasp. 'He couldn't make you leave to save Nigel's career!'

'He could.' Ruthie smiled sadly. 'That's what used to happen. It was another couple of years before employment laws changed to prevent women being discriminated against – and I'm not sure how much the army took those laws to heart, anyway. The CO said that if I truly cared for Nigel, I'd let him get on with his life and not ruin his career. I *hated* him. But with Elsie and the CO both telling me that I was the problem, I told Nigel I was staying in Surrey, and we should make a clean break.'

A silence fell. Ruthie sipped her drink. Raff noticed Maddy looking at him with a peculiar expression. The little cleft between her brows came and went, came and went. He had no idea whether she was thinking: *Damn you for stirring all this up;* or: *Is it hard hearing all this? Are you OK?* Then she blinked and looked away and the connection was lost.

'I told him,' Ruthie said, grabbing Raff's attention again, 'that he had to try and make a go of things with Sindy, and I was going to try and find a nice man who was free to love me back.' She gave a half-sob, half-laugh. 'He was so shocked. He wrote to ask me to reconsider. I didn't keep that letter. It nearly broke my heart.'

Softly, Maddy asked, 'How long were you together?'

'By then, more than two years. But nearer thirty, altogether.' Ruthie wrung her hands. 'I stayed on in the office. The CO changed, as all service personnel did, sooner or later. I didn't meet a nice single man, as I'd told Nigel I would. No one matched up to him. After about three years, one of the other civilian girls asked if I fancied a coach tour holiday in the north of England. She reserved our seats.' Her lips twisted wryly. 'Then, at the last minute, we realised she'd booked the wrong tour. It was one going up into Scotland, including two nights in Aberdeen, where Nigel was stationed. When I heard, I couldn't help myself. I got his telephone number and extension from the internal directory. As we set out on the holiday, it felt as if I had a big red light on my handbag telling everybody that the piece of paper I'd written his number on was in there.'

Maddy's eyes moved in the direction of the clock above the fireplace and Raff's pulse sped up as he hoped it wasn't time for her to fetch her daughter, because that would probably mean her turfing him out, just when he was learning what he wanted to know. But she returned her attention to her great-aunt, and he breathed more easily.

Dreamily, Ruthie went on. 'By the time we reached Aberdeen three days later, I'd made up mind not to contact him. I told myself we'd got over the heartbreak. I still loved him, but I remembered what that commanding officer had said about me affecting his career. As we drove through the streets, I held out this stupid hope that I'd just catch a glimpse of him, just so I could check he was OK.'

Although Raff knew perfectly well that Ruthie and his dad had got together again, as Ffion was living proof, he found himself leaning in to wait for the next twist in the story.

Ruthie blinked behind her glasses. 'I would have stayed strong, I think, except for my friend getting interested in a bloke on our bus. At Aberdeen, he asked her out for lunch and the cinema, and she went off with him. I said I didn't mind – but while I sat on my own, I just couldn't stop thinking that the man I loved was so near to me for the first time in three years.' She stopped and cleared her throat. 'So I took his number out of my bag and called him from the hotel phone booth.'

She drew in a long wheeze but seemed to have trouble letting it out. She coughed, then took a drink. Maddy frowned, but didn't butt in, even when Ruthie's voice became husky. 'Nigel picked up the phone. He said, "Sergeant Edmonds" and my heart almost exploded. I'm sorry,' Ruthie added, in Raff's direction.

She must be apologising for being his dad's girlfriend, so he muttered, 'It's OK.' It was dawning on him that the terms he'd used to Ffion in the first shock of learning about Ruthie – *Dad's bit of stuff*, or *Dad's bit on the side* – were unjustly scornful. She told her story with such dignity, evoking echoes of past joy and pain, that he couldn't help but appreciate the depth of the love affair, and that Ruthie had suffered for it.

After a moment to recover her breath, she began again. 'He told me a caff to go to and in half an hour he was running in, sweeping off his cap and grabbing my hands over the table. Neither of us could speak.' A tear trembled on her lashes and made a slow path through the furrows of her skin.

'Wow,' murmured Maddy shakily.

'We arranged to meet that evening and we clicked again, as if the last three years hadn't happened.' Ruthie gazed in Raff's direction, expression apologetic. 'He told me he and Sindy had adopted a little boy. But when he said it hadn't led to a single improvement in the relationship, I went and let everything start up again.' Her breath broke on a sob. 'He said he'd put in for a posting back to Aldershot and I started to look for other jobs so if there was anything on his record about me, the problem would already be resolved. But when he came down for his promotion board—' Ruthie drew in another long breath '—I had to tell him I was pregnant.'

Again, she began to cough, and this time Maddy jumped to her feet, passing Ruthie her inhaler and murmuring, 'Take your time. Take it easy.'

Ruthie took one inhalation, then waved Maddy away, peering around her niece towards Raff. 'Being a single mum in those days wasn't easy, socially or financially. We agonised about what to do. Divorce was less likely than ever, because he and Sindy had already adopted you, and you were less than a year old. You might not have stitched his marriage together, but he adored you, and didn't want to be an absent dad. I didn't want that for him, either. It would have been even worse than his parents disowning him. Eventually, we agreed that he'd tell Sindy that a woman from his old office had "got in trouble" – that's what we used to call it – and there was this baby coming up for adoption who could be a brother or sister for their little boy.'

'Oh, no,' Raff heard Maddy whisper.

Ruthie didn't even look towards her niece. 'I had a darling daughter. Darling. It broke my heart to give her away, but she'd have a better life with two parents and a brother to love her than as an illegitimate kiddie.' Morosely, she added, 'I came home afterwards, for Christmas. Elsie and Herbert had decorated the house lovely and everything, but all I could think was that if my daughter had been born to famous film stars she would have been referred to as a "love child". But to ordinary parents? She'd have been called a bastard.'

Raff's stomach shrank. Even allowing for child custody problems, the mores of the 1970s, his dad's religious upbringing and his dad's parents, who Raff remembered as having opinions and judgements on everything, it sounded as if Nigel's double life had short-changed both women in it. Had Mum been bitter that she and Dad had 'had' to marry? Had she ever dreamt of another man? Or even had one? Raff couldn't guess, and it was too late to ask. All he had proof of was that Nigel had got himself in a situation where he couldn't have everything so he'd grabbed as much as he could – and sad, sweet Ruthie had ended up with *nothing* she'd wanted.

Apart from a share of Nigel who, with his human weaknesses, had bricked himself into a corner by adopting Raff. If not for that, would Nigel have finally got up the courage to stop living a lie once Ruthie was pregnant, and have left Sindy? That would have meant Raff being brought up in a totally different family. He tried to imagine it, and knew what Ffion had meant when she'd talked about the parallel life she could have had.

Dad – he'd been the one to live both lives available to him. And though part of Raff knew he should feel disappointed in him, he found himself grateful that Nigel had somehow juggled his two lives, so that Raff and Ffion's childhood hadn't shattered.

Then he realised that Ruthie was suffering another wheezing, coughing fit. Maddy, frowning, held Ruthie's drink to encourage her to sip. Finally, the elderly lady managed to calm herself enough to gasp out, 'In the end, Raff, I gave your mother more than I ever took from her.' Then she dragged herself forward in the chair and hunched over, wheezing.

Raff tried to absorb the depth and truth of Ruthie's final comment. Maddy stroked the elderly lady's grey wavy hair back from her face and declared, 'I think that's enough for today. We can invite Raff back another time if you want to talk to him again.' It was quite plain that Ruthie was her concern, not Raff.

But it was a good point for Raff to regroup. He needed to talk to Ffion and confess that he'd been here today. Inwardly, he winced at her likely reaction. Ffion might look waiflike at the moment, but her illness hadn't blunted the edge of her tongue.

He needed to settle his feelings about his dad. He didn't know whether to be happy or sad that his parents had wanted to create a family via adoption, despite their troubled marriage. 'Making the best of a bad job' had been one of his dad's favourite sayings. With Ruthie out of the picture at that point, had he tried any harder with his wife? Had Sindy wanted any more than a sterile marriage?

He rose, closing his bag, the love letters tucked securely inside. 'I'm sorry if I've stayed too long, Ruthie.' He hovered closer to her chair, feeling awkward and unsure about how exactly you took leave of someone who'd been so much to your family, and yet so little. 'Thanks for inviting me. Thanks for the lovely lunch, Maddy.'

'Welcome.' Maddy graced him with the smallest of smiles.

Then he collected his coat and stepped out of the house and into the chill air. As he strode down the path to his waiting car, he tried to untangle his feelings. Sorrow for his parents, trapped in a marriage they didn't want but had never been defiant enough to leave. Wonder at his father's long-ago secret love. Wonder, too, that society had been so different, just a few decades ago. The Seventies sitcoms he occasionally caught on TV had given him an impression of freedom that didn't seem to have entered his parents' lives, or that of Ruthie – who'd apparently simply accepted the shitty end of the stick.

And yet Nigel and Ruthie's affair had lasted twenty-nine years and produced Ffion – he halted, realising that he'd allowed himself to be ushered out of The Hollies without fulfilling his part of the bargain to tell Ruthie about Ffion. Yet Maddy had seemed quite determined that his time with Ruthie was at an end for today.

Uncertainly, one hand resting on the freezing metal roof of his car, he glanced back at the red-brick house and saw Maddy watching him through the kitchen window.

Despite everything, his mind let the secrets of the past float away as he looked back at her. She was gorgeous.

Then he remembered Harris talking about her husband, Adey Austen. He was pretty sure Maddy wouldn't have thrown him off the headland, as she'd mockingly suggested to Harris, so where was he? He had an urge to know.

And also, how Maddy felt about the absent spouse.

When Maddy returned to the front room after watching Raff's dawdling departure, she found her aunt regarding her balefully. 'I'm in a snit with you,' Ruthie announced.

Maddy halted, unbalanced and taken aback. 'Are you?' She couldn't remember Ruthie ever saying anything to her that didn't indicate complete and boundless love.

'I only needed to get my breath back. You've sent Raff off without me hearing properly about Ffion.' She spoke the name with affection and pride, in the same way she usually said 'Maddy' or 'Lyla'.

'I'm sorry if you're upset,' Maddy said evenly. 'But I'm not sorry I thought you'd had enough for today. It would have been irresponsible—'

'Please ring him,' Ruthie cut in. 'Find out when he can come back. Now, if possible. He can't have got far.'

Maddy hesitated. Ruthie looked weird – excited yet determined. Slowly, she took out her phone and tapped Raff Edmonds' name in her contact list. After a few rings it went to voicemail. Flushing, she put the phone away. 'He's not picking up.'

Ruthie glared in a most un-Ruthie way. 'Maddy, if you're going to take the law into your own hands, you'd better give me his number.'

Maddy bristled. 'Probably he's driving and hasn't got the capability to answer hands-free. But if you want to make the call yourself, I'll add him to your contacts.' She did so. 'I'll keep trying Raff, but I have to go to The Green and meet the school minibus.'

Ruthie was already saying, 'Alexa, call Raff Edmonds.' But when the call went to voicemail she whispered, 'Damn.' And Ruthie, for the first time that Maddy could remember, hunched a cold shoulder.

Chapter Five

However great the snit, Maddy didn't properly regret dismissing Raff until the following morning, when Ruthie didn't emerge from her room and Maddy peeped in to find her crying.

Aghast, she breathed, 'Oh, Ruthie.'

Behind her, Lyla piped, 'What's the matter with Grauntie Ruthie?' And then her little body slipped between Maddy and the doorjamb.

Instantly, Ruthie wiped her eyes. 'Just coughing,' she told Lyla gamely. 'Do your eyes water when you cough? Mine do.'

Ruthie coughing was common, so Lyla was content to skip across the carpet and offer as big a hug as her small arms would allow. 'Aw. It makes you look as if you're crying.' 'Aw' and 'yay' were both big in Lyla's vocabulary.

Managing a smile, Ruthie said, 'Why on earth would I cry? What do you think you'll do at school today?'

Lyla beamed. 'We're reading out our lines for the 'tivity play. I'm a star.' She adopted a pose with her arms out and her feet apart, to demonstrate how her star would stand. 'I have to tell everyone to follow me.' She looked smug. 'The angels can't say their words till I've guided the wise men to the stable.'

Maddy, glad Ruthie had mollified Lyla without prompting too many questions, stroked the little girl's head. 'Say bye to Grauntie Ruthie, then get your coat. It's time to catch the minibus.'

'Bye, Grauntie Ruthie.' Lyla turned her head to receive Ruthie's kiss, bestowed one of her own on Ruthie's softly lined cheek, then skipped from the room.

Maddy eyed Ruthie cautiously. 'Be back soon,' she said softly.

Now Lyla was no longer there to put her under scrutiny, Ruthie's smile vanished, but she nodded.

Maddy usually enjoyed the early morning stroll around the curve of Jubilee Crescent with Lyla bouncing with enthusiasm for the day, pointing out the first Christmas lights appearing on houses and wondering when her friend Misty, who lived in nearby Thornham, would bring her birthday party invitations to school. Despite joining the chatter, Maddy felt Ruthie's despondency as if it were her own. Or maybe it was the weight of her aunt's displeasure that was making it hard to enjoy the whorls of leaves freezing to the pavement and discovering on a lamppost a poster for a Christmas fair in the lounge of the Duke of Bronte. Nelson's Bar didn't have a village hall, so the pub fulfilled the community role. The proprietors, Kaz and Oliver, had made it part of their business plan when the extension was built. This strategy had shushed most of those protesting the extension that transformed the B&B into a pub with a generous bar and restaurant with a few guest bedrooms.

'Can we go to the Christmas fair?' Lyla demanded excitedly.

'It's at the end of the month, but try and keep us away,' Maddy declared. Nelson's Bar *loved* Christmas. There would be a Santa race up Long Climb, the Christmas fair, wreaths on doors and enough fairy lights to give the cliffs a permanent festive halo. Every year, it was like living in a snow globe or an advent calendar. As well as the Duke of Bronte already being dressed in its Christmas finery, the village committee had hung strings of lanterns across Droody Road. Several houses they'd seen as they walked around the village had lights already on their trees in the garden.

Lyla gave a squeal. 'There's Jude and Blake. Can I run?' She turned an eager, enquiring face to Maddy like a flower making the most of the wintry sun.

Maddy grinned. 'Let's check the road . . . OK, it's clear, let's go.' They hurried across Droody Road to where Heloise stood with Blake and Jude.

Lyla burst into fresh 'I'm going to be the star in the 'tivity' boasts. Blake and Jude didn't look as impressed as Grauntie Ruthie had.

Maddy enjoyed a ten-minute chat with Heloise before seeing Lyla aboard the silver minibus and waving her off. Lyla managed a cursory acknowledgement, mouth moving as she chattered.

Heloise, her fair hair gleaming in the harsh winter sunlight, huddled into a black woollen coat. 'You up for a coffee in Hunny? I fancy a poke around the shops. Make the most of it while I don't have any kids or dogs.' 'Hunny' was the local name for nearby Hunstanton.

Regretfully, Maddy shook her head. She needed to return and see if she could smooth things over with

60

Ruthie. 'Can't today. Maybe Saturday, if you don't mind Lyla being in tow.'

Heloise nodded. 'Sounds good. I'll have little Daisy. I'll probably be as excited as her and Lyla at seeing whether there are any Christmas trees up yet. Shall we go to the Hunstanton Christmas Festival nearer the end of the month?'

'Absolutely,' Maddy agreed. 'Lyla's already asking about the Christmas fair at the Duke. We can all go together.' Side by side they walked the first part of Droody Road, then Maddy's route took her into Jubilee Crescent. She checked her phone as she went. Raff Edmonds hadn't replied to her texts or voicemail, but she tried him again as she hurried through the crisp morning, so she could tell Ruthie that she had. Voicemail again.

The Hollies welcomed her in from the cold with a waft of warmth, but Ruthie was still in her room. The door wasn't quite shut and Maddy could make out her shape, motionless in her chair, her face turned towards the window, though it was doubtful that she could see much beyond patterns on the light. Maddy shouted a cheerful hello, then went to make hot chocolate, sure that however blue Ruthie was, a steaming mugful would help.

A few minutes later, when she tapped Ruthie's bedroom door, it was to find her aunt sitting in exactly the same position. A tear had tracked down one softly wrinkled cheek, and her gaze was distant, even for her. A white and blue shirt box rested on her lap.

Maddy gave it a curious look, not remembering having seen it before. 'I've brought hot chocolate,' she murmured.

Ruthie sniffed without looking around. 'Thanks.'

'I tried Raff again,' Maddy went on. 'Still no reply. Maybe he's broken his phone.'

'Won't know, will we? If he never answers and never comes back, I'll have missed my chance,' Ruthie said dolefully.

Heart sinking, Maddy put down both cups of hot chocolate – she'd made one for herself in the expectation of being invited to perch on the dressing table stool to drink it. 'We don't have any reason to think that, do we?'

'We don't have any reason not to think it either,' Ruthie pointed out in uncharacteristic pessimism. Her hands stroked the box on her lap, and she turned her gaze towards them. 'These are Nigel's letters – all those I kept.' Her voice caught. 'I can't read them anymore.'

At the sorrow in those five words, any reply Maddy might have made lodged in her throat like a mouthful of sand.

With heavy movements, Ruthie lifted her thick glasses and wiped her eyes, her face puffy with crying, like a doughy bun. 'Will you read me some?' she whispered.

Maddy startled. 'Um . . . yes, of course. If you want me to.'

Ruthie said. 'Yes, please. Only—' She glanced Maddy's way from beneath a wave of grey hair. 'Not the last page. He always got . . . *adult*, on the last page.'

Maddy almost said, 'Oh, crap!' in horror at the idea of reading aloud a long-ago love letter that became *adult*. She swallowed the words. 'OK. Any particular letter?'

'I can't tell which is which.' Ruthie opened the box and stared down into a nest of paper and envelopes in a haphazard pile. 'Just pick one. But read me the date, so I know roughly what to expect.'

'Maddy drew in a breath and took out a long buff envelope bearing the words *On Her Majesty's Service* on the back. 'There are several in one envelope, here.' She peered at the separate folds of lightweight writing paper inside.

'Pick any. I didn't keep them in order.' Ruthie made an impatient motion with her hand, then sat silently while Maddy chose two pale blue sheets folded together. Each, she discovered when she smoothed the paper out, was covered on both sides with small, loopy writing.

She glanced at the top. 'It's the 3rd August 1984. The year I was born.'

Ruthie nodded. 'He'd left the army by then and oversaw repair resources and stock for a big company. Still in Scotland, though. The children were settled at school. Ffion would have been coming up to seven years old.'

Maddy moistened her lips, realising how much of Ruthie's story she still didn't know. 'Nigel never got back to Aldershot?'

Ruthie shook her head. 'He went before a couple of promotion boards, but none were successful.'

'So, by 1984, you'd been together for . . . ?' Maddy tried to remember if Ruthie had given an exact date for when the affair began.

Ruthie wrinkled her forehead. 'About thirteen years, but for three of those years we didn't see each other.'

Maddy smoothed the letter between her fingers, gazing at it without reading the lines of old, ballpoint pen. 'Writing to each other all that time? Never seeing each other?'

The look Ruthie turned on Maddy was what she herself might have called 'old-fashioned'. 'There were occasional visits.'

'Oh.' Maddy cleared her throat, not wanting to delve into what happened then and began to read. '*My dearest, darling Ruthie.*' Unexpectedly, she felt a prickling connection with the unknown man who'd written these words, and the affair that had been going on even as Maddy came into the world.

'*Big news*,' she continued, making her voice excited to reflect the underscoring of these two words. '*I think I'm being sent to Guildford on another course – only twenty-five minutes on the train from you. There's a new computer system they want me to know about. In a way, I feel bad, because every time they put in a new system another bloke loses his job, but at least it isn't me (this time).*'

'He was a bit political,' Ruthie recalled with a reminiscent smile.

Nigel went on to fill half of page two with his views of the government's failings regarding the working man, with occasional underlining and exclamation marks. Eventually, he returned to his original point. '*The course is Weds, Thurs and Fri. There's an induction reception on Tues evening, but I will have Weds and Thurs evenings free, and finish lunchtime on Fri, so we could have Fri p.m. together as well as most of the evening, till I get back to town to catch the sleeper. Can you wangle the half-day off? Please try!! I'm praying the course doesn't fall the same week as your hols because that would be too cruel, if I was in Surrey and you were on a tour of Devon.*

'*Oh, my dearest, darling, Ruthie, I wish you could be in that sleeper compartment with me.*' Maddy's cheeks heated as she turned to page three, hoping that the adult part wasn't about to start early. '*Just with the hope of seeing you, I'm like a dog with two you-know-whats.*' Maddy suspected that 'you-know-whats' didn't mean tails. She read on. '*It's been two months since you were last up in Aberdeen, when you managed a whole five days in that hotel, and I long to see you again, even though it's wonderful to sometimes phone you in the evening and hear your voice. I keep all your photos and letters in my safe here at work, but they're no substitute for having you with me.*

'I know you'll want to know that the children are bonny and happy.

'I do love you so much, Ruthie.'

Ruthie cleared her throat. 'That's probably all you need to read of that one, dear. I remember how the last part would go.' Her cheeks were pink, too, but at least there was now a sparkle in her eyes. 'He always ended, *I love you, Ruthie. God bless you and keep you safe, all my love Nigel.* And a row of kisses.'

'Aw, sweet,' said Maddy, borrowing one of Lyla's exclamations as she folded the two sheets of flimsy paper back together. She ventured, 'He didn't have much to say about the children.'

A huge sigh shook through Ruthie's small, dumpy body. 'That's how I wanted it. It was too painful to know the details. I used to fantasise about him bringing Ffion along to see me, but it would have been too hard for me. I would have wanted to hug and kiss her and burst out with who I was. That would have been wrong – and cruel to Ffion and Sindy. So I just settled for knowing she was OK. And the little boy, of course.' Thoughtfully, she added, 'Funny to think that little dot they adopted turned up here a few days ago, a big man.' She stared ruminatively at the window again, her hands folded over the box. 'I didn't even know what they'd called my little girl, until Raff told me. It would have made her too real. I yearned for her, you see, and if I'd known more, if Nigel had told me the details of her life, I think it would have been worse. I locked her away in my heart how she'd been

– a beautiful baby I'd only had with me for sixteen days.' A wipe of her eye. 'Of course, by giving them my baby, I only made it more likely that he'd stick with Sindy. It was very hard.'

Eyes stinging, Maddy reopened the envelope and returned the letter she'd read out – half love letter and half chat with a best friend. 'Did you never try to trace her? After Nigel died, I mean?'

Ruthie blew her nose as she shook her head. 'I didn't know she knew Nigel was her real dad. I decided to leave it to her, because adopted children often do try and trace birth parents. And then when she did . . . you shut it down.' Ruthie sounded like a hurt child. 'I think that's enough for now. Perhaps you'll read some more to me another day.' She opened the box lid.

Maddy gently posted the envelope inside, again gripped with unsettling guilt that she'd upset Ruthie, even though she'd thought she'd acted for the best. 'I'll read to you whenever you want.'

The unfocused gaze turned her way behind smeary glasses. 'And you'll keep on at Raff?'

'Yes.' Maddy's voice emerged as little more than a whisper. 'I'm sorry if I did the wrong thing by asking him to leave.'

A pause. Finally, Ruthie said, 'You did it for the right reasons.'

The mixed kindness and disappointment in her voice made Maddy feel an inch tall. 'You can sack me as your carer,' she whispered.

Ruthie raised one iron grey eyebrow. 'Don't tempt me.' But then she winked, so Maddy knew all wasn't lost.

Chapter Six

By that afternoon, Raff had still not answered Maddy who, consequently, remained in the bad books of her usually loving and adoring great-aunt. Ruthie was quiet and listless, nothing like her usual warm, funny self, though she made an effort in front of Lyla, who bounced home from school full of reports of the Christmas play, now only just over a month away.

Maddy decided to give Ruthie privacy to brood by taking Lyla to Zig-Zag Beach near the tip of the headland to make the most of a cold but fine afternoon before early winter dusk made it inhospitable. The tiny beach was reached via Zig-Zag Path between its wooden railings, and Lyla raced down it, squealing with glee.

The wintry afternoon turned the sea to gunmetal and the gulls complained as they rode the icy wind. The grey waves made Maddy think of Adey and how, in the same way she was continually ringing Raff now with no reply, on the night of the snowstorm nearly seven years ago she'd rung and rung Adey's number, and then rung his parents, hurling them into anxiety. Finally, she'd contacted Harris, who admitted seeing him briefly on the cliffs. 'Totally pissed off, he was,' he'd said accusingly. 'Said you'd had a huge row.' It had been true, but not unusual. People rowed. People stormed off.

It was just that most came back – if only to get their things.

Finally, she'd called the police. Officers had come out, but the swirling snow backing on a gusty wind that dark night had meant they could do little but make out a 'misper' report. Medium risk, they said. Adult male, no vulnerabilities, no threats to harm himself. But Adey had taken no belongings apart from the clothes he stood up in and whatever cash might have been in his wallet. She'd described his Timberland boots, Tommy jeans and Diesel sweatshirt, all covered with a North Face coat. She'd provided a photo taken only at the weekend. The police had searched the house, as if Adey might have crept in without Maddy noticing.

She shuddered. With no evidence to the contrary, the police had treated Adey ending up in the sea as a possibility, and she couldn't help gazing at the cold, deep water sometimes and wondering . . .

With a shiver, she thrust aside a vision of a long fall and icy black waves.

Not even Harris Soley seemed to have a clue what had happened to Adey, and he hated Maddy for it. Not that Harris had ever needed much excuse to hate Maddy.

Now, on the beach, Lyla sang, as if singing the waves to the shore, and shells crunched under her little boots as she meandered happily, breaking open brown seaweed pods and inspecting pebbles. As if reading Maddy's uneasy thoughts, she paused to swing her enquiring grey eyes

Maddy's way. 'In my class, some people have a mummy, and some have a daddy, and some have both.'

Maddy, stomach dropping, summoned a smile. 'That's right.'

Lyla frowned. 'But Blake, he said that I had to have had a daddy once, or I wouldn't have been borned.'

'That's true.' Maddy hesitated, spooked that Lyla had chosen to talk about daddies at this moment, when she rarely brought the subject up. Maybe it was just that Blake, being older, knew more about the facts of life, and had been puzzling over Lyla's circumstances. 'But I'm afraid I don't know where he is. He left Nelson's Bar a long time ago, and he didn't know you were going to be born. Nobody really understands what happened.'

That was as near as she cared to get to explain to a six-year-old that her daddy had stormed out in a huff one dark December evening to disappear into thin air, and that he hadn't known about Lyla because Maddy had deliberately kept her pregnancy from him. How could she explain those dark days, and her fears that Adey would have wanted a termination?

But Lyla was already switching subjects. 'Is Grauntie Ruthie cross with you?' she demanded, clutching a shell in one small, chilly-looking hand. The wind had half-unravelled the neat plait Maddy had woven into Lyla's fair hair at the beginning of the day, and strands blew across her sweet face.

Maddy continued her honesty-if-possible policy. 'A bit. She gets irritated when I think I know best.'

Lyla's eyes crinkled so that there was hardly any grey showing as she declared mischievously, 'So do I.'

With an exaggerated sigh, Maddy let her shoulders

droop. 'It's sad if the people I love most are annoyed when I try to look after them.' But, inside, it stung to be considered by her aunt to have been well-intentioned but overbearing.

Ruthie had lived a sad life, behind her warm smile. She'd never got her man, and her daughter had been brought up by another woman. Had Maddy lost her the only chance she'd ever have of getting news of her daughter, because Raff was now incommunicado? It had seemed innocuous enough at the time to tell Raff that Ruthie had had enough, but now guilt had lodged like lead in Maddy's stomach.

Could she locate him by visiting Docking? A long shot as she didn't know his address, but she could ask at the shop and pub. Someone might know him.

But maybe he no longer wanted contact. Maybe he'd satisfied his family's curiosity about the woman who'd sent love letters to his dad and would be happy to let her fade away. But then, *really*? If Ffion had located her birth mother via Raff, would she be satisfied with second-hand news of her?

There was no evidence to the contrary and Maddy blinked hard.

Lyla skipped to a rock poking through the sand. 'This looks like a turkle.'

Maddy smiled. 'It does look like a turtle.'

Layla picked up some dripping seaweed. 'Here's the turkle's hair.' She became engrossed in draping it artistically over the 'turkle's' head.

Maddy took out her phone. The signal that the village now boasted was non-existent down here in the lee of the cliffs, but she checked anyway. Nothing. She reread the most recent message she'd sent to Raff.

Sorry if I've made things tricky by getting overprotective of Ruthie. She's v keen to have more news of Ffion. If you have no wish for further contact, could you at least let me know Ffion's OK, so I can tell my aunt?

If she didn't get a reply today, she'd follow up to tell him what Ruthie had said about why she hadn't tried to trace Ffion, in the hopes it might touch a heart.

'My hands are cold.' Lyla gazed at her pink digits covered in damp sand, her small face crumpled in discomfort.

It wasn't Maddy's first rodeo, so tucked in her pocket was a dry face flannel, just the right size to dry small hands. 'Let's get them warm then. Here we are.' She leant over Lyla, absorbing the smell of the cookies the little girl had eaten between The Hollies and Zig-Zag Beach, brushing off as much sand as she could with practised sweeps before rubbing Lyla's hands dry. 'And here are your gloves, if you've finished playing with shells and seaweed.' She produced a knitted purple pair from her other pocket.

Lyla brightened when her hands were snug. 'Can we—'

'Go home for dinner? Yes,' Maddy interrupted deftly. 'Look at those dark clouds marching across the sky ready to pelt us with rain.' Firmly, she took Lyla's small, gloved hand.

Lyla gave in gracefully, skipping every other step to keep up with Maddy as they climbed sandy, stony Zig-Zag Path back to the clifftop. 'Miss Edge says we're going to have *snow*.' Lyla sucked in her breath impressively.

Maddy glanced down at her. This was the second person to warn of a severe winter, which the press loved to term

'A Beast from the East'. 'It's ages since I've seen snow in Nelson's Bar.' *Seven years.*

Lyla halted, face animated. 'Was that in the olden days?'

'Definitely.' Maddy grinned. Time was always relative. Maddy's childhood was the past to Lyla; Ruthie's affair with Nigel was the past to Maddy.

Once home, any lingering sand stamped off on the garden path and Lyla having run into the front room to edify Ruthie with a muddled news bulletin about the beach and snow and marching clouds, Maddy took a big breath and made a big decision. 'Lyla,' she called.

Lyla bounced from the front room to the kitchen. 'I'm being a kangaroo.' She bounced around the table.

Before she could begin a second circuit, Maddy caught her, sinking onto a kitchen chair and pulling Lyla onto her lap. 'Would you like to see a picture of your daddy?' Her breath stuck in her throat. Part of her wanted to leave Adey as a faceless figment of Lyla's past, but Lyla would probably deal with an image better than a figment. Her questions on the beach seemed to indicate that she was old enough for a few details, and if other children like Blake were interesting themselves, Lyla deserved to understand what she could.

'Yes,' said Lyla, sounding unsure.

Maddy took out her phone and scrolled almost to the beginning of her photo collection. She'd deleted many of the photos of Adey after a couple of years, in a fit of annoyance at him, but she'd kept one – a favourite, that dated back to before she'd wanted High Cottage and he'd held her to blame for all the problems that came with it. It was funny to look at the image and think, *we were happy then. We loved each other.* Adey gazed into the camera, full face, half-smiling, looking as if he was about to speak. His fair hair was close-cropped, waving on top, grey eyes ingenuous, as if he'd never shout at Maddy that he just wanted rid of 'that bloody place' and was 'sick of carping over money'. She smothered a wave of sorrow. 'This is him. His name's Adey.' She didn't go into the surname, as she'd registered Lyla as Lyla Cracey, not Austen Cracey or Cracey Austen, and was unwilling to provoke more questions right now.

'Oh,' Lyla said. She examined the picture, zooming in as Maddy had taught her, then zooming out again. 'Is supper soon?' She wriggled down from Maddy's lap and poised her hands in front of her again, obviously returning to kangaroo mode.

Maddy relaxed. Showing her the image had been the right thing to do. Lyla knew there had been a person, once, but Adey had no impact on her present. 'I'll start it now.'

Then, as Lyla kangarooed back into the front room, finally, *finally*, Maddy's phone pinged with a message from Raff, and she was able to forget Adey again. She opened it apprehensively. Sorry for delay. Ffion wanted time to think. Can you and I talk again? Not trying to go behind backs but situation delicate.

Hmm. Maddy wondered why it was delicate when all the players knew the big secret of Ffion's origins. She typed back: Talk on phone or in person? I could come to Docking this time.

Now he'd finally got in touch, he didn't seem to want to mess around as his reply winged straight back. How about in between? Thornham 8 p.m. tonight?

She replied: 8.30 so Lyla will be asleep? and suggested her favourite pub in Thornham, on the main road.

Scrubbing potatoes with a lighter heart, she thought

hard. How much should she tell Ruthie? While she didn't like underhandedness, she didn't want her aunt to get her hopes up only to have them dashed by the 'delicate' situation. With that in mind, even aware of Ruthie's grumbles about Maddy taking too much on herself, she decided that she still needed to know what was on Raff's mind before exposing her aunt to it.

Once the potatoes were boiling, she slipped into the front room, and selected a snippet of truth on which to hang a subterfuge. 'Ruthie, Heloise asked me to go to Hunny. If Lyla's in bed beforehand, do you mind babysitting? We could ask Della if she'd like to keep you company.'

Ruthie smiled, looking more her old self. 'Yes, you go out. I'll ring Della.'

Lyla leapt up from where she'd been playing with her cardboard castle on the floor. 'Can I do it? Hey, Alexa, call Della Hawthorn.' Ruthie's Alexa was used to taking instruction from Lyla.

As Maddy returned to the kitchen, Raff texted to agree to 8.30. Her heart pattered, and she couldn't entirely put that down to keeping her aunt in the dark. She'd lived a quiet life since Lyla was born and meeting Raff in secret for whatever reason felt exciting. And Ruthie would expect Maddy to wear make-up and change her clothes for the supposed excursion into Hunstanton with Heloise, so there was no reason to go in the jeans and sweater she'd worn all day. Her heart put in an extra thump.

The pub was a typical country hostelry with beams, flagstones, and two steps inside the door to trip down. Lights twinkled from a bare branch in a pot and tinsel inched along the beams like caterpillars dressed in finest bling. Perhaps some had metamorphosed into the butterflies that flittered around his stomach. Ffion, as he'd suspected, had not held back when he'd told her he'd met Ruthie without telling her, and had only consented to tonight's meeting on the understanding that he didn't mention Chloe. In fact, she'd been emphatic. 'Chloe's decided that she doesn't want to meet Ruthie after all, and though it's frustrating that she won't say why, it's important her wishes are respected.' Raff had agreed, because Chloe was Ffion's daughter, not his, but he had no idea how he'd answer if Maddy asked whether Ffion had kids.

He secured a table near a fireplace with a woodstove and when Maddy whirled in ten minutes later, her hair caught up behind her head before pouring down her back, she took the chair beside him, using another chair to dump her coat. Her short, black skirt and top of dusky rose suited her colouring. She wasn't petite and stumpy, like her great-aunt, and it was hard for Raff to keep his eyes on her face.

'What can I get you to drink?' he asked, after they'd exchanged greetings.

'Tap water, please.' Her eyes reflected the twinkle lights, looking like miniature solar systems.

Already half out of his seat, he hesitated. 'Tap water?'

She shrugged. 'I like water. No point in the bottled stuff.'

'OK.' He chose his usual low-alcohol beer and soon he was reseating himself beside her.

Her gaze focused keenly on him. 'I'm not sure what the meeting's about.' Her smile robbed the sentence of any snark.

He took a couple of sips while he marshalled his

thoughts, as if he hadn't marshalled them four different ways en route to the pub. 'I don't want to be mysterious or obstructive—'

'Good,' she put in, genially. She flicked back her hair and the silky length immediately slithered over her shoulder again. She didn't spoil the long, silky straightness with curls or waves, he noticed.

Realising he'd forgotten how he'd begun, he started again. 'I moved to Docking in July to be near Ffion.' Slowly, feeling his way, he added, 'I was offered a publishing contract that would allow me to take a break from teaching – which I didn't mind, to be honest – and focus on my writing. I'm renting to see how things go. Ffion's lived there for some time.'

Maddy's expression was polite. She was probably wondering why he was giving her a backstory.

He took a breath. 'I moved here because Ffion's ill.'

'Oh.' The polite expression catapulted into one of dismay. 'I'm sorry.'

A sip of beer eased the tightness that always gripped his throat when he confronted this black cloud that hung over his family. 'It's a bastard,' he said frankly. 'Over a year ago, she got rheumatic fever, which became rheumatic heart disease. She needed someone nearby.' This was what he'd agreed he'd say. No details of impending surgery to replace a heart valve. *No pity party or making it all about me,* Ffion had stipulated. But it *was* about her, and – by extension – Chloe.

'So,' he went on, 'as you asked once whether any further news I had would be good or bad, I want to discuss whether you think Ruthie's well enough to deal with Ffion's ill health.' He tried to give her some idea of scale. 'Ffion's well enough to drive, and to work remotely –

though only four days a week – but she's frail and fatigued.'

'That's tough for her.' Maddy hesitated, tapping her nails on the tabletop. 'We'd have to proceed gently, but Ruthie wants to see or talk to Ffion desperately. Letting Ffion be adopted was what she felt was best, but she's always held her in her heart. I have *not* been flavour of the month since I ended your visit on Monday. I suppose I was high-handed.' Her cheeks pinkened.

Ffion had used the same phrase to describe him, so he let that pass and concentrated on framing the story the right way. 'Ffion's fatigue has made it second nature for me to take jobs off her shoulders and apparently, though we'd discussed it, I jumped the gun visiting Ruthie. Ffion wasn't quite ready. As I've also stirred up a storm for Ruthie by spotlighting a secret, now I'm keen not to make things worse for either of them. I take it Ruthie's loss of sight is irrevocable?'

'Unfortunately.' Maddy sighed, expression darkening. 'Age-related macular degeneration, with occasional bleeds in the eye. She sees an ophthalmologist for injections to try and hold back further sight loss, but what vision she has is mainly around the edges, and straight lines appear wavy, so you can imagine how difficult it is.' Maddy sipped her water. A group of people entered the pub chatting, all middle-aged and cheerful, known to those behind the bar judging from the banter that sprang up. When they'd moved away from the table, her gaze fixed on him as if she could see through his change of subject. The gold flecks in her eyes were like sparks from the fire. 'On Monday, if I hadn't said Ruthie had had enough, what would have happened? I thought you were about to tell her all about Ffion, so it was just a matter of asking you to come another time to carry on the conversation. Instead, you've been ignoring me.'

A staff member arrived to put a log on the fire, and he wished she hadn't as he felt hot already. Apart from the agreeable opportunity to have a drink with Maddy, it would have been better if Chloe had suffered her change of mind before he'd ever got involved. 'I probably would have,' he admitted. 'But now Ffion wants a time-out. She's under a lot of stress.' This was what they'd agreed he'd say, but he tried to create context. 'Ffion's important to me. She's my sister. That's the law of adoption. We were brought up to love each other, and we do. For what it's worth, I think she should meet Ruthie, her natural mother, but it's not up to me to balance her emotional scales.'

The brown-gold gaze warmed. 'I think they should meet too but agree it's not up to us.' Maddy fiddled with a small vase of holly on the table, ensuring its red ribbon lay dead centre, then peeped at him under her lashes. 'This is probably bang out of order . . . but do you think Nigel's your natural father, too?'

'No,' he said briefly.

She blinked. 'Sorry. I just thought that as he'd had an affair with Ruthie . . .'

'He might have had an affair with someone else, and got them pregnant, too,' he finished for her. 'But I know who my birth father is. We email occasionally.' He smiled. 'My birth parents were teenagers, Liz and Dave, and Liz's parents were friends with my adoptive parents, Nigel and Sindy. Liz had kidney disease and died soon after the birth. Dave was unprepared to be a father and his parents were either kept out of the loop or washed their hands of me. Liz's parents were going to have me adopted and Mum and Dad wanted me. Liz's surname was Rafferty, so they made that my new first name.' He looked away. 'When Ruthie said what she did about grandparents giving away a grandchild rather than keep a bastard, it made me wince.'

Maddy's hand came to rest gently on his arm. 'I'm glad you found a nice family to join.'

Ridiculously, his eyes burned. He forced a laugh. 'Did I sound sorry for myself? I was just telling you the facts.'

Her hand remained, warm through his sleeve, and he noticed she wore no wedding ring. 'My parents broke up when I was small. Dad moved down south. Mum went to live in Spain when I was eighteen because she likes sunshine and felt she'd done her duty by me. Only Ruthie and I stayed in Nelson's Bar. So now we know why you're protective of Ffion and I'm protective of Ruthie.' She dimpled at him. 'Another drink?'

Without waiting for his answer, she hopped up and headed for the bar, purse in hand. When she returned, he started to say awkwardly that he didn't feel good about her buying him a drink when she was drinking water, but she bowled on with the previous conversation. 'Rafferty Edmonds is a nice name.'

'Well.' He scratched his chin self-consciously. He'd shaved before coming to meet her. 'I write as Edd Rafferty. And it always feels weird to say those words if I'm not at a writers' conference or publishing party. It feels like Mr Edmonds, English teacher and deputy head, has imposter syndrome.'

Her eyes twinkled. 'But you're a real author – for money.'

He laughed. 'For money now, after a couple of decades of rejections and near misses. On the strength of my first two books my agent got me my current deal with a decent advance. It sounds good that with my savings, I can live modestly while I try and make a go of full-time writing, but in a year I might have to do some part-time curriculum planning or tutoring to augment whatever I make from my books.'

'Still.' She lifted her glass to clink with him. 'Congratulations, author.'

He gazed at the soft light in her eyes and the smile curving her lips and felt a tightening in his groin. 'That's kind, considering I've caused you nothing but upheaval.'

Surprise flickered in her eyes. 'I don't begrudge people success. I was on the peripheries of another type of publishing before I had Lyla. I'd trained as a chef, but I didn't like the time pressures of a kitchen, so I became a food stylist.'

'A what?' He watched her mouth as she grinned.

'A food stylist makes dishes look gorgeous for a photographer. We worked on full-colour cookery books. I painted chickens with wood stain to make them look perfectly golden or balanced blueberries on mousse before it went floppy.'

'Painting chickens with *wood stain?*' he said incredulously.

She gurgled a laugh. 'Disgusting, isn't it? But it works for the camera. We used motor oil instead of syrup, for puddings, too. It looks more like syrup than syrup does.'

'And you left this awesome job when Ruthie and Lyla needed you?' he asked.

A shadow fell over her face. 'I'd been working directly for a studio, which turned out to be a mistake as I was made redundant. Freelancing had seemed scarier but would have turned out the better choice.'

As she added no more, he returned to his own story.

'I'm not sure how my ex-wife Antonella feels about me getting a "big five" publisher.' It wouldn't hurt for Maddy to know he was divorced. 'We met at a writing group, and she was a shining light, not me. She *says* she's delighted, but I think that secretly, she feels she deserved it more.' He grinned.

'You keep in touch?' she asked.

He shrugged. 'As friends. Opposites originally attracted, but that didn't last and our relationship fizzled out. She likes to roast on beaches in the Canaries and I prefer to trek up mountains. She'd hate where I'm living, a converted outbuilding with a patch of concrete. She's more into four-bedroomed new-builds with double garages.'

Conversation was interrupted by a woman in a puffy bronze gilet pausing beside their table, blonde hair wind-tousled. 'Hello, my dears, can I interest you in raffle tickets? Prizes from a spa day to a meal for two. We're raising money for Christmas dinner for the homeless.'

Maddy reached for her purse. 'Of course.' Frowning, she handed over a fiver and scribbled her phone number on the ticket stubs.

Raff tried to read whatever thoughts were clouding her brow, taking his time buying his own yellow raffle tickets. From the well-worn appearance of The Hollies and the lack of labels on her clothing, he thought that a fiver might be a lot for Maddy to give to charity in one go.

He was still mulling this over as the woman moved off. Perhaps misreading his silence, Maddy sighed. 'I suppose you heard Harris Soley in the Duke of Bronte as you were leaving that night? Asking me whether I'd found my husband?'

Seeing hurt in her eyes, he elected not to share that Harris had already enlightened him by then. 'It sounded like a joke in bad taste.'

She grimaced. 'Harris was Adey's best mate and his "jokes" about me pushing Adey off the cliffs are wearing thin. I didn't do it,' she clarified. 'But Adey did disappear.'

Even though he knew that bare fact, Raff couldn't help his lips parting in surprise.

'We were drowning in maxed credit cards,' she went on. 'Adey didn't want to stop buying clothes or running his BMW. It was terrifying.' She paused to gulp some water. 'We left a plumber working at the cottage on Friday while we visited friends and came home on Sunday to a flood. Lights out, ceilings down, carpets sodden, and water running down the walls. It was snowy weather, too, so the place was an icebox.'

'Shit,' he murmured, appalled at the picture she painted.

'Quite.' She gave a mirthless laugh. 'A pipe had been left unsoldered under the floorboards. Adey and I had a titanic row because the plumber – one of his buddies, moonlighting – confessed he had no insurance. So, *I* said—' her voice quavered '—we'd claim on our house insurance and Adey admitted he'd let it lapse. He tried to blame it on me for being made redundant.'

Raff found his hand was resting on her arm, just as she'd offered him a moment's unspoken sympathy earlier.

'He stomped out of the house and into the snow.' She sipped more water and then gave him a half-smile. 'I never saw him again.'

Raff was aware of other voices and the crackling of the fire, but what echoed in his ears was *I never saw him again*. It was bizarre. Incredible.

She blew out her cheeks. 'Harris met him striding

around the clifftop in a temper, but after that . . . nothing. The police never found a trace of him, not financial or digital, or crossing a border. There was a search. Dogs. A helicopter.' Her eyes closed for an instant. 'My life turned into a soap opera. Half the village stood watching, their eyes sliding between the police and me.' She lifted her hands, palms up, as if to demonstrate coming up empty. 'There's been no evidence of foul play but no evidence of life. I was left in limbo.'

Shocked by the story being so close to what that moron Harris had told him, angry that Harris would jibe at her about it, he could see why she clung to her little family unit of daughter and great-aunt. 'If he's alive . . . he left his daughter?' Raff demanded.

'He didn't know she was on the way. We weren't getting on well and I hung on to my news as long as possible. I suppose I was scared he'd pressure me to have an abortion because we'd talked about having kids before, and he'd said he wasn't ready. The pregnancy wasn't planned.' Tears glittered in her eyes.

Raff couldn't help his recoil but, really? She'd thought her husband might want her to abort their child?

She shifted her glass. It had left a wet ring on the wooden tabletop, and she wiped it away. One corner of her mouth lifted wryly. 'Hard to believe that we were happy before we bought High Cottage. He was fun and loving when everything was OK, and relied on me when things went wrong.' She looked at Raff beneath those long lashes again. 'I support homeless charities just in case he's on the streets somewhere. It's where some missing people end up.'

He turned that over in his mind. 'Wouldn't he just come home?'

Brows arched, she said, 'I've studied a lot of missing persons websites and watched TV programmes. People spiral down. They lose their sense of themselves and erect barriers between them and their old lives, whether or not barriers need to exist. Mental illness is a big factor. Nobody could pretend Adey was in a good frame of mind.'

It was such a bleak picture that Raff wished that he'd bought ten pounds' worth of raffle tickets instead of five.

She shrugged. 'Or, Adey might just be happier elsewhere. Some people who "disappear" want a fresh start and might even have a whole new life already lined up.' A sigh emerged from deep in her chest. 'A person's perfectly entitled not to be found, whatever crap they've left behind.'

The author in Raff made him spot the loose end she hadn't tied up. 'What happens if he comes back?'

'I tell the police and they interview him so they can close the case. And I divorce him,' she added with ice-cold unsmiling certainty. 'I would have already if it was possible, but I have to wait seven years and go through a process of asking for him to be "presumed dead", which sounds horrible.' Then her eyes widened comically, as if she'd decided to make light of things. 'Also, I'll panic because he'll try to claim half of High Cottage.'

'You still own it? But you live with your great-aunt.' The Hollies had been the address on the letters to his father long before the period Maddy was talking about, so he was sure the house was Ruthie's.

'High Cottage is in joint names, but rented out,' she said. 'I had to fight like crazy to pay the mortgage, so it wasn't repossessed. I sold everything – all Adey's labelled clothes and posh gadgets, my jewellery, my car – his was

84

repossessed by the finance company. I bought things from boot sales and refurbished them to sell on eBay. I worked shifts at the pub and took zero-hours call centre work. In between, I dried out the cottage and redecorated. Heloise helped, and I guilted the builder into replastering ceilings, but I was pregnant and almost bankrupt. Then Ruthie said she needed a carer, and did I want the job? I leapt at it. Living with her gave me and Lyla a home and renting out High Cottage made me solvent.'

Silence fell. Raff mulled over her delivery of her story – veering between calm and caustic but never into self-pity. If the missing Adey Austen was the weak reed she described, he'd chosen the ideal wife. If he wasn't dead, he was an arsehole. 'I see why you describe it as limbo,' he said eventually.

'It's what it is.' Then she checked the time and picked up her bag. 'I have to be going. Ruthie doesn't stay up late, and she sleeps downstairs, not close to Lyla.'

He rose. 'I'll talk to Ffion again,' he promised, conscious of admiration for this woman and the way she rolled with the punches that life sent her way.

Her smile was tired now, as if reliving the past had been exhausting. 'I won't pressure you, but I'll cross my fingers.' Then she pulled on her coat, gave him a smile, said, 'Bye,' and hurried out.

She'd given him no encouragement to walk her to her car, so he watched her swing out of the door and vanish from his sight.

Next day, Wednesday, was Ffion's day off, so Raff intended to talk to her while Chloe was at school. Ffion's remote working in an IT support role and her four-day week helped with fatigue. She lived quietly since rheumatic fever had given her a beating, so could cope financially, even with a sixteen-year-old daughter to support. Hopefully, by the time Chloe needed funding through university, Ffion's treatment would have restored her capacity for normal hours.

He'd call when he broke for lunch. At the glass dining table that served as a desk at one end and a place to eat at the other, he whizzed through emails from his editor and publicist, grinning with pride at being taken seriously as an author. No more lesson plans or OFSTED for the time being. For now, his name was on the lips and at the fingertips of people who also dealt with top-selling authors.

With a thrill of apprehension, he saw that his editor Vikki had emailed him the suggested front-cover image for the first book in his deal. Opening the file, he paused to drink it in. A sword gripped in a gauntleted hand, *Edd Rafferty* in white capitals and *The Sword of Adeckor* in a spiky red font blazing against a granite grey background. And, Vikki said, she was talking to design about a crown on the back cover, and a silhouette of a centaur with a flowing mane.

A lot of the pages destined to fit within those covers had yet to be written so, after printing out the cover and propping it where he could see it, he opened his first draft and read yesterday's output, fiddling with sentences and cutting empty phrases. Maybe it was because part of his mind had been on incorporating seeds that would eventually lead to the second book in the contract, *The Blood of Adeckor*, that with a sinking stomach he discovered a stupid mistake in the timeline between Chapter Fifteen and Chapter Five. Crap. Frowning, he went back over the pages to gnaw over the best way to smooth it over. And, hell, Chapter Ten was affected, too. Stupid characters who took charge of his imagination and numbed his facility with logic . . .

By the time the flow of the book was restored, and he was happy with the machinations of the king's advisers, his empty stomach and a whispering of sleet against the window pulled him from his writing. He glanced at the time. 'Two-thirty?' he said out loud. He'd have to hurry if he wanted a private chat with his sister before Chloe arrived home on the school bus from Hunstanton.

He made a sandwich, then pulled on his thick jacket and beanie hat against the sleet and stepped outside, covering the distance to Ffion's as he ate, his mind occupied with the conflict he'd been working on before his timeline tripped him up. Absently, he noticed that beside the notice about the Christmas fair at the village hall had sprouted a Christmas tree with red tinsel and silvery twinkle lights. A golden star sat wonkily on the top. It was a cheery reminder of what was only just over seven weeks away.

At about the same time as he ate his last bite of lunch, he arrived at Ffion's, and shook his mind clear of Adeckor's world of craggy mountains and uncharted plains. The terraced house was more about cream and red curtains and comfy armchairs and he was pleased to find Ffion relaxing with a book.

'Good to see you,' she called, as he took the couple of steps necessary to reach the lounge. 'I've just made a fresh jug of coffee.'

'Perfect.' In the kitchen, he found her food shopping had been delivered and waited in boxes on the table. Probably it was one of Choe's jobs to put it away, but Raff decided to do it himself in case Chloe went off to a friend's house and forgot. It was the kind of task that set Ffion huffing and puffing. Then he emptied the filter jug into the biggest mug he could find and joined Ffion in the cosy lounge.

Ffion had known that he was meeting Maddy last night, so he wasn't surprised when she began the conversation with an expectant 'And?'

He dropped into a chair. 'I met Maddy. I told her as much as we agreed about your medical situation.'

Ffion blew out her cheeks. 'What does she think?'

'That Ruthie will be fine, if we go about things sensitively,' he answered promptly. 'Apparently, Ruthie's desperate to meet you.'

Ffion only looked dubious. 'Yeah, but Chloe . . . I don't want to upset her.'

He surveyed her through the steam from his coffee, looking frail and pale, but wearing the slightly mulish look she got if anyone tried to railroad her. Still, no harm in being honest. 'I feel terrible. When I first went to see Ruthie, I thought it was what you wanted, and I was just getting the lay of the land. Instead, I've upset you and possibly desperately disappointed an elderly lady. And it was Chloe who first wanted you to find your natural mother.'

Her gaze slid away. 'I'm sure that it's what she wanted a couple of weeks ago. She's a mercurial teenager. Her list of things to agonise over changes by the hour – GCSEs, dancing, discovering boys, fitting in with friends.' Her expression grew rueful. 'She was scared when she said she wanted to know her grandmother, grappling with the fear that I won't make it through the op in February.'

'Well, it's possible,' said a small, high voice from the sitting room doorway.

Ffion and Raff both jumped when they realised that Chloe had come into the house unheard and was now standing looking mutinous, her bleached blonde hair in a ponytail, her black uniform and coat worn oversized, as befitted a member of a street dance crew. Piercings laced the edges of her ears and a single nose stud gleamed gold.

Ffion smiled. 'You're early, darling.'

Chloe stepped further into the room. 'Got a lift with a Year Twelve who lives in Stanhoe. Lot quicker than the bus.' She offered Raff a fist bump, then let her school bag slide off her shoulders, and her coat slither off to join it on the floor. After stooping to give her mum a hug, she subjected her to a searching teen stare. Raff wondered whether Chloe and Ffion's petite frames came from Ruthie. Was there a resemblance in the way Ffion held her head? Or was it his imagination?

'It's *possible*, Mum,' Chloe repeated, evidently intent on not giving up her stand on human frailty.

Ffion pulled Chloe down to share both the armchair and another hug. 'Things do happen to people, Chloe, but the success rate on this op is high. Raff will move in here to be with you and bring you to see me in King's Lynn hospital, but I should be away less than a week. Once I've recovered, I should be firing on all cylinders.'

'Shoulda, woulda, coulda,' Chloe murmured, tilting her head so that it rested against her mother's shoulder. Raff watched the youngster's lip wobble and couldn't blame Ffion for not pushing the Ruthie thing. His own heart felt as if it was beating its way out of his chest at the thought of the op, so Chloe's fears for her mum were totally understandable. Conceived via an un-Ffion-like Ibiza hook-up with whom Ffion hadn't even exchanged phone numbers, Chloe was born into a family that had only ever consisted of mum Ffion, Grandma Sindy, Uncle Raff and Auntie Antonella.

Sindy and Antonella, for different reasons, had disappeared from the family group.

He wanted to assure her, *I'll always be here for you, Chloe,* but he knew that would only prompt her into conjuring up examples of disaster that might make it impossible for him to keep that promise.

Ffion wriggled around in the shared armchair until she could gaze into her daughter's face. Tentatively, she said, 'Raff has information on my birth mother. Would you like to hear it? Or wait and see if you feel ready another time?'

Chloe stared silently back. Raff could see tiny movements of her irises as if she was gazing into one of Ffion's eyes and then the other. Then she swivelled her head and looked at Raff. 'For real?'

He smiled. 'Yes, I've met her.'

Softly, Ffion recounted the gist of what Raff had learnt in the past five days.

Chloe listened, her legs over Ffion's like a baby who'd grown too big to be rocked – which was what she was, he supposed. When Ffion finished, she murmured, 'Freakin' hell,' her favourite not-quite-a-swearword. As teens do, she examined the situation from her own perspective. 'So, this niece Maddy, her daughter and her mum, are all related to me?'

Ffion smiled tremulously. 'They're cousins to both of us but I never know how to work out that second or third cousins stuff, and who's removed.'

Chloe looked blank. 'What's "removed"?'

As Ffion explained how "removed" related to cousins

of differing generations, Raff experienced a prickling feeling. The only blood relations in this room were in the other armchair, cuddled up like kittens and talking about their family.

Raff was on the outside. Till now, he and Ffion had felt themselves to be in similar situations. Now she had a growing list of blood relations.

Then Chloe swivelled towards him with all the trust and affection she'd always shown him, and the unpleasant feeling vanished. 'Is she nice?' she demanded.

'Very,' he answered promptly.

'Freaky,' she breathed, eyes wide. 'And she's, like, really, really old?'

Belatedly, he realised that she was talking about Ruthie rather than Maddy. He replied, 'She's not very tall, like you and your mum. She has grey hair and wears glasses, though I don't think she can see much even with them.'

'Aw, that's sad.' Chloe adopted the overly sympathetic tone she might use if one of her dancing buddies was out in the first heat of a competition.

'Her great-niece lives with her, to care for her.' Ffion stroked Chloe's hair.

Raff added, 'And she has respiratory issues. Asthma,' he added as Chloe frowned at the term.

Her brow cleared. 'Oh, asthma. Does she have a puffer? Salina at school has a blue one but Murph's is pink. He says it's embarrassing.'

'Ruthie's is red.' Raff suddenly recalled the detail.

Chloe turned back to Ffion, gazing down and looking very young. 'Still not sure.'

For a second, Ffion looked wistful, but still she stroked Chloe's head. 'How about we talk about it again at the weekend?'

'OK.' Chloe began to lever herself from the armchair. 'I'll start my homework.' In passing, she ruffled Raff's hair. 'Like the new cut.' Then she stumped into the hall, dragging her backpack as if she thought it had sprouted wheels.

After she'd gone, footsteps clumping, Ffion gave Raff a tired smile.

As so often, he tried to meet her needs. 'You look as if you need to be left alone to chill. I'll go back to work.' He clambered to his feet, gave her hand a squeeze, and shouted, 'Bye, Chloe,' up the stairs, receiving a faint reply. Outside, the afternoon was winter grey, almost dusk. The streetlamps had come on, wearing halos of light, like on a Christmas card.

This Christmas would be the fourth since he and Antonella split; his second since their divorce had been made absolute, and he didn't miss the old hullaballoo one jot. He kept Christmas simple now there was no Antonella to buy Christmas cards and then insist half were his responsibility; or make hospitality plans and then expect him to shoulder most of the work because teachers got 'so much' holiday. Now, he bought Ffion something frivolous and expensive, like cashmere socks and posh pyjamas, because she deserved to be spoilt occasionally. Chloe liked cash, but he also bought her something to unwrap, like a top okayed by Ffion. He contributed to the food shopping and then turned up at Ffion's on Christmas Day with gifts, wine and flowers, ready to roll up his sleeves and pitch in with Christmas dinner. As he was resident in the village over the Christmas period this year, he had plans to read or watch TV, unless Ffion or Chloe wanted him to go with them to see a choir or a street performance.

Although he'd seen other women since splitting with Antonella, he hadn't so far dated through Christmas. He enjoyed not worrying whether presents would be expected, and if so what; or whether there were things she'd want them to attend together. Christmas time as single time was great.

He wandered home under a darkening sky, his thoughts returning to his book. Should he give Adeckor a love interest? Like . . . how would he react if the *queen* came on to him? Now there was a conflict – love for the queen warring with loyalty to the king. Temptation versus betrayal.

He let himself into his tiny rented home ready to sit down at his computer and find out, because the world he created was one he could control more easily than his family's real life.

Real life could be uncomfortable.

Chapter Seven

Maddy really wanted to get on with her day and the first truly Christmassy entertainment now it was nearly the end of November, and disliked wasting Saturday morning on a doorstep – especially the doorstep of her own house, High Cottage. But one of her tenants, Garth, who evidently was not feeling the Christmas spirit, stood with one arm across the doorway, plainly not wanting her in. As she'd neglected to make an appointment, as per the tenancy agreement, she could scarcely insist. Down the hall, a ginger and white cat ate on the kitchen counter. For an instant, time seemed to shift and Maddy saw Adey standing beside the same counter, fair hair showing off a perfect cut as he made Maddy coffee from the machine he'd just had delivered, presenting the cup along with several kisses, then making them his favourite breakfast of scrambled egg with bacon.

Maddy shook the vision off. 'I see you have a cat,' she said pleasantly. 'I'm afraid pets aren't allowed under your tenancy agreement.'

Garth shrugged. 'It's a polite cat.' In the few weeks

since she'd last seen him, he seemed to have grown bigger and scruffier, with food stains down the front of his sweatshirt. The lines on his face parked themselves in an expression of truculence. 'I answered your email. I said there was no good putting the rent up this year because I can't afford it.'

Maddy felt at a disadvantage, with him on a step above, gazing down at her, but when something worried her she reacted spikily, which was good armour. 'I'm afraid the tenant doesn't set the rent, Garth. The landlord does. I didn't raise your rent last year, but I must this, I'm afraid, by twenty-five pounds a month – which is still below market.'

'But everything's gone up,' he complained with an angry wave of his hand, as if it were her fault.

Maddy stuck her chin in the air. 'Same for everyone, including me. The mortgage on High Cottage has increased—'

'I ent here to pay your fucking mortgage,' Garth snapped, eyes bulging in outrage.

'Yes you are.' Maddy narrowed her eyes in an expression that proved effective with Lyla. 'I rent my home out solely because I can't afford to live in it. The rent must cover my costs.' Plus provide her with income, but that was her business. Maddy knew Garth could easily make up twenty-five pounds a month by cutting his consumption of beer at the Duke of Bronte.

Garth snorted. 'Yeah. Everyone knows about your old man.'

That he'd said 'your old man' instead of 'your husband' reminded her unpleasantly of Harris Soley. Maddy regarded Garth in silence, refusing to discuss that night when the snow had backed and veered around the headland village while Adey chose to rage around the cliffs instead of dealing with a bad situation. No lurid headlines had followed as police divers discovered the worst, yet whiffs of curiosity had always followed her around the village and made people unsure how to deal with her. And now she'd confided the realities of her weird situation to Raff, he'd promptly dropped all communication again.

She calculated dates. Two weeks and four days since she'd met him in Thornham, and then he'd gone off to talk to Ffion. Nothing in all that time.

Maybe he'd been writing furiously. That was what authors did, wasn't it? Locked themselves in attics and abandoned the world? She'd checked Amazon for Edd Rafferty and discovered mainly four- and five-star reviews for already published books, and one, *The Sword of Adeckor*, available for preorder. An author persona made it seem unreal that he'd turned up at The Hollies with Ruthie's love letters and secrets.

Back in real life on the doorstep, Garth fidgeted. 'Leanna, my girlfriend, left,' he blurted sullenly. 'That's why I can't pay more.'

Maddy's stomach sank. Relationships ending could be bad for landlords. Household income shrank and so tenants withheld rent or did a moonlight flit, leaving arrears. Either she needed to formalise the situation or find other tenants.

She tilted her head understandingly. 'I'm sorry to hear about Leanna. Under the tenancy agreement, she should have given me notice to quit.' She didn't know Leanna well as she'd only come to the village to live with Garth, who'd been brought up in Nelson's Bar like Maddy. The second year of his tenancy was well underway, and she hadn't had problems with him before, so she made her voice sympathetic. 'Look, I'll draw up a fresh tenancy agreement in your name only to protect you, shall I? Did you get her key? Or would you like a change of locks? If you want to stay, that is.' She hoped he did because an empty property got expensive.

Confusion, then shock chased each other over Garth's face. 'Shit, I hadn't thought about Leanna walking back in. Do people do that?'

'People sometimes take it upon themselves to break the rules,' Maddy said vaguely, imagining the recently departed tenant moving herself back in again acrimoniously and causing all kinds of arguments . . . such as who was paying the rent.

The fight seemed to go out of Garth. 'Can we change the locks?' Gruffly, he added, 'Rentals in the village are thin on the ground. I'll manage somehow.'

'Of course. I can do it tomorrow, and bring you the new tenancy agreement, OK?' The locks fitted at High Cottage accommodated the changing of the barrel without disturbance to the part fitted to the door. She even had spares from when she'd changed them two tenants ago under similar circumstances.

'Thanks,' he said, and blew out a breath. 'It's horrible when you split up with someone, ent it? All kinds of aggro.'

'It is,' Maddy said drily, remembering her fight to keep this very cottage. She arranged to call back after lunch tomorrow and left, mildly guilty that she'd let Garth think she was doing him a favour in revising the tenancy rather than protecting herself as much as him. To make up, she wouldn't evict the cat. He did look polite.

Beyond the gate, she followed the cliff path towards Marshview Road, gazing down at the angry grey sea far below as waves boomed against the rocks, spouting spray high into the air. Garth had provoked her memories of sleepless nights after Adey vanished. The juggling of payments. Mounting interest. Bank charges. The scraped-together income from unreliable, casual employment followed by stumbling, exhausted and pregnant, into High Cottage to redecorate.

She still had nightmares.

Pausing, leaning into the wind, she opened her banking app to check her balance. She was never likely to be a millionaire but rent plus carer's allowance now kept the sleepless nights at bay.

Yes, her balance told her she was OK. She could afford to take Ruthie, Lyla and Heloise to Hunstanton for the Christmas festival, and meet the costs of stalls and rides and Santa's grotto outside the Princess Theatre.

But when she entered The Hollies, expecting to find Ruthie and Lyla dressed in Christmas jumpers ready to hop in the car and call for Heloise en route to hours of festive fun, she found only Lyla dressed, lying with her legs up the back of the sofa, viewing *The Loud House* on the TV upside down.

Probably keen to deflect attention as Maddy had made it plain that TV watching should be done right side up, she rolled over quickly. 'Grauntie Ruthie's feeling poorly. We've got to go without her.' Disappointment edged her voice.

Maddy's gaze flicked to where Ruthie huddled in her chair.

Ruthie's head moved only slightly in Maddy's direction, as if she couldn't be bothered to try and focus. 'I've got a headache. All I'll see is a blur of lights and flickering anyway, and it's cold out.'

All her points might be factual, but Maddy was alarmed that Ruthie was being so unlike herself. She hadn't even bothered to brush her hair this morning, let alone shower and dress. 'Oh-kay,' she said, keeping her voice light for Lyla's benefit. 'So, Lyla, you need to turn off the TV, go to the loo then find your coat and boots, please. OK? Go!'

Lyla, clearly looking forward to the Christmas festival, fumbled with the TV remote, repeated, 'Go!' then raced from the room. Her hair was already escaping its ponytail but she'd be snuggled under a hat all day so that wouldn't matter.

Maddy went into the kitchen. After a few minutes, she returned with two travel cups filled with tea to leave on Ruthie's table, so Ruthie could have a hot drink without endangering herself by trying to use the kettle. Then she perched on the footstool and studied her aunt. 'I've made sarnies and left them on the top shelf in the fridge. Are you OK?' she asked softly.

Ruthie nodded. 'The Christmas festival would be tiring, that's all.'

'True.' But Maddy didn't think Ruthie was feeling her eighty years any more than usual – she was down because of Raff's continued silence. To Maddy, her quiet suffering was worse than her initial grumpiness and dismay. It was all about Ffion. Ruthie's baby. Lost baby. 'I'm worried about you,' she said. As she did so often, as if touch could make up for lack of sight, she took Ruthie's hand. It lay in hers, wrinkled and soft. 'You're still angry with me?'

Silently, Ruthie shook her head.

'I know it's a while since we heard from Raff.' Maddy was glad she'd never told Ruthie about the meeting in Thornham, because it would only have created a fresh raising and dashing of Ruthie's hopes. Filtering through Maddy's heartache for Ruthie and the guilt that she'd been the one to cut Raff off before he'd told Ruthie all about Ffion, Maddy felt disappointment in Raff. He'd left Ruthie hanging. Couldn't he just *say* that his sister wanted no further contact? Maddy was sure by now that this must be the case.

Ruthie sighed. 'I know.' Her mouth trembled.

Maddy stroked the small, creased hand, knowing that Ffion not wanting contact couldn't be the whole scenario, or Raff would never have met Maddy to discuss his sister's health. Nor would he have seemed relieved when Maddy felt Ruthie could deal with it, if she only got news of her daughter. Tentatively, she said, 'I don't want to leave you alone like this. We'd better stay.'

As Maddy had hoped, this shook Ruthie out of her mood. 'Madeline Cracey, don't you dare disappoint your poor little Lyla,' she scolded, turning to face Maddy properly. 'I'll be fine. I've got the mega remote—' the TV remote control with the oversized buttons '—and Alexa.'

Satisfied with this evidence that the real Ruthie was still in there, Maddy felt better. The sound of the toilet flushing upstairs told her she didn't have long to manoeuvre before Lyla bounded back onto the scene. 'But you're not even well enough to get out of your jammies or brush your hair. I'd better at least tell Heloise that I won't go out with her tonight.'

'Huh,' Ruthie puffed, pulling her hands away and sitting up. 'You could talk your way past a tiger with a toothache, you could. Don't you go putting off your arrangements. You'll make me feel terrible and you know Della's coming this evening. I'll get dressed, if that'll convince you.' She didn't manage a smile, but she paused to find Maddy's shoulder and pat it.

Lyla ran in, dragging her coat by one sleeve. 'Can I wear my silver sandals?'

'No, you need your boots.' Maddy shook her head at the flimsy sandals, unsuitable for a winter's day when the wind from Scandinavia sharpened itself on the sea before flinging itself at the Norfolk shore.

'Awww,' moaned Lyla, trudging from the room.

Maddy stood back as Ruthie climbed to her feet, because helping where help wasn't needed wouldn't help Ruthie maintain as much independence as was possible.

Lyla returned without her coat. 'These boots?' She held up a pair of once-white snow boots with a bedraggled furry rim.

Maddy stifled exasperation that Lyla sometimes felt the need to do five other things before doing as asked. 'Did you get them out of the pile for the charity bag? They're too small. Get your octopus wellies. They have a lining to keep you warm, and if you want to walk on the beach, you'll be dry.'

'Awww.' Lyla trudged off again. Then, as if offering a valuable trade-off, called over her shoulder, 'Can I take my handbag, then?' Lyla's 'handbag' was a pre-loved silver-coloured quilted evening purse that she'd bought at the school jumble sale.

'Of course,' said Maddy, whose law of parenting was to say yes to anything she could say yes to. The evening bag could go in her backpack when Lyla got sick of having the tarnished chain strap over her shoulder.

Ruthie began to move off towards her own room, touching furniture as she went. Then she hesitated and turned back. 'Maddy . . .' She stopped to clear her throat. 'I'm sorry I'm grumpy. But Raff's had time to come back

101

to us. And he hasn't, so she—' The sentence was choked off. She swallowed. 'I'm just sad that I got so close only to miss out. I should never have taken it out on you. He steered the conversation until he'd satisfied his curiosity about his dad and me, didn't he? You just let him off the hook at the perfect moment.'

Hot tears spiked Maddy's eyes. She crossed the small space between them and hugged her aunt's soft body. 'I know. I'd thought about asking Raff to lunch again, but I think that might only scare him off for good.'

Ruthie nodded. 'I usually put up with my bad eyesight, but at the moment I'm frustrated that I can't even walk down to the main road and get the bus on my own, go to Docking and find her.'

Maddy closed her eyes, as if she could share Ruthie's burden of partial sight. 'You know I'll drive you if you want to go.'

A huge sigh blew hot on Maddy's neck, before Ruthie answered. 'I suppose it's a daydream. If she wanted to be found, Raff would have told us.' Ruthie's arms tightened. 'There's one of those letters I'd really like you to read to me. Do you think later, or tomorrow, you could?'

A tear tipped out of Maddy's eye and slipped down her cheek. 'Of course. I'll read every page of every one, if you want.'

Ruthie managed a hiccup of laughter as she withdrew. 'Not the sexy bits, dear.'

'No, not those,' Maddy agreed, blotting away the tear she knew Ruthie couldn't see.

Lyla bundled back into the room, coat on and unbuttoned, octopus-decorated wellies safely on her feet and the battered evening bag over her arm. 'Aren't you ready *yet*, Mummy?' she demanded.

Maddy laughed. 'Just checking Grauntie Ruthie's OK, honey.'

Eventually, Maddy was satisfied Ruthie could spend a few hours alone without ill effect. They called for Heloise at her cottage in Traders Place and drove down Long Climb, through the pinewoods weaving along Norfolk's coast. Heloise was wrapped up in a grey fluffy coat and hat that suggested she was ready for whatever weather the day could throw at her.

From her car seat in the back, Lyla chatted and chirruped. 'Heloise, I'm going to Santa's grotto – aren't I, Mummy? And to see the lights and the tree and sing Christmas songs. It's exactly one month to Christmas Day!' All Maddy and Heloise had to do was add the occasional comment.

Soon they were parking. Heloise had a friend in Old Hunstanton that let her use her drive to save the scrum and the expense of the public car parks. Then they trooped down Cliff Parade and through Esplanade Gardens where benches overlooking the sea would be mobbed in summer, and the shelters looked like bus stops. Lyla insisted on checking whether the ice-cream café was open – it wasn't, in a far from sunny Hunny – and stopping to admire a rowing boat that had been turned into a planter.

Finally, the gardens opened onto a vista – the grassy slope of the green, with the beach and sea beyond and busiest streets of Hunstanton to one side, jaunty in their Christmas finery of bunting and coloured lights. Hundreds of people swarmed between a temporary stage on the grass and the stalls and kiddie rides on the prom that joined the green to the beach. Happy voices filled the air and Christmas songs blasted through a PA.

Eyes shining, Lyla jettisoned her evening bag in Maddy's direction. 'Can I go on the teacup ride?'

As there wasn't too much of a queue, Maddy was happy to say, 'OK, let's hurry down to it,' and pay what she was sure was only one of many fares this afternoon so Lyla could jump into a yellow cup on a red saucer, grinning and waving whenever she passed, her complexion changing with the flashing lights.

Maddy and Heloise shifted foot to foot in the ice-edged wind. Heloise raised her voice over the loud strains of 'All I Want for Christmas is You'. 'Mind if I dump you tonight?' She trained her gaze over Lyla's head where the grey-blue sea frothed like a witch's cauldron at the edge of the beach and rocks smoothed by the sea looked like giant cobbles.

Maddy cocked her head. 'Got a date?'

Heloise tucked in a lock of fair hair that was trying to escape her hat and rounded her eyes impressively. 'It's a *second* date.'

'Whoa!' Maddy gave her friend a giant nudge. 'A *second* date. Get you. That's nearly a commitment.' Mischievously, she added, 'As long as it's not with Harris. If you're dumping me for him, our friendship's over.' Although she laughed, it had been a tricky time when Heloise had unaccountably had a 'thing' with Harris. He'd expected to sit with them in the old bar on Saturday evenings, and Maddy had not only felt the gooseberry, but had also hated the phoniness of pretending friendliness for Heloise's sake. Maddy had often drifted out into the wider lounge bar within moments of him joining them, hoping Heloise didn't mind too much and understood that Maddy still considered Harris a knob, just as Maddy had to understand that Heloise couldn't help who she was attracted to.

Lyla's ride ended and she dismounted her teacup, calling excitedly. 'I was in a *cup*.'

The crowds grew and so did the queues at stalls and rides. They had a lunch of chips washed down with cans of fizzy drink almost too cold to hold, then warmed up again with hot sugary doughnuts. 'Do They Know it's Christmas' deafened them while Lyla danced on the spot in a noisy queue of excided kiddies for Santa's grotto and came away with a pink fairy doll with its own hairbrush. At a nearby stall dressed in green crepe and red lights, Maddy bought Lyla a white fur fabric snowman hat that tied beneath her chin and Heloise treated her to an antler hairband, which wouldn't fit over the hat so joined the doll, hairbrush and discarded evening bag in Maddy's backpack.

All around, excited voices and Christmas tunes carried on the frozen air. Lyla rode a tiger on a carousel while seagulls came to roost on a roof, pigeons on another, and Maddy and Heloise joked that they looked like rival gangs muttering about each other.

Darkness drew in as if brought on by the clouds rolling over the sea. Kids ran by waving illuminated wands. Strings of lights came to life between the Princess Theatre and the Golden Lion Hotel, then the PA squeaked, and a man's voice boomed out, 'Time to light up the stage and welcome local choir – the Seagate Singers. A big hand, everybody. They're going to start with "Jingle Bells" and they hope you'll all join in.'

'I will, I will!' Lyla jumped up and down, hand in the air as if she was at school. Soon Maddy and Heloise were holding hands with her to jig in front of the stage, singing 'Jingle Bells', then 'It's Beginning to Look a Lot Like Christmas' and Lyla danced so energetically that her face went red within her snowman hat.

Soon she began to flag, though it was still more than an hour until the Christmas tree switch-on. 'I'm thirsty,' she grumbled.

'I am, too,' said Heloise. 'But I need the loo.'

'So do I,' declared Lyla, taking Heloise's hand expectantly.

'Then I'd better get the drinks.' Maddy clomped down the slope to the prom to the snaking queue at a kiosk, stamping her feet.

Then a familiar voice came from behind her. 'Hello, Maddy.'

Turning, she saw Raff, hair covered by a red woollen beanie, collar around his ears. 'What are you doing here?' she asked stupidly. Then, on a laugh: 'Sorry, I expect you're here for the festival like the other hundreds of people.'

'And looking for coffee.' He pointed at the refreshment kiosk with his elbow without removing his hands from his pockets. Then, uncertainly: 'Is Ruthie with you?'

'She stayed at home. I'm with Lyla and Heloise.' Should she call him on being silent for so long? Should she ask him to consider how poor Ruthie was feeling? Or would that just make him vanish again? There was a big enough crowd for him to vanish into. More than anything, she wanted to demand, 'Are you with *Ffion*?' If so, she wished Ruthie had come, so they could stumble over each other and the decision about whether to meet would be moot. But that was the kind of thing that didn't happen in real life, and Ffion was entitled to make that decision rather than have her birth mother thrust upon her.

With these thoughts jostling for space in her mind, she shuffled forward a couple of steps, stealing a glance at his profile. If he felt awkward after more than two weeks

106

of silence, it didn't show. Instead, he stepped forward again when she did, while the choir on the stage up on the slope burst enthusiastically into, 'It's the MOST WON-derful time . . . of the year!'

Maybe noticing the lack of small talk, he asked, 'Going to the Duke of Bronte tonight with your friend, Heloise?' He glanced at Maddy, and the lights strung around the drinks van reflected in his eyes.

'I thought I was,' she said ruefully, following his lead and not addressing the subject of Ruthie and Ffion. 'But she has a date.' Nearby, teenage boys began shaking cans of Fanta and Coke and she edged a step away from them and closer to Raff.

'Do you date?' Raff asked unexpectedly.

She turned back. A crack and hiss along with a shout of laughter warned her one of the cans had been opened even before a few drops landed on her ear, which gave her an excuse to look startled. 'Occasionally.' They were nearly at the head of the queue, now. 'But my dating profile would look interesting, wouldn't it? "Single mother with missing husband. Police aware".' She reached the counter and ordered three hot chocolates from a man in a brown coat and white apron. 'Can I get you something?' she asked Raff.

He smiled, but shook his head. 'I'm buying for others. But thanks.'

Were any of the 'others' Ffion? Quashing the impulse to demand the information Ruthie craved, she turned away, her three disposable cups wedged in a cardboard carrier, ready to say goodbye.

But then he said, 'Would you come on a date with me? Tonight?'

Almost dropping her cups of hot chocolate, Maddy

stared at the smile glittering in his eyes, and could keep her aunt out of the conversation no longer. 'Would it be awkward? I'm thinking about Ruthie. And your sister, for that matter.'

Raff waved the person behind him in the queue past him. 'Truthfully . . .' Then he hesitated.

Maddy realised that her heart was speeding. Lightly, she prompted, 'I'm a fan of honesty.'

'My sister . . .' He glanced towards the sea, which was lost in late afternoon darkness now apart from ragged reflections from the shore. When he met her gaze again, his expression had become rueful. 'Recently, I've become aware of my adopted status, specifically that everyone else in the Dad-and-Ruthie scenario is connected genetically.'

Maddy paused to consider this turn in the conversation. 'I don't suppose I'd thought of it. But I think I see.'

'I've never felt excluded, not even when Ffion admitted that Dad was her birth parent, but when we went out for Ffion's birthday recently, I couldn't stop thinking about it. So, I've stopped asking her about Ruthie because I'm worried she thinks it's not up to me to push, as I'm not her "real family".' He drew air quotes with his fingers. 'But then, seeing you standing in the queue, looking pretty, your hair blowing—' a lopsided grin '—I was glad not to be connected to *you* genetically. Because it means I can ask you out.'

'Oh!' Fire bloomed in Maddy's cheeks. Then she laughed, because, in a fizzy moment, she realised she'd like to go on a date, and do something so normally adult. More, she'd like to go on a date with Raff – and not just because she wouldn't have to explain the Adey situation or because he'd just intimated that the silence regarding

108

Ruthie was coming from Ffion, rather than him. It was because she liked his company and his conversation.

She liked him.

She said, 'That would be great.'

But Raff continued as if she needed persuading. 'We could make it at the Duke of Bronte, if you want to be near to Ruthie. They have a restaurant, don't they?'

She pulled a face. 'Thanks, but that would be like dating in a goldfish bowl. By Monday, half the village would be asking me what I'm buying you for Christmas and others would ask how Adey would feel.' And she could just imagine Harris's sneers and jibes . . .

Raff's lips thinned. 'Don't they think you're entitled to go on with your life?'

'Not all of them.' *Harris*. She adjusted the tray of hot chocolate in her hands, breathing in the sugary scent that warred with the briny tang of the sea now rolling in up the beach, its usual hiss drowned out by the music from the green.

He frowned, his eyes fixed upon her face. 'But you consider yourself separated.' A statement, not a question.

She laughed. 'I *am* separated. You can't get much more separated than not having seen or heard from your husband for nearly seven years. I can't begin the legalities that will lead to divorce until the New Year, that's all.'

His smile returned, crinkling his eyes at the corners. 'How about I book a meal somewhere outside the village but not too far? Eight-thirty again?'

She beamed. 'Text me the venue and I'll meet you there.' She began to move away, indicating the hot chocolate. 'Better get these to the others before they get cold.'

'See you later.' He smiled.

As she hurried up onto the green, towards the stage,

her heart soared as if it had been filled with helium. Lyla, still in her snowman hat, shrieked when she saw her. 'Where have you been, Mum?'

Suddenly aware of how long she and Raff must have been talking, Maddy kept her eyes on her carrier of hot chocolates. 'There was a queue. Here you go.'

Then the lights around the stage began to flash white, red and green, and a snow king and snow queen on stilts, white costumes studded with flickering lights, made their long-legged way towards it, waving to the cheering audience.

Lyla waved back so energetically she almost dropped her cup. 'Their crowns are icicles!'

More cheering as Santa emerged from his grotto in his rich red suit, the cast of the panto from the nearby Princess Theatre filed up on stage dressed as elves and princesses and led everyone in a countdown to join in the switching on of the tree lights. 'Three . . . two . . . one . . .' And then a huge, 'Hooray!' as not only did the coloured lights of the nearby Christmas tree spring to life, but white lights encrusting the bare branches of all the trees on the green, making them a winter wonderland.

'Yay, yay!' Lyla joined in gustily, now wearing a moustache of hot chocolate.

Under cover of the applause, Maddy turned to Heloise to murmur, 'Now I've got a date tonight, too.'

'Who?' Heloise hissed, eyes enormous.

Maddy smiled loftily. 'You didn't tell me who your date was.'

Heloise frowned, then shrugged. 'His name's Jon and he'll be coming from King's Lynn. Now, you.'

'He thinks you're worth the petrol from King's Lynn?' Maddy enquired, straight-faced.

'*Maddy!*' Laughing, Heloise gave her a shake.

Maddy laughed at being shaken like a bell. 'Raff.'

Heloise's brows flipped up. 'But he has a beard and scruffy hair. He's my type, not yours. You said you'd only met him to discuss Ruthie.'

'He's shaved, and been to the barber's,' Maddy reported. 'My type after all.' She hoped so, anyway, because she found she was looking forward to this evening, very much indeed.

Lyla fell asleep as they drove out of Hunstanton. She barely stirred as Maddy eased her from the back of the car and carried her indoors to be undressed for bed. Lyla had plummeted far beyond the reach of human voice, so Maddy kissed her smooth forehead, stroked her hair from her face then went to find Ruthie.

She found her in the front room, listening to football transfer news on TalkSPORT 'Nice time?' Ruthie asked, after telling Alexa to drop the volume.

'Very. Sorry I didn't shout hello when I came in, but I was carrying Lyla. She's zonked.' Maddy ran her eyes over her aunt, who was sporting brushed hair and clean leggings and a jumper. She filled her in on the events at the festival. Carefully, she added, 'I met Raff there, in the queue for hot drinks. We're going out for a meal tonight,' she ended, having decided that she wasn't in the habit of lying to Ruthie and didn't see why she should begin now.

The corners of Ruthie's lips went down while her brows flew up, a comical expression of surprise. 'Raff?' She mused for a moment, appearing, as so often, to stare into nothing. 'On his own, was he?' she asked eventually.

'In the queue, at least,' Maddy agreed.

Ruthie's nod was slow. 'And he didn't say anything about Ffion, or you'd have already told me.'

'He mentioned they'd been out for her birthday, that's all. And I felt as if the silence is coming from her, not him.' Maddy didn't see any harm in the slight paraphrasing. Raff might not like Maddy to pass on that he felt that Ffion was excluding him deliberately.

Ruthie swallowed audibly. 'November 10th. She'd have been forty-six.'

Stomach sinking, Maddy moved further into the room, though she'd been about to put Ruthie's meal in the oven and then go upstairs to the shower while it cooked. The significance of Ffion's birthday hadn't struck her. What a moron to have mentioned it so casually. BIRTHday. Probably it was part of the bad case of the blues Ruthie had been suffering from. 'Sorry if that was insensitive,' she murmured.

Rather than reply, Ruthie leant over the arm of her chair and retrieved the blue and white shirt box containing Nigel's letters. 'The letter I want to hear should be easy to pick out. It's the only one on yellow foolscap paper. Goodness knows where he scrounged that up from.'

Maddy's mind flew back to this morning, when she'd agreed to read a letter to Ruthie. She tried not to glance at the clock as, unsure what foolscap was, she perched on the footstool and opened the box, stirring the layers of paper and envelopes. Sure enough, there was only one slim sheaf of yellow. 'Here we are,' she said, and Ruthie nodded in satisfaction. Maddy opened the folds and discovered that foolscap seemed to mean sheets a touch longer than A4. The pages were ruled, with a margin and punch holes, and looked as if they'd come from a pad on an office desk.

'What's the date?' Ruthie whispered. 'Is it 30th November 1977?'

Maddy checked in surprise as she realised today was the 25th, almost forty-six years later. 'It is. It must be etched on your memory.'

Ruthie only nodded. Her knuckles were white, she clasped her hands in her lap so tightly, and she tilted her head, as if preparing to pay close attention.

Maddy began to read aloud. '*My dearest, darling Ruthie.*'

She went on, her voice growing husky as the emotions bled from the page. '*I know we agreed I wouldn't share details about the baby, but I have to tell you, just once. I'm so happy, and yet the saddest ever. I can't stop thinking about you all alone. Four days ago, when you passed our baby into my arms, I thought my heart would stop.*' A quick glance showed her that Ruthie had sucked her lips inwards, as if to stop them trembling. '*She is the preciousest gift any woman ever gave any man.*' Maddy had to pause to swallow. '*And all the little cardies and mittens you knitted to send with her, all white with ribbons. Ruthie, darling, my love, my poor love! I feel as if all I have brought you is pain and you have given me everything.*'

Maddy could see where he was coming from with that. How different would her aunt's life have been if she hadn't fallen for the wrong man? Or if that man had never offered Ruthie a lift to those gardens they'd visited together, and fallen in love he wasn't free to feel? She read on. '*I want you to be happy that she's settled here in the room I decorated for her. She woke up once for her bottle and went back to sleep like an angel. I stood by her cot and watched her, and I held you close in my thoughts. I stood there two hours. Dearest love, I thought you should know, just once, that she's being looked after and is safe. God bless you. I love you. Nigel xxx*'

By the time Maddy got to the end, she was blind with tears.

Ruthie blew her nose in a hard, determined way, as if daring herself to cry. 'He was right to send it,' she said gruffly. 'I've read it a thousand times.' She coughed, then let out an enormous sigh. 'I couldn't steel myself to meet Sindy,' she murmured. 'And I couldn't let a stranger pass the baby over. So, I told Nigel to tell his wife that I would only give the baby to him, because I knew him from work. He made out I was a scared young thing and a bit rubbish at coping. We didn't go a very official route. The baby had lived with them for a while before they put in for adoption. Social services came and saw me to check I knew what I was doing, giving the baby away. Horrible, it was. They asked if I wanted to see her or have contact. I pretended that I didn't know who the dad was and that I just wanted the baby to go to a nice family so I could get on with my life. It all went through all right. In the end, it came to paperwork.'

Maddy's heart ached for Ruthie and even a bit for Nigel. His outpouring of love and grief had been genuine and grammatical mistakes like 'preciousest' had humanised him. Just an ordinary bloke who'd taken several wrong turns in his life and had skewed, sometimes self-serving priorities, but recognised where he'd been lucky. And Ruthie hadn't. 'Did you ever regret it?'

'No,' she said with certainty, mopping a tear. 'With Nigel, she'd never have anyone pity her for not having a dad or call her a bastard. And Sindy never worked, you know, so she stayed home and looked after her.

Nigel and her, they brought up two good kids, seems to me.'

The room wasn't very warm, Maddy suddenly realised. The weather was getting so cold outside that the heating needed to go up and the fire should be set roaring. She gave her aunt a hug, returned the yellow letter back to the box and then set about these mundane tasks.

Once she'd put Ruthie's dinner in the oven, she returned to the front room. Ruthie had the TV on. She called it 'watching' TV but heard more than she saw, enjoying quiz shows and panel games, because you didn't really have to see what was going on. Ruthie glanced her way. 'Della's coming about eight-fifteen.' She lifted an admonishing finger. 'So, don't you go saying you won't go out on that date. Della's busy with those Christmas cards she makes, and she's bringing them to do while we chat.' Her voice softened. 'Thanks for reading out that letter. I just had a yearning to hear it again.'

Maddy's heart gave a giant squeeze. 'Are you sure you don't mind me going? Raff has just texted but if going will hurt your feelings—'

'Text him back and say you'll be there,' said Ruthie pragmatically. 'There are no enemies in this situation, dear. Just complications.'

Chapter Eight

When Maddy arrived at the pub Raff had chosen, breath racing in the winter wind, she found a warm and cosy welcome. The pub's dining area was strung with fairy lights and a luxuriant pine Christmas tree strained under the weight of gold and silver ornaments. The optics and glasses reflected the many twinkling lights from the bar side, and the copper ornaments on the green-painted walls reflected them right back.

Butterflies turned backflips in her stomach. She hadn't gone out with a man since the summer, an American holidaymaker she'd met on Hunstanton beach. It probably counted as a 'meet-cute' as he'd overheard her talking about mace, the spice, and thought she'd meant pepper spray. The actual date was not as funny, as it became clear that he thought 'a date' automatically included retiring to his hotel room after dinner. He'd actually had the neck to say he'd be willing to pay for the meal, as if that would sway her decision whether to sleep with him, and when she'd said she'd rather go Dutch he'd giggled and asked if 'Dutch' was a sex position. She'd scarpered home telling herself that that's what you got for dating tourists.

Raff should be good for more than stilted conversation and an unwelcome pounce.

He waited at a small square table at one side of the room and greeted her with a quick hug and an easy grin. 'Hope this place is OK. It has great reviews.'

'Good reputation locally, too,' she said, hanging up her coat before taking her seat. 'Which is great, because I'm starving. Getting Ruthie's meal sharpened my appetite.' Against the background hum of happily chatting fellow diners, they studied a menu bordered with holly leaves and Christmas pudding, and then both chose the turkey dinner.

Cheerfully, Raff decreed, 'It's one month before Christmas, so it would seem rude not to. Enjoy the festival? How was the rest of your day?'

Maddy told him about her morning meeting with her tenant. 'I want to retain him because, apart from him being a local who needs somewhere to live, it's an expensive faff to find new tenants. I'd make more money in the summer renting the place out as a holiday cottage, but it would be difficult for at least four months of the year, if not six. Winter weather in Nelson's Bar just about takes your skin off.'

Raff touched his face, as if checking.

It drew Maddy's attention to his fresh shave and healthy colour. Impulsively, she said, 'I thought an author would be all white and weedy, shut up indoors all day.' Then she turned to smile at the waiter, who'd appeared beside them.

After the waiter had gone off with their order, Raff repeated with mock wrath, 'White and weedy? Because

I'm trapped in my garret all day, working by the light of a candle?'

'And starving,' she joked. 'I've read everyone wants to be an author but hardly anyone can earn a living,' she added, enjoying the light in his blue eyes.

His smile faded. 'It's a competitive field. I'm living on less than I used to get from teaching to try and subsist while I write these two books. My advance is miles more than I used to get from my old publisher, but the author receives the money in stages. I keep thinking my new publisher will ask for it back, instead.' He pulled a mock-scared face, making Maddy laugh, before he continued more seriously. 'I've a financial cushion but there wasn't a massive sum to divide with Antonella when we sold the house. We'd added a new kitchen and conservatory to the original mortgage.'

The waiter returned with drinks and a Christmas cracker to place before each plate, presumably because they'd chosen their meals from the festive menu. When he'd hurried off, Maddy said soberly, 'Financial worries are the pits. I still have bad dreams about the avalanche of bills and financial shocks that almost sucked me under.' She stopped, realising that by talking first about her tenant and now the financial nightmare caused by Adey leaving, she'd vaguely alluded to her ex twice in a few minutes.

But Raff didn't seem worried, just continuing the conversation naturally. 'I can see how you might have felt it was you against the world. Were Adey's family around? They must have been out of their minds with worry for him.'

She curled her lip. 'They were distraught for him, but somehow managed to cast me as a villain. His mum Tilly said, "It'll be on your conscience if you've driven him to do something silly. Your marriage was all at sea, because *you* were always trying to navigate via a different lighthouse." That was after I'd told them about the debts. She assumed I'd been the one spending money that we didn't have and blamed me for being made redundant.' She picked up the Christmas cracker, absently smoothing its gold paper ruff. 'Usually, she was the one to have a go at Adey for his extravagances, so I think she deliberately created a rift to discourage me from asking them for money – not that I'd planned to. Anyway, we ended up screaming at each other.' She shrugged, though the memory of Tilly's brick-red face still drove her heart rate up. 'My father-in-law stepped in and said they'd open their own lines of communication with the police, so I needn't trouble to keep them informed of developments.'

Raff's expression set like concrete. 'You're not serious?'

'Yep.' She picked up her drink. 'They were the kind of people who could start an argument in an empty barn. They moved from Nelson's Bar while Adey was at uni because Tilly was a nurse and got a good job in a Liverpool hospital, and they left behind a lot of relieved neighbours.'

His blue eyes were warm. 'Do they know about Lyla?'

Her stomach gave the anxious little churn it always did when this thought intruded. 'Not unless someone in the village passes news to them.' She tilted her head. 'I do sometimes wonder whether I ought to try to contact them, for Lyla's sake.'

His eyebrows quirked and his usually affable expression switched to grim. 'But for all your in-laws know, you could be starving in a gutter. If they do know about her, that's unconscionable.'

She nodded, warmed that he was clearly ranging himself on her side. 'So being out of touch is a relief, rather than a worry. I'm not sure they'd be a positive in my daughter's life.' Ruthie and Heloise were her usual confidantes regarding her beloved Lyla, but she felt sufficiently at ease with Raff to add, 'Occasionally, I wonder whether Adey might be in touch with his parents. If so, I suppose I'm kind of glad they know he's OK. At the same time, I hate them for not telling me.'

'I can imagine.' He hesitated. 'It's the kind of thing I usually only read about.'

She lifted an eyebrow. 'Or write about?'

He laughed. 'No. I write about a fantasy kingdom and its politics.'

'OK.' She nodded. 'I'll tell you, then. If you have author friends who write crime novels, it felt just like being trapped in one – the police getting no feedback from Adey's phone and saying that meant it was disabled or *in water*. Police dogs, search and rescue volunteers, the marine unit. The police searching the house and his things for evidence of addiction or coercion, checking his laptop, doing credit checks to see if he had bank accounts I wasn't aware of. Asking what he was wearing, taking his DNA from his toothbrush, making appeals on social media. But nothing. The police called me every day for a couple of weeks talking about national and international markers, assuring me they were checking hospitals, mental health units and his GP. Apparently, borders for sea crossings aren't monitored as closely as for air, but his passport was at home and there was no record of him applying for another. They referred me to a missing persons' charity who suggested I put up posters and circulate them to bus and taxi companies.' She lifted her hands, palms up. 'But if Adey doesn't want to be found, then he's entitled not to be. That's the law.'

Their meal arrived, two beautifully presented plates of steaming turkey, golden roast potatoes and every festive add-on the chef could think of. 'Awesome,' Maddy changed the subject with relief, already mentally sacrificing some potatoes and sprouts to ensure she'd have room for Yorkshire pudding, bread sauce, pigs in blankets, stuffing and crispy balls of sausage meat. The turkey looked succulent, though she knew how hard it could be to keep turkey breast moist when cooking on a large scale.

After carefully drizzling the perfect amount of gravy, she set to, forking up turkey and bread sauce together, then turkey and stuffing, to make certain she got all her favourite taste combinations. The sausage meat crispiness was only surface deep, as it ought to be.

Then she became aware of him twinkling at her. 'What?' she demanded, giving herself a quick wipe with her festive red paper napkin in case she'd slurped gravy over her chin, and then checking the front of her blue top for spatter.

The creases around his eyes deepened. 'It's refreshing to see a woman with an appetite. Antonella's go-to when we ate out was a small salad and Ffion finds eating big meals makes her breathless.'

The steam from her turkey seemed to warm her face. 'I like food,' she said defensively.

'Me, too.' He sliced into his Yorkshire pudding. 'Food should be enjoyed and I'm glad you're not – what was that phrase? "White and weedy"?'

Laughter almost made her blow half a pig in its blanket off the end of her fork. 'Definitely not. I eat like a horse, but I'm always on the go, so I'm able to.'

He nodded, but the teasing light had left his eyes. 'That's what I see when I look at you. A woman who gets on with things.' Matter-of-factly, he added, 'It's attractive, your zest for life. You're an attractive woman.'

It was a while since Maddy had received male compliments, apart from the American tourist who'd trotted out a couple of rehearsed tributes as he'd tried to steer her into bed. She found herself reacting clumsily. 'Considering eating attractive – is that current dating etiquette?'

Raff lowered his knife and fork to laugh. 'My experience with students means I'm well practised in spotting deflection. But if you prefer to pretend you don't look amazing, that's fine.'

Wrong-footed first by him seeing through her so easily and then sliding in a further compliment even as he said he wouldn't, she found herself deflecting again. 'You're nothing like my old teachers – most of whom I didn't like.'

He tilted his head questioningly. 'What was the problem?'

She dipped a carrot in bread sauce and gravy. 'I felt like school was only about exam results. I remember a teacher saying I was "all about doing" when he meant I wasn't academic enough. I didn't sit still and hang on his words; I fidgeted and talked until someone gave me something to do with my hands.'

His brows drew down between his eyes. 'Academic achievement is no more or less valuable than vocational or physical achievement.'

'Not according to Mr Thompset.' She wrinkled her nose. 'And then Mrs Dulwich told me that I had to get used to being looked at.' At his ludicrous expression of non-comprehension, she almost choked on her Yorkshire pudding, which would have been both embarrassing and a horrible waste.

'What the hell?' he queried, treating her to a fascinated stare.

She sobered. His expression might be funny, but the situation never had been. 'One boy in our year ogled me all the time and followed me around. It was unsettling. I became self-conscious about my body, and teens don't need pressure in that department.'

'And this teacher dealt with your unease by telling you that you had to get used to being looked at?' he demanded.

She looked down at her plate. 'She sort of wrapped it in a compliment – like: "a pretty girl like you will have to get used to being looked at". It would have been more helpful if she'd taken the boy aside and explained that he was making me uncomfortable by leering. Instead, his behaviour escalated into suggestive comments and jokes. I talked to Adey about it when we were married, and he said that teenage boys don't know how to engage the interest of a girl they fancy, so they act like morons.'

He stopped eating to sip his drink, which caught the Christmas lights and fragmented them. 'There's something in that, but you should have been protected, and the boy would have benefitted from some advice. What about your mum?'

She waggled her head in a 'so-so' gesture. 'Mum covered the basics, like food, clothes and decorating my bedroom, but wasn't good at emotional support. I suppose I should have ignored his behaviour, but it was . . . incessant.'

They ate on in silence, and Maddy was just wondering if she could fit in the rest of the crunchy roast potatoes if she sacrificed dessert, when Raff said, 'Are we talking about that character Harris?'

Quickly, she looked up, startled. 'How did you know?'

He wiped his hands on his napkin with quick, irritable movements. 'That night in the Duke of Bronte, he told me you'd been at school together and went through some stupid nickname rigmarole.'

'Mad Crazy,' she said, wondering how many times she'd heard that ringing from Harris's lips.

His brows slanted in a thoughtful frown. 'I try to be open-minded about what drives people, what pressures they're under, what their mental state is and why, but I failed with him. I didn't like him, and I joked with him that he was obsessed with you. Maybe he is.'

The thought sent a roll of nausea through Maddy. 'Oh no, not that,' she protested, dismayed. 'Even though he was Adey's best mate, he was always bloody rude and sneery. Eventually, Adey would tell him to shut up, and he'd sulk. Adey vacillated between exasperation and thinking it was funny, with occasional excursions into saying it wasn't as bad as I made out.' She rolled her eyes. 'Sorry, now I'm going from crime novel to psycho thriller. If your publisher ever asks you to change genres, you'll have an idea to run with.'

'I'll mention you in the acknowledgements,' he joked.

Maddy began to relax. 'Damn. I was hoping for the dedication. I suppose I'd have to save your life or something to get that.'

'At least,' he agreed solemnly, and the mood of the evening flipped. He made her laugh with funny anecdotes about his teaching days, including a student who poked something between Raff's shoulder blades and growled, 'Just keep walkin', shitface.' Another teacher had 'disarmed' the student – of a banana – and Raff had laughed so hard he'd cried.

Maddy watched the laughter glowing in his eyes, as

124

they finished their meal. 'But, still, you're glad you stopped teaching to write?'

He nodded. He'd almost cleared his plate. 'A more creative life, without a timetable – except for deadlines. My amazing agent Elinor got me a good contract, so I grabbed it with everything I had. Now, if I work all evening, it's because the book's going well, not because a teacher's personal planning time is woefully inadequate.'

He put his knife and fork together on the plate and sat back. 'Tell me what it's like to grow up in a tiny community. I grew up in Aberdeen. A nice residential area, but much different, I imagine.'

'Taking a minibus to school from an early age was scary at first,' she said. 'But then it was exciting. Now I'm scared for Lyla, but she loves it, so I don't let it show.'

He asked, 'How many generations of Craceys have grown up in Nelson's Bar?'

She paused to consider, surveying her plate and deciding she'd just about reached capacity. 'My great-grandparents, grandparents, Mum, me and Lyla, at least. I don't know before that.'

He pushed his plate aside and settled himself with one forearm comfortably on the table. 'Do you think you'll ever leave?'

She tried to imagine not living high up on the headland, where the wind blew a gale one day, and the clouds engulfed the village the next and then summer brought forget-me-not-blue skies. 'I love Nelson's Bar. Not seeing the sea every day would be weird. Or living in a block of flats along with a hundred others—' she pulled a face '—no thanks.' Then she sighed. 'You never know though, do you? What if it becomes financially impossible for me to stay? What if Ruthie needs more care than I'm able to give her, and her house has to be sold to support that?' A wave of sadness swept over her, but it was a possibility she and her aunt had talked about. Passing a certain age and state of health made those conversations inevitable. 'If I didn't live with Ruthie, to stay in the village would mean me getting a job and having enough money left after after-school and holiday childcare to move back to High Cottage – which would be a lot more expensive to run than my share of Ruthie's household costs.' She smiled mistily. 'Ruthie declares that she'll just "fall off her perch" and leave The Hollies to me, so I'll be fine financially. I tell her that I want her to live forever and that inheriting a lovely property in the village would be no consolation for losing her.'

'That's sweet,' he said.

The server appeared beside them, her ponytail swinging. 'Would you like the dessert menu?'

Maddy clutched her sides inelegantly. 'I think I'd need to come back and make it a meal all of its own.'

Raff's eyes crinkled at the corners. 'Fine by me. Tomorrow evening for dessert, then?'

As the server took their plates and whisked off, a giggle escaped Maddy, a breathless one that didn't even sound like her.

Then Raff reached over the table for her hand, lifted it to his mouth and kissed it.

And just like that, the desire to give uncharacteristic nervous giggles faded, but the breathlessness remained, as if her lungs had tightened so she couldn't filter quite enough oxygen from the warm air, rich with the aroma of food and wine. Her gaze felt locked onto Raff's, trying to read the expression in his intent blue eyes.

His hand closed more tightly around hers. 'Want to go on somewhere? How late can you stay out?'

Regretfully, she said, 'I'll have to go home soon, I'm afraid, for Lyla. I'd love to suggest we go on to a sophisticated bar or a nightclub, but that's not my life.'

He smiled. 'Of course. Ruthie's quite elderly to be left in sole charge late into the evening.'

A tide of warmth swept over her, not because it had been a lovely date, nor even because he hadn't made a pass, but because he was demonstrating an understanding of her two big responsibilities. Some men would have groused, 'Your great-aunt's with her and she's asleep. You have your phone if anything happens, haven't you?' Not every childless man would appreciate that she needed to always feel comfortable that Lyla was not 'safe enough' or 'OK', but properly secure, and that Ruthie found life as a sight-impaired person challenging enough without Maddy laying undue obligation on her.

She didn't even feel pressure to explain that it felt too early in the relationship to invite him back to hers, what with the possibility of her 'responsibilities' waking up. She said, 'It's not quite ten o'clock, so Della will only just be packing up her crafting kit and going home. I'll leave after coffee.'

When Raff smiled, ordered coffee and asked for the bill at the same time, so they wouldn't be held up waiting for it, there was a little bump in Maddy's chest, as if her heart had received its first nudge towards falling for him.

His hand remained around hers until the drinks arrived, but then he let her go, so they were free to tap credit cards on the contactless machine. Heloise had once told Maddy that although she didn't expect a man to foot the bill on a date, it was a tiny black mark against him if he didn't. In contrast, Maddy preferred people to pay their way, male or female – especially since that idiot tourist had felt he was buying sex with her, along with the meal.

They opened sugar sachets and poured milk. Raff audibly inhaled the fragrant steam. 'It's been a great evening.'

'For me, too,' she answered. But the final minutes of the date soon drained away and Maddy judged it time to gather her things.

Raff rose to pull on his coat. They walked out to discover a dusting of snow, the air cold and crisp.

Maddy gazed at the glittering pavements, and the lampposts wearing white caps. 'How pretty. It's like icing sugar.' As the car park behind the pub was cramped, she'd parked on the road outside, half on the grass verge along with a line of other cars. Raff took charge of her scraper to clear her side windows while she started the engine and turned on the wipers and rear-window heater. The sparkling white powder spurted and sprayed from his energetic, rasping sweeps.

Maddy climbed back out of the vehicle to thank him and take back the scraper. When she saw the front of his black coat was powdered with ice, she laughed and brushed it off. He caught her hand, his skin as cold as the snow yet warming in the seconds that they touched. She gazed at him in the light of the twinkle lights all over the front of the pub, his hair lifting slightly as another car approached, its headlights capturing them like a searchlight as it pulled in nearby.

Ignoring it, Raff edged closer. Then he slanted his head and brought his lips to hers in a tiny, questing kiss. He paused, giving her time to step away.

Instead, she closed her eyes and stayed where she was. His lips brushed hers again, warm and soft and sizzling right down into the core of her. Tiny, heated kisses fell on her face and down her jaw to the crook of her neck – about as much of her as was available above her thick parka. Then his mouth returned to hers and her lips parted, inviting him to kiss and lick until their bodies melted together and it felt as if his caressing tongue stroked her soul.

As first kisses went, it was perfect.

Eventually, dazedly, she eased away. The recently parked car was dark and silent now, the engine ticking as it cooled. The occupants must have got out while they were kissing, and Maddy hadn't even heard their footsteps crunching in the snow.

He murmured. 'Can I call you tomorrow?'

'Sure.' She smiled in the darkness and pressed one last kiss beside his mouth. 'Speak then.'

She got into her car, its engine running more smoothly than hers was, and pulled away to drive the dark lanes back to Nelson's Bar filled with a delicious sense of something awesome happening.

Tomorrow he'd call. She knew he would, despite the silence he seemed to have felt it necessary to keep on behalf of Ffion, because everything about Raff Edmonds said 'decent guy'. He wouldn't play games or keep her waiting. Sometime tomorrow she'd talk to him again.

Chapter Nine

On the afternoon of the next day, Sunday, Nelson's Bar's Christmas Fair got promptly underway in the Duke of Bronte. Twisted crepe streamers hung like a Christmas rainbow, intertwined with enough tinsel to be visible from space. The Christmas tree stood sentinel over stalls selling mince pies and Christmas jumpers and Maddy's ears rang with the clamour of voices from amongst the youngest in the village – a crying baby – to the oldest, which would include Ruthie, Della and their friends at a nearby table. Watching Ruthie smiling as she listened to the conversation, Maddy wondered whether her aunt had shared the Ffion news with her friends. Maybe, if she feared her own generation harbouring the attitude that illegitimate children and single mothers bore a stigma, Ruthie would wait to see if Ffion ever became a part of her life. And that was looking less and less likely with each uncommunicative day. Only this morning, Ruthie had sighed and said that it was Ffion's choice, and Ruthie's cross to bear.

After ages touring stalls and entering tombolas, Maddy

and Heloise flopped down in the corner by the bar which, today, was set up as a coffee shop. Lyla had skipped off to the soft play area and bestrode a sponge crescent moon, giggling with her friends. Now it was officially less than a month before Christmas – if only by one day – Lyla had set her mood on 'permanently excited', boinging around like Tigger at every sight of tinsel.

Maddy, content that Ruthie and Lyla appeared happy, relaxed with her coffee and asked Heloise, 'How did last night's date go? You look great today, by the way.'

Heloise looked pleased. Her fair hair was freshly trimmed, catching in the collar of a herringbone coat she lovingly termed 'vintage'. She wore make-up, though the fair was low-key as social engagements went, and she'd been light-hearted all afternoon, joking with stallholders and tickling Lyla. 'I was about to ask you the same.' She waggled her eyebrows as she picked up a mince pie.

'I asked first,' Maddy declared. 'Spill.'

Heloise glanced around, obviously checking for gossip radars pinging in her direction. Nelson's Bar had an active bush telegraph. 'It was great. He was lovely and attentive. I think people are too quick to—' she hesitated, flushing '—well, too quick to judge men who look alternative. Some think that makes them bad people.'

'Oh, judging on appearances, you mean? I get that. So, this Jon is your usual long-haired surfer dude type?'

For an instant, Heloise hesitated, eyes surprised. 'I forgot I'd told you his name's Jon. He has a ponytail sometimes, if that's what you mean.'

'It's more important that he's attentive and lovely,' Maddy said. Then she became aware of Ruthie's friend Della hovering at her elbow, wearing a reindeer-strewn jumper and her usual beaming smile. 'Just letting you know that I'm going back on the craft stall now, but Norma's with your auntie.'

'Thanks, Della. You're the best.' Maddy rose to give the kindly older woman a hug, stooping because Della, like Ruthie, was on the small side. As Maddy resumed her seat and Della toddled off towards a craft stall gaily hung with Christmas stockings, wreaths, tinselly headbands, knitted toys and glittery baubles, Maddy noticed Harris at a nearby table. He winked, to which Maddy returned the smallest of nods, annoyed he'd parked himself quite so close. Idly, she wondered what he'd look like if he shaved and took himself off to the barber's, as Raff had.

Raff. He'd texted this morning. Is this a good time to call? X

She'd liked the kiss, having lain awake last night, thinking of his touch burning through her like wildfire, revelling in the almost forgotten feeling of a hard and hungry man containing himself. Because of today's fair, they'd agreed to postpone their chat until evening, after Lyla's bedtime.

Being a single mum was restrictive. The stigma Ruthie had been so scared of might have largely gone, but the parenting was all on her. How important would Raff become? Would he and Lyla ever develop a relationship? Would Maddy ever meet his sister Ffion? Her stomach lurched. It would break Ruthie's heart if Maddy met Ffion and Ruthie never did. She wondered if Raff had thought of it.

'Hey, daydreamer,' Heloise broke in. 'You haven't told me about *your* date.'

Not about to confess to Heloise that, mentally, she'd just been taking things with Raff a lot further than a date, she smiled. 'We got on well enough to kiss goodnight.'

Heloise's eyes lit up. 'And did the earth move?'

Maddy laughed. 'It did a bit,' she admitted cheerfully, because Heloise was her best friend, and she knew she would only ever want Maddy's happiness. 'He's going to call later.'

'Mummy!' Lyla bounded over from the soft play area. 'Mummy, can we look at Della's Christmas cards again? I love them.' She teetered on her toes.

Maddy smiled at the bright-eyed little face. 'Again? OK, then.'

At this time of year, Della's crafting skills were firing full power on Christmas cards and advent calendars. She always made Ruthie a card with lots of sequins, so Ruthie could feel whatever she couldn't see. Maddy had bought Lyla's: a hand-stitched black cat watching Santa's legs emerging down the chimney, and let Lyla choose one for Ruthie: a foil Christmas tree with buttons and sequins for ornaments.

Heloise accompanied them to the stall, continuing the conversation, albeit in a way suitable for Lyla's young ears. 'I could have Lyla sleep over one night, if you want to . . . ?'

'Yes, *please*,' piped Lyla, with a fresh bout of pogoing. 'If Mummy wants to what?'

Maddy stifled a giggle.

'If Mummy wants to paint the town red,' Heloise said solemnly, proving that her years as a nursery nurse and childminder had equipped her for such conversations.

Lyla wrinkled her brow as they zig-zagged towards the stall between all the other fairgoers. 'Which town? Hunstanton? Paint all of it? Our school's already red . . . or at least a sort of dark pink.'

This time, Maddy let her giggle escape. 'I suppose the

133

bricks are pinkish. It's clever of you to notice.' She felt happier and lighter than she had for ages, and could only put that down to yesterday evening with Raff.

Lyla grabbed Maddy's arm, grey eyes alight. 'Can I sleep over at Heloise's? When can I come, Heloise? Is it just me, Mummy, or are you coming? I want it to just be me, because Heloise gives me lots of chocolates,' she concluded seriously.

Maddy laughed. 'Ouch! Don't mind my feelings, will you?' She linked arms with Heloise to prevent the three of them being separated as a fresh bunch of people burst in, a gust of freezing clifftop air breezing in along with them.

Heloise grinned at Lyla. 'How about Friday? I'm looking after a black and white cat called Tuxedo for a long weekend, so you could feed him. On Saturday, we can go to Docking for their Christmas fair.' She sent Maddy a mischievous look. 'Maybe Mummy would like to meet us there.'

Maddy tried to look reproving. 'I'm not sure what's happening on Friday, yet. Nothing's *decided*,' – 'decided' relating to whether she'd take advantage of the sleepover to go home with Raff. It might not even be possible as it would mean asking Della whether she could keep Ruthie company. Norma occasionally stepped in for Della, but Ruthie wasn't as comfortable with her.

Heloise assumed a face of mock-innocence. 'Lyla's sleeping over with me; that's what's decided.'

Lyla crowed, 'Yay!'

'I'm not going to be railroaded,' said Maddy, as they finally reached the craft stall, which was thronged with people no doubt from all the villages around, not just from Nelson's Bar. Della waved from behind the stall.

Lyla glanced behind her at the soft play corner, then snatched her hand away from Maddy's. 'Misty's here. I'm going to see her.'

'Just when we'd barged our way to where she wanted to go,' Heloise murmured, smiling after Lyla as she threaded through the crowd.

Maddy grinned. 'Now I've fought my way here, I'm going to buy Ruthie one of the chunky cardigans Norma knits,' she said, reaching out to trace the neat cable stitch on a cheerful purple number.

Heloise snorted in amusement. 'Look at the length. It'll be a woolly tent on Ruthie.'

'It'll keep her warm.' Maddy fished in her pocket for her purse. When she'd paid and the cardigan was squashed into a recycled-looking carrier bag, Maddy edged away from the busy stall, but then Heloise caught her arm and tugged her to a standstill.

For once, Heloise's pleasant face wore a deadly serious expression. 'You ought to go for it, if you want him,' she said bluntly. 'How many men do you meet, stuck up here in Nelson's Bar? Oh, it's a gorgeous spot,' she added, as Maddy opened her mouth to object. 'But you see the same people all the time. You're Lyla's mum and Ruthie's carer but you're also entitled to a life.'

She was so warm and earnest that Maddy's heartstrings pinged. Impulsively, she hugged her friend. 'Thank you, Helly. You're right, but Friday's five days away. Let's just see what the week brings.'

Of course, if the week improved on the developing heat between Maddy and Raff, then Maddy would be very grateful that Lyla would be sleeping over with someone Maddy absolutely could trust.

* * *

135

By eight-twenty that evening, Lyla was in bed and Ruthie listening to a podcast about Cold War détente in the Seventies. Beyond wondering exactly what Ruthie had been involved with at the Ministry of Defence, Maddy had been happy to fill the woodstove for her aunt and then retire to her bedroom ready for Raff's call.

She'd barely closed her bedroom door when her phone tinged. She snatched it up with an anticipatory smile, thinking it might be Raff texting to check Lyla was safely abed. But instead of *Raff Edmonds*, it was *Number withheld* that appeared on her screen. Though expecting it to be a marketing message, she opened it and read:

Sorry to be away so long. Think of you often. How are you? ILU x

The room swam.

Maddy's heart ricocheted off her ribs. 'ILU' was a sign-off she'd once known very well, but hadn't seen for almost seven years. Adey's code for 'I love you'. Hot and cold, she read and reread. Then, with trembling fingers, she replied. Adey???

The phone was silent.

She waited.

Her heart pounded.

The screen remained blank.

Then the phone rang.

She jumped so hard that she almost hit herself in the head with it.

But, this time, what flashed onto the screen was *Raff Edmonds*. Shaking, she answered with a squeak. 'He-hello?'

Raff's low laugh sounded in her ear. 'You sound astonished to hear from me. Isn't this the arranged time?'

136

Obviously, he had no knowledge of what had just happened, or of the shock and disbelief that raged in her veins. His voice was low. 'Last night was the highlight of my week, by the way. In fact, of my year.' He paused.

Maddy realised that he expected a reply, but her throat seemed to have gone rigid.

'Maddy?' he said uncertainly.

'I'm here,' she managed. Suddenly, she had no idea what to say to the man she'd kissed last night. Her happiness deflated like a leaky balloon. *Idiot,* she thought bitterly. *What made you dare think about a happy ending with Raff? A future, however distant? You jinxed yourself. Thought it was over after seven long years? Well, it's not if your missing husband has just turned up.*

'Maddy?' Raff's voice came again, kind and concerned. 'Is something wrong?'

She gulped, queasy from a whirl of emotions. Was it only this afternoon she'd been planning Lyla's sleepover with Heloise to allow Maddy the freedom to spend adult time with Raff? That suddenly seemed as unlikely as Christmas on the moon. 'I just received a text, and it might be from Adey,' she burst out, her voice thin and quavering. 'I told you my situation was a mess,' she added, as if it was Raff's fault. Voice giving out, she ended the call.

For some time, she sat, head in hands, too shocked to even go downstairs and tell Ruthie. Too dread-filled to cry. Would there be another text, confirming or denying it was Adey? As she sat, and her breathing calmed, she realised she must have sounded like a deranged witch. No wonder Raff hadn't called back.

When she finally tucked her silent phone in her pocket and trudged downstairs, it was to find Ruthie, reassuringly familiar in her armchair, eyes closed. It was impossible to tell whether she was asleep or concentrating on the podcast as a male voice spoke earnestly about something called the Strategic Arms Limitation Talks of 1972 and 1979.

Unwilling to disturb her peace, Maddy prowled restlessly into the kitchen. Occupation was what she needed – not silence and free time. The uncovered kitchen window showed a sea mist, blank and impenetrable, and she was sufficiently unnerved to pull the blind, as if Adey might even be out there, watching. 'Don't be stupid,' she muttered to herself. But she left the blind down.

The thin barrier between her and the stealing mist didn't prevent her mind from whirling, though, and panic surged. *Money*. What could Adey lay claim to? The law regarding joint possessions might not consider how she'd fought tooth and nail to haul herself from the edge of bankruptcy. It might only see that now she was solvent and High Cottage was in joint names.

The future was suddenly as opaque as the night outside.

Her gaze fell on her to-do list, stuck to the fridge door. One of the few items left unticked was 'make Christmas cake'. Grateful for something useful to occupy her, she grabbed her mixing bowl and the kitchen scales.

A jar of mixed fruit had been soaking in brandy for several days. She took it from the shelf and gave it a good shake before opening it and the rich, alcoholic smell pervaded the air. She measured butter, sugar, eggs and treacle into the mixing bowl, wishing it was fear, anxiety, dread and misery she was beating the hell out of with her wooden spoon. Before she could weigh out and add the flour, she became aware of a gentle but insistent tapping. Bemused, she took a couple of steps across the hall to peep in at Ruthie, who still appeared to be deep in concentration-slash-nap.

The tapping came again. *Tap-tap-tap*. Pause. *Tap-tap-tap*.

It couldn't be Della or Heloise, both of whom were familiar enough with the household that they'd knock and walk in with a 'Hi, it's me.' The black-painted door boasted no chain or peephole, this being Nelson's Bar, but for the first time, Maddy wished for them.

Adey? It would feel like coming face-to-face with a ghost.

Tap-tap-tap. She hovered closer.

Her heart kicked itself into a bumpy gallop. Adey could have visited High Cottage. Her tenant Garth would have directed him to Ruthie's house.

Tap-tap-tap at the door.

Bump-bump-bump went her heart.

Tap-tap-tap.

Bump-bump-bump.

Holding her breath, Maddy lifted the Suffolk latch and twisted the doorknob, then yanked open the door. She gasped as the outline of a man loomed and her heart bounced so hard it felt as if it had bruised her ribcage.

But then the figure stepped into the light and smiled.

Giddy with relief, she breathed, 'Raff? Oh, come in.' Recovering her wits, she stepped aside so he could enter and she could shut the door against the icy sea mist shrouding Nelson's Bar.

One of his dark eyebrows arched. 'I thought ringing the bell might wake Lyla, but I wanted to see why you hung up on me.' His voice rang with concern, rather than anger.

'I didn't mean to,' Maddy said, dismayed to realise she had. 'And it takes an earthquake to wake Lyla. Come in.'

She led the way into the kitchen, which smelled of brandy and sugar.

He unzipped his ski jacket and shrugged it off to drop it over the back of a kitchen chair, gave her his long, slow smile and cut straight to the chase. 'Has hearing from Adey changed everything?'

But before she could reply, Ruthie's voice came from the doorway. 'Hello, is that Raff's voice?' She stood, framed by the light, cardigan rumpled and thick glasses askew.

Raff took a step away from Maddy. 'Yes, hi, Ruthie. I just came to talk to Maddy.'

After a hesitation, Ruthie said, 'Oh. Good,' but Maddy didn't miss the wistful expression that drew its sagging lines across her face. With a twinge, she realised that Ruthie would have got her hopes up for news of Ffion. 'Right then,' Ruthie went on, valiantly. 'I'm off to bed to listen to the radio, so I'll say goodnight. You stay here, Maddy. I don't need anything.'

With an unconvincing smile, she turned towards her room, marking her route by touching the hall table as she passed. The door closed behind her, and Maddy and Raff were alone.

Chapter Ten

Raff saw Maddy's face fall as her aunt left. She looked so unhappy that despite his head telling him that it had probably been a bad idea to come to the cottage unannounced and let Ruthie see him, he slipped his arms around Maddy and pulled her close. Baking paraphernalia filled the kitchen, and her hair smelled faintly of sugar. 'The text must have come as a shock.'

For a second she stiffened. Then she softened and slid one of her arms about him, while she fished for her phone with the other. 'It might not be him, because it came from an unknown number.'

He drew back enough to focus on the screen of her phone. Sorry to be away so long. Think of you often. How are you? ILU xxx

'ILU stands for "I love you", and it was how he usually ended texts to me,' she explained dolefully. 'I've been complaining about being in limbo, but this development's unnerving.' Putting away her phone, she leant her head on Raff's shoulder.

He stroked her back, following the soft curve of her

spine to her waist. 'What's worrying you about him turning up? You don't have to resume your marriage . . . unless you want to?' He held his breath. This limbo business was beginning to affect him, and it was uncomfortable. She had history with Adey, the tie of marriage, and they shared a child – even if he didn't know it.

She pulled back to give him an incredulous look. 'I *know* I don't have to take him back, and I *won't* want to,' she said shortly, as if he'd accused her of being spineless or clueless.

Relief unknotted his belly. 'Then the legalities will just be different, won't they? You'll be able to get a divorce.'

'It's not that easy,' she said slowly. 'How will anyone weigh up the crap he left me in versus the income I've been able to achieve? Those things come back to High Cottage being in joint names. Where the hell do I begin? Citizens' Advice Bureau? A solicitor? How will the law react if he protests that I sold most of his possessions in my efforts to avoid bankruptcy?' Her head landed back on his shoulder with a *thunk*. 'I'll have to tell the police about the text. But the most worrying thing's Lyla, of course. Would she want a dad, given the choice? Would he want to be in her life? A court would probably grant access to the birth father.'

He suspected she was correct. It wasn't the time to comment, but he wondered whether she'd ever considered giving Lyla a stepfather. He hadn't even begun to consider possibly, *maybe*, potentially reaching that place with her himself, but if he hated children, he wouldn't be dating a woman with a child, would he? Right now, what he hated was the idea of some other guy fulfilling the role. Feeling her trembling, he tightened his arms, wishing he could tell her everything would be fine. 'What does she know about him?'

Her voice became husky. 'An age-appropriate truth – that I don't know where to find her dad and he didn't know she was going to be born. I try to make him non-essential. Our family is her, me and Ruthie.'

'There are lots of different versions of "family",' he agreed, thinking of Ffion bringing up Chloe alone and doing a damned fine job of it. It crossed his mind that Ffion might like Maddy – if they met. Wordlessly, he dropped a kiss on her hair.

'Mummy? Who's that?' piped a voice, and he swung around to see a small, sleep-creased girl, her toes curled away from the cold flagstones, her lilac pyjamas sporting a pirouetting fairy and the words *If you can't be good, be magic* on the front.

Raff released Maddy even as she ducked from his embrace. 'Lyla.' She scooped up her daughter. 'What are you doing awake, my beauty?'

Lyla rubbed an eye, gazing at Raff through the other one. 'I had a bad dream, so I wanted you.'

'Of course you did,' Maddy declared, smoothing down the waves in Lyla's blonde hair. 'I'll cuddle those bad dreams away, won't I?'

Lyla nodded. Her gaze remained on Raff.

With a resigned set to her shoulders, Maddy turned. 'Lyla, this is my friend Raff. Ruthie knows him too, and so does Heloise.' Her voice was gentle and matter-of-fact.

Raff understood that she was presenting him as a generally friendly figure, not particular to herself. 'Hello, Lyla,' he said genially, but wondering again whether he should have come here tonight. For himself, yes. He'd wanted to be there for Maddy, and a simple call back hadn't felt enough. He'd wanted to see her face when she talked about the astonishing fact that long-missing Adey might have contacted her. But for Maddy? This was the second time he'd presented himself here uninvited. Maddy hadn't closed the door on him but hadn't expected her daughter to come downstairs, judging from her earlier remark that it took an earthquake to wake Lyla. Single parents were understandably chary of introducing their kids to their dates.

He waited for her to give him a lead, like *Raff's just leaving* or for Lyla to demand to know why Raff had been cuddling her mum.

But Lyla's attention was elsewhere. She yawned. 'Can I have hot milk to help me sleep?'

Maddy nuzzled Lyla's neck to make her laugh. 'You're supposed to be in bed, young lady, not cadging treats.'

Lyla giggled and peeped at Raff as if inviting him into the moment. He grinned back.

'You can have half a cup.' Maddy slid Lyla onto a kitchen chair.

The notes of Lyla's laughter were like music on the air. 'Mum-*mee*, I'm not a baby. I won't wet the bed if I have a full cup.' She knelt up and propped her elbows on the table, her eyes following her mother taking down a white mug decorated with a unicorn leaping a rainbow.

Raff's heart gave an unexpected twist. Chloe used to kneel up on chairs at Lyla's age – adapting her small self to an adult-sized world.

Spotting that Maddy was lining up two mugs beside the unicorn one, Raff took it as an invitation to stay and sat at the table. A teacher and an uncle, he had no trouble opening a conversation with Lyla. 'Do you like living in Nelson's Bar? I've only been a few times.'

Lyla tucked her sleep-bedraggled hair behind her ear. 'Yes. I like Zig-Zag Beach and the playground on The Green. And I like the sea lots.'

He smiled his thanks when Maddy put a mug of coffee before him. 'My house isn't as close to the sea as yours. I live in Docking.'

Lyla turned to Maddy. 'I'm going to Docking on Saturday with Heloise, aren't I? To their Christmas fair.'

Maddy kept her attention on Lyla. 'I think Heloise mentioned it. Drink your drink. It's not too hot and you need to go back to bed because it's a school night.'

Lyla's brows curled in puzzlement. 'Heloise said you might meet us there, Mummy.' The child turned wide blue eyes on Raff. 'I'm going to have a sleepover at Heloise's house on Friday so Mummy can paint the town red.'

Raff turned an interested gaze on Maddy. Her face had turned the colour she was apparently going to paint the town. 'That's great. Heloise gets a treat and Mummy gets a treat.'

Lyla regarded him over the rim of her cup of milk, before pausing to lick her lips. 'What's Heloise's treat?'

'Having you to stay.' He grinned into the guileless grey eyes.

Lyla looked gratified. 'And Mummy goes to —' A pause. A frown. 'Mummy, where will you be?'

Maddy was still pink. 'Come on. Drink up. Bed.'

Raff found himself wishing she was talking to him.

With only a small sigh, Lyla drank, her eyelids heavy now as if the reminder of bed had made her drowsy. Then she deposited her cup on the table. 'I've had enough.'

Maddy rose and gathered her up off the chair. 'I'll carry you, so your feet won't get cold. Say goodnight to Raff.'

'Night.' Lyla yawned, waving in his general direction.

'Night,' he called back and watched the pair cross the hall and disappear up red-carpeted stairs. Maddy hadn't told him to leave so he finished his coffee, listening to the cosy bedtime sounds of murmuring voices, footsteps, a flushing loo. Then just Maddy's voice, gentle and soft. He imagined her reading a sleepy-time story, as Chloe used to call it, maybe about unicorns and magic.

Maddy's voice stopped. A pause. Then down the stairs appeared her feet, her legs and then the rest of her. A variety of next moves flitted through his head, but he opted to demonstrate that he knew not to outstay his welcome by rising and tugging on his coat. 'Dare I hope I'm invited on the town-painting excursion on Friday? Or do you have other plans?' It would be a bummer if he didn't get a second date, especially if she was seeing some other bloke.

But she smiled. 'I'd intended to ask if you'd like to go out to dinner again. Heloise suggested the sleepover, and also meeting at the Christmas fair in Docking, as Lyla can't get enough of Christmas.' Her colour heightened anew. 'I'm sorry if our banter, regurgitated by my daughter, made me sound calculating.'

He moved closer to her. 'It sounded great. Shall we call it a date?' He particularly liked the idea of her being in Docking the morning after – if it meant she would have spent the night there with him. He hadn't forgotten the text that had brought him here, though. 'I'll understand if anything happens to prevent it.'

Her smile switched off. 'If my disappeared husband reappears, you mean?'

Rather than confirm it directly, he asked, 'Could the message have been from someone else?'

Her shoulders hunched. 'They would have to know his

sign-off – which I suppose Harris or someone could have. And have a reason not to reply when I asked if it was him.'

Raff took her hand. 'Replies to a withheld number don't go through, I'm afraid.'

She stared a moment, understanding and dismay dawning in her gold-flecked eyes. 'I'd forgotten that. How stupid am I?' She gazed meditatively at her phone. Then she tapped a couple of times and held the handset to her ear for several seconds, before pulling a face. 'Just tried calling his old number. The recorded messages says disconnected or out of service.'

Raff didn't think she was stupid. He thought she was beautiful, distressed yet valiant, warm, and lovely. He kissed her gently on the mouth. 'I hope Friday works out for us, and I hope you can sleep after all this.'

She pulled a wry face. 'So do I.' She didn't sound too optimistic. A text that might be from your missing husband must take some processing. He felt uneasy and unsettled, so could only imagine how Maddy felt.

Another kiss, then Raff drove home through a fog that made the pine trees look as if they were floating without trunks as he eased down Long Climb, his headlights barely penetrating the grey murk. At the foot of the hill, the fog cleared to a barely misty evening, as if it was just Nelson's Bar that had its head in the clouds. He picked up speed past a garden centre with brightly lit trees outside.

Despite his preoccupation with the odd text this evening, he hadn't missed the raw expression on Maddy's face as Ruthie had looked so hopefully at Raff. One thing he could do that might have the potential to ease the load on Maddy's mind was to speak to Ffion again. He'd do that tomorrow.

* * *

As it turned out it was another three days, Wednesday, before Ffion's schedule allowed Raff to visit. Her Monday and Tuesday working calendar had involved a plethora of video conferences and deadlines; on Monday evening she and Chloe had driven into King's Lynn to an open evening at the school Chloe had chosen for sixth form. The evening of Tuesday had seen Ffion fetching Chloe from a dance rehearsal and, knowing her limitations, then having an early night.

Raff understood. Ffion was exhausted by everyday life. Chloe's current school had no sixth form and her further education had to be arranged. He bided his time until morning coffee on Wednesday, Ffion's day off, when a lie-in might help recharge her easily depleted batteries.

At ten-thirty, he wrenched himself from mulling over how practical it would be to give growing but forbidden feelings for the queen to shape-shifting hero Adeckor. He'd have to conduct an affair as a man rather than a centaur . . . because, well 'hung like a horse' would be tricky to get around.

Raff pulled on hat, ski jacket and the boots that usually carried him on hikes along the coastal path. After the small snowfall on Monday, an iron frost had gripped Norfolk. Roads were gritted but paths were mini-ice rinks. On the familiar route along High Street, every leaf wore a white icy jacket and at Church Place the white-painted walls of Ffion's dinky house looked to have risen from the twinkling frost. He clattered the front door knocker and let himself in.

He discovered Ffion at the kitchen table, frowning over her laptop. She greeted him: 'I thought Chloe was set on transferring to the school we visited on Monday, but now she wants to visit a sixth form college.'

He set a chair so he could view her screen, which depicted enthusiastic-looking students. Without commenting on Chloe changing her mind a lot these days, he said, 'Can't blame her for wanting to be sure of the right choice.'

Ffion looked tired and drawn, as well as rueful. 'But a little notice would make life easier. Someone's said there's a great performing arts programme so now she wants to go to their open evening – tomorrow, in King's Lynn.'

'I could drive you,' he offered.

Her brow cleared. 'Really? That would be great, especially in view of the weather. It's amazing how much extra concentration tires me out.'

'No prob.' He treated her to a gentle punch on the shoulder. 'What else are big brothers for?'

'I've always wondered.' She twinkled at him. 'I can't believe it's only two years before Chloe starts university. How fast she's growing up.'

As Ffion had made Chloe the subject of the conversation, Raff felt able to bring in, 'Are you and Chloe any closer to making a decision about Ruthie Willson?' Even he was beginning to see that Ruthie was getting a rough deal and beginning to wonder why he couldn't at least give her a little news about Ffion. 'I've been trying not to badger you, but I saw her again, briefly, and she looked so hopeful.' Although he wouldn't normally keep his sister informed about his love life, he'd already mentioned he was dating Maddy, deeming openness essential in this case.

Ffion closed her laptop. 'Chloe and I talked in the car coming back from King's Lynn.' She looked up with a faint smile. 'It's a good way to make a teenager talk – trap them in a moving car and hide their headphones.'

He laughed. 'I don't suppose we were any different. I used to go to great lengths to avoid Dad's lectures.'

'True,' Ffion said. 'After talking it over—' She drew out a pause so long that Raff had time to think that his sister would spend the rest of her life wondering what she and Chloe would miss out on if her answer was 'no'. That Maddy wanted the meeting too, he tried not to take into consideration. He'd support Ffion and Chloe's decision and hope that the attraction bubbling between him and Maddy wouldn't prove dependent on whether Ruthie met her long-lost daughter. *Although* . . . A strange feeling gripped his chest. What if he and Maddy ever committed, and their two little family units felt unable to meet? It seemed ludicrous, but it could happen.

'—we'd like to meet her,' Ffion finished. 'What do you think?'

Relief seeped through him, but he had to swallow an unexpected lump before he could speak. 'I think she'll be over the moon,' he said simply, picturing Ruthie's soft, plump face wreathed in an enormous, emotional smile.

Ffion flushed, a light in her eye suggesting she was more excited than she was letting on. 'Are you able to set up a meeting? Chloe and I thought that might be the best way forward.'

'Of course.' He found himself sitting straighter. 'But I should tell her about Chloe's existence first.'

Ffion laughed, a real sparkle in her eyes now. 'Yes, of course.'

'Are you thinking of visiting her in her home? Or to meet on neutral ground?' he asked.

Ffion gnawed her thumbnail, a mannerism he thought had been left behind in their teens. 'Visit her, I think,' she said uncertainly. 'It might be easier for her emotionally, and the niece would be there to take care of her if necessary.'

'Maddy,' he supplied, finding he wasn't keen on hearing her referred to so impersonally.

'Oh, yes,' she said with a sisterly dig to his ribs. '*Maddy*. How did the date go?'

'Good,' he answered economically, not about to confide how the text Maddy had received on Sunday had blighted things though he'd told Ffion the basic details of Adey's 'missing person' status, as it would have been strange not to mention something so significant. The mystery text was still uppermost in his mind, though Maddy hadn't said much more about it.

His little sister looked intrigued. 'You could call her now.'

He laughed. 'Yeah, right, with you earwigging. No, I think I should get Maddy on her own first. She'll know the best way to tell Ruthie so that she doesn't get excited or stressed into an asthma attack.'

Another dig in the ribs. 'What wouldn't you say to Maddy with me listening?'

He rubbed his side in exaggerated discomfort, though actually he was glad to see Ffion being playful rather than dog-tired. 'Mind your own business, you nosy bag,' he retorted rudely. But then gave her a quick hug. 'I'm glad you're going to see Ruthie. I think you'll like her.'

Smile fading, Ffion gazed into his eyes. 'I hope so.' Then she sighed. 'I've been reading more of her letters. She never asked much about me. Usually, just a line like "How are the children?" or "Thank you for telling me the children are well". It feels a bit cold.' She gave a theatrical shiver.

He digested this. 'I think there's more that went on

151

between Ruthie and Dad than appears in their love letters. The affair lasted twenty-nine years, remember.'

'Yes.' For several moments she looked far away. 'I'm not likely to forget.'

He reminded himself that the story Ruthie's letters had told concerned Ffion and Chloe much more than himself and that Ffion alone had nursed the secret for the twenty-one years between Nigel's death and Sindy's. Raff hadn't wanted to read many, but it was understandable that Ffion had felt entitled to know the story of how she came into being. He had nothing more than an adoption certificate to remind him that he'd once had a mother other than Sindy, and an email now and then from a bloke who always signed himself Dave rather than Dad. Just thought I'd check you're OK. Raff would answer, Good, thanks. You? Dave would say, Fine, and that would be it for another year or two. They'd met a couple of times in Raff's teens, but they'd felt like strangers and nothing more than their brief emails had come of it.

He hoped Ffion would feel more for Ruthie, because Ruthie evidently harboured intense love for her.

After an hour of comfortable conversation and a cup of coffee, he returned home to work, jotting ideas on a big white pad, then scribbling them out again. Adeckor didn't seem to want to tell Raff whether he would fall from grace by having a thing with the king's wife, or would rise above temptation. Raff thought about sending his hero off on some fresh battle to delay the decision, but that would only let Adeckor off the hook.

He threw down his pen and stared at his screen. He'd written about ten words today and had no idea if they were even in the right order. He snatched up his phone and texted Maddy. Can we talk, when you have a minute free? X He didn't want to say, 'when you won't be overheard', but that was what he meant.

Half an hour passed. He made Adeckor a pros and cons list: *sleeping with the queen.* Pros: *the queen and Adeckor want it, love is a strong emotion;* and cons: *if the king finds out he will exile Adeckor or have him put to death. Where will Adeckor's loyalty lie?*

He could be banished, then earn redemption by saving the king's life in some way Raff had yet to decide. But the queen would still be around to tempt him . . .

His phone buzzed. Maddy had texted, Now OK? X

Leaving Adeckor and the faithless queen to sort out their own mess, he made the call.

'Hey,' her smooth, sexy voice said in his ear. 'I'm on my way to meet Lyla off the bus. Freakin' freezin', too.' She laughed.

He had a vision of her huddled into her coat, the wind tangling her hair and the cold pinching colour into her cheeks, snatching a few moments with him. 'You sound happy,' he said, feeling his way into the conversation.

'Much happier,' she confirmed. 'No more texts. Must have been some crazily coincidental wrong number. I decided not to bother the police with it.'

Relief swept over him, not just at the news but because she'd understood his need to know. He shoved aside the fact that coincidence didn't explain the ILU part of the text and he was pretty sure the police might have felt the same. But he had no right to try and make Maddy's decision. 'How do you feel about that?' It was a good, open-ended question, one that had allowed many a child to confide without feeling pressured.

'Relieved,' she said. 'Whoo! Hang on.' A scuffling noise,

a curse, running footsteps, then she was back. 'Wind blew my hat off,' she said. 'It's blowing a gale in Nelson's Bar.'

'Freezing in Docking.' Why was he talking about the weather when he didn't know how long he had her undivided attention? 'Do you still have a babysitter for Friday?'

'I do. Heloise seems to be seeing a lot of someone, but not on Friday.' She sounded as if she was smiling.

Mindful of what Lyla had let slip about Maddy perhaps being in Docking on Saturday morning, he said, 'Have you been to the pub here? I'm told it's good.'

The smile remained in her voice. 'It is,' she confirmed.

And his heart gave a little hop because without saying so, each was acknowledging that she might stay the night. He could not wait.

Chapter Eleven

After giving Lyla and Ruthie their dinner and welcoming Della to spend the evening with Ruthie, Maddy rushed into Heloise's cottage in Traders Place, Lyla's mittened hand in hers. 'We're here, Heloise.' She shut the door behind her and peeped into the kitchen, then the sitting room.

'We're heee-yar, Helo-ee-eeze,' Lyla carolled in her sweet, sing-song voice.

The sound of a door opening upstairs, then Heloise jogged down the stairs, her fair hair swinging either side of her face. 'My two favourite women, looking excited and happy,' she said with a wicked glance at Maddy. 'Shall I take your backpack, Lyla my lovely?'

Lyla wriggled free of the straps. 'I've got my jammies, and my toothbrush and my stuff.' Lyla's stuff encompassed whatever seemed vital to her six-year-old self, from an empty nail varnish bottle to a pencil case and the plush pony she cuddled in her sleep. 'I want a new backpack for Christmas, with unicorns on, like Misty's at school.'

Heloise had already purchased exactly the backpack

Lyla had put on her Christmas list, but in blue as against Misty's pink. Now, though, Heloise pulled a doubtful face. 'Let's hope Santa has enough. I expect the unicorn merch is popular.'

It was doubtful that Lyla knew what 'merch' was, but she nodded, evidently ready to allow Santa some latitude. 'Can I put my stuff in my room?' She had no hesitation in claiming Heloise's spare room as hers, and it was true that it was rarely occupied by anyone else. A sleepover at Heloise's was a treat that happened every few months.

'Good idea.' Heloise caught Maddy's eye. 'Then I can talk to Mummy a minute before you say bye.'

'Cool.' Lyla sprinted up the stairs, backpack banging on the banisters.

As soon as her footsteps passed over their heads, Heloise reached out questing hands. 'What are you wearing?' As if Maddy were a teenager, she unzipped her coat and surveyed the burgundy velvet dress beneath, perused Maddy's topknot and smoothed the rest of her hair, which had been left to hang heavy down her back. Then she inspected Maddy's black ankle boots, which were tied with ribbon. 'Excellent. Sexy and demure both at once. I've been preparing a dating lecture for you.'

Maddy snorted. 'I'm thirty-nine. I'm totally aware that I don't need to do anything I'm not comfortable with. Neither do I need telling how to get help if I'm scared.'

Heloise nodded approvingly. 'Good. But what about the rest?'

Maddy frowned, less certain of her ground. 'What rest?'

'First—' Heloise held up a finger '—you don't need to automatically repel boarders if a man comes on to you.'

'Oh, come on.' Maddy laughed. 'I wouldn't *automatically*,

just because I didn't sleep with that up-himself tourist last summer. He was a knob.'

'But Raff isn't a knob, so you're allowed to fancy the pants off him,' Heloise pointed out reasonably.

Maddy opened her mouth to say she was quite well aware, thank you, but paused, realising Heloise might have a point. Maddy was date rusty and her run-in with the entitled tourist might colour her thinking. 'OK,' she allowed.

Heloise held up another finger. 'Second, if you *do* fancy the pants off him, you can tell him. Strong women let prospective bed partners know what they want.'

'Yeah,' Maddy agreed dubiously, trying to imagine herself telling Raff that she'd like to go to bed with him.

Heloise giggled. 'I don't mean you pay for dinner and act entitled, but a woman making the first suggestion is *OK*. OK?'

'OK,' Maddy repeated. Maybe she should have paid more attention to Heloise's dating adventures to remind herself how it went. She'd started seeing Adey at the end of their schooldays, and limbo and Lyla hadn't encouraged her to focus on replacing him. But she had no opportunity to ask exactly what sort of thing Heloise might say in that situation, as Lyla bounced downstairs, two steps at a time.

'Isn't it time to go, Mummy?' she asked bossily, the feet of her tights sagging over her toes, her boots evidently abandoned upstairs.

'It is,' Maddy agreed. There was no need to go through the 'Will you be OK without me?' routine. Lyla loved Heloise and Maddy had confidence in her, not just because she was a qualified nursery nurse and childminder, but because she was Heloise, utterly on Maddy's side always.

She rezipped her coat, said her goodbyes, and was soon driving through tiny dancing flakes of snow to Docking, admiring the snow already sparkling on the hedges in the moonlight. The pub had its own car park, and she pulled up there fifteen minutes later.

Inside, broad, worn floorboards and painted panelling around the lower half of the walls gave the pub a country chic feel. Pictures ornamented the plastered section, and tinsel and strings of shiny red beads looped like bunting between them. Raff was waiting at a table, and she got the feeling that it was indicative of the way he treated women – not with ostentatious door opening and chair settling, which always made her uncomfortable, but by making sure they weren't kept hanging around.

He rose when she approached, unwinding her scarf and smoothing her hair, slid his arms around her in a quick, hard hug, and dropped a soft kiss just beside her mouth.

She felt that kiss all the way to the soles of her feet. It jangled through her as she seated herself on one of the wooden chairs. 'Nice place,' she said, hoping that she sounded breathless because of the icy air outside rather than because her veins were humming with anticipation.

A young female server arrived with green menu folders, a pocketed apron over black jeans. 'December specials are on the board, including our festive feast. If you want the black pudding in panko breadcrumbs starter I should grab it now, because it's popular. I'll bring water for the table.' With a smile, she was gone.

Raff pushed up the sleeves of his white Henley top. A couple of the buttons were open at his throat.

Maddy liked the look. A *lot*.

His smile always reached his eyes. 'Good to see you.'

158

Warmth trickled into the pit of her stomach. 'And you.' Remembering Heloise's pep talk about it being OK to show interest, she added, 'I've been looking forward to it.'

'Same.' Anything else he might have said was lost in the process of the water jug arriving and Raff ordering beer, having walked to the pub. They perused their menus, Maddy deciding on chicken with creamed leeks and bread sauce bon-bons and Raff saying cheerfully, 'Steak and chips, please.'

Finally, the server hurried off again. Raff picked up Maddy's hand from the tabletop and planted a soft kiss on her fingers. It tingled. He seemed comfortable with gestures of affection. His greeting kiss had been equally sweet, brief enough for a public place yet intimate enough to declare their connection. She found her gaze dropping to his mouth, which smiled as he was divining the direction of her thoughts.

He dropped his voice. 'I wish now I hadn't picked a venue quite so crowded.'

She didn't seem able to stop smiling. 'Fear of crowds?' she hazarded impishly.

His blue eyes gleamed. 'Fear of missing out.' When she tilted her head enquiringly, he clarified, 'Fear of missing out on repeating the more meaningful kiss at the end of our last date.'

Heat thrummed through her, as if she was made of harp strings, which he'd just run his fingers lightly over. 'It was very nice,' she agreed.

His fingers tightened around hers. 'Then I need to try harder, until I score an "amazing" or "awesome".'

She skated her thumb over his palm, feeling the slight roughness to his skin then leant forward far enough to just brush his mouth with hers, ignoring the table digging uncomfortably into her.

His eyes lit up, belying his mock-sorrowful sigh. 'And you scored "awesome" straight away.'

She laughed, enjoying the flirting, the feeling of their fingers interlacing. She heard herself say, 'I don't have to rush home tonight. Heloise has taken Lyla, as planned,' though she felt blood rushing to her cheeks.

His eyes softened. 'We could always have coffee at my place. It's not far away – just behind a house in High Street.'

She pretended to muse on the question. 'We could.'

Then the brisk, smiley server returned with two steaming plates of food, and they pulled apart to allow their meals to be placed before them. Raff picked up his cutlery. 'I have news,' he said.

Maddy had begun investigating her bread sauce bon-bons, which she'd chosen partly because they were new to her – stiff bread sauce shaped into balls and rolled in breadcrumbs then shallow fried, she surmised. She paused with half a bon-bon speared on her fork. 'Good news or bad?' Then she recognised suppressed excitement in his gaze, and dropped her fork onto her plate. 'Ffion?'

His smile blazed, crinkling the corners of his eyes. 'Yes, Ffion.' He paused to eat a mouthful of steak.

She wanted to say, 'And? *And?*' but forbore, instead eating her half bon-bon – or was that just a bon?

'But first, I have to tell you something.' He cut up several chips as if he needed something do while he summoned the right words.

Maddy's heart sank. Was he about to pull out some unpalatable fact? Was Ffion sicker than he'd disclosed?

Finally, he lifted his gaze to hers, level and clear. 'I

didn't tell you before as Ffion didn't want me to mention it to begin with, but Ffion has a daughter, Chloe. She's sixteen.'

'Wow.' Maddy halted, the other half of the bon-bon abandoned. 'Didn't I ever ask if she had a husband and kids? It seems a glaring omission, but I don't think I did. I was just so focused on her, and what she is to Ruthie.'

'No husband, one kid,' he confirmed, watching her face, obviously awaiting her reaction.

'So, Chloe is Ruthie's granddaughter. Wow,' she said again. 'She'll be stoked.' A horrible thought occurred. 'Chloe's OK, isn't she? She hasn't got the same heart condition as Ffion?'

'No, Ffion's condition isn't genetic,' he answered. 'But one of the reasons Ffion's taken so long over the decision is Chloe.' He sighed. 'She's a lovely girl but—' he rolled his hand in the air as if searching for the right word '—teenagerish. And she's scared by Ffion's impending surgery. The idea to search Ruthie out originated with her. To have another family member around must have felt attractive.' His gaze flickered away and then returned. 'I think maybe she's old enough to be intrigued by blood ties, always having known that Ffion and I were adopted.'

They turned their attention to their food for a while, conversation from other tables swirling around them. A dog lay beneath a nearby table, watching human feet pass by. The fire crackled and the ornaments on a Christmas tree jingled if anyone brushed too close. Maddy was full of this new information. She didn't mind that Raff hadn't told her about Chloe because that would have been Ffion's call to make. That Ffion had been giving Chloe space to make up her teenage mind suddenly made sense of the silences that had felt so brutal at the time. 'You're close to Chloe?' she asked.

'Love her to bits,' he confessed easily. 'I've loved her from the day she was born. Her life's been full of angst recently – GCSEs this year and sixth form next, her mum being ill . . . I've reassured her that Ffion should be fine after her op, and she knows that if anything went wrong then she'd have a home with me. But you can't blame such a young person for feeling fear and looking for comfort. She lost a grandmother she loved when Mum died more than two years ago and then she learns about Ruthie and wonders if she'll be someone else she can lean on.'

Maddy nodded. 'I think I understand.' She gave a wriggle. 'I feel as if I want to dash home and tell Ruthie right away.' She even swiped a sip of his beer to steady herself.

Raff's eyes twinkled understandingly. 'Ffion and I agreed that I should ask you the best way to go about the meeting. Ffion suggested we – her, Chloe and me – visit Ruthie at The Hollies, on the supposition that Ruthie would be most comfortable in her own home. If she prefers neutral ground though, that would be fine.'

Maddy's mind leapt ahead, visualising Ruthie's joy. 'I think she'd agree to visit Lapland if it meant meeting her daughter. And *grand*daughter! She's going to be delirious.' A choked little laugh emerged, and she had to sip her water to prevent it turning into a sob. 'Sorry. I'm just *thrilled* for her. She's been so sad, and she means so much to me.' Her eyes burned and she had to use her napkin to blot under them so her mascara didn't smudge.

His eyes looked a touch misty, too. 'I think Ffion and Chloe have made the right decision – so long as you think

Ruthie's health will be up to a meeting.' The sentence went up at the end, like a question.

'A little thing like breathing won't stop her,' Maddy said frankly. 'I know she had an asthma attack when she first met you, but it was quite different. It was a big shock out of the blue, and she got emotional about your dad. A meeting she knows about and can look forward to will be different. I'll tell her the good news as soon as I see her tomorrow.'

'After you meet Lyla and Heloise at Docking village hall for the Christmas fair?' he queried with a wicked grin.

Her blush at this reference to Heloise's assumption that she'd still be in Docking in the morning burst across her face and ran down her neck with a feeling like warm syrup.

He must have realised he'd embarrassed her, because he sobered. 'I know you were suspicious of me when we met, but I hope by now you realise that I'm an OK guy.'

Her heart quivered at his earnest expression. She swallowed. 'I was suspicious. I get touchy when I think someone's threatening my loved ones.'

'So do I. I'm glad we haven't ended up on opposing sides.' They finally got around to finishing their meals, and afterwards he took her hand over the table again, as if that was the natural place for it.

He told her some more about Chloe, who lived for her street dance group – which was called a 'crew', apparently – and the educational decisions underway.

'Weird to think she attends the same school I went to,' Maddy commented. 'I hope she enjoys it more.'

'I think she likes it OK.' He looked down at their joined hands. 'I feel as if I'm always hedging about telling you things, but when I explained about Ffion's heart trouble, I didn't mention that the surgery was in February.'

Maddy could see shadows in his eyes. 'I'm sorry to hear that,' she said gently. It was a down in an otherwise gloriously happy conversation.

He blew out his cheeks. 'I admit I'll be glad when she's safely through it. But she should be *much* better if it goes well, so we're holding that thought.'

They talked about Ffion and Chloe for a while, then he edged the conversation back to matters nearer to hand, rubbing his chin, which Maddy had noticed was a 'tell' whenever he was uncertain. 'What are you hoping for? You know – us.'

Involuntarily, her fingers twitched in his. 'I haven't looked past promising beginnings, I suppose.' It seemed a safe answer.

His eyes smiled. 'And what are you hoping for tonight?'

Heart rate quickening, she was about to say, *you, ideally,* when her phone beeped to alert her to a text. As it could be Heloise about Lyla or Della about Ruthie, she delved for it in her bag. 'Sorry. Just let me check if I'm needed.' Then she read *number withheld* on the screen and her breathing hitched.

The message opened in response to her shaky tap. Can you ever forgive me? There's nothing I want more. ILU x

She actually felt the blood drain from her cheeks.

The cheery young server chose that moment to reappear. 'Clear these plates for you, can I? Would you like to see the dessert menu? Or coffee, maybe? Another drink?'

Maddy heard Raff answer as if from a distance. 'Just the bill, please.'

Her throat dry, she fumbled her phone back into her bag, too shaken to think about whipping out her credit card to pay her half of the bill. *Adey. It must be Adey. ILU once could be a crazy coincidence . . . but twice? Adey. He was alive and he was contacting her.* The dining area's cheery tinsel suddenly felt out of place, and the relaxed chatter coming from tables around her unnerved her. She wanted to get away.

'Maddy,' Raff said, in a tone that suggested he'd said her name more than once. 'Here's your coat. Let's get that coffee.'

'Coffee?' she repeated incredulously. Did he really think that she was going home with him now?

His hands settled on her shoulders, heavy and somehow comforting. He murmured in her ear. 'You're white as a sheet. I don't think you should drive home yet. Come and have a hot drink. There's no—' he paused '—other expectation. It's obvious why you'd react like that to a text. It's like the other one?'

She nodded. The fun and awareness between them had drained away. 'I'll be OK to drive to your place,' she said, and then they braved the ice-edged wind to hurry to her car. Remnants of snow remained in corners and crevices like white streamers that had blown about in the wind. In silence she drove, feeling distant and odd, the words *forgive* and *nothing I want more* circulating her brain. Raff directed her down Station Road and Well Street into High Street and she followed his directions like a robot. He indicated a narrow drive at the side of a larger, flint and brick house, and she turned left into it, glad she didn't drive anything wider than her old green Vauxhall Corsa as the walls seemed ready to scrape her door mirrors as it was. Relieved to get through unscathed, she came to a stop on a patch of concrete.

'Just pull in there,' he said, indicating a meagre space beside his ruby red Mazda.

Glad to see there was just about enough room to back out and turn when she left, she did so, then let him usher her to a brick building, a narrow two storeys with a pointed roof.

Inside turned out to be cute enough to intrude into her preoccupation. The whole of the ground floor was a warm and welcoming living space, with cream-coloured kitchen units with black surfaces that gave way to an area for a glass table and metal chairs, and then blue sofas. A flight of open-tread wooden stairs rose from halfway along the opposite wall. Raff waved her to the sofas while he busied himself with a kettle. Glancing about, she took in a black laptop on the table and a notebook with a pen and loose papers sticking out of it. 'So this is where Edd Rafferty works,' she said, remembering his pen name.

He glanced up with a smile. 'And sighs and swears a lot.'

This bijou residence was warmer than The Hollies, where the window frames and doors seemed more suitable for ventilation than insulation. 'What was this place originally?' she asked.

'It's described as a former workshop or outbuilding,' he answered. 'The owners have only lived in the village a few years and it was in disrepair when they moved in. They walled in some garden for themselves and converted this as an income stream.' He let a teaspoon clatter in the sink then carried two plain white mugs with him when he came to join her and placed them on a small table that was conveniently positioned before the biggest sofa. She imagined him propping his feet on it while he watched TV.

He sat beside her and slipped an arm around her shoulders.

Sorrow was a weight inside Maddy as she rested her head on his shoulder. Why did Adey have to pop up just when her life had been moving forward? It wasn't that she wanted to declare him dead if he wasn't, but she'd waited so bloody long. Sweat moistened her hairline. Trouble was all she could envisage from his return. A voice nagged from the back of her head. *You didn't keep any money back for if Adey returned.*

But he left me in a mess! I got us out of it with hard work. He didn't do his share.

And WHAT about Lyla?

She reached for her coffee and swallowed a gulp, heart speeding. Maddy couldn't claim a majority share in Lyla, and she needed no paternity test to know that Adey was Lyla's father.

Beside her, Raff reached for his cup. 'Are you more convinced it's him, this time?' His voice sounded as if he was keeping it carefully neutral.

With a sigh, she dug out her phone and reread the text, tilting the screen so that Raff could see it too. Can you ever forgive me? There's nothing I want more. ILU x 'ILU again,' she said grimly. 'I don't think I ever will forgive him, and I certainly don't love him.' She tried to order her thoughts. 'I told you before how prevalent mental illness is among people who go missing. It's something I always try to bear in mind, but if this is the first step to him returning, I'm going to find it difficult.'

'Could he have been in prison?' Raff asked meditatively.

She shrugged, feeling so much weight on her shoulders she was surprised she could move them. 'From what the police said, him hitting any system like that would bring him to their attention. They'd have notified me, even if they just said he was safe and well but didn't want contact.' Exposing some of her deepest held fears prompted a tangle of emotions, including a heart-stopping, bone-deep fury. Even the roots of her hair felt hot. 'Do you have any alcohol?' she demanded abruptly.

She felt his head turn her way. 'Of course. Wine, beer, brandy . . . ?'

'I'd love a big glass of wine, preferably red.' She shut her mind to the consequences of exceeding the drink-drive limit. Heloise was with Lyla and Della with Ruthie. If her daughter or aunt needed her, she'd just have to get a taxi.

He unwound his arm from around her and a few long strides took him into the kitchen. Soon he was pouring healthy measures of dark red wine into two glasses, before returning to his place on the sofa.

She took the glass he offered.

He kicked off his shoes and, just as she'd imagined, propped his feet on the table. 'I can't conceive what it's like to be in your situation.'

'It's uncomfortable.' The first mouthful of wine made her taste buds zing. 'The gossip's never completely died down. Harris's "jokes" help keep it fresh in people's minds.'

He hugged her into his side. It was lovely to be the receiver of comfort for once, instead of the giver. She put down her wine glass and snuggled into him, winding her arms about his neck. 'I'm not usually needy,' she confessed, her voice half-smothered against his shoulder. 'You should have fancied Heloise. No kids, no baggage, not even an ex-husband.'

He stroked her back, softly soothing. 'Heloise is a pleasant, attractive woman – but she's not you, Maddy.

You're great company. You make me laugh. You growl like a tiger if you think Lyla or Ruthie are being threatened. You're beautiful. And we have . . . chemistry.' His body curled more fully around hers.

Only moments ago, she'd felt heavy with dismay and sorrow, but suddenly she felt . . . hot. Fizzy. Floaty. Heady. The sensations of desire she hadn't felt for so long. Heart thudding against his body, she whispered, 'Is it wrong to be turned on right now?'

His voice low, he murmured, 'Not in my book.' His mouth just below her ear shot through her like a firework.

She nuzzled his neck, feeling the first prickle of stubble along with the warmth of his skin. And back into Maddy's head floated Heloise's advice. But she felt awkwardly tongue-tied. 'Are we . . . Is it the right time . . . ?'

His hand slipped down to cup her buttock. A smile coloured his voice. 'I'm desperately hoping for wonderful endings to those sentences.' He shifted so he could look into her eyes. He must have been satisfied with what he read there because as she melted into him, he kissed her, a deep, hot, tender kiss that felt like an all-over caress. She closed her eyes to better enjoy the velvet of his mouth while his stroking hands turned her spine to jelly. Finally, she broke away long enough to gasp a complete sentence. 'Are we going to bed?'

'I would love to,' he growled against her mouth. 'Certain?'

'Yeah,' she said, wriggling astride him. 'Sooo certain.' It felt like his lap was meant for her and she cupped his head, tracing his scalp and neck, his thick dark hair sliding between her fingers.

He nibbled the crook where her shoulder met her neck. 'Sooo am I,' he murmured, then pulled back to inspect the front buttons of her dress. He began to flick them open one by one, pausing after each to kiss and nuzzle the flesh he'd exposed. When he uncovered the lace of her bra he murmured, 'White, I love white,' then pushed it aside to put his mouth to the swell of her breasts.

'Mm,' she groaned, pleasure ricocheting inside her skull, her body answering the silent call of his.

Raff broke off to fumble at the buttons at the neck of his top and then yank it over his head. His chest was firm, sprinkled with dark hair on smooth skin that seemed to cry out for her nakedness against it.

Somehow, they managed to angle themselves without breaking contact until they were more horizontal along his capacious sofa, tugging at clothes. Maddy kicked off her black, beribboned boots.

Raff paused to protest, his blue eyes gleaming down at her. 'I really like those boots.'

'If I keep them on, I'll only worry about the fabric of your sofa.' Maddy slipped her fingers past the waistband of his boxers. Raff gasped and forgot all about the boots as she began to stroke him.

They didn't make it upstairs. At least not for ages. And, even then, it was hours before they got to sleep.

Chapter Twelve

Maddy surfaced slowly, languorously. The warm, male body cupped around hers reminded her that she'd spent the night with Raff. Something about his stillness told her that he was already awake. Remembering his disappointment at being told his kisses were 'very nice', she kept her eyes closed as she murmured, 'Awesome.'

The big male body nestled still closer as a husky morning voice rumbled encouragingly, 'What about amazing?'

Laughing, she wriggled around within his arms. Then her phone rang. 'That's Heloise's ringtone,' she sighed, and wriggled the other way, so she could ferret in her bag beside the bed.

Lyla's young voice piped in Maddy's ear. 'Mummy, I've slepted at Heloise's house, now. We're going to the Christmas fair. Can you come, too?'

Automatically in mum mode, Maddy glanced at Raff's black bedside clock, which read 8:36 a.m. 'Have you had breakfast?'

'Just cereal,' Lyla reported. 'Heloise says we can have

croissants, too. With Nutella?' she asked, her voice fainter, as if she'd turned away with the question. Maddy heard Heloise answering firmly that, yes, *definitely* with Nutella. Lyla's voice returned. 'Only one each, though, because we have to leave room for snacks at the Christmas fair.'

Maddy's heart filled with love at hearing Lyla's happy voice. 'OK, I'll have breakfast, too, and I'll meet you at the Christmas fair.' They chatted for a few minutes until Lyla ended the call in favour of croissant with Nutella.

Raff was smiling when Maddy turned to face him again, his thick hair rumpled. 'Christmas fair and Santa?' he hazarded jokily.

'But I don't have to be there until ten.' She waggled her eyebrows.

Raff closed the inch of space between them, his smile turning hot and sexy. 'So, you have time for breakfast and a shower . . .'

'And you,' she confirmed, hooking one of her legs around his.

In the event, they were ready to leave the house with only just enough time to walk to Docking's village hall, taking a slice of toast each to munch on the way. 'Lyla's too young to jump to the obvious conclusion but Heloise will probably give you knowing looks,' she confided cheerfully, before taking a bite of toast that was rapidly turning cold. 'Look at the frost on the remains of the snow. It's like white glitter! At least my car should have thawed by the time I come back for it.'

They linked the hands that weren't holding toast and set off down the narrow, walled drive, At the end, they swung right onto High Street.

Two petite figures halted coming the other way. 'Oh,' they chorused in twin tones of surprise.

'Oh,' Raff echoed. He glanced at Maddy. 'This is Ffion and Chloe.' And to them, 'And this is Maddy.'

Maddy added the final, 'Oh,' to the crisp morning air and went crimson. Their entwined hands and the toast was like holding a great neon sign saying, *spent the night together!*

Teenage Chloe, blonde hair escaping from a slouchy blue woollen hat, looked as big-eyed as a wild animal before it bolts. Her hands were stuffed in the pockets of a purple puffa coat, and her feet were encased in high-top once-white trainers decorated with zips and diamanté.

Ffion, wan and strained-looking, was first to recover her balance. 'Great to meet you, Maddy.' Her head sported a traditional bobble hat, a bright scarlet that exaggerated her pallor.

'Nice to meet you, too,' Maddy answered with mechanical courtesy. 'Raff gave me the fabulous news that you want to meet Ruthie. She'll be overjoyed. What a wonderful Christmas present it will be for her.' Though she wanted to add heartfelt thanks, to explain how sad and upset Ruthie had been, she suppressed the urge, aware that it might come across badly. *I'm Ruthie's great-niece and applauding you for meeting your mother.* 'I hope we can arrange it soon. It's fantastic that you've found each other.' She halted, awkward and unsure how to go on. Feebly, she added a tangential, 'So . . . you and I are related.'

Ffion looked grateful to hear something to which she wanted to respond, yet still looked shy and uncertain. 'Yes. I checked a chart on a genealogy site. We're cousins once removed, and you and Chloe are second cousins.' She smiled at Chloe in a clear, *don't just stand there* appeal. 'And Chloe and your little girl are second cousins once removed.'

Chloe sent her mother a silent look, as if not appreciating being brought into the conversation.

They all gazed at each other; four figures stiff as if frozen by the wintry air blowing off the sea four miles away. Maddy found herself rushing in to fill the silence. 'Ruthie's lovely. You'll love her. Everyone does. She's very independent – well, except for being partially sighted, of course, and her asthma getting worse, which is why she needs a carer. Me.' She tailed off.

Ffion's waiflike appearance made Maddy feel a towering clodhopper. Chloe was like a graceful elf. Neither of them carried a spare pound. Both gazed at her. She searched their expressions. Apprehension? Resentment? Did they see her as an obstacle? A threat? Trying to reassure them while wishing they'd rush in to arrange a time and date to meet her great-aunt, she only found herself becoming clumsier. 'Don't think I'm the gatekeeper to Ruthie. Well, I kind of am, as her carer, but I realise . . .' She couldn't think of a way to acknowledge that they were more nearly related to Ruthie than Maddy herself was. 'I can fade into the background when you meet her, if you want,' she ended hesitantly, feeling no rapport with the two females silently scrutinising her. She swallowed, imagining telling Ruthie about coming across Ffion and Chloe like this. Ruthie might be hurt because she hadn't been at the meeting, her dim eyes dull with disappointment. *Oh, poor Ruthie.*

'We're just on our way to the Christmas fair in the village hall.' Raff stepped in. He hadn't freed his hand from Maddy's while she'd stumbled through the one-sided conversation and if he felt ridiculous that they were both clutching cold toast, he didn't show it.

Ffion gave him an affectionate smile. 'That's where

we're going. We tried to call you, Raff, but there was no answer, which is why we walked here.'

Maddy felt her entire head set fire in an enormous blush. He must have put his phone on silent while they made love.

He just smiled easily at Ffion. 'Then let's walk together.'

Ffion and Chloe turned and led the way. Maddy chucked her toast under a hedge where she hoped a hungry bird might find it. Raff ate his, as if cold toast was one of his favourite breakfasts, chatting to Ffion between bites. Both Chloe and Maddy walked silently until Maddy realised that she should say something about Lyla, as she'd be at the hall, with Heloise. 'My daughter and my friend should be at the Christmas fair already,' she put in when Raff paused for breath.

Ffion cast a polite smile over her shoulder. 'I'll bet your little girl's excited about Christmas, isn't she?'

Grateful for this small acknowledgement of common ground, Maddy replied, 'Madly.'

But it only led to fresh silence. Maddy was so disappointed in her new-found relatives that she could have cried. Chloe appeared to be either awkward or sulky and Ffion had all the warmth of a puppet. Well, she wasn't going to subject Lyla to this stilted atmosphere, which she was old enough to notice but too young to understand. She decided on honesty, halting in the village hall car park and giving Raff's hand a final squeeze before letting it go and turning to Ffion and Chloe. 'I'm gladder than I can say that you're going to meet Ruthie, but can we leave introductions with Lyla for another day? She's young and more interested in buying baubles for the tree than that her family's about to expand.'

Ffion nodded and murmured politely. Chloe looked the other way. Raff gave Maddy a hug. 'We understand.'

Gratefully, she kissed his cheek, then turned and hurried for the doors to the hall.

Aware that the meeting had gone badly, Raff watched her whirl away, letting his gaze rest on her swinging ponytail and her neat back view. He still liked those boots.

Then he heard Chloe hiss to Ffion, 'Can we just go? I have assignments and dance practice. I don't want to keep meeting her round the stalls. It'll be weird, especially when she obviously didn't want us to meet her precious daughter.'

Resignedly, Raff turned to face the situation. He'd known and loved his niece all her life and was under no illusion that her silence had been bashfulness. She hadn't taken to Maddy, and she hadn't tried to hide it. He dropped a friendly hand on her shoulders. 'I don't think she meant to offend you. She just didn't want things sprung on Lyla – much like you and your mum didn't agree to meet Ruthie until you felt ready.'

Chloe toed the tarmac. 'So, she's getting her own back?'

Even Ffion objected to that. 'I doubt it. She'll want to sit down and talk to her little girl beforehand. "By the way, these people are cousins you don't know about" would be hard to understand. I'd be the same with you at sixteen, let alone six.'

Chloe sent Raff a sidelong look. 'How come you've got a thing going with Maddy?' She made it sound as if he'd been caught shoplifting.

He hung on to his patience. 'The normal way. We met. We liked each other. We're both single so I asked her out.' Then, not giving her a chance to say anything else confrontational, added, 'I understand if you feel it'll be awkward bumping into her at the Christmas fair, as you've only just met. You go. I'll catch you up when I've spoken to Maddy.' He turned towards the double doors through which Maddy had just vanished.

From behind him, Chloe called, 'No, we'll wait for you here.'

The attempt at manipulation didn't escape him, but refusing to be hurried, he paid his entrance fee to a bulky middle-aged man in a jolly elf costume. Inside, he crossed to the larger of the two halls, unzipping his coat at the welcome warmth generated by dozens of happy fairgoers. As it wasn't a massive space, he spotted Maddy in seconds. Her cheeks were two red patches in an otherwise pale face, underlining his impression that the chance meeting had not gone well. Her friend Heloise was talking to little Lyla, who was jumping with excitement. Maddy's gaze met his, and she broke away to approach him, expression quizzical.

Quickly, he said, 'I wish you'd all met in more convivial circumstances but I'm glad you'll be able to tell Ruthie that they'll meet her soon.'

Happiness entered her eyes. 'She'll be as excited as a kid at Christmas.'

Then Lyla bounded up, gaze full of curiosity, while Heloise followed, wearing the kind of knowing grin Maddy had told him to expect.

'Hello again, Lyla,' he said easily. 'Having fun?'

It was all the encouragement she needed to treat him to a run-down of all her activities last night and today, explanations about Heloise, Mummy, Christmas, the fair and – for some reason – a cat, all jumbling into one another.

He listened, nodding and friendly. Eventually Lyla ran down, and he said, 'Better go. I have family waiting,' which earned him a fascinated look from Heloise, who'd watched the scene in silence.

As they all turned away in the direction of a nearby stall of colourful yoyos, he checked Lyla wasn't watching and made a phone shape of his hand, mouthing at Maddy, 'Later?'

Her smile was brief but brilliant, and she nodded before letting herself be towed away.

Back outside, he found Ffion and Chloe shifting from foot to foot in the cold and felt guilty he hadn't thought of Ffion's health when he'd gone off to find Maddy.

His sister was obviously trying to keep things cheerful though, because she said, 'How about lunch at the pub?'

Before Raff could agree, Chloe broke in sarcastically. 'Uncle Raff's only just had his breakfast.'

His patience ran out. If he remained in the company of his sister and niece, he was going to have to tell Chloe to improve her attitude, and that wouldn't make for family harmony. He gave Ffion a hug. 'Can I take a rain check? My end-of-February deadline's on my mind. If I want to take time off at Christmas, I need to make sure I'm on schedule.'

Chloe's eyes glittered. 'If you want to go off with your girlfriend, just go. Don't make excuses.'

'Chloe!' Ffion gasped.

Raff regarded Chloe steadily. Whether she was upset or angry, his answer was the same. 'Seeing Maddy won't make me love you and your mum any less, you know. You two are my priority, especially up until Mum gets her new heart valve.'

Chloe looked suddenly vulnerable. 'Then why aren't you coming to lunch?'

He didn't say that her crack about breakfast had gone

down badly but kept up the reasonable tone he'd perfected over the course of hundreds of confrontations with teenagers. 'Because I want to write today. Unless you or your mum need me?' He put slight emphasis on the word *need*.

'Not really.' Chloe looked away.

After muted goodbyes, Ffion shaking her head at her teenage-stropper, Raff strode back to his tiny house feeling both out of sorts and short-changed. If he'd known Chloe was going to be so difficult, he could have stayed at the fair with Maddy instead of saying goodbye to her.

Even when he'd made himself a big mug of coffee and more toast, he stared for ages at his laptop screen, scrolling backwards and forwards over his most recent chapter and frowning, while he tried to get his head into the story. Then he went to Amazon to check his new cover was up, getting a kick – or maybe motivation? – from the striking image with 'Edd Rafferty' emblazoned in bold font, up there with real writers like George R.R. Martin and J.R.R. Tolkien.

Finally, he wrote the scene that had been trying to come out of him, where Adeckor was discovered alone with the queen by one of the king's aides. From the triumphant glitter in the aide's eyes, the 'discovery' had been engineered. He paused to mull over the aide's motivation. To discredit Adeckor? Or the queen? Or even to set the king free?

Human relationships could be hard to understand – just look at his own morning and Chloe's prickly reaction to Maddy. With the noticeable exception of Harris Soley, Raff had only seen people liking and admiring Maddy and he was troubled about Chloe. He briefly considered changing his mind about lunch, but then decided that Chloe shouldn't be rewarded for negative behaviour.

He grabbed a piece of scrap paper and tried to mind-map his way out of Adeckor's predicament, only looking up when he received a text. Ffion's name appeared on the screen and her message was brief.

Can you give me Maddy's number so I can fix up meeting x

Cheered by this hopeful sign, he broke off to send it.

Chapter Thirteen

It was so warm in the village hall that Maddy had to carry her coat and hat, and Lyla's too. Lyla teetered on her tiptoes as her little hand indicated a stall selling hoops hand-decorated with crochet and feathers. 'Can I have a dreamcatcher? And one of those wooden puzzles? And a hoodie?' The pointing finger swivelled about like a weathervane. 'And—'

Maddy laid a tender hand on the small head. 'Whoa,' she admonished gently. 'Christmas isn't an excuse to be greedy.'

'Except when it comes to mince pies and gingerbread,' Heloise murmured, peering at a cake stall.

Maddy ignored this unhelpful aside. 'You've already asked Santa for too much in your Christmas letter, Lyla.'

Lyla's eyes glittered like fairy lights. 'But he's going to bring me a pink electric scooter, isn't he?'

Heloise smothered a laugh.

'I think we just asked for an ordinary scooter,' Maddy reminded her, glad that this was the first time she'd heard about the scooter being powered, a vision arising of her chasing her six-year-old through the village while Lyla hung on screaming, unable to remember how to brake. 'And don't rely on it being pink. Santa has lots of presents to find. We can't be picky.' And Maddy had bought a silver one with purple wheels.

'But he's magic,' Lyla objected.

Santa's powers of simultaneous delivery of gifts around the globe, reindeer flight and entering via chimneys were hard to support even for a mum who'd had more sleep than Maddy had. She changed the subject. 'Shall we buy some Santa cupcakes for Grauntie Ruthie?' She indicated the cake stall.

With a loud, 'Yay!' Lyla darted towards the tabletop bearing cookies and cakes in all shapes from brown reindeer to green and red Christmas wreaths. The cheerful ladies behind the stall in Christmas jumpers looked delighted to bag up cupcake Santas, cinnamon stars and virulent green Grinch cookies, but Maddy drew the line at 'reindeer poo' chocolates, no matter how often Lyla giggled, 'Please! Plee-ee-ase, Mummy!'

Finally, they crossed to the smaller hall where a café had been set up, and lunched on triangular sandwiches laid out in the vague shapes of Christmas trees, cherry tomatoes to decorate the top and squares of cheese to make the tubs at the foot. Maddy had been feeling hungry after only a few bites of toast for breakfast. 'Afters' was Christmas scones made with mincemeat in place of dried fruit. Maddy watched Lyla tucking into the scone. 'Bet we could make these ourselves at home.'

'Yep,' Lyla agreed, with every confidence in her mother's kitchen prowess.

'By the way,' Heloise murmured, when Lyla was occupied cutting the final part of her scone into bite-sized

182

pieces with a plastic knife, 'I don't know if we talked about going out tonight, but I've got a date.'

Maddy met the note of apology with interest. 'Is it Jon again? How many dates is that? Five? Surely you've graduated to "seeing each other"? Or even "seeing a lot of each other"?'

Heloise blushed as she fiddled with her coffee cup. 'Let's not go mad. "Seeing" is all I'll admit to.' But her eyes sparkled.

'Ooh,' teased Maddy.

The sound caught Lyla's attention. 'Ooh what?' She looked expectantly from one woman to another.

'Ooh, that was a lovely scone,' Maddy said solemnly, well-experienced at having conversations that were designed to go over Lyla's head. Lyla gave her a suspicious stare.

Lunch over, Maddy checked the time and said they must get home. 'Della said she could stay till about noon, so Ruthie's already on her own.'

After only the usual protest from Lyla, who saw it as a six-year-old's duty to object to plans not originated by herself, they rose. 'Well, I'm going in Heloise's car,' Lyla declared pugnaciously, as if searching for something she could get her way over.

Maddy, remembering that her own car was at Raff's, returned mildly, 'If you *ask* Heloise, if you're lucky, she might say yes.'

Lyla turned on Heloise her most meltingly appealing smile. 'Please, Heloise, may you drive me home in your car?'

Heloise pretended to think over this quaintly phrased request before saying, 'OK, then, seeing as it's you. But you need to go to the loo here, first.'

'Yay!' Lyla gave a little skip.

Maddy imparted the usual instructions about being a good girl and Lyla nodded with the usual lack of attention, and they parted ways on a hug. 'See you in a bit at Heloise's house,' Maddy called after her daughter. She wouldn't mind a few minutes with Raff to discuss her unexpected meeting with Ffion and Chloe, and whether Chloe's attitude had just been typical teenage ways. Her manner had felt hostile, but maybe she was just awkward and shy. Zipping her coat, she left the village hall and hurried down High Street.

But when Maddy turned into the yard outside Raff's bijou residence, she could see him sitting at his table near the window, frowning as he stabbed ferociously on his keyboard with a finger of each hand, and decided not to disturb him after all. It gave her a warm feeling to see him like that, presumably mid-creative flow, and it was exciting to think that what he was writing would be on the shelves in autumn. She had lots of warm and exciting feelings over Raff. Her lover the novelist.

That thought, their night together, and even the event-filled morning that followed, hadn't been quite enough to expunge from her mind the latest text that she was beginning to term 'maybe Adey'. Her car started, despite the chill, and she backed it round before setting off for Nelson's Bar in a sudden gloom. She'd have to report the texts to the police. They might even have a way to discover whether the texts were really from Adey.

But if they were from someone else – who? And why?

The gnarly problem absorbed her as she bimbled along Brancaster Road between the hedges and fields that still twinkled with frozen snow in shaded areas. She'd told Ruthie about the first text after a while, and they'd mulled it over together. Why would anyone but Adey send such texts? To make mischief? As a joke? Or to discourage her from formally applying for a Presumption of Death certificate? The only reason for the latter that they'd thought of was financial – someone didn't want her to be able to lay sole claim to what was presently jointly owned. From her research so far, though, even though she was Adey's beneficiary under wills they'd made when they bought High Cottage, it was only a probability that she'd be awarded Adey's estate, not a certainty. And even if she was awarded his estate, if Adey reappeared he might be able to apply to get it back. It was much harder to move forward on the basis of lack of evidence that a person lived, rather than evidence of death.

The only thing certain about trying to formalise her position regarding Adey was that it would automatically end her marriage.

Unfortunately, the texts meant that if someone was trying to delay her application, they'd done a great job. This brought her full circle, though – *who?*

Troubled and preoccupied, she turned right and then left towards the village, enjoying the car pulling up Long Climb, which was so steep that she couldn't see the tarmac in front of her at times but steered a course between the trees of the pinewood that edged the road. Then she burst out onto Long Lane, where flint or chalk cottages gazed at her from behind walls and hedges, past the Roundhouse on the end of Roundhouse Row into Droody Road, then Traders Place, and drew up outside Heloise's cottage.

Unsurprised at the absence of Heloise's car, as she and Lyla had paused at the ladies, which might involve a queue, she switched off her engine and took out her phone to consult the internet about anonymous texts.

Then her attention was drawn to a familiar figure lounging along the pavement, the wind blowing his hair out from his head like a chimney brush. And the first reason she'd thought for someone other than Adey to send the texts hit her. *To make mischief.* Scrambling out of the car, she slammed the door behind her. 'Harris!'

He swung around, his hair now blowing back like dog's ears. 'Hey, Mad Crazy. You want me?' He smirked, putting undue emphasis on *want.*

She ignored his juvenile double entendre. 'Have you heard from Adey?'

His smirk vanished and he looked so unsure it could almost hint at vulnerability – if douchebags like him could have finer feelings. 'No. Why should I?' He took a couple of steps towards her. 'Have you? Is he OK?'

He looked so genuinely startled yet hopeful that it gave her pause. Then, seeing no reason for subterfuge, she pulled out her phone, opened the conversation thread from the withheld number and wordlessly handed it to him.

Harris's eyes moved as he read, his beard twitching in the icy blast swirling over the little village so high above the sea. She watched closely for a flush of guilt or a glint of triumph, but the face he turned to her as he handed back her phone wore only blank astonishment. 'Fuck me,' he said hollowly. Then hope flared in his eyes. 'You think he's coming back?'

Wrong-footed by him speaking to her without trying to annoy her, she accepted the phone and reread Adey's last message. Can you ever forgive me? There's nothing I want more. ILU x

As if he were arguing with her, she observed, 'That's how he always ended his messages to me. ILU meant—'

He snorted. '"I love you" – yeah, I know, Mad Crazy. Think I didn't know that stuff? I was his best mate.'

She recoiled from his tone and returned to the confrontational pissing match that was their usual mode of communication. 'Always jealous of him loving me, weren't you? He put me before you and you couldn't stand it.'

'That weren't it,' he denied in quick outrage. 'You're just against me and always have been.'

She wanted to retort, 'You started it, with moronic jokes about me at school,' but caught herself, aware that childish tit-for-tat would get them nowhere. Instead, she took a deep breath and tried to be the better adult. 'Look, Harris, we both have our problems. I heard you were made redundant, and I know how shitty that feels. Why don't we just stop baiting each other?' It was mainly him baiting her, but it wouldn't improve their interactions to point that out.

His brows clanged down, but he was silent, as if undecided.

Then she heard an engine and turned to see Heloise's car turn into Traders Place. She waved, standing back from the entrance to Heloise's drive. When she looked again, Harris had gone, either into a nearby house or up the footpath that led to the curve of Long Lane.

'Mummy!' Lyla jumped out the instant Heloise opened the car door for her and raced towards Maddy, hair and unzipped coat flying. Almost knocked from her feet by the power of her daughter's hug, Maddy reflected that no one would believe that less than half an hour earlier Lyla had scorned travelling in Maddy's car. 'Hiya, sweetie,' she crooned. 'Let's get your stuff and thank Heloise for having you, then we'll go home to see Grauntie Ruthie.'

'Grauntie Ruthie, yay!' Lyla yodelled, wriggling away and then racing off to collect her backpack from Heloise's house.

While Maddy didn't exactly share that level of excitement, she did feel fizzy at the prospect of telling her great-aunt that she could expect to meet her long-lost daughter any day now. How thrilling was *that*? Ruthie might even yell, 'Yay!' and caper about, too.

She just hoped that Ruthie's meeting with Ffion and Chloe went better than Maddy's had.

It was past three o'clock when Maddy felt Lyla was sufficiently settled at the kitchen table with an activity book and a pot of coloured pencils for her to have a discreet word in the front room with Ruthie under the guise of taking her a drink.

All too aware of the acuteness of Lyla's hearing and the shortness of her attention span, she said, 'Coffee, Ruthie,' in her usual voice, checked an inhaler was on her table at her hand, then said more softly, 'I have good news.'

Ruthie's face creased into its familiar smile. 'Your date went well and you're seeing Raff again?' She could probably glean that from Maddy's overnight absence.

Maddy's face warmed as she laughed. 'Yes – and I hope so. But that's not it.' She took the soft, crepey hand in hers. 'Raff asked me to tell you something. For some reason it never occurred to me.' She squeezed Ruthie's hands. 'You have a granddaughter. Ffion has a daughter, Chloe.'

Air escaped Ruthie in a high-pitched wheeze. 'Really?' she breathed. Her eyes behind her glasses shone with tears. 'Oh, Maddy. *Maddy*. Oh, my dear. Isn't that . . .

astonishing?' She paused to gulp. 'Did he say much about her?'

'Better than that,' said Maddy, enjoying bringing joy to her great-aunt's face again. 'Raff says Ffion and Chloe want to meet you.'

Ruthie gasped and sat bolt upright, her gaze on Maddy as if she could read every detail of her expression. 'Really? *Really?* Truly?'

Hot tears burned the backs of Maddy's eyes. 'Really, truly. I met them myself.' She'd deliberated over sharing this detail in case Ruthie felt put out or left out but now elected to emphasise both the unexpectedness and brevity of the encounter. 'We hardly knew what to say to one another,' she declared, in a diplomatic representation of the awkwardness. 'Except that I told them how lovely you are, of course.'

Ruthie laughed, then choked. 'Oh, Maddy, Maddy! I don't know what to do with myself. When will they come?'

'I don't think any of us was organised enough to suggest anything concrete. But I'm sure Raff won't mind being the middleman.' Her heart sang to see the joy in Ruthie's face, even when her aunt fell back in her chair, breathing audibly. 'Inhaler?' she asked gently.

Ruthie waved away the idea. 'Just give me a minute. I'd almost given up hope. I thought she'd decided that she'd gone on all her life without me and didn't need me now. And there's a *granddaughter*.' She glanced in the direction of the TV. 'Turn that off a minute, so I can think.' She fumbled for the remote from her table and shoved it at Maddy. 'I wonder what they'll think of me?'

But Maddy had other information that must be imparted before she could speculate on things like that.

189

'I have some less-good news, though.' She watched Ruthie's gaze sharpen with apprehension and made her voice gentle. 'Ffion has a heart condition – a result of her having rheumatic fever, apparently. But she's due surgery to replace a heart valve in February and should be much better after that. She's pale and a bit drawn-looking, but if I didn't know the situation, I would have assumed she was getting over flu.' She didn't want to admit to even herself, let alone Ruthie, that her disappointment had not been that Ffion had had 'illness' written in the lines on her face but her general air of uncertainty and apprehension about Ruthie . . . though Maddy did suppose it was a big thing to meet a mother you knew nothing about. She could almost feel jealous of Ffion having had two mothers, when Maddy's only one was so distant.

'Bless her,' Ruthie said quietly. 'I hope to goodness her operation goes well. Forty-six is no age to have that trouble. Modern medicine is wonderful, though.' She frowned over the news for a minute, then brightened. 'Does Chloe look like Ffion?'

Maddy considered, recalling the teenaged girl, whose mood she hadn't been able to pin down. It firmed her resolve to remain in the background when the three first met – though within easy earshot in case Ruthie needed her. 'They're alike in build – both petite, like you.' Ruthie could be described as 'dumpy' rather than petite, but Maddy knew from old photos that Ruthie had been small and slender before age had settled cushions around her tummy. 'But with them muffled up in coats and hats, it was hard to tell. Chloe's in a dance group,' she added, thinking Ruthie would like to hear something personal.

Judging from her fond smile, she did. 'I can hardly

wait,' she crowed, literally wriggling with joy. 'Why don't you ring Raff and make him hurry them up?'

'Erm . . .' Maddy pretended to consider. 'Because he might not appreciate being "made"? And he's working this afternoon. I think it would be better to arrange a call for this evening, after Lyla's in bed.'

Face falling, Ruthie protested, 'But you'll be going to the Duke with Heloise tonight. You'll forget.'

'No, I won't. She's got a date, and I thought it was a bit much to ask Della to keep you company again this evening anyway.'

Ruthie allowed herself to be temporarily distracted. 'Have you met Heloise's new chap?'

Maddy shook her head. 'I just know his name's Jon and he's from King's Lynn. She's being mysterious about him, but if he makes her happy then that's what matters.'

Ruthie returned to the subject that was obviously preoccupying her, giving another exaggerated wriggle. 'I can hardly wait to meet up with Ffion and Chloe. I think we ought to have those Santa cupcakes to celebrate, don't you?'

As if by magic, Lyla appeared at the door, her snub nose decorated with a dash of pink felt pen. One of her shoes had come off. 'Are we having cake? Please can I get the tin down?'

Both Ruthie and Maddy burst out laughing. 'Down from where you're not supposed to be able to reach it?' Maddy asked in mock severity.

Lyla giggled and rolled her eyes. 'I can climb up the units now.'

Nevertheless, Maddy thought it better if she stretched up and reached the container from the top of the cupboard, an old Dairy Milk tin that Ruthie liked to keep

191

stocked with snacks. Soon they were back in the front room and biting Santa's hat or belly, depending on where each cake-eater began.

Lyla, as usual, was a conversational flea. 'In my activity book I did a maze and only went wrong once. Me and Misty sit together at school now, but Miss Edge says we talk too much. A lady at the fair today said it's going to snow tonight. She told me and Heloise in the queue for the loo.'

'The radio said the same,' Ruthie put in. 'I bet you haven't seen much snow, Lyla, have you?'

'Only the thin little bits. Not thick white like on telly.' Lyla heaved a huge sigh, as if she only just realised how terrible that was.

'I suppose that's right. The last time we got proper snow here would have been just before you were born.' Maddy could date it as it was the night that Adey had disappeared. Her mind strayed to the latest text. Shit. She had yet to telephone the police.

When Lyla asked for another cake and Ruthie looked as if she might indulge her, Maddy put in, 'She's already had a scone. If she has more sugar, I'll never get her to bed tonight.'

Ruthie's mouth shut with a snap and Maddy grinned, knowing that Ruthie wouldn't want anything to put off the planned call to Raff. As she enjoyed the thick, sugary butter icing atop the cupcake, she took out her phone and sent the promised message to Raff. Are you free for a phone call later, when Lyla's in bed? x ☺

A reply returned within the minute. Certainly am free. Can I call after 9? Have a supermarket delivery 8–9 X

She confirmed, then passed on the news to a beaming, excited Ruthie before giving in to Lyla's pleas that as it was December – if only the 2nd – it was time to put up the Christmas tree.

Lyla abandoned her activity book, then crawled into the cupboard under the stairs with Maddy to heave out the tree and a box marked 'baubles' and another marked 'lights'.

'I'll take it, I'll take it,' yelled Lyla, thoroughly overexcited, cradling the top of the tree in her arms and dragging the foot across the carpet into the front room.

Maddy followed, the boxes piled in her arms and uttering cautions about scratching the walls or knocking over Grauntie Ruthie's table.

Ruthie lowered herself gingerly to the floor and began taking the ornaments out and laying them on the carpet near the tree. Maddy knelt beside her and untangled the lights – multicoloured, because Lyla had chosen them last year – and Lyla hopped about, yelling sentences that began: 'Can I . . . ?' or: 'Let me . . .' or: 'Yay!'

It was a task to keep Lyla's excited gyrations from sending everything flying and Maddy had to reprove her. 'Lyla, you're going to break something. Look, you're standing on the knitted monkey that Dilys gave you a couple of years ago.'

Lyla dropped to her knees in sorrow beside the squashed brown monkey in a red Santa suit. 'I'm sorry,' she whispered brokenly.

Maddy's heart melted, and she stroked back Lyla's soft hair. 'It's OK, my lovely.'

Lyla looked at her askance. 'I was talking to the monkey.'

Ruthie laughed so hard she almost rolled over backwards.

Finally, the tree was up, a jolly mix of shop-bought

ornaments and things Lyla had made over the years, glittering and shining with every imaginable colour, and it was time to embark on the bath and bed routine for Lyla, who was so shattered by a busy day that she was asleep before eight.

As Raff wouldn't be available for an hour, Maddy went down to check that Ruthie had everything she wanted. She found her sharing her armchair with a familiar blue and white box. 'Would you read me one or two, dear?' she beseeched. 'I'm restless, waiting to find out what's going to happen. I can't talk to Nigel—' she paused to swallow '—but it will feel a little bit as if he's talking to me.'

A rush of sympathy made Maddy's eyes brim. 'Of course,' she said, fighting a wobble that wanted to creep into her voice. 'Any particular letters?'

Ruthie held the box out. 'They're all jumbled up. Just choose one.'

Like being asked to pick a raffle ticket, Maddy thought. She perched on the footstool beside Ruthie's slippered feet and dipped into the box, stirring up a faint scent of old paper. She picked a letter at random, flattening the lined paper across her knees. 'It's dated December 1971.'

'He was still at Keogh Barracks.' Ruthie nodded, her spectacles glinting, a reminiscent smile flickering over her lips.

Maddy cleared her throat. 'He begins with *My dearest, darling Ruthie*, as usual.'

'He was very loving,' Ruthie acknowledged wistfully.

In a light, neutral voice, Maddy began.

'*Oh, what an empty weekend without you, my darling. Woolworths is full of Christmas decorations and the Sally Ann band was playing carols in Aldershot, but all weekends are empty. I can't wait for Mondays, to be near you, see you, speak to you, even if I have to keep my hands to myself and call you "Miss Willson".'*

She mentally sidestepped the image of Ruthie and a man who struggled to keep his hands off her. 'Were colleagues in the same office really that formal?'

Ruthie nodded. 'Different offices would be different, I suppose, but that was the norm in the barracks – Miss Willson and Sergeant Edmonds. I might call the other typists by their first names, especially at lunchtimes or if no one senior was listening.'

Maddy had never called anyone she worked with by anything but their first name. She went on, reading with a melting heart about how Nigel had not been able to wait for Wednesday afternoons and any time he and Ruthie could be together. The stationery room got more than one mention.

Ruthie twisted her fingers and gave a grin that was both impish and embarrassed. 'You'd better leave that letter now. Pick another, dear.'

Maddy folded the first letter away, thinking that Nigel had seemed a lovely man, despite his duplicitous life. As her fingers hovered in the air above the disorganised mass of folded sheets and opened envelopes, she had a sudden vision of what might have happened if Raff and his family had never come looking for Ruthie, and a future version of herself discovered this box in Ruthie's things once she was no longer around. Her heart recoiled. How would she have felt? Would she have read them?

Probably, she acknowledged honestly. And then would have been flabbergasted by Ruthie's secrets as she pieced them together.

Shoving away such unwelcome thoughts of losing her

dear aunt and friend, she went to the bottom of the heap for her next choice, picking a letter still in its envelope. It bore an unfamiliar address in Hampshire. Ruthie had lived near Aldershot garrison in those days. When she pulled out the two sheets of paper folded together, something else fell out – a photo of a man, his purple shirt open and showing his naked chest. The faded colours spoke of the picture having been shot some years ago, and she couldn't remember such enormous shirt collars being fashionable in her lifetime. Short, military haircut tousled; the man laughed into the camera. It could only be Nigel. Maddy was struck by the ordinariness of him. He wasn't gorgeous. He wasn't ugly. He was just like any bloke you might see in the street.

She turned the photo in her fingers. She knew its type from its black backing and thick, plasticky feel. She even remembered Ruthie owning the kind of camera that produced them – a Polaroid. At about Lyla's age Maddy had been fascinated by the white squares whirring out of the bottom of the camera and then the image developing as she watched.

This photo had been cut off, just where that open shirt ended . . . Maddy realised what must have shown below and knew simultaneous, contradictory urges both not to let Ruthie know what she'd found and to giggle and squeak, 'Euw!' Gently, she tucked the photo back into the envelope.

'What does it say?' Ruthie prodded Maddy's shoulder, evidently bemused by the long pause.

Hurriedly unfolding the thin sheets, Maddy said, 'August 1973.'

A long sigh gusted out of Ruthie. 'He'd heard about his posting,' she said flatly.

Maddy was sorry if she'd happened on a letter full of bad memories. 'Do you still want me to read it?'

Ruthie nodded, so Maddy went through the customary '*My dearest, darling Ruthie*' part. Then:

'*You know my bad news, because the CO announced it to the whole office before I could get you alone or write a note. A fucking posting, just what I didn't want. And fucking Aberdeen! Hours away from you. What shit luck. I couldn't believe it when he called me in to drone on about the army sending me where I was needed and although there was no promotion in it, opportunities would arise. Bastard. I came out of his office and couldn't look at you.*

'*Ruthie, I can't bear it. I can't. This is very wrong of me, but will you consider moving up there, too? It is wrong of me, isn't it? But please don't say no right away. You're the only good thing in my life.*'

Maddy felt a lump in her throat. Nigel sounded so woebegone that it touched her heart.

Ruthie whispered, 'I wanted to move – till Elsie and the CO both gave me a bollocking about seeing a married man.' Ruthie blew out her cheeks. 'I did love him, you know.'

Maddy succeeded in swallowing the lump. 'I can see that. And he loved you.' It could rarely be considered OK to have a thing with a married man, especially one who strung you along for decades, but Maddy was beginning to feel she was seeing the real Ruthie Willson for the first time. The lifetime of being single. The self-reliance, until failing sight took that away. The air of being on the sidelines. But she knew what Nigel had seen in her – she was one of the best people Maddy knew. Impulsively, she scrambled onto her knees and gave her aunt a big hug. 'And you know I love you too, right? I'll always be here for you, Ruthie.'

'Aw.' Ruthie gave a strangled laugh as she returned Maddy's embrace. 'Aren't we being a couple of wet nellies?'

Then Maddy's phone sounded, and Ruthie half-pushed her away in eagerness. 'Is that Raff? Answer it. Find out whether he thinks Ffion and Chloe will come soon.'

Amused and half-indignant at her ejection, Maddy checked the screen. 'Yes, it's him. I'll talk to him upstairs and let you know what he says.'

Ignoring a tut of disappointment from Ruthie that she wasn't to overhear the conversation, Maddy headed for the stairs, answering as she went.

Raff's soft 'Are you free now?' sent a prickle up her neck.

'Now's good,' she answered, arriving in her bedroom. Movement at the window caught her eye, a whirl of white flakes dancing on the evening breeze. 'Oh! It's snowing. Lyla said it would. I hope it stays till morning so she can play in it.'

Raff said, 'It's snowing here, too – big flakes, so it might settle.' Then, before Maddy could ask about Ffion and Chloe, he went on. 'I could drive over, if you're not busy. We could talk in person.'

She was instantly distracted. 'That would be great,' she said, speaking slowly but thinking rapidly. Caring for Lyla and Ruthie didn't allow her much freedom. Heloise was a wonderful friend and babysitter but had her own life – and man, currently – and cheerful, obliging Della couldn't be expected to sit with Ruthie more than a couple of times a week. If she wanted to date more than casually, her household would have to admit Raff as a visitor. 'Come over for a couple of hours.' Lyla was already firmly asleep, and if Maddy knew Ruthie then her aunt would soon leave the front room for what she'd probably call 'the courting couple'.

'See you soon.' He sounded pleased and anticipatory, then ended the call promptly as if he thought Maddy might change her mind.

Maddy felt breathless and skippy as she cleaned her teeth, applied mascara and changed into a dark, sapphire blue top. Next, she'd pop down and tell Ruthie that she'd be able to hear about the eagerly anticipated meeting directly from Raff. The unexpected visit felt like Christmas come early. Christmas. It was only just over three weeks away.

Might it be . . . different this year?

She'd planned Christmas dinner here at The Hollies with Lyla, Ruthie and Heloise – though she wondered if Heloise would soon make plans with her bloke Jon instead. But now she dared to imagine inviting Raff, Ffion and Chloe too. The table could be carried into the front room and the extra section put in to fit seven around it. To produce a meal for that number was no problem for someone who'd once worked in restaurants.

Still turning this idea over, she pulled the scrunchie and clip out of her hair to give it a quick brush. And that was when the text came.

Stomach shrinking, she picked up her phone. When she read the message, she turned cold with dismay.

And then hot with anger.

Deep, burning anger.

Chapter Fourteen

The Hollies was a grand name for a sweet little cottage, Raff thought, as he parked his car beside a hedge, the leaves of which had turned into a million tiny cups of snow, sparkling white in the light of the streetlamps. Seeing Maddy this evening was such a bonus that he strolled up the path whistling, taking a childish satisfaction in being the first to make footprints, enjoying the squeak of snow beneath his boots as flakes twirled and dived around him, making tiny cold spots on his cheeks. A holly wreath had appeared on the door of The Hollies, with a fistful of silver baubles attached with tartan ribbon.

He'd raised his hand to the doorbell when the door flew open. Maddy reached out and grabbed his arm. 'Come here.' Startled, Raff found himself bustled across the hall and into the front room. He might have thought that she'd been watching for him and couldn't wait to get her hands on him . . . if she hadn't been wearing a murderous glare.

He gaped at her. 'Whoa. What's up?'

'Who the actual *fuck* do your family think they are?' she spat. 'Ruthie's in her room, crying.'

Too baffled to notice it was the first time he'd heard Maddy swear, Raff was at a loss. How had they got from a phone conversation full of excitement and promise to Maddy shaking with fury? Her hair was loose and tossed around her shoulders, reminding him tantalisingly of how it had looked in bed. Her eyes, though, were as hard as pebbles. 'I don't know what you're talking about,' he said calmly. 'Why's Ruthie crying?'

A tear formed on Maddy's lashes, too, and she dashed it away. Her voice shook. 'She was so excited. Over the moon. Hardly able to sit still because Ffion and Chloe had agreed to meet her. Then – bam! – they don't. Is raising poor Ruthie's hopes only to dash them a belated revenge on her for being your dad's "other woman"?'

'They don't want to meet her?' He blinked. 'Who said?'

'Ffion.' Maddy snatched her phone from the pocket of her jeans and thrust it at him. A text bubble showed on the screen, time-stamped 21.55 today. This is Ffion Edmonds. Very sorry but have decided not to meet Ruthy. It is causing trouble in my family. We r OK as we r.

He reread it, then took out his own phone and checked his contacts. 'It's Ffion's number,' he confirmed stiffly. Maddy's furious upset was not without justification.

'I was joking when I said you were giving me good news to get me into bed,' Maddy hissed. 'But I couldn't understand why Ffion and Chloe were so muted while I was babbling on about them meeting Ruthie. I bet they didn't even know what you'd told me.'

He recoiled as if she'd slapped him. 'Look,' he said hoarsely, 'I'm stuck in the middle of this. I can see how it looks but—'

201

'Here,' she said, literally shaking with anger, 'I want you to read this.' She snatched up a piece of yellow lined paper from the arm of a chair. '*Read* it.'

His heart clenched as he recognised his father's handwriting. Slowly, his eyes travelled over the page, wincing over the phrases . . .

I'm so happy and yet the saddest ever . . . when you passed our baby into my arms, I thought my heart would stop . . . all the little cardies and mittens you knitted to send with her, all white with ribbons . . . all I have brought you is pain and you have given me everything . . . I want you to be happy that she's settled here . . . I thought you should know, just once, that she's being looked after and she is safe. God bless you. I love you.

Nigel xxx

He barely had time to read the final *x* before the paper was pulled from his fingers.

'Now leave,' Maddy growled. 'I need to be with Ruthie. This is breaking her heart and I can't even look at you anymore.'

With as little ceremony as she'd bundled him into the house, she hooked a hand through his arm and bundled him out again. He found himself with the porch at his back and snowflakes sliding down his neck. His heart felt as if it was beating right through his body, with horror, with embarrassment, with shock. With anger.

He stood immobile while he cooled off.

When he could hear the whisper of falling snow rather than the sound of blood pounding in his ears, he strode back over his own footprints, which hadn't had a chance to cover over during his speed-of-light visit. He yanked open his car door and swore all the way home, peering into the snow that danced in the beam of his headlights, furious and upset for himself, distressed at a mental picture of Ruthie, tears streaming from her half-blind eyes.

He drove straight for Ffion's cottage in Church Place. Seeing lights brightening the downstairs, he let himself in with scant ceremony. Ffion and Chloe started in surprise from their respective armchairs, Chloe poised with her hand in a bag of popcorn. 'What's the matter?' asked Ffion, blinking, as if she'd been nodding off before the TV and the roaring open fire.

A cute little Christmas tree had appeared in the alcove beside the fireplace, but he didn't stop to admire its twinkling lights. 'Do you have your phone?' he asked shortly.

Wonderingly, Ffion fished it out from the pocket of her purple fleece.

'Can you unlock it, please? Go to your messages.' Raff stooped beside her so he could read the list. Without asking permission, he stabbed the top message so that it opened in full. This is Ffion Edmonds. Very sorry but have decided not to meet Ruthy. It is causing trouble in my family. We r OK as we r.

Ffion's mouth dropped open. Her gaze turned slowly to Raff and dull colour stained her usually pale cheeks.

Raff heard a rustle behind him. 'Stay there, Chloe,' he said, utilising the eyes in the back of the head developed by every teacher. 'I know your mum didn't write this text. She knows Ruthie ends with *ie* rather than with *y*, and she never uses the letter r in place of the word "are".'

203

Ffion's gaze turned to her daughter and this time her colour drained. 'Did you use my phone?' she whispered.

Raff glanced at his niece who was hunching in her chair like a cornered animal.

When she didn't answer, Raff said grimly, 'Ffion, if you check your last text to me, you'll find a request for Maddy's number – also Chloe's handiwork I assume. She obviously doesn't want you to meet your mother and chose an underhand way to prevent it. Ruthie's in tears and Maddy's furious with *me*.'

From her chair, Chloe struck back, 'Sorree if I stopped you getting your leg over.'

His head whipped around, anger roaring in his ears. 'I think more of Maddy than just a leg over! Don't you understand? She thinks I gave her good news to get her into bed. She thinks badly of me, Chloe. Anyone would. You've behaved disgracefully to put me in this position.'

When Chloe's face crumpled, Ffion leapt in. 'You're upset, Raff, and saying too much.'

He swung back to her. 'I think I'm being restrained.' He snatched up the TV remote, silenced whatever they'd been bingeing on and dragged a chair around so he could face them both. 'I am upset – you're right. Aren't you, Ffion? Chloe's broken your mother's heart. I don't know if it's childish jealousy because I've fallen for Maddy, or an immature lack of empathy or consideration for others. Yes, I can see you crying, Chloe, but it's time you realised that you're not the only one with feelings.'

Though plainly taken aback, Ffion frowned at Raff. 'Hang on. Give Chloe a chance to explain before you rip into her.' Her voice softened as she transferred her gaze to her daughter. 'Tell me why you did it, Chloe.'

Chloe's bag of popcorn had spilled in her lap. She

covered her face with her hands. 'I just didn't want to meet her anymore.' Her voice was thin and uncertain.

'Why?' Ffion persisted, still in the kind of non-confrontational voice Raff knew he should have been using.

One of Chloe's shoulders rose in a shrug. 'I realised it wasn't worth it.'

With a huge effort, Raff managed to speak calmly. 'What wasn't?'

Chloe gave a big sniff and took her hands away to wipe her eyes on the sleeves of her hoodie. 'Maddy said Ruthie's asthmatic and half-blind.'

Ice formed around his heart. 'You mean she'll be no use to look after you if anything happens to your mum and me?'

Quietly but emphatically, Ffion jumped back in. 'Or, Raff, Chloe's scared to get close to Ruthie in case she dies, just like Grandma Sindy and just like she's afraid I will.'

Silence, apart from the crackle of the fire and a car passing outside. Raff felt some of his anger drain away. 'I can see that,' he admitted eventually. 'But she's old enough to say it, rather than pulling a trick that hurts so many people.' His gaze travelled back towards his niece. 'Chloe, if your mum's right about your motives then I'm sorry I hadn't thought of it that way. But you've trampled on the feelings of your own grandmother. You've hurt me because it's made Maddy think badly of me. Your actions were unacceptable, and my reaction reflected that.'

Ffion spoke through pale lips. 'Thank you, Raff. Chloe and I are blood with—' Her eyes widened. 'I mean—' She faltered to a halt, eyes enormous and face white.

Slowly, he rose. 'I'm not blood, so I should butt out,'

he concluded for her. 'But it hasn't done Ruthie much good being *blood*. Look what Chloe's done to her. Perhaps I've been as guilty as you in trying to shield her from your medical reality and she's ended up with the idea that she's the only one who matters. Well, she's not. She can't trample on Maddy and Ruthie as "not worth it" without accepting the consequences.'

He took a long deep breath, fishing for his car keys. With deliberate emphasis he said to Ffion, '*Your mother* has only ever done her best for you, and in difficult circumstances. Maddy showed me a letter from Dad to Ruthie after she'd given you to him and Mum. He reassured her that he was looking after you and loving you. It's obvious, despite you thinking her cold for not enquiring after you all the time that she only distanced herself in order to be able to cope with giving you up. You ought to read for yourself about her sending little clothes she'd knitted for you, and Dad saying Ruthie gave him everything and all he'd ever done was bring her pain.' He paused. 'Maybe bringing pain to Ruthie Willson is in that Edmonds blood.'

Then he turned and left, closing their door quietly behind him and driving the few minutes home through softly falling snowflakes that were turning roofs and gardens into fields of cotton wool, driving slowly not because of the treacherous slush on the road but because of the pain thumping through his veins.

When he'd parked in the yard, he switched off the engine and watched snowflakes land like stars on his windscreen. The stars melted into drips that slid down the glass. Finally, becoming aware of the cold, he heaved himself from the car. Losing his footing, he had to put a hand down in the soft, crisp whiteness on the ground to save himself. He straightened and shook the freezing crystals from his fingers, then went indoors to a silent house with no one waiting for him except the characters that occupied his mind and his laptop.

Knowing he wouldn't sleep, he sat down and opened his computer.

Maybe he could channel his anger and bitterness and let Adeckor rip the head off the conniving royal aide trying to poison the king against him.

Or maybe he should just let Adeckor and the queen run off into exile. Then they'd be happy, even if Raff was miserable.

Chapter Fifteen

Maddy could hardly stand the sorrow that had bowed Ruthie for the six days since she'd told her great-aunt of Ffion Edmonds' unfeeling text. She hadn't even laughed when Lyla, wide-eyed to learn that if there was much more snow school might close before the term's end, demanded, 'Does that mean Christmas will come early, too?' At least Lyla filled Ruthie's silences, chattering about snow, muddling up Santa's home in the North Pole with the snowy world in which she found herself.

On Monday, Maddy had finally called 101 to report the texts that might be from Adey. Someone from missing persons had called her back and then a female officer had called in to read the texts for herself, but *number withheld* meant it was untraceable even to the police, apparently. Maddy had agreed to forward any further texts and report any developments.

Though her Christmas spirit had taken a hit, Maddy persuaded Ruthie to accompany her to the school play on Friday, to see Lyla back across the stage holding a gold cardboard star before her while three wise men followed her to Bethlehem. Ruthie usually loved to attend Lyla's school functions. Unable to see what was happening on stage, she relied on dialogue and the occasional whispered explanation from Maddy. She'd whisper back that it sounded as if the children were having fun and the teachers as if they were expecting an anxiety attack.

This time, though, she was silent, barely nodding at Maddy's description of tinsel framing children's paintings of Santa on the wall and yoghurt pots inexpertly painted silver to look like bells.

Ruthie seemed to have aged before Maddy's eyes. Her cheeks sagged and her mouth turned down. Her movements were slow and heavy. Maddy had tried to brighten her aunt's life by preparing favourite meals and trying out the Christmas scones as she'd promised Lyla, but her efforts had prompted only fleeting smiles. 'I'm all right, dear,' she'd said once, evidently aware that Maddy was trying to cheer her, but she still seemed to be wearing her own personal darkness like a cloak.

The children sang 'O Little Star of Bethlehem' and Maddy clapped, beaming in case Lyla searched the audience for her. But inside she was not much cheerier than poor Ruthie, who clapped listlessly at her side.

Raff had been in touch only to text: I can only apologise for the actions of my adoptive family. I wish you and Ruthie nothing but happiness. It had given Maddy pause as she remembered Raff speaking lovingly of his family and declaring his adoptive status irrelevant. And the second sentence sounded a lot like 'goodbye'.

Goodbye.

Had she expected goodbye? When she'd shoved him out into the snow, so angry she'd barely known what she was doing, had she thought she was seeing him for the last time?

The truth was, she hadn't been thinking at all. She'd been reacting, heart scoured by Ruthie's sobs. It hadn't even been a case of shooting the messenger, as the message in this case had leapt onto Maddy's phone screen without Raff's involvement. It had been anger-transference. He'd been there and she'd unfairly made him responsible for what his sister had done. Worse, she'd accused him of getting her into bed under false pretences when she'd been the one to make the first move.

Her conscience was raw.

Lyla and her star made the return trip across the stage – had the wise men needed a guide for the return journey? Maddy didn't remember that – and the children left the stage at the end of the act, two shepherds clutching soft-toy sheep and Mary swinging the baby Jesus doll negligently by one foot. Maddy, like the parents and grandparents around her, clapped enthusiastically. A teacher took to the stage to explain that the children would now sing their favourite Christmas songs.

One small boy piped up from the row of children at the front of the stage. 'They're not my favourites. I don't like any of them.'

Children and audience laughed. 'Thank you, Damien.' The teacher calmly qualified her earlier comment. 'The favourite Christmas songs of all the children but Damien.' More laughter.

Maddy wondered what Raff was doing. She hadn't answered his text, too horribly scared of increasing Ruthie's agony if Maddy . . . what was the phrase used in war films? *Fraternised with the enemy*. Maddy's family was one side of a gulf and Raff's, adoptive or not, on the other. And the gulf was filled with emotional spectres and monsters of the past, too fierce and ugly to dodge.

Ice formed in her stomach as she acknowledged that it was probably going to be impossible to see Raff. Ever.

She clapped again at the end of 'Jingle Bells' and then at a funky rendition of 'Santa Claus Is Coming to Town' complete with tinsel-holding and arm-swaying. Finally came 'We Wish You a Merry Christmas' and then the applause rang out for the last time.

The head teacher announced that as it was nearly home time, any parents who wished to take their child early should come along to the appropriate classroom in ten minutes. Ruthie sat still, stolidly staring into space. Maddy felt too low to try to lift her spirits and checked her phone, which had been silenced for the performance. Her heart sank when she saw a text from *number withheld*. She opened it.

We should talk about logistics. ILU x

Talk? Maddy stared at her phone, beyond frustrated that she had no way to reply. Mechanically, she forwarded it to the number the police officer had given her, with a brief explanation.

It occurred to her to wonder whether the police had been in touch with Adey's parents. Maddy should have checked. Tilly and Gwyllm, despite being a pair of grumpy guts, had a ferocious love for Adey.

As people were now heading off to pick up their kids, Maddy said to Ruthie, 'You sit here while I get Lyla.' Ruthie nodded. Maddy sped off to room two, where she collected Lyla and her belongings, then watched Miss Edge mark Lyla as having been collected.

Lyla brimmed with excitement. 'I didn't forget to walk slowly or to hold the star up high, did I? Did you see

211

Misty being an ox? She chewed like a cow all the time. Oxes are kind of cows—'

Maddy nodded and exclaimed and agreed in all the appropriate places, until she was back in the hall, where a couple of teaching assistants were packing up chairs. Ruthie hadn't moved.

'Grauntie Ruthie!' Lyla bellowed. 'Did you see me being a star? I was *the* star who guided the kings—'

Ruthie managed to assume a listening face while Lyla recounted the play as if they hadn't just witnessed it. Slowly, they made to leave, Lyla chattering all the way back to Maddy's car.

Then Ruthie turned to Maddy, blinking her unfocused eyes. 'Can we go down to the beach?'

It was so unexpected that Maddy floundered. 'Now?' She could see the sea about half a mile away from where they stood in the car park but knew her aunt couldn't.

Ruthie nodded. 'I'd like to listen to the waves, and I'm not sure I'm up to Zig-Zag Beach because of the walk back up.'

As Ruthie made so few demands, Maddy simply replied, 'OK. We'll have about an hour's daylight.'

Lyla skipped, delighted at the unexpected after-school activity and bundled into the car in a whirl of open coat and half-on shoe, leaving Maddy to place her backpack on the seat beside her and shut both Lyla's door and Ruthie's before opening her own.

Like any self-respecting local, Maddy knew where to find on-street parking rather than paying for a car park, which meant they had a hundred metres or so to walk to the promenade, Ruthie taking Maddy's arm to navigate the uneven pavements safely. At the beach, a dirty layer of snow overlaid the stony sand. There was little happening apart from dog-walking, the humans – and some of the dogs – wrapped in warm jackets. Maddy bought tea and hot chocolate from the café in the aquarium. Ruthie, huddling deeply into her winter coat and scarf, found a bench, its metal parts wrought in the shape of sea serpents, and sipped her tea, gazing towards a sea that could be no more than a pale grey area in her vision.

Down on the snowy sand, Maddy sipped her own drink, while Lyla chatted and sang, hopping on and off rocks. Gulls rode the wind, their calls as bleak as the cloudy sky.

In half an hour, the hot drinks were just a memory, and Maddy felt that her flesh was crystallising, like ice. With a glance at Ruthie's pinched face, she said carefully, 'It'll be dark soon and Lyla's getting cold.'

'OK,' Ruthie answered flatly. Then she gave a great sigh and creaked to her feet. 'No point crying over what can't be changed.'

There was a finality to the words, as if Ruthie were putting her terrible sorrow to bed. Perhaps those born and brought up near the sea, took comfort from its vast agelessness. Ruthie had made sorrowful peace with the knowledge that she'd never have a relationship with the person she'd brought into the world. Maddy had gone down onto Zig-Zag Beach often to think about Adey and worry about life in general.

They drove the few miles home with the car heaters turned up.

After the excitement of the play and the beach, Lyla flopped on the sofa, watching CBeebies. Ruthie, though still subdued, huddled near the kitchen radiator while she and Maddy composed a grocery list at the same time as Maddy peeled vegetables. The winter evening felt like a time of mourning: Maddy for something she'd barely started with Raff; and Ruthie for what might have been with Ffion and Chloe. A few short weeks was all it had taken to make Ruthie yearn for Ffion and Maddy ache for Raff, but in these small, familiar, everyday tasks, time dragged by until Lyla went to bed.

By the time Ruthie was in bed too, it was half past nine. Maddy had run out of excuses to put off the call her conscience was nagging her to make. Her phone seemed to burn a hole in her pocket as she dragged herself slowly up the red-carpeted stairs to her room, where she bunched up her pillows as a backrest, pulled up her contact list on her screen and, for the first time in seven years, tapped on *Tilly*. It rang six times, making her expect voicemail to kick in.

Instead, the line clicked open, and her mother-in-law's voice answered cautiously. 'Maddy?'

'Yeah, hi, Tilly,' Maddy replied flatly. 'Sorry to call out of the blue but something's cropped up that I think I should tell you about.' She'd mentally rehearsed this much of the conversation. Now she added, 'I'm receiving texts that look as if they're from Adey.'

For several moments, she thought the connection had dropped and she was going to have to ring back and start again, but then Tilly replied, strained and choked. 'You've taken me by surprise.'

'Yeah,' Maddy agreed, trying to keep her voice neutral. Her feelings and Tilly's would not be on the same part of the emotional scale. Tilly would be stunned but euphoric at this sign that Adey might be alive and well – as Tilly had always maintained he was. For Maddy, his reappearance would be more problematic. In fact, washing up after supper, she'd found herself toying with ways of

214

stashing money away to appear poorer than she was in case she had to come to a financial settlement. She'd paused for a full minute with suds running down her hands as she imagined transferring her small savings into Ruthie's bank account under the guise of paying back a loan. Unfortunately, courts could investigate people's bank accounts and would soon prove the loan a figment of Maddy's imagination.

She blinked and returned her thoughts to the here and now. 'Sorry if this is upsetting,' she said. 'I've tried his old number, but it's disconnected. This could be someone messing with me. The number's being withheld so I can't ring or text back.' As Tilly didn't reply, she added, 'People can withhold their number in their settings, or use burner phones.'

When Tilly still didn't answer, Maddy thought she might not know what a burner was. 'A burner's a pay-as-you-go phone, with no contract. You can bin them – or "burn" I suppose – when they've served their purpose.' When Tilly still didn't comment, Maddy asked as kindly as she was able, 'I presume this is a complete shock? You never heard from him?'

And just like that, the waspish, difficult Tilly found her sting. 'Are you suggesting that I would be in touch with him without telling you?'

Maddy thought it a distinct possibility but saying so wouldn't make this conversation any easier. With an attempt at diplomacy, she answered, 'I'm asking everyone who was close to him the same thing.' 'Everyone', in truth, had only been Harris Soley so far, but she hadn't stayed in touch with any of Adey's university friends or wider family. She'd been too busy keeping her head above water since that dark, snowy night when she'd last seen him. 'Is Gwyllm there?' she asked in a friendly way, as if she'd like nothing more than a chat with her father-in-law. In fact, she'd really like to ask him the same question, hoping to catch him off-guard. He might be as truculent as his wife, but he didn't possess the same mental agility.

'He's out,' Tilly said swiftly, sounding pleased.

Damn. Maddy should have just called him separately without alerting Tilly to the fact that she wanted to talk to him. 'Never mind. I'm sure you'll fill him in.'

'Have you told the police about this proof of life?' Tilly put in, evidently over the initial shock.

Maddy didn't lie. 'Yes. And it's a possible indicator, but not proof.'

'I always said he wasn't dead.' Then Tilly changed tack, sounding eager. 'Did you manage to save the house? Or was it repossessed?'

Slowly, Maddy closed her eyes, wondering, not for the first time, how bitchy Tilly and tight-fisted Gwyllm had ever produced extravagant, happy-go-lucky Adey. Dark memories swept up to swamp Maddy, not just of the financial mess Adey had left her in but of the lack of support from her parents-in-law. Her reply reflected her bitterness. 'Kept it . . . by the skin of my teeth.' Maddy gazed around her bedroom at Ruthie's house, at the thick curtains that didn't keep out the draught from the diamond-paned windows, at the uneven beams and the bright rug over the faded carpet. It was hard to remember sharing High Cottage with Adey. Now, if Adey came back, she'd have to get used to sharing the rental income with him, at least. She shivered. That would leave Maddy struggling again, just when she'd got herself into a place where she could save a little most months.

Tilly's brisk voice came again in her ear. 'If that's all,

I'll say goodbye.' She hesitated, then added awkwardly, 'Thanks. Keep me updated.'

'Yeah, bye,' Maddy returned without warmth. The end of the call left her restless and uneasy. She jumped off the bed and stepped softly to the open door of Lyla's room, watching her darling daughter by the light from the landing. Lyla's eyelashes rested on her perfect skin, her hair a tangled skein across her pillow. Tears pricked at Maddy's eyes, and she knew she could bear to share the rent from High Cottage more readily than share Lyla.

But what about Lyla's wants and needs? She knew she'd had a dad who had disappeared. How could Maddy possibly keep it from her if she learnt Adey's whereabouts? And if her dad came back . . . Lyla was a lovely, affectionate little girl. She wouldn't see a daddy's unreliability or extravagant spending habits; she'd just see the big smile and ready hugs and, quite likely, treats and presents. Adey was great at treats and presents. It was just responsibility he was so crap at.

Using the side of her hand to wipe beneath her eyes, she returned to her bedroom and got ready for bed before slipping under the heavy duvet and picking up her laptop from the bedside table. Over the next half hour, she investigated anonymous calls and texts. One site told her: *'private number' in place of a number is usually a call from the UK; 'unknown number' usually indicates the call is international.* The next site, conversely, stated: *there is no difference between 'withheld number', 'private number' or 'unknown number'.*

She already knew that dialling 141 before a number would disable caller ID in the UK on a per call basis so wasn't surprised to see that information on every site she visited.

Although most of the conversation was about malicious calls or texts, scammers and marketeers, it led seamlessly to her next area of research – burner phones. She learnt that actual burner phones were becoming passé now it was possible to buy burner apps more cheaply. With a burner app, as well as simply blocking caller ID, you could 'spoof', so the recipient saw a fake number. The fake could be replaced by a different fake at regular intervals, or even after each call or text. Burner apps were used not just by scammers and pranksters, but by serial daters who found burning a phone number a convenient method of ghosting.

Maddy shook her head and blew out a sigh.

Evidently, a missing husband had any number of methods available when it came to contacting the wife he'd left behind without allowing the conversation to be two-way. Ditto for anyone *pretending* to be said husband.

She could try and block the anonymous texter, but if he – or she – was using an app that changed numbers, it would be pointless. And what if it really was Adey reaching out, in trouble whether mental, physical or emotional? It would be horrible of her to block him. Stories of long-term missing persons sometimes depicted lost and wandering souls, subsisting on the street far away from home, unable to surmount the obstacles they felt blocked their way back. One man had described his wife messaging him from a computer in a library for two years before she felt able to come home. She, too, had seemed to be initiating conversation, yet making replies impossible. Confusion? Warring emotions? Ready for so much but no more?

The man didn't describe what happened once his wife returned, which Maddy would dearly have loved to know.

Images of Adey living on the street or in a hostel had haunted her ever since he'd disappeared. It might be inconvenient for him to show up, but Maddy couldn't ever turn her back on him, despite the appointment she still had with a solicitor in January. If Adey was alive somewhere, she'd have to grit her teeth and deal with it.

Huddled beneath her duvet, it was a long time before Maddy found sleep.

On Saturday afternoon, Raff tried to conjure up an idea for a short story, requested by a magazine that came free with a weekend newspaper. It had come as a shock to learn that authors frequently supplied free content to earn the publication of their latest book cover alongside. Eight hundred words seemed a woefully small number with which to convey both characterisation and plot. Gloomily, he wondered if the magazine would settle for one or the other.

He wasn't in the mood to write a short story.

Yesterday, his editor Vikki had sent a friendly email asking how *The Sword of Adeckor* was going, and he wasn't sure whether to admit that his supposedly political fantasy was caught up on Adeckor's love for his queen, or to plough on because falling in love happened in the middle of real life all the time. He imagined himself negotiating with Vikki. *If Adeckor goes into exile with the queen, that makes him a renegade. He can fight other renegades, still protecting his king's interests. Then the king will realise his marriage to the queen had run its course anyway and divorce her, so Adeckor can return to the king's household.* Adeckor's world hadn't so far boasted divorce courts, but, as the author, Raff could introduce some. Unless . . . who said there had to be

219

marriage at all? He frowned, scribbling on his pad: *without marriage, how does the queen get to be queen? By appointment? If so, the king doesn't have to be in a relationship with her.*

Which took away his nice new conflict.

But if king and queen are both political appointments, then Adeckor would simply change his allegiance from king to queen. Civil war??? Pleased with this idea, he turned to gaze through the window to mull it over, but his attention was whipped from his work when he saw Ffion and Chloe picking their way slowly across the concrete.

Obviously spotting him through the window, Ffion raised a hand and gave a tentative smile.

Briefly, he waved back. Since the unpleasant scene last Saturday evening, a week ago, a couple of *Are you OK?* texts had been the only communication between himself and Ffion. Slowly, he got up to open the door.

'Hey,' he said politely, ushering them in.

'Hey.' Ffion met his gaze, her arm around Chloe, who looked anywhere but at him. 'We've come to clear the air.' Her gaze fell on his open laptop. 'Oh, sorry – you're working.'

He waved them towards the sofa, closing his laptop in passing. 'I can work later.'

'But you hate to be interrupted when you're writing,' Ffion objected, nevertheless pulling off her hat and unzipping her coat.

Pale and unsmiling, Chloe sank onto the sofa without removing either her slouchy blue hat or the thick, black, oversized hoodie that reached to her knees.

Raff threw himself down beside her. 'Being friends with you two is more important.' He touched Chloe's arm. 'Are we friends?'

She turned a tragic face on him. 'We haven't seen you all week.'

He slid an arm about her. 'I've been feeling hurt and sorry for myself.'

'And pissed off with me,' she returned half-accusingly.

'True,' he acknowledged. 'But I suppose you were looking at things from your own perspective. I was collateral damage.' When she looked mystified, he said, 'That's when things other than the main target sustain damage, inadvertently.'

'Oh.' Chloe looked crestfallen.

'Which is why we're here to apologise,' Ffion said meaningfully.

Chloe nodded. 'I'm sorry, Raff. I didn't mean you to get hurt.'

He hugged her. 'And I apologise for not understanding why you did it. Are we cool?'

She gave him a watery smile. 'We're cool.'

Ffion visibly relaxed. 'And how are things with Maddy, Raff?' Her grey gaze was steady.

It was he who looked away. 'She texted me during the week.' *Thursday. It had been Thursday.* He'd jumped on his phone like an idiot when he'd spotted her name on the screen only to be disappointed by the contents of the text.

Ffion waited expectantly.

He rubbed his stubbly chin. He hadn't bothered shaving since Maddy had thrown him out of her aunt's house. Vividly, he remembered the shock, the snow falling around him while he stood – appropriately – frozen. Should he fib, to protect Ffion and Chloe's feelings? But the contents of Maddy's message were like something raw and sour, and he knew he was incapable of smiling it away. 'She

221

doesn't feel comfortable seeing me, now. It's a non-starter.' But it had started, right here on this sofa, where they'd made love. He pictured her naked, hair tumbling, head thrown back. He swallowed. 'She's putting Ruthie first. And I understand,' he added hastily, 'because that's how I feel about you two. OK, who's for a frappé? I cooled some espresso earlier and I have squirty cream and ice.' He and Chloe shared a weakness for frappé, despite frost on the ground.

Silently, both Ffion and Chloe nodded, and he strode off to the kitchen fridge, talking about the email from his editor, explaining that he'd had an idea that would mean a bit of rewriting, talking fast and loud in the hope that they'd get the message. *Don't ask me anything else about Maddy. It's too sore and too soon.*

And they must have caught his unspoken plea, because Ffion told him that they'd strung their Christmas cards around the lounge and Chloe told him that she had dance at five. Her friend's mum was driving them there and Ffion would fetch them back.

'Sounds great.' Raff's previously effortless uncle role felt unfamiliar and strange. He tried to recapture it. 'Why don't I drive in with Ffion and we can all have dinner somewhere? My treat. Ask your friend if she's free for it, Chloe.' Then he turned on the blender to crunch up the ice, glad of the noise to cover any cracks in his avuncular manner.

Chapter Sixteen

Maddy mulled over the Adey texts for much of Sunday. Ruthie was still subdued and even Lyla noticed, leaning over the arm of Ruthie's chair to hug her and plant a big 'Mwah!' of a kiss on her soft, wrinkled cheek.

Maddy saw tears glisten in Ruthie's eyes and felt her own eyes prickle, because she wasn't much cheerier than Ruthie. Ridiculous, when she'd known Raff such a short time, but when he'd turned up at the door for lunch that day, shaved and with his hair smartly cut, her heart had leapt. Apparently, that troublesome organ hadn't settled back into its proper place because it ached whenever she thought of him.

And she thought of him often.

But now she shoved him from her mind. 'I've had a nice idea,' she said, injecting cheer into her voice. 'Why don't we go out for Sunday lunch? We haven't been to that family pub near King's Lynn for ages. They always have a festive menu.'

For several seconds, she thought Ruthie would refuse, but then she took a breath, and said with an obvious effort, 'That would be lovely. And give you a rest from cooking.'

Before long, they were bowling along the A149, Lyla singing 'Jingle Bells' in the back seat and spotting Christmas trees.

Ruthie was trying to be cheerful. 'Even though I can't see much now, I always enjoy a run out in the car. If I was a dog, I'd probably be one that sticks its head out of the window and lets its ears blow back.'

Maddy giggled at this mental picture. 'I can open the window if you want.' She touched the button to make the window open a crack.

Ruthie creaked a laugh, and Maddy did the window up again, spirits lifting. She made sure to keep the conversation light, to encourage Ruthie's good mood. Either it worked or Ruthie played along, as the three of them talked about Christmas for the rest of the journey, Lyla enumerating her Santa requests and Maddy and Ruthie pretending they'd put enormously extravagant things on their own Christmas lists.

'Shoes with diamonds on the toes and a bath full of chocolate,' said Maddy.

'A trip to Bermuda,' Ruthie put in. 'And a speedboat.'

'Then I'm asking for a zebra and a camel,' Lyla declared. 'And I want a whole *swimming pool* full of chocolate.'

They arrived at the prettily named Pearl from the Sea, which was about six miles from the edge of the bay known as The Wash. According to the backs of the menus, the pub's name alluded to the treasure of King John, lost in The Wash in 1216. Maddy wanted to giggle at the phrase 'lost in The Wash' as it sounded as if it concerned laundry rather than the rectangular estuary where four rivers met the sea.

'Aw,' Lyla breathed, gazing around at the decoration-encrusted interior of the pub. 'It's so pretty.' And, indeed, the pub did look almost like a Christmas decoration shop, with baubles and tinsel sparkling from every available surface.

A server paused at their table. 'Have you entered the Santa competition? Here's a competition card.' He pointed at the beams that graced the ceiling of the pub. 'See that Santa on the white, pearly bauble, peeping out from behind that bell? There are another fourteen. You mark them on the picture on the card and if you get more than a certain number, you get a prize.'

'How many do you have to get? What's the prize?' Lyla demanded, all business.

The server said, 'There are prizes for ten and up. See, there are lots of other children hunting. You're not allowed to look for Santa baubles when your food arrives, though,' he added solemnly, with a wink at Maddy.

Sure enough, children with pens and cards were squinting along beams and peering into the depths of a luxuriously laden Christmas tree, occasionally saying, 'Oh!' and then covering their mouths as they realised that they might be giving away a Santa sighting to other contestants.

Maddy said, 'The beams are lined with baubles and so are all the vases. It's going to take you ages, Lyla.' She helped mark the Santa ornament the young server had shown them, to give Lyla the idea. Each time she spotted one of the Santa baubles, complete with curly white beard, she ran back to the table, so Maddy could supervise the placing of the cross on the card because diagrams were hard for six-year-olds.

Then, one eye on her daughter, Maddy read the menu

225

to Ruthie. 'What about puddings?' Ruthie demanded, who always picked dessert first and then judged what main course allowed room for it.

'Christmas pudding, mince pies with ice cream, Christmas trifle, yule log, cinnamon cookies with butter cream or fruit pavlova,' read Maddy, obligingly.

'Yule log,' Ruthie decided. 'With ice cream. What are the mains?'

Maddy fell into her usual role as the able-bodied adult in the family. After consulting Lyla, she had all three orders ready for the server, who'd acquired a candy cane headband since they'd last seen him. When lunch was served, Lyla raced back exclaiming loudly, 'I already have *eight*. And I know where there's one more.'

The server paused to check Lyla's card. 'Wow, eight!' He made an exaggeratedly impressed face. 'You only need another two to win something.'

'Ohh,' Lyla breathed, eyes enormous.

Despite the sad week since Ffion had reneged on meeting Ruthie, and Maddy had fallen out spectacularly with Raff, they had a lovely, Christmassy time. Ruthie allowed herself a large glass of wine. 'With my eyesight, it won't make any difference.'

After lunch, Lyla went off on the Santa hunt again and scored twelve circles on her competition card, which won her a set of 'pearl' beads, to her beaming delight. All the way home in the car she pestered Maddy. 'Can I wear them to school? Can you take a picture and send it to Misty's mummy, please? And can I show them to Heloise?'

As Maddy had again missed out on Saturday night at the Duke, Heloise having a date, she promptly agreed to the latter. 'Let's phone Heloise while we're driving and see if she wants to come round.' She used the voice-dialling on her phone, but the call went to voicemail, so she left a message and she and Lyla chatted the rest of the way to Nelson's Bar, as Ruthie snoozed comfortably in the front passenger seat.

They were nearly home, in Droody Road, when Maddy noticed a familiar figure striding along the pavement, hands stuffed in the pockets of her vintage coat. She opened her mouth to exclaim, 'There's Heloise. I'll stop.' She'd even taken her foot from the accelerator. But then she saw her friend turn at one of the cottages that directly fronted the street. An almost equally familiar male figure opened the door, grasped her wrist and pulled her into his arms.

Maddy almost drove off the road.

Harris had just pulled Heloise into his house.

And Heloise had been laughing . . . not protesting, not being kidnapped, but falling into his arms.

'Oh . . . she's gone into someone's house. We'll have to talk later.' Numbly, Maddy returned her attention to the mechanics of driving: checking mirrors, indicating, turning into Jubilee Crescent. All the time she silently tried to process what she'd seen.

Heloise and Harris again?

But what about the man called Jon who Heloise had been seeing?

When she'd parked outside The Hollies, she checked Ruthie was sufficiently awake to trundle into the house under her own power; let Lyla out of the back seat and saw her safely indoors, catching the coat and scarf Lyla thrust in her direction and agreeing to send a photo to Misty's mummy *soon*. She fed the woodstove and then hung up coats and scarves.

All the time, *Heloise is back with Harris* circulated her brain.

227

Smiling smiles she didn't feel, Maddy took eight photos of Lyla in her faux-pearl necklace, then let Lyla help send them.

'When can I have a phone?' Lyla demanded, handing back Maddy's with evident reluctance.

'I haven't quite decided,' Maddy hedged. Some children in Lyla's class had their parents' superseded phones to use on the household Wi-Fi, presumably with appropriate parental controls in place. She'd been anticipating upgrading her phone and letting Lyla have her discard, but with the financial worries around Adey's possible reappearance, she'd carry on with her existing phone for now.

'Aw.' Lyla let her body flop like a puppet whose strings had been slackened, then trailed with melodramatic disappointment across the hall and upstairs to her room.

Maddy debated reproaching her about sulking, but as Ruthie had found a documentary about the Falklands to listen to, at least Maddy now had the opportunity to vanish upstairs to her own room. There, she stood by the draughty window, watching through the old diamond-shaped leadwork as the streetlights came on in the dusk, wearing golden halos in the cold air. A silver car swished by, its headlights wavering, illuminating tracks in the frost.

Maddy felt heavy, as if bad news came in the form of lead. Heloise was having a thing with Harris. Images came to her of Harris loitering outside Heloise's house that day she'd accused him of sending the Adey texts and it seemed more likely than ever that he was the culprit. He could be wheedling information from Heloise and know that Maddy had become properly interested in a man for the first time since Adey left. Did Harris think he was somehow protecting Adey's interests by keeping his spirit alive?

Regardless, Heloise had hidden her relationship with him from Maddy. That wasn't how you treated a lifelong friend.

Isolation swept over her. Things with Raff were over before they'd begun. Heloise was in a relationship that promised to exclude Maddy, if last time was anything to go by. Then, Maddy had suspected Harris displayed his affection for Heloise just to make Maddy uncomfortable, watching and gauging how she felt about him smooching her lifelong friend. Ruthie was too sad for Maddy to talk over her own problems with her. Even Lyla was in a strop. If Adey showed up it was going to bring nothing but problems.

She had Christmas shopping still to do for all three of them – much of it online, because long trips around the shops didn't go together well with being mum to a six-year-old and Ruthie's carer – as well as present wrapping and card writing. Christmas felt like the most enormous chore. For several moments, she let herself feel self-pity.

Then Lyla came to the bedroom door saying, in a small voice, 'Can I have a hug? And hot chocolate with marshmallows to cheer me up?'

Maddy's smile was tremulous, but she said, 'If you promise not to be upset every time I can't buy you things you want,' and swept her darling daughter into a big hug, wishing all disappointments were as easily eased.

Later, after much thought, Maddy sent Heloise a text. Is there an evening soon when you can come round after Lyla's asleep? If you're here earlier, she won't go to bed.

The reply arrived quickly. How about tonight?

Maddy's stomach turned over, but she replied. Awesome. See you then.

Then she went to fib to Ruthie, who was pottering

about in her room while she listened to the radio. 'Heloise is coming round. She wants to talk about this bloke she's been seeing.'

Ruthie was never tricky about allowing Maddy space. 'I'll go to bed early, dear. No point you shivering up in your room when there's a fire down here.'

'Thanks.' Maddy gave her aunt a grateful hug then went to put a bottle of white wine in the fridge in the glum assumption that she'd need it, and then rounded Lyla up for a bath.

Heloise arrived brandishing a tin of shortbread. 'I've broken into the Christmas goodies.' She shucked out of her coat and struck a pose. 'Ta-dah! The 10th of December is a good day to break out Christmas jumpers. Do you like it?' Her sweater was royal blue and depicted Santa with a white pom-pom on his hat.

'Great.' With a wriggle of unease, Maddy recalled that Heloise was due to spend Christmas with them, as usual. What if she'd rather be with Harris? Or – horror – she asked to invite him along to The Hollies? 'Wine?'

'Not half.' Heloise followed her, chatting about an enormous dog she'd agreed to pet-sit over New Year. 'Honestly, she's half horse. Do you think Lyla will want to meet her?'

'Almost certainly.' Maddy poured wine into two stemless glasses, which Heloise had bought her for her birthday, and led the way into the front room, where the woodstove was burning. She felt trembly with dread. None of the gentle openings she'd been mentally rehearsing would return to her now. Instead, she regarded her best friend through hot eyes and asked huskily, 'Are you having a thing with Harris again?'

Heloise halted, mouth half-open, the flickering flames from the stove reflecting in her glass.

Into the silence, Maddy added, 'I saw you in a clinch on his doorstep today.'

Heloise unfroze sufficiently to take a sip of wine. All the gaiety had left her voice when she spoke. 'Yeah. We're together again.' Her gaze fixed on Maddy's face, she wore the same look of dismay that Lyla did when she'd been caught eating snacks without permission.

Carefully, as if her words might turn into knives and sever their friendship, Maddy said, 'Obviously, you've been hiding it from me. And what about the bloke called Jon from King's Lynn? Is he in the picture as well?'

Heloise's colour changed, so her cheeks were red and her lips white. 'I didn't say he was *from* King's Lynn. I once said he was *coming from* King's Lynn, which he was on that occasion.' Then, with the air of someone making a clean breast of things: 'And Jonathan is Harris's middle name, so . . .' She tailed off.

'So, you weren't lying?' Maddy said woodenly. 'Just arranging the truth in a certain way?'

Heloise's chin jutted. 'If that's how you like to see it.'

Maddy's heart fluttered like a bird trying to break free of a net. There was something ominous in Heloise's expression. And despite a feeling of impending doom, Maddy heard herself croak, 'How do you see it?'

'I see the whole picture.' For several moments, Heloise stared down into her wine.

Maddy couldn't leave the conversation like that, obfuscated by evasive replies. 'Spit it out, Helly,' she said quietly.

Heloise sighed, winding her legs up under her in the armchair and hunching her shoulders. 'I didn't tell you

I'm back with Harris because I knew you'd be upset and give me shit.' She held up her hand as Maddy made a small note of protest. Her gaze was steady, now. 'You did before, Maddy. If he wanted to sit with us, you looked all panicky and went silent or hurried off. That's as bad as right out saying, "I don't like Harris".'

'Harris and I don't like *each other*,' Maddy corrected, taken aback to find herself under attack. 'It goes right back to school – as you know – and he's *still* calling us Mad Crazy and Hell's Bells. Doesn't that bother you? And he hated me being with Adey.' Shaking, Maddy broached her wine, feeling a hit of alcohol might steady her. 'You being with him was awkward. I admit it. I was glad when it ended. Sorry if that makes me a bad person.'

Heloise shrugged a shoulder. 'No, but it felt like I couldn't have your friendship if I had him, and that's how it ended. *I* ended it, though you seemed to assume it must have been him. Then, a few weeks ago . . . well, we're not overburdened with single men here in Nelson's Bar, are we? You've got a lot in your life, with Lyla and Ruthie. I live alone and look after other people's kids and pets. When Harris cosied up to me again, I thought a one-nighter might be fun. It turned out to be the most exciting thing that happened all year, so I carried on.'

Maddy turned over her friend's words while Heloise morosely drained her wine glass, then got up and fetched the bottle from the fridge. What was it about Harris? Adey had never really called him on his attitude to Maddy, and now here was Heloise overlooking it, too.

Heloise returned, poured herself a generous slug of wine and resumed her seat. 'Last time, I thought I liked him more than he liked me, but this time . . . I'm not sure why, but he wants to see more of me.'

'I know why!' Maddy heard the words before she even realised that she'd half-yelled them as everything fell into place with a 'clunk' in her mind. 'He's been getting info from you and he's behind those texts that are supposed to have come from Adey—'

Then Heloise was on her feet, her glass lying on its side on the rug and the wine puddling beside it. 'This isn't about you, Maddy.' She gathered herself with a visible effort and lowered her voice. 'I made it about you and your feelings before, but now I'm wondering why, as I seem to have been called here to get a bollocking.'

Dismay stained Maddy's cheeks scarlet. Guilt warred with hurt – hurt to be seen through so easily? Or that Heloise would think the worst of her? Then guilt took over. 'I'm sorry if my lack of tolerance for Harris made you give up a man you cared for,' she whispered. But she couldn't help noticing that Heloise hadn't actually said that Harris wasn't responsible for the texts.

Yet, how could she guarantee that? She wasn't with him twenty-four hours a day.

Heloise righted her glass and fetched the kitchen roll. They knelt side by side on the carpet, blotting up the wine. Then Heloise sat back on her heels and sighed. 'I'd better leave.' Fairly gently, she added, 'Maddy, why don't you sort out your own weird life instead of worrying about mine?'

It was the pointed kind of friendly advice, yet Maddy hugged Heloise, hating to think that bloody Harris the knob might disrupt their friendship. 'Sorry if I'm guilty of viewing things through my own lens. But sorting out my life is easier said than done.'

'Really?' Heloise retrieved her coat from the newel post and shrugged into it. 'The Adey situation and Ruthie's

233

disappointment about her daughter might be out of your control. But it seems to me you really liked Raff. Why let things end badly?'

Maddy trailed her friend to the door, pausing when she opened it to see snowflakes whirling down like white confetti. 'Oh, it's snowing again.' The garden looked magical, the white coating glittering and gleaming in the light streaming from the windows while flakes danced down from the sky. 'Lyla will love it if it stays till morning.'

Heloise pulled up her hood. 'And Maddy loves the chance to change the subject.' But at least she treated Maddy to a bemittened wave with both hands.

'Maybe I did leave things badly,' Maddy conceded, stepping into the porch in her slippers so she could pull the door almost closed behind her and preserve the house's heat. She shivered. 'But I must think of Ruthie. Now Ffion's let her down, Raff and I are on opposite sides.'

Heloise began to crab down the path, leaving sideways footprints in the snow. 'I get that. But Raff hasn't done anything wrong. Now, go in before you freeze.'

As Maddy was shivering violently, she followed this advice, locking up, checking the woodstove was firmly closed, turning off lights. Finally, she went up to bed wondering dismally whether she and Heloise would become distant, just as Maddy and Raff had, and all because of their loyalty to others. She wrapped herself in the duvet sitting up, shifting the curtains aside to gaze through the window. Snow twirled around the streetlamps, filling wheel ruts and footprints as the village went to sleep. If it kept up, by morning the hedge would look like a wonky white caterpillar and her car look like a blancmange turned out of a giant jelly mould.

Sort out your own weird life. Raff hasn't done anything wrong.

The snow was mesmerising, spinning, and knitting thick hats for cottages, taking the edges off sharp points and straight lines. The garden bench would soon look like a white sofa.

Finally, she picked up her phone. The screen told her the time was eleven-thirty-five. The lateness of the hour gave her the perfect excuse not to call – and what could she say, anyway? *I'm calling to say that nothing's changed.* Cue awkward, baffled silence. Finally, she composed a text. I'm sorry things ended because we've found ourselves on opposite sides of a fence, and that I was angry with you when you'd done nothing wrong. I just want you to know that. Enjoy Christmas. The 10th – nearly the 11th – of December was early for Christmas wishes, but he'd know it was a parting pleasantry rather than a bridge to put things back as they were.

Fatigue hit her and she slid the curtain back into place. Still wearing the duvet like a cocoon, she rolled down onto the bed and began to drift into sleep.

Just before the final moment of unconsciousness, her phone beeped. The sensible thing would have been to put it on 'do not disturb' and close her eyes again. But she saw *Raff* on the screen and extracted her arm from the duvet to snatch up the handset. The message read: Ditto, saw where your anger was coming from, agree. Ditto. So, he too was sorry about the way things had ended, agreed it wasn't his fault, and reciprocated her Christmas wishes.

She had no right to expect more, but the message was as chilly as the night outside.

Chapter Seventeen

The next three days were incredibly exciting – for Lyla, if not for Maddy and Ruthie.

The snow continued, sinking to earth in an unending shower of white confetti, and schools closed to ensure the safety of children, parents and staff. The *Eastern Daily Press* ran snowy photos of Hunstanton lighthouse and the beach, which looked a bit like a giant had been washing up in the sea and left suds along the shore. Rural villages throughout Norfolk were isolated by the tricky conditions and Nelson's Bar, higher than all the land around and reached by steep Long Climb, was one of them. As there seemed little point digging out a car when it was impossible to leave the village, the roads remained snowy, part of the Christmas card perfection.

Children shrieked in joy as they pushed each other around on sleds on The Green. Front gardens were filled with snowmen and, indoors, radiators were festooned with gloves drying after snowball fights. Adults ruefully predicted running short of bread, milk and fresh veg. The Duke of Bronte had no draught beer as brewery delivery drivers were no keener to hazard the steep slope of Long Climb than anyone else. Bothered about the food situation rather than the shortage of beer, Maddy – with help from Lyla – made bread, then they bundled up in coats, boots, hats and scarves and slipped and slithered their way around to Heloise's house to present a fresh loaf as a peace offering.

Heloise let them in with raised eyebrows and the cryptic comment, 'This is interesting.'

Maddy plunged in. 'I came to say— Oh.' She came to an abrupt halt as she spotted Harris lounging in the kitchen rocking chair. It hadn't occurred to her that he might be there. But why shouldn't he spend time with the woman he was seeing? If she wanted Heloise's friendship, she'd have to adjust. Remembering Heloise's criticism about her hostility towards Harris, she said politely, 'Hello, Harris. Lyla, say hello.'

''Lo,' said Lyla. She turned straight to Heloise. 'I've made snowmen in the garden and Mummy let me put my old hat on one. Will you come and see them? Oh, and Mummy's brought you some bread.' She quirked an eyebrow as if to signal that this must be the worst gift ever.

'Mm, it smells lovely.' Heloise took the still-warm parcel and gave Lyla a hug. She gave Maddy a hug, too, but not until Maddy had tentatively opened her arms for one.

Harris, as if he'd caught 'best behaviour' from Maddy, concurred. 'That bread smells delicious.'

Lyla was already pulling off her hat and shucking her coat. Maddy hesitated, aware of barging into a cosy twosome, but Heloise indicated it was OK by saying to Lyla, 'How about we have a slice of this with Nutella, then we can make a snowman in my garden, too. I've been waiting for you to come round and do it.'

'Yay!' yodelled Lyla, pulling out a kitchen chair with a screech on the flagstone floor.

Maddy had little option but to take off her outdoor clothes and join the fresh bread and Nutella feast. Harris did too. To avoid being accused of treating him to silence, she said, 'Any luck with the job hunt?'

Surprise flickered in his eyes. 'Got my fingers crossed for one in procurement for a King's Lynn company but won't hear till January.'

She nodded. Lyla saved her from having to come up with anything else by chatting happily about Grauntie Ruthie not going out in the snow, and that Mummy's car was completely covered and looked like a marshmallow.

Harris asked Maddy, 'You hear any more from Adey?'

Her gaze flew to his face, expecting to see the assumed innocent expression that came with one of his incendiary questions. 'Or the person purporting to be Adey? No.'

Once the snack had been eaten, Heloise said, 'Shall we make that snowman, Lyla?'

Lyla, blithely oblivious of Maddy's wish to reignite friendly relations with Heloise, answered, 'Can you look after me here while we make a snowman and Mummy goes home to check on Grauntie Ruthie?'

This was so much the type of arrangement often initiated by the adults that Maddy and Heloise both laughed. Comfortably, Heloise said, 'I can, my lovely.'

Deciding that she'd get no warmth from Heloise while Harris was there anyway, Maddy said, 'I know when I'm not wanted. When shall I come back for her, Heloise?'

'I'll drop her off when the snowman's finished,' Heloise answered, leaving Maddy little option but to reach for her coat.

She was halfway into it when Harris spoke up. 'It's time I was going, too.'

As she could hardly change her mind about going at that point, Maddy had to watch Harris kiss Heloise and Heloise blush prettily.

Then she found herself walking out onto the snowy street with Harris. The air that greeted them was bitingly cold, so she pulled up her hood and made a show of concentrating on where she placed her booted feet amongst the slippery footprints of those who'd passed this way since the last snowfall.

Harris burrowed his hands into the pockets of his ski jacket and fell into step. 'You don't think those messages came from Adey, then?'

She glanced at him. He wasn't wearing the sarcastic smile that so often accompanied their conversations, so she bit back a comment that she'd hardly have accused Harris of being the culprit if she'd been convinced that Adey was the texter. 'I don't know what to think, to be honest.' Then, when he only walked beside her, his hair blowing in the wind, she added, 'I called the in-laws to ask if they'd heard from him, but Tilly said not.'

He snorted. 'Did you and Tilly have a cosy chat?'

For once, she laughed at his ironic tone. 'No. She was as chilly and disagreeable as ever.'

At the corner of Traders Place, Harris paused. His house lay to the right along Droody Road and Jubilee Crescent lay in the opposite direction. His face was pink with cold, and his breath hung in a cloud. 'Maddy,' he said, proving that he remembered that she had a name other than 'Mad Crazy'. 'If you do find out it's Adey, will you tell me? I know I piss you off a lot – on purpose,' he added, as if he didn't want her to think he was a knob

239

by accident. 'But I'd love to know he's OK. It's haunted me, being the last one to see him. What if he did chuck himself off the cliffs and I could have talked him out of it? When he told me to sod off, I just did, because I was sick of all his moaning about money.'

Maddy's jaw sagged. Never had she thought that Harris might be irritated by Adey's complaints. And as for guilty feelings on Harris's part – they'd never entered her head. To her, the subtext of his stupid half-sour, half-teasing comments about her having driven Adey to hurl himself into a freezing, stormy sea had been, *I resent you for causing my best mate to leave.* Never once had she read the message, *I'm pointing the finger at you because I can't face it being my fault.* Stunned, she said, 'I don't think harming himself is in Adey's nature. But running away because we were up shit creek with the house being flooded and no money to fix it . . . ?'

Harris kicked at a drift of snow, sending glittering spicules hissing into the afternoon air. 'Except you did fix it.'

'Well, yes.' She thought back to the long freezing days of battling pregnancy nausea while ripping out ruined carpets and drying out the house, literally screaming down the phone at the contractor until his conscience made him turn up to do the replastering. Of evenings spent listing items on eBay. Of fitting in scans and midwife appointments around her desperate struggles. The utter relief of letting out High Cottage in week thirty of her pregnancy and moving in with Ruthie, trading exhaustion for afternoon naps. She struggled to explain her gut feeling. 'It took a lot of hard work. But Adey liked things to come easy. When he realised how badly he'd stuffed up by letting the household insurance lapse and employing a builder who wasn't insured either, he felt trapped.'

240

Curiously, she asked, 'Have you been feeling guilt for the last seven years?'

Without meeting her eye, he nodded.

For the first time ever, she felt sorry for Harris Soley. She repeated, 'I don't believe it's in Adey's nature to do himself harm.'

Harris's gaze became distant. 'He could have had an accident.'

That thought had been Maddy's companion since the snowy night he'd gone missing, but she said, 'Wasn't he too smart to have gone close to the cliff edge?'

For the first time in the conversation, the customary resentment crept into Harris's voice. 'If you don't think he jumped, and you don't think he fell, then why try and get him presumed dead?'

Maddy didn't let the question trigger an angry response, though he could only have got information on this from Heloise or Ruthie – and no way was it Ruthie, who hadn't come into direct contact with Harris for years. 'Because I need to get on with my life,' she said gently. The wind nipped her exposed face. 'While he's missing, I can't divorce him or sell the house. If there was an alternative method, like "Presumed not wanting to face up to his responsibilities", I'd use that. But there's not.'

'Divorce. Heloise said you're seeing someone. Do you want to get married again?' he challenged.

So, definitely Heloise, despite yesterday's indignation. At the attendant lance of pain, and the blunt reminder of Raff, Maddy's patience snapped. 'That's my business.'

Harris snapped right back, the usual frustrated anger drawing lines on his face. 'I don't like Adey "presumed dead" if he's not. It's disrespectful.' He pronounced the last word grandly.

241

'Oh, piss off,' she said tiredly. '"Presumption that Adey deserves respect" would never stand up in court.'

He stared at her for several seconds. Then he blinked, and it was as if he came back to himself. He even laughed. 'You know what, Maddy? I don't know why we're arguing. Everything you've said is true. Adey would have come back if he were able or wanted to. He hasn't. We both need to get on with our lives. I've let my loyalty blind me.'

'OK,' she said, not understanding this U-turn but taking a step away because if she stood there much longer, she'd be as cold as the snowman Heloise and Lyla were probably making as they spoke.

His beard twitched, as if the mouth half-hidden by the fuzz had twisted wryly. 'I'm glad we had this talk. You've made me look at everything differently.' Then he said a quick goodbye and hurried off, his step as light as the snow would allow.

Maddy stared after him, confused at his suddenly changed world view. Then she turned for home, having to steady herself on a lamppost as her boots scrabbled for purchase on the ice.

As she slithered on, fresh snowflakes began to float down around her, as if the God of Winter had decided that Nelson's Bar needed another snowfall to paint the trampled areas newly white. On a whim, instead of taking the turning into Jubilee Crescent she continued along Droody Road and crossed onto the clifftop near the Duke of Bronte, where a Christmas tree burned bright in the window.

Today, as often in winter, the sea was restless and grey. Perhaps because of Harris's hypothesis that Adey had slipped from the cliff in the snow, she kept back from the edge, then stood still for a full minute, trying to sense how Adey might have felt that night. An enraged Adey hadn't been given to sensible decisions. *Could* he have ventured too close to the edge? Both she and Harris had occasionally spoken of him in the past tense, even while wondering if he was alive.

No wiser when the minute had ticked by, she turned and trudged back through the falling snow to The Hollies.

'It's only me, Ruthie,' she called, as she balanced awkwardly, pulling her boots off to leave on the doormat to drip. 'My hands and toes are frozen, despite my gloves and boots.'

Ruthie's reply was faint. It came from the direction of her room.

Alarmed, in case her aunt had fallen or was too breathless to lift her voice, she crossed the hall in her socks, knocked and opened the door. There, she found her aunt sitting on her bed, the duvet drawn up around her, and she started as if caught doing something naughty.

'Are you OK?' Maddy began. Then she took in tear tracks on her aunt's cheeks and the box that Maddy now recognised, clutched on her lap.

Ruthie's chin wobbled. 'I'm having a bit of a moment. I still miss Nigel,' she said simply, though she tried to force a laugh.

Maddy's heart gave a squeeze. In all the anger and dismay about Ffion's capriciousness, she'd almost lost sight of the fact that Ruthie had lost a love she'd felt unable to mourn. 'Should I leave you alone? Or do you want to talk?'

Ruthie's face creased into a grateful, if watery, smile. 'Would you mind reading me a letter, dear? It brings him closer. If I could read them myself, I would.'

'Of course. Let me just hang up my coat.' Being a carer was all about doing things that the other person wished they could do themselves. You put away your embarrassment or reluctance and did what you could.

On her return, she crawled onto the bed and tucked her legs under the duvet beside Ruthie's, settling her back against the old-fashioned quilted headboard and took a letter Ruthie pulled from the box, opening the folds of the cheap, thin grey paper. Maddy barely had to read the salutation to know it would say, *My dearest, darling Ruthie.* It proved to be a fairly boring missive of wishes they could meet again soon and that though Nigel lived for Ruthie's letters and whenever he could phone her, they were no substitute for having Ruthie in his arms. When he began to reminisce about *last time* and *saying hello properly*, Ruthie cleared her throat and turned pink.

'Time to stop that one?' Maddy suggested, letting the letter fall back into its folds. 'Choose another, then.' Ruthie handed her a pale blue one. Dated late September 1977, it proved to be more poignant.

'*I hate to think of you at home alone awaiting the birth. I know you said they were keen for you to stop work as soon as your maternity leave could start, but there's no one with you. I can't bear it when you say you're treated like an embarrassment with people looking the other way rather than greet you in the street. I bet half those bitches and bastards had to get married themselves. Once they're married, they can point their fingers at others.*'

'That was true,' Ruthie observed sadly. 'Wedding bands did quieten wagging tongues. And putting the baby up for adoption gave some people amnesia, and they treated me as if I'd never been pregnant – apart from a bit of an atmosphere when I went back to work.' She snuggled further into her duvet. 'I was too sad to bother moving away and starting afresh, though, so I just ignored it. In the end, the gossips found something else to talk about.'

Instead of a sexy end to this letter, Nigel remained grim.

'*I've got to check with you one last time. Are you certain you want me to give the baby a home for life? I wouldn't blame you if you changed your mind and would understand but, at the same time, I have got everything ready and waiting here. I've painted the nursery and ordered the cot.*'

Maddy blinked away a hot tear.

Ruthie sighed. 'I could have kept her with me for longer than I did. They encouraged it, in a way, the midwives and social people. But I gave her up quickly because it was best for her to get attached to—' she gulped '—Sindy.' She hunched her shoulders. 'I did my best for Ffion then, and I've made up my mind to do the same now. If she doesn't want contact with me then that's what's best for her. I'll never see the adult she grew into or meet my grandchild, but I made that bed a long time ago and it's too late to complain. Ffion thinks of Sindy as her mother. Nigel and me, we pretended Sindy didn't exist in our letters, but I borrowed her husband, and she got my child.' She found a tissue up her sleeve and blew her nose.

Maddy slipped her arms around her aunt's round shoulders and, when Ruthie said no more, described to her what she couldn't see. 'It's snowing again. The flakes are floating down. Occasionally they land on your bedroom window and slip down like . . . like little white feathers.' She'd been going to say *like tears* but Ruthie had enough tears in her life. 'Nelson's Bar looks like the decoration on a Christmas cake, with all the cottages

245

made from icing. The Phillipses, across the road, they've got an absolute riot of different-coloured lights on the front of their house and on their fir tree. The Grants next door have gone for all white fairy lights.'

'I like a bit of colour, myself.' Ruthie felt for Maddy's hands and took the last letter from her, holding it, her face turned towards the window. After a few moments, she murmured, 'Isn't it funny how bad things have happened to us at Christmas? I gave Ffion up. Adey went missing.' She heaved another deep, heartfelt sigh. 'It's a good job we've got each other and lovely little Lyla, isn't it, dear?'

'It's all I need,' Maddy lied, thinking how much she wished she could have had Raff, too.

Ruthie, more honestly, said nothing, because they both knew that she craved a meeting with her daughter and granddaughter, and was tormented that it was out of reach.

Her yearning was the most natural thing in the world.

By Friday, no fresh snow had fallen, and Long Climb had been ploughed. People cleared their cars and gritted the roads. Snowmen melted into nondescript grey blobs and the schools said they hoped to reopen on Monday, after a weekend thaw.

'So, you'll have the last three days at school and won't miss all the Christmas fun,' Maddy told Lyla on Friday afternoon as she picked up shiny silver baubles from around the Christmas tree because Tornado Lyla had just swept by and knocked them off.

'That'll be lovely,' said Ruthie, from the depths of the throw she'd huddled up in because she seemed to be feeling the cold more this year. 'Mm, those mince pies smell good. When will they be ready?'

Maddy and Lyla had been busy in the kitchen after lunch and the fruity, spicy aroma was mouth-watering. 'They're ready, they're ready!' Lyla crowed, dancing around in an apron with a robin on the front.

Maddy caught her hands before she knocked the Christmas tree over entirely. 'The last batch of pies has just gone in the oven and the others have only just come out. Grauntie Ruthie would burn her mouth if we brought her one now.'

'Aw,' mourned Lyla. 'I suppose that's the way the cookie grumbles.' Then she danced up to Ruthie's armchair. 'Mummy gave me my own pastry and I made a mince pie pasty with four glassy cherries on top. I'll share it with you, if you like.'

Ruthie's eyes might be dim and watery, but they hadn't lost their twinkle. 'What a kind girl you are. I won't take your special mince pie pasty, though. I'll just have one of the ordinary ones.'

'Good call,' Maddy murmured. Lyla's pastry had been enthusiastically kneaded, rolled, squashed and crimped, and filled with too much mincemeat so it was flooding out to singe the edges of the 'mince pie pasty'. She was pretty sure Lyla would soon abandon it in favour of the more traditional variety.

'Door!' Lyla bellowed, a split second after the doorbell rang out, then bounced and skipped from the room.

Maddy got to the door just as Lyla threw it open with a bright, 'Hello, who are you?'

But Maddy didn't need to ask – though she stared in silent astonishment. She'd already met the small woman hovering outside the door wearing an enormous coat and a nervous expression. 'Ffion,' Maddy breathed.

'Who?' Lyla demanded.

It took Maddy a second to gather her wits. 'Come in,' she managed. 'This is a surprise.' Or a shock. Her mind flew immediately to Ruthie. Thank goodness she'd had her inhaler only a few minutes ago because in seconds she was likely to scale the heights of emotion. As Maddy ushered Ffion through the door and took her outdoor things, she satisfied Lyla with a quick, 'Ffion is Raff's sister.' But her mind was whirring, turning over the best way to deal with the unexpected visit.

Ffion was pink in the face. Tautly, she smoothed her hair. 'Forgive me for just turning up. I had to come while I had the strength and the nerve. Ever since Raff told me what had happened—' she didn't mention the text in so many words '—she's been on my mind. Then it snowed and made leaving Docking tricky. But today the roads are much clearer. Chloe's on a video call with a teacher. I thought it would be better if I saw her on my own this first time.' She obviously assumed that Maddy would know when 'she' and 'her' referred to Ruthie. Lowering her voice, she added. 'Raff gave me and Chloe plenty to think about. My brother can make his feelings plain when he needs to.'

The words speared Maddy. Raff had made his feelings plain in his bed too.

Lyla, never one to be left out for long, butted in. 'We've been making mince pies.'

Ffion turned her attention to the beaming little girl. 'How yummy. I can smell them.' She smiled, then turned back to Maddy. She slapped a hand to her heart. 'I'm so panicky I can hardly see straight. Do you think she'll see me?'

Maddy couldn't help the laugh that bubbled out of her. Feeling a warmth towards Ffion that had been absent till now, she said, 'I think you'll make today one of the best of her life.'

Relief smoothed away Ffion's anxious frown, though she took three audible breaths before she let Maddy show her into the front room.

Ruthie peered in their direction. 'Who was it, dear? A delivery?'

'A visitor,' Maddy said, heart thumping in excitement at what was about to play out before her eyes. 'For you.'

'Who is it?' Ruthie asked with a touch of impatience. 'Della?'

Maddy looked at Ffion expectantly.

Ffion took another deep breath before she quavered. 'It's Ffion.' Her voice was small, questing.

Ruthie's jaw sagged open. Then she heaved herself to her feet. 'Ffion?' she whispered, incredulity in her thready voice. She took several hesitant steps, her arms out, but tentative.

Ffion hesitated too. Then she took two quick strides and slid into Ruthie's embrace like a boat finding its dock.

No one uttered a word.

The small round figure hung on tightly to the small slight figure. Maddy watched through a blur of tears.

'Is Grauntie Ruthie crying?' demanded Lyla, sounding bewildered by the emotional tableau.

With a quick swipe of her sleeve across her eyes, Maddy put her arm around Lyla's shoulders. 'Only with happiness,' she whispered. 'Grauntie Ruthie hasn't seen Ffion for a very long time.' Explanations had been forced upon her without notice, but she found she didn't mind. What was important was the joy in Ruthie's snuffling sobs as she rocked Ffion, as if hinting at all the decades her arms had yearned for her baby.

249

Maddy ushered Lyla into the kitchen, where they could keep out of the way by busying themselves with pragmatic tasks like checking whether the first batch of mince pies were cool enough to eat and then boiling the kettle to make everyone a drink. Maddy moved the mince pies from cooling rack to plate, chatting absently to Lyla. She felt overjoyed for Ruthie. The woman had given Maddy love all her life, never once hinting that she hadn't seen her own child grow up.

'Can I have it, can I have it, can I?' Lyla wheedled, eyes alight as she gazed at her 'mince pie pasty', its glacé cherry decorations askew.

'Soon,' Maddy promised. 'How about you tear off sheets of kitchen roll for napkins?' All the time she was dealing with small, practical details, her heart was daring to peep out of the bruised depression it had been in all week.

If Ffion and Ruthie are OK, there's nothing to get in the way of seeing Raff.

'You could start a new kitchen roll, the one with snowflakes on. Yes, that looks Christmassy. Put one on each plate.' *If Ffion and Ruthie are OK, there's nothing to get in the way of seeing Raff.*

She hovered closer to the kitchen door so she could peep in at Ruthie and Ffion. Ruthie was back in her armchair, beaming, wiping her eyes. Ffion had pulled up the footstool, as Maddy so often did herself, so she could hold Ruthie's hand and talk.

Maddy went back to make strawberry milk for Lyla and tea for herself and Ruthie, strong and milky as Ruthie liked it. *If Ffion and Ruthie are OK, there's nothing to get in the way of seeing Raff.* She closed her mind to how exactly she was going to approach him, but she was sure it would be OK, somehow.

The tray was heavy as she carried it into the front room, asking Lyla to pull up a small table. Checking what Ffion wanted to drink and darting back to make a quick cup of white coffee, trusting that Ruthie and Ffion wouldn't mind Lyla burbling about mince pie pasties and strawberry milk for the short time it took.

It wasn't till she returned, and Lyla demanded, 'Mummy, are you crying too?' that Maddy realised that she did, indeed, have two wet patches on her cheeks.

Ruthie creaked a laugh. 'You must think we're very odd, Lyla, to cry when we're happy. But Ffion's my daughter, just like you're your mummy's daughter. For a long time, I didn't know where she was, but now she's found me and I'm very, very, *very* happy indeed.'

Maddy waited for Lyla to ask what that made Ffion's relationship to herself.

Instead, Lyla regarded Ruthie seriously for several seconds. Then she said, 'Like my daddy and me? He went away and got lost. Will he come back and find me someday, like Ffion?'

Shock tingled through Maddy. In the silence, she delved inside her heart for the right answer, while Ruthie and Ffion looked on. Eventually, she said, 'It's a little bit like that. But because your daddy left before you were born, he doesn't know about you.'

Lyla's grey-eyed gaze fixed on Maddy. 'So, he won't come?' There was woe in her voice, making Maddy wonder if all the time she'd thought Lyla barely thought about not having a dad around, she'd actually been harbouring anticipation or hope.

She had to clear her throat before she could reply. 'We can't tell.' She wrestled with a need to be truthful while not giving Lyla false expectation. 'I don't think he will, but

I'm not right all the time.' Maddy's heart sank and ached at the same time. Poor Lyla must have been hiding her thoughts about daddies all this time, thinking that – like Christmas – some things took a lot of waiting for . . . but they arrived in the end. She slipped her arm about her darling little girl. 'We live with Grauntie Ruthie, don't we? And we have Grandma in Spain. Except . . .' She drew out the word to indicate that she was about to produce a nice surprise. 'Ffion's your family, too. She's a kind of cousin.' And Ffion chimed in as if they'd arranged it, with an explanation of their cousinship and that she had a daughter herself, Chloe, who was also a cousin to Lyla.

Lyla listened, wearing a tiny frown of concentration. 'And Grauntie Ruthie's my great-great-auntie.' Then she turned her luminous eyes on Maddy. 'Can I hand the mince pies round?'

Maddy's heart nearly burst with love for her little one, for any sadness a lack of daddy might bring her. 'Thank you, that would be lovely. Remember to hold the plate nice and flat.'

They munched their pies and sipped their drinks. Ruthie kept touching Ffion and saying, 'I can't believe you're here.'

Every time, Ffion would answer, 'I can't believe it, either,' or 'I feel as if we could talk for hours.' Finally, she added, 'But I'm beginning to get tired, so I'll go soon. I know Raff told you I'm waiting for an op.'

'What's an op?' Lyla demanded.

'It's short for "operation". Ffion's going into hospital and having a tiny part of her heart fixed,' Maddy said reassuringly.

'How?' demanded Lyla disbelievingly. 'Do they cut her open with scissors?'

Maddy tried her best to take the scariness out of something that really was alarming, with: 'No, sweetie, and Ffion will be in a deep, deep sleep and won't feel a thing.' But one ear was on the conversation going on between Ruthie and Ffion.

'Will you come back?' Ruthie asked.

'Definitely. It's been so wonderful.' Ffion's voice caught. 'But I'm not sure about Chloe yet. She's struggling, and her mood swings are wild.'

Ruthie's voice grew husky. 'I understand. Just tell her I'd love to meet her when she feels ready.' They spoke to each other in a low, intimate way, as if they'd last met days ago, rather than the forty-six years it had been.

Maddy took a bite of her now cool mince pie, enjoying the crumbly pastry – she'd got great marks for pastry making during her training – just as her phone began to ring. On the screen it said *number withheld* and her stomach gave a twist. She swallowed fast so she could answer, climbing to her feet at the same time. 'Hello?'

'Mrs Madeline Austen?' asked a male voice. 'This is DS Novak of Norfolk Police. I'm calling to let you know that I've been contacted by the police in Cornwall.' Hesitation. 'This might be unexpected, but I've been informed that your husband Mr Adrian Austen is in the Royal Cornwall Hospital. He was injured in a road traffic accident this morning.'

'What?' Maddy whispered, blood pounding in her ears.

DC Novak repeated the information, slowly and clearly. 'Mr Austen has been missing for some time?'

'Seven years,' she whispered. Her knees turned to water and she had to plump back down on the chair.

With a tiny part of her mind, she heard Ruthie say to Lyla, 'Would you go upstairs and fetch your new pencil case to show Ffion, please, dear? I think she has a young friend who needs something like that for Christmas.'

Lyla stepped heedlessly over Maddy's outstretched leg. 'We got mine from Amazon.' Then she ran out, her feet clumping on the stairs.

In a dream, her voice far away, Maddy cut across whatever else DS Novak had to say. 'Can you give me ward details, please? I'd better go to see him.' And she ended the call without even checking whether DS Novak had finished speaking.

Ruthie whispered something to Ffion. Ffion murmured, 'Raff told me about it.' Then Maddy was aware that Ffion was speaking on the phone.

Maddy felt hot as the fire that burned in the woodstove and then as cold as the melting snow outside. It was odd. She could hear Lyla return, then her voice, agitated and high. Ffion's soothing, Ruthie saying, 'Oh, dear.' Then Maddy felt the carpet against the side of her face, and she had to close her eyes to stop the room from spinning.

Whispers. Murmurs. Footsteps.

Ffion murmuring, 'Maddy, if I help you sit up, can you sip this water? You've obviously had a shock.'

And Ruthie: 'Don't cry, Lyla, love. Mummy will be all right in a minute.'

Maddy knew she should sit up and drink the water so she would come round, for Lyla. But the memory of the words, *Adey's turned up* closed her eyes . . . and darkness swallowed her.

Chapter Eighteen

Raff had put his character Adeckor in the position of having to choose between his love for the queen and his fealty to the king. It had seemed like a meaty conflict, but he'd been scribbling and typing all day and hadn't found a satisfactory way through it. Maybe he'd take up Vikki's standing offer to chat over knotty plots . . . but it always felt like a sign of weakness.

He tried not to take phone calls while he was working but whenever his phone rang, he couldn't resist reading the screen, in case it was Elinor his agent with news of a sale to a foreign publisher, or – his secret desire – news of a massive film deal.

Ffion. OK, that was another person who got an answer. 'Hey,' he greeted her economically. 'OK?'

'I'm OK,' she replied, as if there was nothing ever wrong with her. 'But something's happened to Maddy.'

Reactively, Raff shoved back his chair and glanced around for his coat and car keys. 'What sort of something?'

Ffion wasted no words. 'She passed out after getting a phone call. She's woozy but she was able to tell us that the call was from the police. They've found her husband in a hospital in Cornwall. I can't leave her just with Ruthie and Lyla.'

Raff halted in his tracks. 'You're with *Ruthie*? And Maddy's husband's turned up?' It was almost too much to take in, and he had to lean against the table.

'She got a call out of the blue.' Ffion sounded harassed and wobbly. 'I don't know what to do. Maddy says she's got to see him in hospital and Ruthie's stressing out. A friend of Maddy's is coming to look after Lyla.'

'Heloise,' he supplied mechanically.

'That's it. I can't leave Ruthie if Maddy goes off. I'm not sure if it's best to bring her home with me, but then there's Chloe . . .' She sounded as stressed out as she said Ruthie was.

Raff's brain began to shake itself free of the effect of the shock news overdose. He started slotting together options. 'How about you ring Chloe and tell her the situation? You can give her the choice of bringing Ruthie home or you staying in Nelson's Bar, so she feels in control. I'll come over to you.'

He didn't give her a chance to ask why. He needed to help . . . and it wasn't necessarily Ffion he wanted to check was OK. He ended the call and grabbed his keys. He was indicating to turn into High Street when his phone rang, and he answered on his car's built-in system.

'It's Chloe,' said a high-pitched voice. 'Me and Mum think it'll be best if you take me with you. If I'm not comfortable with—' she took a breath '—Mum's mum, then you can bring me back and Mum will stay there. I'm going to try and be OK, though, because it will be lots easier for Mum.'

Raff had little difficulty following this slightly garbled

speech and got ready to turn right at the church. Warmly, he said, 'That's great, Chloe, thinking of your mum. I'm already in the car so I'll be outside your house any second.'

''K.' Then the line went dead and as Raff pulled up Chloe scuttled through the front door, tucking her phone into the front pocket of her hoodie, a coat over her arm, treading cautiously over what remained of the snow. She hopped into the car with a loud, 'Brr. Freezing.'

He turned his car and drove out of the village, sticking to the middle of the lanes to avoid the snowy, icy margins that looked ready to spin them into a hedge.

He spared Chloe a glance. 'OK?'

'S'pose. It'll be weird, though,' she said, with the air of one not sure she was doing the right thing.

From that, Raff felt he was meant to deduce that Chloe had decided to accept the situation but felt apprehensive about being catapulted into meeting Ruthie. As he didn't want to say, 'Good girl,' as if she was six, he opted for: 'I'm just grateful you're supporting your mum. I might be helping Maddy.'

'Yeah,' she said turning to him. 'That's freaky. Mum says her missing husband's turned up in a hospital somewhere.'

'Cornwall, about as far away from Norfolk as you can get while remaining in England,' he supplied, easing up at a staggered crossroads in the hope that his car wheels wouldn't lock up. The car found grip, and he took the right-left smoothly.

Apart from a sideways moment on Long Climb, they arrived at The Hollies OK. Ffion opened the front door before they'd even pressed the bell. Smiling, though pale and anxious, she drew Chloe towards the front room, whispering as they went. Chloe visibly squared her shoulders before stepping over the threshold.

Raff's attention was chiefly on Heloise, who hovered in the hall, an expectant gaze on him. She spoke in hushed tones. 'I'm taking Lyla home with me. Frickin' Adey, showing up. Maddy shouldn't drive all that way. She's shaky since she got the phone call and her car's ancient. I don't drive. I'd send Harris with Maddy, because he was Adey's best mate, but she won't hear of it. Keeps saying she'll drive herself "in a minute" when she feels better.'

'I'll drive her,' he said calmly. He couldn't let her set off on a long car journey alone and shaken.

Heloise's face cleared. 'I was hoping you would. I'll pack bags for Maddy and Lyla.' She turned and hurried up the stairs.

Lyla cannoned into the hall from the front room, bouncing with excitement, yet also looking anxious. 'Mummy's going to see a friend who needs her help. Heloise is going to look after me. She's pet-sitting a little dog and she's going to let me help walk it. Ffion's going to look after Ruthie. And I've got a second cousin once moved called Chloe.' Each short sentence was delivered in a breathless, almost defiant way, as if daring herself to get upset at the bewildering succession of events, seeking comfort from reciting details.

She must have learnt a valiant attitude from Maddy, as Lyla even managed a smile as she squeezed by him and followed Heloise upstairs.

Raff strode into the front room, where the woodstove blazed. Ruthie was standing before her armchair, speaking to Chloe, who looked unsure, but was nodding. Ffion was observing intensely, a half-smile on her face.

Maddy was sitting statue-like on the sofa. She, too, was staring at the group, but blankly. Probably her mind was in Cornwall, he thought, and crossed the faded green carpet to settle gently beside her, cutting out any awkward bridging of the chasm that had opened between them by focusing on what was important. 'How are you doing?'

She switched her gaze to him, and, as if complicit with his mental shortcut, said, 'I have to see him.'

He ignored the sinking of his stomach as the various reasons she felt the need to go to Adey flashed through his mind like nightmares. Though plainly dazed, she didn't look ready to be swayed from her purpose, so he just nodded. 'I'm driving you. Heloise is packing your overnight bag. We'll swing by my place to grab mine. It's a long trip to Cornwall, but by travelling through the evening, you'll be able to visit him as soon as they'll let you in in the morning.'

Maddy looked grateful but unsurprised, as if she'd been waiting for him to arrive and take over. 'Thanks, Raff.' When Lyla and Heloise came in together, Lyla swinging a backpack and Heloise a sports bag, Maddy went into parent mode and talked softly and calmly to Lyla about Mummy only being away a short time. She helped Lyla button her coat and Heloise plonked a woolly hat with two tassels on her head.

While that was going on, Raff ascertained the name of the hospital from Ffion, whipped out his phone and googled nearby B&Bs. Scrolling rapidly, he found a family room with two beds. He'd be able to satisfy his urge to take care of Maddy, while not taking anything for granted.

Everyone called goodbye to Lyla, with: 'Have a lovely time!' and 'See you soon!' so the little girl smiled as if she was in for a lovely treat, rather than being shunted off the scene while her mum went to find the dad who'd been absent for all of Lyla's life.

Raff received a confirmatory text from the B&B with the code for the key safe where he'd find the room key, and returned thanks, grateful that even if they arrived after midnight, they'd be able to access somewhere warm and comfortable.

Ffion turned to Maddy. 'Is it OK if we stay here with Ruthie? I'll take her to our house if you'd rather but—'

'—she's more comfortable here, where she knows where everything is,' Maddy finished for her, looking as if she were beginning to regain her grip on things. 'You'll find clean bed things in the cupboard on the landing.'

Chloe said to Raff, 'I'll stay too, to make sure Mum doesn't do too much. We'll drive back to ours later to pick up our things.'

Proud of everyone trying to look after everyone else, Raff gave his niece a hug, and then hugged his sister for good measure.

Looking pale and spaced out, Maddy fetched her handbag, coat, boots, hat, scarf and gloves, then picked up the lilac sports bag Heloise had packed for her. Her gaze settled on Raff.

'Ready?' he said. She was behaving like Stepford Maddy, and though he recognised it as a coping mechanism brought on by intense stress, he didn't like it. Stepford Maddy gave Ffion house keys, hugged Ruthie, and strode towards the front door.

Raff hurried to catch up. In no time, they were heading back out of the village, skidding down Long Climb, where dripping trees created treacherous ice rivers across the road.

Maddy opted to remain in the car while he raced around his house, packing a bag, including his laptop so he could work if sidelined in a waiting room or left at the B&B while Maddy . . . did whatever Maddy chose to do. He locked the front door. Then he unlocked it again and sprinted in for the chargers for his phone and laptop, cursing because he seemed to always forget these essentials, locked up and slid into the car beside Maddy.

She was still unnaturally calm and silent while he programmed the postcode of the B&B into the sat nav. He'd only filled up with fuel a couple of days ago, so there was nothing holding them up.

They headed for Cornwall.

It was, as he'd said, a long, long drive.

At first, Maddy just stared out of the passenger window. Raff drove through the Birchams and joined the road to King's Lynn, the gateway south and west from their part of Norfolk. Traffic was heavy, especially at roundabouts. It was dark and oncoming headlights were like a constantly moving string of fairy lights.

Maddy stirred only when her phone rang. From Maddy's end of the conversation, it was Lyla. 'I'm in Raff's car. What are you doing? Oh, the dog sounds lovely. What colour is he? If he belongs to someone in Titchwell he hasn't come far for Heloise to look after him. Oh, yes, I know you're looking after him too. OK, sweetie. Enjoy your sleepover.' Pause. 'Hi, Heloise. No, I know you wouldn't let Lyla play with him unless he was friendly. She'll probably walk his little legs off, if you let her. I will. Yes, of course. Don't worry.'

When her call ended, she lapsed again into silence, eyes on the glitter of frost on the verges and the occasional twin points of light in a hedge that meant a lurking animal.

They were through King's Lynn when she suddenly said, 'Thanks, Raff.'

He was glad of the sign that she was beginning to function more naturally. 'No problem.' He told her about the B&B arrangements. She asked a few questions, like a thawing icicle dripping sentences. Then she thanked him again and turned back to the passenger window, where lighted house windows now flashed by.

Later, she said, 'I don't know what to do.' While Raff was debating his response, she added, 'At least he can't run off before I get there. He has leg injuries and had surgery this afternoon.'

'Right.' He entered yet another roundabout, waiting for a gap in the traffic. 'Have you been in touch with the hospital directly?'

She shook her head, and he caught the movement in the corner of his vision. 'Better he doesn't know I'm on my way – unless the police have passed on that I intended to go.'

She seemed so dazed that Raff didn't ask how Ffion had come to be with Ruthie this afternoon, what Maddy thought of Chloe's change of heart and how blissed out Ruthie had looked, standing with her daughter and granddaughter. He especially didn't ask exactly why Maddy wanted to see Adey, because there were too many potential answers and some of them, he didn't want to hear.

As for whether she'd noticed that there were apparently no more familial sides to be taken . . . now was *not* the time. She was dealing with something else.

They made OK time past Birmingham. The traffic became lighter as the evening wore on and they continued south and west. Maddy received a text and bent over her

262

phone, her plait lying over one shoulder. 'Ffion and Chloe have been to fetch their things and are back in Nelson's Bar. They're taking Ruthie to the Duke for fish and chips. I'll just remind them not to tell anyone where I'm going.' Not long after, she reported another text, from Heloise this time. 'Lyla's asleep in bed. So's the dog, who's called Bozo, and Heloise has treated herself to a glass of wine.'

Near Bristol, they took a break at a service station, visiting the loos, buying sandwiches and hot drinks in carry-out cups. Raff refilled his petrol tank before they rejoined the mesmerising flow of headlights.

In Devon, the roads became busy again, until the long stretch of the A30 to Bodmin, which was quieter. As they drew nearer their destination, Maddy sank into her thoughts once more.

Finally, nearer one a.m. than midnight, they found the B&B in Truro, parking on one side of an expansive tarmac drive and tottering on stiff legs around the back of the house, motion-sensitive lights flicking on at their approach. They found the key safe at a door as promised, retrieved the key and entered directly into a large room with two beds and a sofa.

Maddy inspected it tiredly. 'Looks as if it might have been a granny annexe, doesn't it, with the little kitchenette thing.' There was also a wet room leading off the main room.

A further door was firmly shut, and Raff read out the notice stuck to it. 'Welcome! Breakfast between seven-thirty and ten through this door. Grateful if you'd remain in your own comfy room till then. Tea, coffee and biscuits near your kettle.' The writer of the note had drawn a smiley face.

Maddy asked, 'Which bed do you want?'

'This will do.' With studied casualness he tossed his bag on the bed nearest the bathroom. He didn't want to risk stumbling into her bed if he had to get up during the night. OK, he did want to, because not only was he screaming to have her body against his again, but he wanted more than anything to soothe away that shuttered, shattered look on her face. But that same shuttered look kept him at a distance, because if ever a woman looked as if she needed space to think, it was Maddy Cracey.

Maddy Cracey Austen, he reminded himself. Maddy Cracey *Austen*.

After they'd each used the bathroom and then turned out the lights, he did find sleep. But it took a long time to come, and it didn't last long.

Chapter Nineteen

It felt surreal to awake in a strange room and realise that Raff was only a few feet away. For a second, Maddy fantasised about slipping from her bed and into his, cuddling up to his strength and letting desire wash her away from real life. But she realised how ill-advised it would be, in these crazy circumstances.

When she reached for her phone to check the time, Raff's head turned. 'It's nearly eight,' he said. 'I just looked.' His voice was flat and gravelly.

She rubbed her eyes. 'Better get breakfast. The hospital's website said visiting is ten a.m. to eight p.m.' It was even more surreal to say something so commonplace when here they were sharing a room but not a bed. She felt as if the memory of their lovemaking was being projected onto the ceiling for them both to watch.

'Yes, and I'm hungry,' he said, politely. 'You can use the bathroom first.'

From him it seemed like a courtesy, but she was hit by the memory of Adey saying that kind of thing when he just wanted another few minutes in bed. *Adey*. She knew he was alive, after all this time. No longer could she think, 'if ever Adey turns up', because she knew where he was. Of course, she was *glad* he was alive, but panic skittered up her spine like a rat, and she shivered. When she confronted him in a couple of hours, would she remember the loving Adey he'd once been? Or the one who'd left her to sink or swim?

She hurried through a shower, having taken her overnight bag in the bathroom with her for clean undies and top. Then, while Raff was in the bathroom, she called Lyla who, reassuringly, only wanted to talk about the dog Heloise was looking after. 'Do you know that Bozo is another word for stupid?' she gurgled excitedly. 'So, we can go out with him and shout, "Bozo, Bozo!" and it's like shouting "idiot!" We can't have a pet, can we, because of Grauntie Ruthie's asthma?'

Maddy laughed at Bozo's name and agreed that furry things were bad for Ruthie, all the time wondering what life held in store for Lyla after Maddy had faced Adey in his hospital bed.

After the call, Raff emerged from the bathroom and they stepped through the green door into the main house, finding themselves in a small, neat room with a table covered in a pink cloth. A round-faced woman appeared a few seconds after the door closed behind them. 'Morning, welcome! I'm Ina. Glad you got here OK. Always a bit odd when someone books online late at night. Usually, it's someone for the hospital, being as we're so close.' She had a pleasant sing-song voice and a mellifluous Cornish accent.

'That's right,' said Raff, politely but without offering details.

The woman beamed. Her hair was too dark for her

pale complexion and done in a doughnut-shaped bun. 'Do sit down. Tea? Coffee? Full English or something lighter?'

Raff chose the full English. Maddy thought men must be genetically wired never to turn one down and as he cleared his plate of eggs, bacon, sausage, beans, tomato and mushrooms, she toyed with scrambled egg on toast. Knowing she'd only eaten half a sandwich last night, she forced some of it down, but enjoyed the piping hot coffee more.

They talked desultorily about the breakfast, like people who had nothing to say to each other when Maddy supposed they had *a lot*.

But Lyla was Maddy's priority. If anyone had asked her a few days ago, she would have declared Lyla to be adjusted to her circumstances and that just as she knew furry pets weren't part of her family, she knew that neither was a dad.

Until Lyla's haunting question about her daddy finding her one day . . .

That had been hard to hear, especially when Ruthie and Ffion had just been looking as if finding each other was like a win on the lottery.

Life was never easy – hers, anyway – but Adey being found alive and kicking almost exactly seven years since he'd vanished was going to be especially hard.

Those moments when she'd thought that Ruthie and Ffion reuniting solved everything between her and Raff had been short and sweet. In fact, almost too short to be sweet.

Ina returned with more toast and little pots of things to spread on it. When she spied a tub of Nutella amongst the jam and marmalade, Maddy found herself suddenly missing Lyla. Hot-eyed, she swiped the tub to take home to her.

If Raff noticed, he didn't comment.

An hour later, they drove to the hospital. Raff found a parking space, and Maddy fought the almost paralysing knowledge that she'd be fronting up to Adey in a matter of minutes. She cleared her throat. 'You could wait at the B&B, if you want. I don't know how long I'll be.'

His smile held a hint of incredulity. 'I'd rather know you're OK.' He indicated his bag on the back seat. 'I have my laptop. I'll find a waiting room and work.'

She managed a smile. 'Aren't authors meant to write in coffee shops?'

His smile fleeted again. 'That's also an option.'

Inside the hospital, they found their way to the ward. Outside of the double doors was a row of chairs. Raff pointed at them. 'I'll be here if you want me.'

She swallowed. 'Thanks.' In a dream, she pressed the button to gain admittance to the ward and was soon being directed by someone in uniform, like any other visitor. Adey was in a room of his own.

Maddy marked off the bays until she reached the designated door, heart pumping so hard she could scarcely see. She paused in the entrance.

A man was seated in a big carrot-coloured chair beside the bed, his leg elevated before him and encased in plaster. The fair hair was right, the colour Adey had bequeathed to Lyla, but it was long and unstyled. This didn't look much like the Adey who'd driven into King's Lynn every five weeks to have his hair cut at a salon.

His head was bent over a magazine. Until the moment when he licked his thumb before turning a page, she harboured a secret hope that it wasn't him, removing

268

obstacles from Maddy's path and sweeping aside the necessity for tricky decisions. Perhaps the person in the hospital would have stolen Adey's identity, or simply shared the same name.

But that old habit of licking his thumb . . .

As if sensing her scrutiny, he looked up. Their eyes clashed, his eyes grey and surprised. Then shocked.

It was really him. Maddy pulled composure around her like a force field and stepped closer. 'Hello, Adey. Long time, no see.'

Judging from the colour draining from his face, Adey had not been told she was on her way. His mouth moved silently, like a fish making bubbles.

Scared her legs wouldn't hold her for much longer, she made a show of perching on the side of the bed as if giving him notice that she was in no hurry to leave, her manner studiedly casual. 'Catch me up on what's been happening with you.' Her mouth was dry and her heart thudding, but she manufactured a faux-sweet smile.

'Maddy,' he said, as if he was having trouble believing it.

'Me,' she agreed equably.

Shock and chagrin argued for supremacy in his face. He cleared his throat. 'I don't know what to say.' The blood had returned to his cheeks now, colouring them dull red.

She crooked a leg and propped her elbow on it. 'Well, you can begin: "One snowy night, I raged out of High Cottage. My wife was furious because the house had flooded, and I'd let the insurance lapse. I met Harris, and ranted to him about how shitty my life was, and then . . ."' She made a cycling motion with her hand. 'You take it from there.'

269

Slowly, he reached for a glass of water. 'It seems so long ago.'

'Seven years?' she suggested softly.

He sipped the drink, replaced the glass, then dropped his head. 'I suppose I had some kind of breakdown.'

She was willing to entertain the possibility, but not without question. 'Mental illness has a lot to do with people choosing to leave their life. Others are running from responsibility. I expect the truth is often somewhere between those two.' She wished she'd brought a bottle of water, because her throat felt as though it was coated in sand. The days when she might have sneaked a sip from Adey's beaker were long gone. 'You didn't care you were leaving me in the shit?'

'I cared.' His eyes slid away from hers. 'Just . . . maybe not enough to stop me.'

'Maybe?' She let her chin rest on her fist.

He blew out a sigh, lips curling resignedly. 'I didn't want to face reality,' he admitted. 'I was in a panic. Overwhelmed. I just started walking. I walked out of the village and along the main road to Hunstanton. It was snowing, but I had my ski jacket.'

'That's right. You grabbed it before you ran,' she remembered aloud. 'It was red. You bought it for snowboarding in Bulgaria.'

His quick glance was surprised. 'You remember a lot.'

'I had to describe it to the police.'

Another sip of water, and again the delaying tactic of returning the glass to the bedside locker. 'I decided to hitch.'

'Where?' she asked.

'Anywhere. Out of the mess.' He sank back into the big chair. Its covering was vinyl and it squeaked as if

270

making a doubtful sound. 'This guy in a truck stopped. He had a pile of scrap in the back. I got in the cab, and he headed inland. He asked where I was going, and I said I hadn't made up my mind. It was like a dream, or like one of those rites of passage movies where a teenager hits the road and has an adventure.'

'You weren't a teenager,' she observed, then made herself stop. All the wondering and not knowing of the past seven years coalesced in this meeting and she didn't want him to clam up.

He gave her a pained smile. 'The guy's name was Vano. He was touring the area, picking up scrap. He was going to fetch a caravan from somewhere and tow it down to Cornwall. He had this phrase he kept saying: "Don't tell me and then I won't know." It was like he was giving me permission to do as I wanted, so I said Cornwall sounded good, but I didn't have more than a few quid on me, apart from my phone. He said the cost of the trip would be one phone, plus me helping him load and unload. He threw the phone's SIM card out the window.'

So, that was why the police had never traced it. Maddy held back from saying so, still worried about spooking him.

He went on. 'We picked up the caravan. After four days of buying and selling—' he paused and rubbed his nose '—I got the idea the caravan was nicked, and he was going to Cornwall to unload it. Vano turned out to have a whole network of contacts. In Cornwall, he introduced me to Pat, a guy who supplied labour to farms on an informal basis.'

'Not bothering the tax authorities,' she guessed, as that, too made perfect sense with Adey being able to drop out of sight. She made sure her voice was intrigued rather than judgemental.

He nodded. 'Pat knew someone who let out rooms—'

'Equally informally?' she suggested.

He nodded. 'Cash only. After a few jobs, I ended up working on a farm and I got a room there. The farmer was a woman called Gina. Eventually, we began a relationship. After a good while, though,' he added hastily, as if realising belatedly that this was *his wife* he was talking to. Another of those dull red flushes. 'Sorry,' he added sheepishly. 'But by then it seemed too late to go home.'

'Right,' she said, neutrally. 'And there was never a payphone handy to let me know you were alive? Or even ask how I was coping with being up Shit Creek without a husband?'

'Sorry,' he mumbled again. 'I realise I was an arse. But when everything gets on top of you . . . well, you're not rational are you?'

'Evidently you weren't,' she agreed, without rancour. 'I usually am. I take it Gina was not exactly one to play by the rules, if she not only employed "informal" labour but lived with one of them?'

A slow smile crept across his face. 'Some people might call her anti-authority,' he conceded. 'She's a good woman. Strong and capable. She says it suits her that I don't exist, and she's never cared why I was living under the radar, because the fact that I am would make it tricky to make any claim on her or the farm if the relationship fails. She's legit, and ultra-keen on keeping the farm in her hands. She's great,' he added, as if Maddy wasn't getting from his admiring tone that he held this rule-breaking woman in deep affection.

Curiously, she didn't mind. Didn't care, in fact. She felt no warmth or rekindling affection for the man sitting before her and it was a relief. A growing anger, yes; a resentment mingled with a need to know the facts; but no love. She neither liked nor disliked him. It was very strange.

'If anyone ever asked my surname, we said Smith,' he went on, looking more relaxed as he got in his stride. 'Everything's in Gina's name. I was driving one of her cars when I had the smash.'

Maddy registered this. '*One* of her cars? It sounds as if the attraction is that Gina has money and Adey has zero responsibility.' Adey's girlfriend being wealthy explained why he'd got a single hospital room, she supposed.

He hunched a defensive shoulder and didn't dignify this snark with a response. 'I was dazed when they got me out of the car, and I gave my real name. But I'm uninsured, obviously, so the cops stuck their noses in. I expect I'll get a fine and a load of grief. They'll tell the taxman and everything.' Then he brightened. 'Still, if I officially exist again, I'll be able to renew my passport and have holidays abroad. Gina's been going without me.'

Maddy bit back an urge to say, 'Aw, you poor guy,' in tones of mock sympathy. She hadn't been able to afford holidays abroad herself.

A silence fell. Maddy's mind worked furiously, prioritising what she wanted to know and what she needed to know. Though it was tempting to demand contact details in case he was spirited away from hospital before she'd finished with him, she discarded the idea as unworkable. He'd come up with a 'Smith Farm, Smith Street, Smithsville' form of reply, not worth the breath he used on it.

Playing for time, she resettled herself on the bed,

wedging her bottom against the bedrail. 'I'm intrigued about the texts I've been getting. You know about them, I take it? They've got to be from someone close to you, because they used your old ILU sign-off, which not many people would know. I'm beginning to believe Harris when he says it wasn't him, because he wouldn't have been able to resist letting me know that he knew where you were when I didn't. It must have been your parents.'

He rolled his eyes. 'I told Mum not to.'

Anger coiled inside her like a snake. Those texts had been causing her stress, and not only had it been her mother-in-law responsible, but she'd also listened to Maddy's conjecture about whether they were genuinely from Adey without a hint of sheepishness or guilt. After a couple of deep breaths, she managed, 'Why did she do it?'

He shrugged, turning his gaze to the door as if hoping someone would come through it to rescue him. 'You know what she's like about money. She kept going on about keeping my options open, in case.'

'In case . . . ?' Maddy let her question hang.

He waggled his head in a 'you know what I mean' gesture. 'Half of the house is still mine. She thought I ought to claim it. She said that after seven years you could have me presumed dead, and then it would be harder.'

She let her head nod slowly, when actually she felt like screaming in outrage. *Your mum said she never heard from you. Both your parents left me to drown in financial shit.* Aloud, she mused, 'Half the debts are yours, too.' She deliberately didn't say 'were'.

With a shrug, as if the debts were a minor detail despite their dire finances having apparently been enough to make him have 'some kind of breakdown', he eased his plastered leg. Probably he thought she'd ease up on him.

She didn't. 'You've been in touch with your parents all along, I take it?'

He cast down his eyes. 'Since a couple of weeks after . . . Sorry.'

She wasn't sure whether he genuinely was sorry that he'd wanted to let them know he was OK and keep up their relationship but had left Maddy in limbo. It mattered less and less, because it was evident that their worsening relationship had allowed him to be OK with abandoning her to their sinking ship while he scrambled to safety. And she'd always suspected it, which painted a stark picture of the death of their love. She chose her next subject. 'Harris says he never heard from you.'

Regret entered his expression. 'No. He was a casualty of the situation, but I missed him.'

You shit. You bastard, she seethed inwardly. Nobody had been a bigger casualty of 'the situation' than she had – unless it was Lyla – but apart from uttering 'sorry' casually, he hadn't acknowledged it.

A nurse in dark blue bustled on a waft of air from the corridor. 'Sorry to interrupt. These nice people are here to see you, Adey.' She beckoned in two police officers, one male, one female.

'Oh,' said Adey. 'S'pose it's about the accident.'

The female police officer smiled. 'That will come. We're here at the request of Norfolk police.'

Maddy made a lightning decision not to get involved. She had nothing to hide but could only imagine that explaining who she was would be harder than wafting away, and she already knew that the police would be obliged to close a case that had been hanging around for years. Coolly, she said, 'This is obviously private. I'll come back later.' She slipped out and managed to catch up with the nurse outside. 'I don't suppose he'll be discharged today?' She made her voice regretful, as if there was nothing she'd like better.

''Fraid not,' the nurse confirmed with a professional smile.

Great. She could relax for now. 'OK. Thanks.' Maddy walked steadily away from Adey's room and out of the ward to where Raff – decent, normal bloke that he was – tapped on a laptop balanced on his knees.

He glanced up and, despite the impossible craziness of what she was up to her neck in, he had a warm, reassuring smile for her. 'I don't think I can be a real author because I didn't say "just got to finish this thought or I'll lose it" before I stopped writing. But I did find a café.'

She laughed, then watched as he packed his laptop into its bag. They traversed the long corridors, following the smell of coffee to a warm, busy area where tables huddled together around a glass-fronted counter filled with sandwiches and cake. Maddy chose a brownie to go with her coffee, not feeling a need for much food, but Raff bought a filled roll along with his Bakewell tart.

Over a surprisingly relaxed snack, she poured out everything she'd learnt. He listened without commenting, although his facial expressions flitted from interest to blank surprise, with an occasional glower.

Pouring it all out brought back her appetite, and she ate a toastie, too.

When they'd whiled away a couple of hours to let the police get well clear, they made their way back to the ward. This time, Maddy took a bottle of water. Raff returned to the seats with his laptop. He was so kind and understanding. She wanted to take his hand and ask, *Is there a future for us, do you think?* How she wished . . .

But she couldn't grant herself wishes. She had others to think of and decide what to do with a husband she didn't want.

Chapter Twenty

Once back outside the private room, Maddy wondered what she'd do if Adey had flown the nest in her absence. The nurse had been confident that he wouldn't be discharged today, but what if he'd discharged himself? All it would take was help, a wheelchair and a suitable vehicle. She'd be left high and dry all over again. By the time she opened the door she felt sick and panicky.

But not only was he there, half-lying atop the bedclothes, but a woman was seated in the chair he'd vacated.

Slowly, Maddy entered, mind working on this new development. Adey regarded her as she approached. When she stood at the foot of the bed, gazing at the seated woman, he said, 'This is Gina. I've just been telling her about you.'

The woman rose and for a moment Maddy wondered if she was going to meet aggression. Gina was Amazonian, tall and curvy. Some of her black hair was slipping from a careless bun on the back of her head and her black leather jacket was matched by high-heeled leather boots. Her imposing figure was matched by the intensity of her considering stare. Maddy mentally prepared to stand her ground if necessary, glad the door stood open so there might be witnesses if things got scary.

But Gina only stuck out a hand. 'Seems we have a mutual friend.' She cocked her head in Adey's direction, and he sent her a naughty-boy smile. 'I might as well be honest,' she went on. 'He never told me about his past and I never asked.' There was no Cornish in her accent. More Sussex. 'But now there's stuff to sort out. We've been talking about what it's best for Adey to do.'

Maddy shook hands, regarding Gina thoughtfully, wondering how much influence she had over Adey and how much Maddy wanted her to have. She'd intended to tell Adey about Lyla, but now she paused. She knew nothing about Gina, but she *looked* tough and no-nonsense. She was in Adey's life. How much did Maddy want her in Lyla's? On the journey down, while Raff drove, she'd had time to think, to evolve scenarios. She'd considered Adey visiting Lyla. But what if one day he wanted Lyla to visit him? Adey couldn't exactly be relied upon to stay where he was meant to be.

Shit. How had it not occurred to her that he might have a woman in his life, too?

Unexpectedly, Gina laid a solicitous hand on her arm. 'You all right, love? Sit down. Adey's been a rat. I don't blame you for looking sour.'

Maddy sat. Gina towered over her.

Adey must have caught discomfort on her face. 'Gina's legit, Maddy,' he said encouragingly. When he'd used the term before, Maddy had assumed he meant Gina paid her taxes and appeared on the voters' roll, and that now his world was divided into those who were legit and those who were under the radar. But maybe he'd meant Gina had a genuine nature.

Gina backed up to perch on the side of the bed, beside Adey's good leg. 'Look,' she said briskly. 'Adey wants to come to a financial arrangement. He understands that old debts have to be considered, but a cottage overlooking the sea – there must be something coming to him.' She looked expectant, as if Maddy would whip out a statement of account for the last seven years.

In a heartbeat, Maddy's mood flicked from fear to anger.

Damn it, Adey was sitting back and letting Gina take the lead, a smile tugging at his lips, as if this was what he was used to – Gina calling the shots, Gina protecting Adey and making his life easy. Just like Maddy used to make Adey's life easy, by leaving him to be an irresponsible charmer while she attended to all the financial worrying and making do. It was just what she'd been afraid of – Adey claiming some of what he'd abandoned when things got tough. There was a 'do your worst' cockiness about his manner. Maddy was a blast from the past, but most people had an ex or two. He hadn't known she'd turn up, but once she had . . . well, he might as well try and get a few quid out of the marital home.

Maddy and Adey had set out with hopes and dreams like any other couple, but what sprang into focus was the realisation of what Adey Austen really was. A marshmallow, with a thin veneer on the outside but soft and weak on the inside. And that took her back to wondering whether she wanted this man in her daughter's life.

But then a vision swam into Maddy's mind of Lyla asking about her daddy.

Shit.

Her thoughts raced. Could she pretend to her daughter

that her daddy had never been found . . . ? No. When Lyla was older, she might even trace her father. Lyla would realise Maddy had lied, and hate her.

She'd spent so much of the last years living with uncertainty, she refused to spend the rest of her life in fear of the truth.

It was going to come out now.

Before either of the others could speak again, she leapt in. 'There's nothing to come to you from the house, Adey, because you owe me over six years' child support for our daughter.'

Gina swung on him, her expression stony. '*What?*'

Adey paled, leaving his few freckles standing out. 'Our daughter?' he asked Maddy blankly.

Maddy eased back in the chair, feeling weak from an adrenalin rush. 'I was pregnant when you left.'

Even Adey's lips were white. His eyes beseeched Gina. 'I swear I didn't know.'

If anything, Gina looked grimmer. 'Really?' she drawled. Then her voice dropped to a growl. 'If you abandoned your kid—! You know my father dumped my mum. I won't have anything to do with blokes like that.'

'I didn't. I didn't know. Honestly. It's a complete shock.' For the first time he appeared truly rattled, looking imploringly at Maddy, as if waiting for her to chirp up in support.

Maddy, taking the time to study the dynamics of their relationship, said nothing until Gina too turned a questioning gaze her way. Still she let seconds tick past. Then, finally, she agreed. 'I hadn't told him. I was worried he'd put pressure on me to abort because of our awful money situation.'

Gina's mouth set in a hard line.

281

Adey's denial was immediate and vehement. 'I wouldn't have. Never.' But the protest was weakened when he added, 'I knew you wanted a kid sometime, Maddy. To be honest, though, being a dad wouldn't fit well into my life.'

Maddy sighed, and in an echo of Gina's words just moments ago, murmured, 'And *I* had a dad like *that*, who left and hardly bothers with me.' She'd lived her life with the hurt that both parents treated her more like friendly acquaintances than beloved family, and she had strained every nerve to give Lyla the opposite.

She'd considered her life tricky when Adey was missing, but now she was beginning to wish he'd never been found.

But, with Gina looking forbidding and Adey visibly shocked and miserable, she had no choice but to turn to the practicalities of securing the life she'd made for herself and her little girl. 'Let's go claim for claim. You sign the house over to me, and I won't ask for child support.'

Instantly, Gina arched one eyebrow at Adey in the universal 'not a bad deal' look.

Adey raised a confirmatory eyebrow back, swiftly saying to Maddy, 'OK. Seems fair. We'll do it via solicitors.'

Really? Suddenly he'd found a use for formality in his life? But Maddy hadn't finished expanding on the deal. 'And then we get divorced.'

'Right.' Adey gave a shrug and a nod.

Surreally, Gina put in some financial advice. 'In the next tax year, or you'll have to pay tax on the half of the house he gives you.'

'Thanks,' Maddy said, trying to get her head around Gina's forceful personality that prompted her to show support for Adey then Maddy, Adey then Maddy, depending what precisely was under discussion. Maddy turned back to Adey. 'I want to tell Lyla you exist, though.'

On this, Adey and Gina seemed united, if their matching dubious expressions were anything to go by.

Maddy leant forward. 'I can't make you, Adey,' she said earnestly. 'But Lyla knows she has a father somewhere. She's started asking about you and it's quite . . . heart-wrenching.' Her voice quavered. 'It was one thing when I could look her in the eye and say that I didn't know where you were, but now it's different. I accept that I don't have your actual address,' she stuck in as Adey opened his mouth to speak. 'But as I know Gina's got a farm, it wouldn't take long to track you down. I'm only interested in what's best for Lyla and how she'll feel to know she has a daddy somewhere who never comes to see her.'

As Maddy had hoped, Gina responded to this trigger, frowning disapprovingly at Adey.

He shifted uneasily under her regard and fiddled with the hem of his T-shirt. 'I don't know. It's all a bit of a mess.'

'Lyla's not a *mess*,' Maddy snapped. 'She's a lovely little girl who's excited about Santa but won't ask for the biggest presents because she knows that we don't have much money. She's considerate of my great-aunt, who we live with because I had to let out High Cottage or have it repossessed.' Then, in fresh outrage, added, 'You're the mess, not her. And your parents are a mess so I'm in no hurry for them to know about her. They dumped me just like you did. I could have starved for all you lot cared – the weak reed and two grasping old grouches.'

Gina regarded her half-admiringly. 'So . . . why do you want Adey to meet your girl?'

Maddy closed her eyes in frustration. 'Because I care about Lyla. She doesn't understand what he is and what he's done. She just wants a daddy like her friends have.' Tears prickled beneath her lids.

The hush could be felt.

Maddy heard Gina say, 'You better tie up your loose ends, Adey.'

Without opening her eyes, Maddy snapped, 'Lyla isn't a loose end, either. She's a darling little girl.' The hot tears began to ooze out onto her cheeks. 'You don't deserve her, Adey, and she doesn't deserve you, but you need to man up and do your best.'

He sighed.

Gina said, 'She's got a point.'

Adey murmured, 'Fuck it.'

Gina answered, 'No. Face it.'

Maddy felt something touch her knee and her eyes flew open. Gina had slipped off the bed and, apparently, prodded her to get her attention. 'Can you drive?' she demanded in a business-like way. 'Good. When he's discharged, I'll get you on the insurance for my camper van and you can drive him to Norfolk to meet your girl. I'll come and fetch him after a couple of days. I can't leave the farm for longer than that.' She frowned at Adey again. 'I'm already short-handed with Adey crocked.'

Adey looked abashed.

Maddy stared, wondering at this strange relationship where Adey acted up and Gina treated him like a naughty boy. Maybe what he'd been looking for all along was a generous version of his mother. Still, Maddy had got what she wanted – or what Lyla wanted, which came down to the same thing. What would happen if Lyla fell in love with her father and wanted to see him regularly, and perhaps his unlovely parents, too, was another battle. For now, Maddy would look no further than winning this one.

She hauled herself to her feet and addressed Gina. 'Thanks for your help and input. It's a tricky situation for you.'

Gina shrugged this off. 'I can cope with most things.'

Maddy laughed. 'I don't doubt it.'

They exchanged phone numbers and Maddy left Adey's room lighter of step and strangely exhilarated by her triumph. It had been a mad day, dealing with a wild situation, but she'd loosened the knots around her problems financial and parental. It painted a stupid grin on her face.

She was still beaming when she arrived back in the corridor and found Raff wrinkling his nose at the screen of his computer, as if not liking what he saw there.

'I'm so sorry that you've been stuck out here half the day,' she said. She might still be amused by the clown show she'd left in Adey's room, but it wasn't fair to lean on Raff now she had the situation under control. Though, when he saw her, he snapped shut the laptop balanced on his knees, for perhaps the first time she glimpsed what it meant to be on a deadline, and that no one else could do your work even when your attention was elsewhere. How uncomfortable the hours must have been on a plastic chair. Impulsively, she took his hand. 'I think you should go home. I'm staying for a day or two before I bring Adey home to meet Lyla.'

Raff jerked back, freeing his hand and lurching to his feet. 'Oh,' he said, sounding unbalanced. Then his dark brows snapped down over his blue eyes. 'I understand.' He shoved his laptop into its bag and slung it on his shoulder.

'Raff,' she began, taken aback at the speed with which he turned away.

He waved an impatient hand. 'No thanks necessary.

Glad to help. Anyone would be.' Then he turned his back on her and strode away, weaving between people and trolleys in the corridor.

'Raff!' Too late, Maddy realised she'd presented the situation clumsily. She started after him, intending to explain that Adey was visiting Nelson's Bar under protest, and mostly because his girlfriend was making it hard for him to dodge his responsibilities.

But . . . but . . . Her feet faltered and stopped.

There was an ocean of other unresolved questions between them, and she couldn't answer all her own questions, let alone his. She had to deal with Lyla and had no idea when she'd have time for Raff.

She should let him go.

To his retreating figure she whispered, 'I think you're overestimating what "anyone" would do.'

She watched him till he was out of sight, aware that others occupying the seats were watching the scene as if it were a soap opera.

Maybe it was.

Since the night Adey had vanished into the blizzard, her life had borne all the hallmarks of the worst, most sensationalised and unbelievable of soap operas. But, unfortunately, that's what she had to deal with.

And so she would.

Chapter Twenty-One

It was one week until Christmas and the afternoon was darkening as Maddy drove the blue camper van cautiously up Long Climb. Her headlights illuminated grey tracks in a field of white, where earlier vehicles had passed in fresh snow. If she ventured outside of the tracks the surface proved treacherous, where icicles were falling from the trees.

'Whoops,' she gasped, as the tyres skidded before finding grip.

From his place in the back, his plastered leg laid along a bench seat, Adey sucked in a breath. 'I haven't even seen snow since I left,' he groused.

Maddy had had hours and hours of Adey's grumbles. She'd also had hours of wearing hat, coat and gloves as she drove, because the ancient camper's heaters were useless; hours of traffic jams; and hours of sleet. As they'd climbed Long Climb, the sleet had changed to snow, to Adey's evident displeasure.

Loudly, she called back, 'You could be a better travel companion, you know.' As Raff had been. She was trying to concentrate on the delicate matter of introducing Lyla to her father, but Raff kept intruding into her thoughts – smiling his sexy smile or, as she'd last seen him, hurt and angry. Grief, as cold as the ice clinging to the pine trees, formed in Maddy's stomach whenever she thought of Raff, and his bleak, hurt, shocked expression as he'd turned away from her at the hospital.

Since then, silence. As she'd twiddled her thumbs all day Sunday while Gina, Tilly and Gwyllm visited Adey, she'd had plenty of time to think about him. Her message, I hope that you and I can talk when I get home Xx had earned no reply, discouraging her from following up with a call. Over and over, she'd rerun their last conversation. Despite the resolve not to hurry after him down that busy hospital corridor, an entire day to reflect had made her realise that, yes, she had to concentrate on Lyla for now. But after that . . . ? She should have made it crystal, crystal clear, that Adey's return to Nelson's Bar was temporary and strictly for Lyla's sake. She should have told him Adey had agreed to divorce.

After much toing and froing, she'd decided that when she had firm news, like, 'We've agreed that Adey will see Lyla once every couple of months,' which is what she thought might be vaguely acceptable to everyone concerned, *then* she could go to Raff's house in Docking and see if they might be able to work their way back to what had once been promising beginnings. Till then, she'd leave the ball in his court.

Finally, the camper crested Long Climb and the road levelled out. Maddy slowed to enjoy skeins of silvery lights twinkling amongst the bare branches of an oak, red and green illuminations dangling from lampposts and light-bedecked Christmas trees glittering in gardens full of snow. She was home.

Her heart kicked up. The end of this journey was only the beginning of a new one, because no one knew Adey was with her. Whenever she thought of telling someone, it had been trumped by a compelling reason not to.

Ruthie might begin to wheeze and only Della would be with her because she'd agreed to join Ruthie for lunch and then spend the afternoon. Ffion, once she knew Maddy would arrive today, had wanted to drop Chloe at school in time for Ffion to sign in on her computer in her office at home. Maddy had left on Friday evening and today was only Monday, but she felt as if she'd been away much longer. Luckily Ruthie, from her phone calls, had loved spending time with Ffion and Chloe.

Heloise had taken Lyla to and from the school minibus, so Lyla would be waiting with Della and Ruthie at The Hollies.

Once Adey had received the information that Heloise was seeing Harris, he'd made it plain that he didn't want Harris to know he was coming. Maddy wasn't sure whether he expected to be a nice surprise or to sneak in and out of the village without explaining seven years of silence to his old friend. She suspected it was the latter. On reflection, though, she decided not to tell any of them that Adey was with her. As with Lyla, she felt more equal to the task of providing explanations face-to-face than over the phone.

She indicated right into Jubilee Crescent where a line of icicle lights hung across the road, twinkling gently. Entering the final stretch seemed to shock Adey out of his plaintive silence. Sounding panicked, he muttered, 'What are we going to say?'

Maddy slowed the van to a crawl because Jubilee Crescent saw much less traffic than Long Climb or Droody

Road and was like a skid pan. 'Who you are, I suppose.' Maddy sighed. 'It was wanting to do the best for Lyla that made me push for this meeting, so I'll introduce you. It wasn't the kind of news I wanted to give such a little girl over the phone.' Maddy had no idea what to hope for, except for Lyla not to get hurt.

The camper arrived outside The Hollies in an ungainly whoosh of slipping wheels, bouncing off the kerb. Adey swore. 'Sorry if it jarred your leg,' Maddy said. 'The snow's banked and I misjudged the road edge.' For several seconds they sat, snowflakes drifting, weaving and veering around the van. It was like a reverse snow globe, Maddy thought inconsequentially. Sitting behind glass, looking out at a world of snow.

Then a movement caught her eye and she saw the door to The Hollies open, light streaming yellowish along the snowy path. Lyla stood on the threshold, balancing on one leg, trying to force the other foot into an octopus boot. Della was huddling into her flowery cardigan and trying to restrain her.

'Here we go,' Maddy murmured, more to herself than Adey. Then, assuming her mummy-smile, she opened the camper's door with a loud squeak, lowered herself carefully into the snow, then tramped gingerly around the front of the vehicle and onto the path. 'Hiya! Just stay there, Lyla. I'm coming in, and I have a surprise for you,' she called brightly.

Lyla stopped fighting her boot. 'Why are you driving that van? Have you seen the snow?' *Erm, yes.* 'You've been gone ages. I walked Bozo three times, and we kept calling in to check on Grauntie Ruthie, and Chloe played cards with me. I like Chloe. Heloise has brought me back now and Della's here. The snow didn't start till lunchtime, so we stayed at school, but if it's snowy again tomorrow school will be closed.'

Maddy crunched up the path and swept Lyla up, disrupting the news bulletin as she stepped into the square hall. 'Hello, Della,' she said to the sweetly smiling woman. Then as Ruthie felt her way out of the front room, her usual beaming smile at the ready, 'Let me shut the door, Lyla. Poor Grauntie Ruthie will freeze.'

She exchanged one-armed hugs with Ruthie and Della, Lyla still clinging to her like a monkey. After checking with Ruthie that she'd had her inhaler quite recently, with a deep breath she turned back to her daughter. 'Now, I'm popping outdoors to get your surprise. Stay here like a good girl because I'm bringing someone special to meet you.'

Lyla's eyes grew big and round. 'Santa Claus,' she breathed.

Her childish vision of a mystery visitor made Maddy burst out laughing. 'You'll have to wait and see.'

She returned into the cold, heart thudding. Adey's face at the window was the picture of apprehension. At Maddy's approach, he rumbled open the sliding door and swung his plastered leg off the seat.

Wordlessly, she reached in and hefted his overnight bag, which Gina had brought to the hospital, then steadied his arm as he edged onto the step, checking how his crutches gripped in the snow before putting weight on them. The leg of his jogging pants had been slit to accommodate the plaster, and a thick blue sock stretched over his protruding toes. He made his way up the path, one gingerly hop at a time.

At last, they stood together outside the door. Maddy met his gaze and read nervous curiosity. Then she reached out and opened the door and let him hop over the doorstep.

In the hall, Della gaped. 'Well, damn me.'

Ruthie frowned, obviously unable to make out details. 'Is it Raff?' she asked uncertainly.

Lyla looked blank.

And Adey looked down at Lyla, eyebrows half lifted in a way that could have signalled surprise or dismay or half a dozen other emotions. Then his tentative smile bloomed into a wide grin.

'Who are you?' Lyla demanded. 'I wanted Santa Claus.'

Maddy knelt beside her, discarding her hat and gloves. 'Sweetie,' she said gently, gathering Lyla into a hug. 'This is who I went to help because he had an accident. It's your daddy.'

Ruthie spluttered, 'Hellfire.'

Lyla looked Adey up and down. 'But he's broken.'

Adey laughed. 'Only my leg is. The rest's fine and my leg will get better.'

Lyla looked at Maddy and her eyes filled with tears. 'He doesn't look like his picture,' she whispered, and Maddy's heart ached as her little girl buried her head against her coat and began to cry.

Adey's smile faded.

Maddy hugged Lyla to her. 'It's OK, that you don't recognise him. People change as time goes by. His hair's different, isn't it? You don't need to cry. He wanted to meet you.' A horrible, sick dread began to well. Had she done the wrong thing by taking the words of a small child as a mission to bring her daddy to Nelson's Bar? She could have said goodbye to Adey and Gina in Cornwall, quietly divorced Adey and let the future take care of itself. She'd considered coming home to speak to Lyla and then arranging a meeting, but had been dogged by the idea that she needed to get Adey to this meeting before he could have second thoughts, or even vanish again.

Ruthie broke in cheerfully. 'Not quite as good as Santa Claus, but exciting, eh, Lyla? Mummy and Daddy have come a long way today, so we need to let them take off their coats and come and sit by the fire. You can show Daddy our Christmas tree.'

''K.' Lyla sniffed, not looking at Adey as she let Maddy take her hand and usher her into the front room.

Della prepared to slip away, refusing to hear of Maddy walking her home. 'I bought grips that fit over my boots, so I won't fall. You stay with Lyla and . . . everyone.' She pulled on her coat, which humped over her bum rather than fitting around it, and made her escape.

Ruthie took her usual armchair, Maddy wriggled out of her coat and sat in the other chair with Lyla on her lap, and Adey took the sofa, propping his crutches beside him. 'Hello, Ruthie,' he said tentatively.

'Hello,' she said, with a small smile. 'Fancy seeing you here.'

He blinked at this mild irony, then gave Lyla a tentative smile. 'I haven't come to worry you. I've booked a room at the Duke of Bronte B&B. I won't be sleeping here.'

This was news to Maddy, who'd intended to give him her bed while she camped on the sofa. She shot him a glare at this typically slippery behaviour, but his attention was on Lyla.

Lyla nodded, but kept her face turned against Maddy's shoulder.

Maddy tried to reassure and distract her. 'Have you made more snowmen? I didn't see one in the front garden.'

293

This time, Lyla shook her head. 'I made a snow dog for Heloise and Bozo.'

'Fab,' she said encouragingly. 'Grauntie Ruthie, could you pass us a tissue so Lyla can blow her nose, please? Here you are, chicken. Give a good blow. There, that's better.'

'Thank you,' Lyla snuffled. She slanted a look at her father. 'Did you get lost?' she asked candidly.

His smile turned wary. 'Sort of. I've been living a long way away.'

'Why?' Lyla's grey eyes, so much like his, gazed at him, evidently aware there was more to the story.

Maddy swallowed a lump in her throat. What a lot for her little girl to deal with.

Adey coughed. 'It's where I'm working.'

Lyla swung her leg, catching Maddy's shin a painful clout. 'Mummy said you didn't know I was borned.'

Adey looked grateful to have a conversational support to clutch. 'That's right,' he agreed.

Lyla's unwinking stare grew thoughtful. 'Why not? Mummy and Grauntie Ruthie knew. Heloise knew.'

'Erm . . .' Adey fidgeted. 'They were here,' he pointed out. 'I was away.'

'Yes, but *why*?' she persisted. 'Why did you go away and get a job and not be here?'

Ruthie murmured what sounded suspiciously like, 'Out of the mouths of babes.'

Maddy debated whether to jump in and rescue Adey, but she was curious to hear his explanation.

Adey's eyebrows met in the middle, as if they could knit him an answer. Finally, he said, 'I just did.'

'That's not a reason, it's an excuse,' Lyla returned scathingly. She hotched round in Maddy's lap, her grey eyes stormy as she studied her mum's face. 'You tell me never to say that because it means I'm fibbing, don't you?'

Her grey gaze was so virtuous that Maddy had a job holding back a giggle.

Then Adey blurted, 'I was very unhappy. That's why I left.'

Slowly, Maddy turned on him the most murderous glare she could muster. How *dare* he lay that on a six-year-old, one who'd been so plainly upset? How *could* he say anything so bloody dickish within the first minutes of meeting his daughter? Didn't he have a brain in his head anymore? Had Gina's cosseting of him stripped away any maturity he'd once had?

Adey looked taken aback, then a repentant flush bathed his face.

Lyla didn't let him off the hook. 'If you were unhappy, why did you come back?' She slid off Maddy's lap. 'Mummy, are you going to take him to the Duke of Bronte in that van? Then can you do my reading with me? I haven't got spellings because it's nearly the end of term.'

Maddy's heart felt very strange, filled with pride that Lyla was such a together kid; stuffed with sorrow that Lyla's father was evidently a disappointment. 'In a little bit,' she said in a brisk mummy-voice, not wanting to leave Lyla looking so much as if the stuffing had been knocked out of her. 'Did you enjoy having Chloe and Ffion here?' She knew she had because Lyla had repeated it often the two or three times a day they'd chatted on the phone while Maddy had been in Cornwall.

Lyla gave a skip of delight. 'Yes! Chloe helped with Bozo's walkies, and Heloise, too, and I showed Chloe the cliff path and The Green, because she hadn't been to

Nelson's Bar before. She's going to come again, and I'm going to visit her house.'

'Lovely,' said Maddy, glad that the missing branch of the family had turned up just when extra hands had been needed on deck. They chatted for another couple of minutes, then Maddy sent her to get her reading book while she took Adey to the Duke of Bronte.

Lyla scampered off. Adey, seeming dazed, exchanged a few words with Ruthie, and then Maddy saw him back down the snowy path. Once he was settled in the van, she paused in the open doorway, huddling in her coat as the icy air seemed to swirl up from the lying snow. 'Maybe I should have talked to her before I brought you in and got her used to the idea. Sorry if I fluffed it.'

His mouth twisted in a smile. 'I don't think you've fluffed a single thing, Maddy. I don't know how to behave with kids. She sensed that, I think. Expected something better.'

Maddy heaved shut the sliding door without a comment. She'd once expected better of Adey, too. Expected that he'd take marriage seriously and not fritter away money they didn't have on things he didn't need. Expected that if he couldn't stick it out, their past love would have made him summon the courage to tell her to her face.

Feet sliding, she circumnavigated the van, then climbed into the front seat. 'You know,' she said quietly before she started the engine. 'I never thought you were dead, which meant accepting you were alive and not contacting me. I suppose a part of me always hoped you'd lost your memory or some such fairy story, like you see on TV, rather than leaving me in a mess.'

He met her gaze in the rear-view mirror. 'I suppose it wasn't so much leaving you in a mess—'

'—as getting yourself out of it?' she suggested.

After a moment, Adey laughed. 'You're too good for me, Mad.'

'However you mean that, you're right.' She started up the camper. 'I'm knackered and I expect you are. Try not to take this evening too much to heart. When Lyla's had a sleep and a chance to think, she might be completely different. I expect there will be people you know in the bar at the Duke. It's been extended a lot since you lived here, so it's a proper pub.'

He raised his voice as she pulled away from the kerb, sounding dubious. 'Can I get to my room without going through the bar?'

'You can.' She concentrated on weaving gently between parked cars. 'Don't you want to see Harris?'

'Of course,' he said heartily. 'But on our own. I'll call him from my room.'

'OK,' she agreed. 'That makes sense – though I don't know why you didn't ring him from the van on the journey. Anyway, I'll take you to the old B&B front door rather than the bar.'

Five minutes later, she was standing in the hall of the Duke of Bronte, watching Olly, one of the proprietors, carrying Adey's bag as Adey hauled himself upstairs with his crutches and the banister, listening to Adey explaining that he'd rather Olly didn't tell anyone he was here, 'as there's someone I want to speak to first, rather than letting them hear through others.'

'Sure,' Olly agreed without much interest. 'Me and Karen took the Duke of Bronte over after you'd left, so I wouldn't have known who you were if you hadn't told me. I've just heard the story, like everyone.'

Yeah. Everyone had heard Adey and Maddy's story.

Maddy dragged herself back to the van, shattered after a day's driving and dealing with Adey. She wanted nothing more than to curl up with Lyla so they could read to each other until it was time for bed.

Well . . . that, and for Raff to answer her text. Once inside the camper, she took out her phone and texted him again. I'm back in Nelson's Bar. Ruthie seems to have had a great time with Ffion and Chloe. She pondered how to end the message. *Speak soon? Hope to speak soon? Can we arrange a time to meet? I need to explain why I brought Adey back? Why didn't you answer my last text? I'm getting a divorce?*

Finally, she opted to just add a kiss to the message and send it.

Chapter Twenty-Two

Raff's week had been shit, and it was only Tuesday. He glanced at his inbox and saw Antonella's name flash up with a subject line of *At last!* It piqued his curiosity, especially as her Christmas card had contained nothing more interesting than seasonal wishes. They kept in touch, but he felt nothing but mild affection for her now, and she seemed to feel much the same. He opened the message, to discover that she'd signed a deal with an independent publishing house. 'Good for you,' he murmured, and typed out hearty congratulations, forbearing to mention that her publishers would never get books into supermarkets, whereas his publisher did.

Then, as if to mock his hubris, an email from his editor Vikki dropped. He felt queasy, as, after skimming the greeting, he read:

> As we all sign off for Christmas, I want to let you know that I'll be moving on to pastures new at the end of February to pursue interests outside of the publishing world.

Did that mean she'd got the sack and Raff had had a duff editor without knowing it? Or maybe working with Raff had made her want to give up? Either way, his deadline was at the end of February – just when Vikki would be heading out of the door.

I'll be leaving you in the safe hands of my fantastic colleagues until the appointment of my successor.

Successor? It was with Vikki he'd chewed over plotlines and conflicts; Vikki who'd championed his books through the acquisition process; Vikki who never wavered in her ambition for him. 'Fuck it.' He propped his elbow on the glass table to glare at his laptop screen, desire to write draining away. All morning he'd been pouring his bad mood into a confrontation between Adeckor and the king, who was seriously miffed at his queen having a thing with his once-trusted man at arms. To introduce external conflict, Raff had brought to the borders of the kingdom a lizard-riding enemy army. Adeckor had put aside the estrangement with the king while he rallied the renegade bands from the mountains, and now Raff had got this fucking email, just when he was about three chapters away from finishing the first draft.

So close . . .

He sat up and clicked on his electronic calendar. If he could finish the first draft by New Year and spend two weeks on the second draft, he'd get the book to Vikki by mid-January. Maybe she'd do the edit, and by the time he got the successor, the book would be too far through the process to be messed with too much.

He could work through Christmas . . . His heart sank even further, though it had already felt at rock bottom.

He could work through Christmas because he had scarcely any plans. He'd hardly stuck his nose out of doors since Maddy had told him she was bringing her husband back to Nelson's Bar. Her laughing eyes and the almost careless way she'd announced bringing Adey 'home' had felt like a snake bite. And he'd recoiled. Red mist dancing before his eyes, he'd raced back to the B&B, grabbed his things and roared off as if Cornish piskies had set his arse on fire, seared by the knowledge that he cared about Maddy but, evidently, she didn't care as much about him.

How she was going to bring Adey back – how she'd return to the B&B, for that matter – now he'd cleared off in the car, made him stop at a roadside café van and huddle in the car drinking coffee, shaken he'd reacted so uncharacteristically. He'd invited himself along on this jaunt, then abandoned her. Shame had crept over him, sweat prickling under the collar of his coat. What a bastard.

But he couldn't envisage turning back and inserting himself into the situation now, though returning good sense reminded him that Adey was Lyla's father. Raff might have distanced himself in a fit of anger, but essentially, the situation wasn't about him. He cared about Maddy too much to get in her way while she attempted to sort things out.

He'd almost given way to the urge to reply to her text about wanting to talk when he'd received another, saying she was home. She hadn't said 'with Adey' but he now knew it to be true, because transporting Adey in a borrowed camper van had trickled through to him via Maddy to Ruthie to Ffion.

He gazed unseeingly at the unsettling email from his editor while he wondered for the hundredth time what

Lyla had made of Adey. She would only see a father, not a man who'd buckled under financial strain and left Maddy. Adey must have been an OK guy once or Maddy wouldn't have married him, so maybe he was a charmer. Maybe Lyla would be besotted with him. Maybe Maddy would be, too.

Maybe Raff should be glowing green, he was so jealous.

A loud knock on the window made him jump and he looked up to see a grinning Ffion. Behind her, the day was growing dusky, reminding him how much of Tuesday had passed.

He rose to let her in. 'Hey,' he said briefly, as she entered, her nose red with cold in her pale face.

'I'm stopping you working,' she said apologetically.

Automatically, he headed for the kettle and coffee mugs. 'It's OK. I was emailing. My editor's leaving and Antonella has signed a book deal. She's stoked.'

Ffion presumably didn't get the import of Vikki leaving because she seized on the latter point. 'Good for Antonella. I got a Christmas card from her.'

'Me, too. I'd already sent her an electronic one, so I guess that makes me look a meanie.' He glanced at the cards that overflowed the top of his bookcase as he had no mantel in this tiny house. He had no Christmas tree or sprays of holly, either.

'I haven't even written my cards yet. I was going to do it at the weekend, before events overtook us. Ruthie's friend Della makes gorgeous cards, but I'd already bought mine.' Ffion unwound her scarf and threw off her hat and coat before crossing to a sofa and landing in it with a *flumph*.

He made the coffee, stirring it until islands of froth rotated on the surface, and took the sofa at right angles to Ffion's. 'How did the weekend with Ruthie go?' He didn't ask about Maddy because she felt like a wound in his chest that he shrank from probing.

Ffion sparkled. 'We got on really well. She's a lovely person.' She paused for thought. 'She's likeable and easy to be with. I wouldn't say that I felt as if I was finding the missing part of me or a replacement or improvement on Mum, but more that I knew her already. All my angst about meeting her just melted away.'

He nodded, pretty sure he'd already mentioned how lovely Ruthie was. 'You're going to call her Ruthie? Rather than Mum?'

Her expression softened. 'Our mum will always be Mum to me. Ruthie's fine with Ruthie.'

'What about Chloe?' He blew gently across the surface of his drink, enjoying the scent of coffee.

'She's calling her Ruthie, too.' Ffion grinned. 'Oh, you meant how did they get on? Really well. And Ruthie didn't mention before, when we changed our minds about meeting her.'

'Great.' It all sounded cosy. He was glad for Ffion. He'd wanted her to meet her natural mother. This feeling of being sidelined, and that there was no place for him at Nelson's Bar, was only because he was out of sorts.

Ffion sighed, leaning forward to perch her cup on the table. 'I have a conscience about Maddy, though.'

Against his will, his attention sharpened. 'Maddy?'

'I left while she was on her way home.' Ffion sounded guilty. 'I had to get Chloe to school, my work stuff was at home and the forecast was for more snow. I let Ruthie call Della to come and make sure she got lunch. I didn't even think to change the beds we'd slept in. I just left Maddy to it, and from what I understand of her husband's story, Maddy's had quite enough of that.'

He imagined Maddy returning with an injured husband after driving for hours and being thrust back into her caring duties without even a clean bed to drop into. His heart twitched at the thought of her being exhausted but, as usual, coping. Then he wondered where Adey had slept, and his fingers tightened around the handle of his mug.

Hesitantly, Ffion said, 'Raff, how are things between you and Maddy? I was shocked when I realised you'd left her behind.'

Like Adey. A slimy feeling of remorse slithered inside him, but he cocked an eyebrow in assumed surprise. 'Slow down,' he advised. 'We started something, but now her husband's around, I can't be in the picture. He wanted to meet his daughter, didn't he?' He sipped his drink to hide his expression.

His sister eyed him shrewdly. 'You can't be in the picture for Lyla's sake? Or Maddy's? Or yours?'

'All of the above.' Then, more moderately: 'She'll need space to sort her life out.'

They drank in silence. Though aware of Ffion's scrutiny, Raff chose to stare out of the window at cottage lights showing above the wall of the yard. Then, as if Ffion had wheedled the information out of him, he added sharply, 'Maddy loves her little girl. What if she's considering a future with Adey for Lyla's sake?'

Ffion gave a sniff. 'From what Ruthie said on the phone this morning, he's staying at the B&B and has a partner in Cornwall. Maddy's met her. It's her camper van she's borrowed.'

These sentences, though terse, were like drops of balm on his tender heart. 'Good,' he answered. 'But I still think I need to butt out until she knows what Adey's going to do next.' He meant until *Raff* knew what Adey was going to do next. Until he got over this horrible feeling of being surplus to requirements. 'Let's see what the New Year brings.'

Ffion drained her mug. 'OK. I'll leave you to get back to work and I'll go home to do the same. I'm finishing for my Christmas break tomorrow, when the schools break up. How about you?'

His gaze had found its way to the window again. Nearby roofs had thin coverings of snow as if dusted with sugar but for once he felt no urge to step out into the cold, fresh air. 'I need to finish my book.'

A beat of silence. Ffion shifted. 'But you're coming to the village carol concert on Saturday afternoon, as arranged? And there's some festive thing on in Nelson's Bar on Christmas Eve Sunday and Chloe and I said we'd go with Ruthie, Maddy and Lyla. I thought you'd come. It's a village Christmas party, with mince pies and mulled wine; then there's a lantern walk around the village. Lyla says Maddy's bought her a lantern in the shape of Santa's head to carry and Chloe's taking glow sticks that bend into bracelets.'

I thought you'd come. For a moment, fiercely, he wanted to. He'd see Maddy. But . . . 'Is Adey still there?' he asked. When Ffion only looked at him, sympathy in his eyes, he said, 'I've got a tight deadline, Ffi.'

'But you'll definitely come to ours for Christmas Day?' She got to her feet, her forehead furrowed in concern.

He hesitated. 'You'll want to see Ruthie and . . . and your new family.' Then seeing her startled horror, he pinned on a big grin. 'I'm a single grown-up. I can enjoy Christmas in all kinds of ways.' He waggled his eyebrows to convey that he had very grown-up plans.

'Raff,' she breathed. 'Is this because I made that horrible

comment about blood when I was upset? I was hoping you'd forgotten but I should have apologised before this—'

'No.' He cut her off. He pulled her into a brotherly embrace, so she couldn't see his face. 'It's about Maddy, and it's about work. I want to be a party pooper. Just let me. Please?'

Wordlessly, Ffion hugged him back.

She dressed again in her outdoor things. He made himself ignore her woebegone expression.

When she'd gone, he closed the curtains and reseated himself at his machine. As he was about to force his mind back to Adeckor's rallying of the renegades, he saw Antonella had replied to his congratulatory email.

As he read, he became very still.

It was unexpected, out-of-the-blue, but in his current state of mind, it was an email full of temptation, a proposal for a grown-up Christmas that appealed to him in every way.

Not giving himself time to second-guess, he clicked *reply* then began to type. Thanks for the invitation. That would be great. I'll go pack.

Chapter Twenty-Three

Maddy's Tuesday had felt long and tense.

In the morning, Adey had called her to say he needed to 'tie up some loose ends around the village' and there was no point meeting up until Lyla had finished school, as the school hadn't, as Lyla had hoped, declared a snow day.

Relieved, she'd agreed, the most obvious loose end she could think of being Harris. 'I usually walk Lyla home from the school bus, but I could fetch you in the van.'

Adey had grunted. 'I can get myself to your place. See you about four.'

Now, Maddy waited with the other parents and grandparents, joking about the horizontal wind that sent her hair swirling, despite her hat being crammed firmly on her head. She'd just checked her phone for messages, wishing Raff hadn't elected to ghost her, when Heloise wandered up.

'I haven't got Jude or Blake today because they've got a tummy bug,' she announced cheerfully, hunching her shoulders against the cold. 'I thought I'd see if I could scrounge a home-time coffee.'

'And maybe get a look at Adey?' Maddy hazarded, holding back her hair so it couldn't blow into her mouth. A long, late-night call from her to Heloise last night had filled her friend in on every step of Maddy's adventure since she'd left the village on Friday. To Maddy's relief, the uncharacteristic tension between them about Harris had abated as if it had never been.

Heloise pulled such an innocent face she ought to have sprouted a halo. 'I'd forgotten he was here.' Then she grinned. 'OK, I'm curious.'

'I think he was going to see Harris this morning,' Maddy said, as the silver minibus swung into The Green ready to discharge its load of village children.

Before Heloise could comment, Lyla jumped down, her eyes zeroing in on Maddy. 'We had special assembly today and I got a five-star snerkiffycut,' she shouted almost before her feet hit the ground, brandishing a piece of thick cream card.

'A certificate? Wow, well done.' Maddy read it out loud. *For being a sensible and caring member of the class. Proud of you, Lyla.* She bent down and scooped her into a big hug.

Lyla allowed the hug and then squirmed away to let Heloise hug her, too. While Maddy did up Lyla's top button, tied her scarf more securely and then pulled up her hood, Lyla asked, 'Is he still here?'

Maddy's sinking feeling was so strong it made her feel as if her stomach was dragging on the ground. 'Daddy, you mean?' It felt so weird to say that. 'He's meeting us at home at four. I haven't seen him today.'

Lyla nodded. Then she passed Maddy her backpack to free her to walk with one leg and skip with the other, providing terse answers to Maddy's questions.

'What have you done today?'

'Nothing.'

'Who have you played with?'

'Misty.' Then Lyla plied Heloise with questions about Bozo and whether Heloise might look after the dog in the future, until they reached The Hollies.

Maddy unlocked the door and Lyla careered into the front room, reanimated as she yelled, 'Grauntie Ruthie, I got a five-star snerkiffycut!'

The next few minutes passed in the usual after-school bustle of milk and biscuits for Lyla, and coffee for Ruthie, Maddy and Heloise. Lyla recovered her sunny smile under a milk moustache, telling Grauntie Ruthie about all the 'nothing' she'd done at school, which, as well as the special assembly, had included a reading test, PE in the hall, a boy called Simmy getting a nosebleed from tripping and banging into Lyla's shoulder – it had hurt her, but she hadn't cried – and helping take down paintings from the classroom wall.

Then the doorbell rang and Maddy went to admit Adey, who grumbled as he swung in on his crutches. 'It's much colder up here than in Cornwall and I had to get Kaz at the B&B to put a plastic bag round my cast so the plaster doesn't go soggy.' He handed his crutches to Maddy while he pulled off his coat with a theatrical shiver.

Maddy, nettled at being treated so peremptorily shoved his crutches back at him. 'I did offer to pick you up.'

His expression turned sheepish. 'Sorry,' he muttered. 'I've never been on crutches before and it's harder work than it looks if you have to go any distance. My arms and shoulders are killing me, and I thought I was going to fall on my bloody arse in a patch of slush.'

'Lyla's here,' Maddy said automatically.

He frowned, his hair sticking out from a black knitted hat, which he hadn't removed. 'I know. I've come to see her, haven't I?'

OK, he wasn't exactly broken into his daddy role, so she summoned a smile to take any sting out of the words. 'We don't swear in her hearing.'

'Oh.' He flushed. 'Right.'

'Coffee?' she offered, trying to be civilised. 'Lyla's watching TV with Heloise and Ruthie in the front room.'

He eyed the doorway, probably, like Maddy, noting that Lyla hadn't come out to see him, then followed her to the kitchen on his crutches, step-clonk, step-clonk. This meant she had to find conversation while she waited for the kettle to boil. 'Comfortable at the B&B? Have you seen Harris?' She halted when Heloise appeared in the kitchen and quietly closed the door.

'Long time, no see,' she greeted Adey with false affability.

'Hell's Bells.' He cried her nickname in glad tones that didn't completely ring true, flinging open his arms for a hug.

'Heloise,' she corrected him, remaining where she was. Her gaze ran critically over him. 'You've forgotten all your old friends.'

''Course not,' he began, and then the doorbell sounded again.

Maddy left the kettle and crossed the hall. Once more, Lyla was conspicuous by her absence, apparently preferring children's TV with Ruthie to her usual vetting of every caller, so Maddy was alone when she found Harris on the doorstep.

His scowl made a black snake of his eyebrows. 'Is *Adey* here?' he demanded, a hint of incredulity in his tone.

Maddy stepped back to let him in. 'I thought he was calling on you earlier.'

'That would have been nice,' he snapped.

Intrigued, she indicated the kitchen, and then followed him in.

Adey leant against the pot sink, eyes wary, though his mouth widened in a beaming grin. 'Harris! I'm so glad to see you—'

'You been here since last night,' Harris accused in a funny, tight voice. 'Heloise told me. I been waiting indoors all day, expecting you. I still live in the same house. My phone number hasn't changed.'

Maddy glanced at Heloise, realising why she'd invited herself for coffee. Perhaps she'd been with Harris today, waiting for Adey to seek out his old friend. Then, when he didn't appear, she'd offered to try and find out what was going on. She'd probably texted Harris that he was here.

Adey looked abashed. 'It's hell on these crutches, man. I only came out of hospital yesterday, so I gave myself a duvet day, watching TV. I was going to get Maddy to give me a lift to yours in a bit.'

The two men stared at each other. Though ready to step in if Harris kicked off and scared Lyla and upset Ruthie, Maddy watched them, fascinated, trying to think back to the conversation she'd had with Adey this morning. Had he said he was going to look for Harris? Or had Maddy merely construed it from his statement about tying up loose ends?

Adey stuck out his hand. 'Well, great to see you again, man.'

Harris just continued to stare. His slack mouth and furrowed forehead spoke of a multitude of scudding thoughts. Slowly, he shook his head. 'For seven years I worried about you, blaming myself in case you went off the cliff and I could've stopped you. *Seven years* without a word.'

Hand falling, Adey fidgeted with the grips of his crutches. 'I was in a bad place,' he began.

'So you just left us all behind.' Harris stuck out his chin. 'Fuck me, Adey—'

Maddy pushed the kitchen door closed but decided not to interrupt the confrontation with another reproach regarding bad language. Heloise looked rapt at the drama, too.

Harris's throat worked as he fought to get out the words. 'Fuck me,' he repeated. 'I been *grieving* you, sure you must be dead, or you'd have been in touch. You know I wouldn't have told Maddy if you didn't want me to.'

Maddy rolled her eyes at Harris. 'Charming.'

Both men ignored her. Plainly, what was simmering was about to boil over.

Harris glared fiercely. 'We've been friends our whole lives. I got in fights for you when we were kids and gave you money when yours ran out. I swallowed it when you went out with Maddy, even though you knew I fancied her like mad. And I never hit on her while you were missing.'

'You *what*?' Maddy and Heloise said in unison, their heads swivelling towards each other, Maddy in shock and Heloise in horror.

Harris hunched his shoulders inside his black coat. 'Sorry,' he said to Heloise. 'That didn't come out right.'

Stiff, pale, her arms folded as if defending herself, she demanded, 'How was it meant to come out?'

Maddy wanted to fling her arms around her and say, 'He didn't mean it. He's just hurling knives at Adey because he's upset.' But the devastated expression on Heloise's face told her that she shouldn't get between her and Harris right now.

Adey made a strange movement, like shrugging off an uncomfortable coat. 'But Maddy didn't go for you.'

She swung on this man – her husband! – aghast. 'You *knew* he had a . . . a *thing* about me? That's what Harris's juvenile leering and teasing was about? You're joking.'

Adey shifted on his good foot, his plastered leg held awkwardly. 'You didn't need to know. You didn't like him.'

'Anyone would dislike that moronic behaviour. You should have been honest,' she hissed. 'Instead, you grouched that Harris and I didn't get on. You used to make out it put you in a difficult spot.'

Adey lifted a protesting hand. 'It was a difficult spot, Maddy. He's my best mate—'

'*Was*,' Harris snapped.

Whatever he'd been going to say next was lost as Heloise whirled and fled the room. Maddy took a step after her, but Heloise had already snatched her coat from the newel post and was out of the door before Maddy had even reached the hall. She turned back, disgusted. Disregarding her own rules about swearing, she looked at Harris. 'That was shitty.'

He had the grace to look ashamed. 'I do like her,' he volunteered gruffly.

Maddy passed her hand wearily over her face. 'You'd better go,' she said. 'Maybe even go after her.'

'All right.' Harris began to back from the room, though not before he'd sent Adey a last offended look.

As the door closed behind him, she turned to Adey. 'You, too.'

His awkward expression turned to shock. 'But I'm here to spend time with Lyla, aren't I?' He sounded uncertain.

'True.' Maddy crossed to the front room doorway and peeped in. Ruthie's head turned towards her, eyebrows raised, silently questioning what was going on. In a bright voice, Maddy said, 'Daddy's here, Lyla. Do you want to see him?'

Lyla gave her a long considering look from the corner of her eye, then shook her head, making her hair dance around her face.

Determined to be seen to be fair, Maddy wheedled, 'Not even for five minutes? You could show him your certificate.'

The headshake only became more violent. 'Watching telly.'

'OK.' Maddy made sure her voice was soft and sympathetic, so Lyla knew whose side Maddy was on. She strode back into the kitchen. 'She doesn't want to, today. You can try again tomorrow. It's been a big upheaval for her and—' she tried to lighten the moment '—I'm afraid you're suffering for not being Santa Claus. That's all she's interested in right now. Would you like me to drive you back to the B&B?'

He looked shellshocked. 'She doesn't want to see me? She doesn't even know me.'

A long deep breath. Maddy counted to ten, mentally comparing Ruthie's joy over finding her daughter with Adey's mild interest at being brought to meet his. 'That's pretty much the point.'

He blinked several times, as if trying to process events. Then he pushed himself upright and settled his crutches.

'A lift would be great, please. It really was hard work getting here.' But he sounded dazed.

Maddy wondered what had flattened him most – Harris calling him out, or Lyla not wanting to see him. Probably a mixture, she thought, as she went back into the front room to tell the others she'd be gone for ten minutes, then she grabbed her coat and retrieved the camper van keys from the hook by the door.

Adey was silent as he step-clonked his way gingerly down the path, which was beginning to twinkle with frost now the sun had disappeared, and hauled himself into the back of the camper. He didn't bother putting his plastered leg up but left it sticking out in front of him for the short journey to the Duke of Bronte.

When she pulled up in the car park and jumped out of the driver's seat to go to the sliding door, he let her take his arm to steady him down the step to the ground. Then he sighed, looked around himself at the jolly lights blazing all over the Duke of Bronte and on every nearby cottage, then back at her. 'Would you mind walking back to Ruthie's and leaving me the camper keys? I'm going to call Gina to come and get me.'

Shock rippled through Maddy, but at the same time she shouldn't have been surprised that he didn't want to hang around. He clearly felt as welcome as a power cut on Christmas Day, and she could feel nothing but relief. She locked the doors and then held out the keys. 'How will Gina get here?'

'One of the workers on the farm will come with her and drive the camper home,' he said. He looked around again, as if trying to place himself in this village high up above the sea, which he'd once called home. He turned back with a weak smile. 'Kiss goodbye?'

She wrinkled her nose. 'Nah. Gina's scary.'

'True.' He smiled fondly, evidently admiring Gina's bulldozing ways. 'What happens now?'

Maddy blew out her cheeks as she considered. 'Lyla might easily want to see you sometime. I could get in touch with you. Bring her down.' Now she knew that the cottage was her own and therefore where she was about money, she could afford to change her old car for something more reliable.

'OK.' He nodded.

Though he appeared relieved, fairness compelled her to add, 'And if you want to contact her, just let me know. Maybe when she's talked to you on FaceTime a few times . . .' A vision of the firmness of Lyla's headshake floated into her mind, and she let the sentence trail away.

'OK,' he said again. 'You take care. Merry Christmas.'

'Merry Christmas,' she answered. 'I'll be in touch about the house and the divorce after Christmas. Get the solicitors onto things.'

He grinned, looking for a moment like the Adey she remembered. 'But no divorce till the tax year after the property transfer, like Gina said.' Then she watched him step-clonking across the car park to the entrance that avoided the bar, pretty sure she'd never see Adey Austen again and only experiencing the becoming-familiar melting relief.

Christmas lights winked and blinked from the cottages in Droody Road, the icy mist stealing in off the sea creating the surreal quality of colouring the very air around her. As she hurried for the warmth of The Hollies and the meal that waited to be prepared, the child and aunt to be loved, bedtime stories to be read, chatter and laughter to be had, she texted Heloise as she walked. I had NO idea.

It's bizarre. I'm so so so so sorry. Unlike Adey, I know the value of a best friend, and would never hurt you. Xx

It was later, after supper, when she was doing the washing up, that her phone signalled the reply. I was more into him than he was me, but it was still a shock. I'll see you soon, but tonight it's just me and a bottle of wine. Xx

Maddy flushed with relief that she wasn't being blamed, noting Heloise's use of the past tense regarding Harris. If Heloise was no longer with him, it cut some turmoil from Maddy's life.

No text from Raff though. Her fingers hovered over the screen. Should she tell him Adey had gone?

But she thought about his lack of contact since he'd stomped out of the Royal Cornwall Hospital compared to her eager checking of her messages, and she tucked her phone away. Ruthie chatted to Ffion regularly now. Ruthie would tell Ffion that Adey had gone, and no doubt Ffion would tell Raff. Whether he did anything about it . . . ? Maybe that was a ball best left bouncing in his court.

At home, she was greeted in the hall by Rocket Lyla, apparently restored to her usual ebullient self. 'When's supper?'

'Soon,' Maddy promised. 'We need to talk, first.'

Apprehension crept into Lyla's eyes. 'Yes?' She stood on one foot and caught the toe of her tights behind her in the other, looking like a gymnast.

Maddy threw her coat on the newel and sat on the second step, pulling Lyla down beside her. 'Daddy's decided to go home for now.'

''K,' answered Lyla, not giving much away.

Maddy had always spoken to Lyla in the most grown-up way appropriate but had never needed to instigate a conversation that could have quite so momentous an effect on their lives. She said in her most reassuring voice, 'But if you want to see Daddy again, I can drive you to Cornwall or he and his girlfriend can come here.' She slipped in the girlfriend information, judging that Lyla was a long way from entertaining any 'Mummy and Daddy together again' fantasies or demanding details of current marital status.

''K,' Lyla said again, propping her chin on her hand. 'What's Cornwall?'

'It's a place. Daddy lives there on a farm. Cornwall has a lot of sea around it, like Norfolk.' Maddy stroked the fair hair Lyla had inherited from Adey.

'Is it a long way?' Lyla raised soft eyebrows.

'About seven hours in the car,' Maddy answered honestly.

'Oh.' Lyla screwed up her forehead. 'Is it today we're having chicken and roasties?'

Maddy gave her narrow shoulders a squeeze. 'Yes. I'll start it now, shall I?'

'Yay!' Lyla launched herself off the step on a trajectory for the kitchen, shouting, 'Grauntie Ruthie, I'm not coming back to watch telly yet. I'm going to help Mummy with supper.'

'OK, dear,' Ruthie returned comfortably, and the soundtrack from a kiddies' programme was swiftly replaced by a choir singing 'Silent Night'.

Maddy followed Lyla, reflecting that she ought to feel sadder that Lyla put chicken and roasties above talking about her father. That could change at any time, but Maddy would facilitate whatever Lyla needed. That was the kind of mum she was.

* * *

318

Lyla tumbled off the minibus on the last day of term, her coat half-on at one side and her backpack half-on at the other, and a folder creased against her chest. 'I've brought my paintings home,' she gasped, thrusting the folder at Maddy. 'Are you sure Santa can't bring me a dog?'

'Positive,' Maddy answered, catching the folder and its contents in one practised hand.

A familiar laugh came from behind Maddy, then Heloise's voice said, 'You can help me walk dogs any time I'm looking after them, Lyla.'

Maddy spun around, joy filling her at the sight of her dear friend, muffled up against the first flakes of snow that were once again drifting down on Nelson's Bar. 'Heloise!' In front of Lyla and the adults ushering away the kids they'd come to meet she couldn't express her gladness at her friend strolling up to meet them as she'd done countless times, so flung her arms around her instead in a hard hug of unspoken joy that Harris's harsh words hadn't come between them.

Then Lyla hugged Heloise, too, saying, 'You look like a dog in that hat.'

'That goes in the charity bag as soon as I get home then,' Heloise said drily, taking off the faux fur with earflaps to examine it dubiously.

Maddy laughed, letting Lyla slip between them so she could hold a hand of each. 'OK?' she asked Heloise, hoping she'd garner from it, 'Are you OK? Are *we* OK?' without anything said that might prompt Lyla to spout questions.

'Yeah.' Heloise gave a crooked smile. 'Is the invitation to spend Christmas with you still open?'

'Of *course*,' said Maddy, heart and eyes filling with equal speed. 'In fact, we all need to make the most of the

Christmas holidays and do something really Christmassy every day.'

Lyla pogoed on the spot. 'Yes, because it's only three more days and then it's Christmas Eve and four days then it's Christmas. And Santa. Hooray!'

'Hooray,' Maddy echoed, smiling down at her gorgeous, lively, full-of-curiosity daughter. 'And the very first thing is mince pies when we get home.'

'And mulled wine?' Heloise asked hopefully.

'Banana milkshake,' Lyla declared.

Heloise pulled a face. 'Ordinary wine, then? After all it is Christmas.'

'Christmas! Mincie pies and 'nana milkshake,' Lyla squealed and, now they were in Jubilee Crescent, where she was allowed to go on alone, she ran towards The Hollies, elbows pumping and heels flying. Then she skidded to a halt – literally, as the snow was beginning to create a fine mantel where it landed – and turned and raced back. 'Ffion's car's outside our house,' she panted. 'I'm going to see her.'

Heloise cast Maddy a glance. 'Ffion's making up for lost time, isn't she? They've only just spent Friday to Monday together.'

'Ruthie's very keen, too,' Maddy acknowledged. 'Who can blame them? It's what I wanted for Ruthie once I knew about Ffion.'

Heloise frowned at the little turquoise car at the pavement edge. 'You've been closer to Ruthie than to your mum. Then Ffion comes along . . .'

Maddy sighed. 'But you can't argue with biology. Ruthie is Ffion's mum.' Though part of her had been a touch surprised that since Monday evening when Maddy returned from Cornwall, Ruthie and Ffion had spoken by phone at least four times and this was only Wednesday. Ruthie had recounted to Maddy how long it was until Ffion's operation, when Chloe was next dancing in a competition, and that Ffion had read some of Ruthie's letters to Nigel out to her. Maddy hadn't enquired whether Ruthie had had to cut her off before any sexy bits, as she did with Nigel's letters.

Displaying sensitivity to Maddy's unease, Heloise said, 'Want me to clear off?'

'No, you're my guest,' Maddy said firmly, and they turned up the path. When they stepped into The Hollies they found Ffion already in the kitchen, and Lyla perched on Chloe's hip as if she was a toddler. Ruthie sat at the table beaming while Lyla explained earnestly that Maddy had said it was Christmas from now on and telling them where she kept the mince pies.

'Shall we just start the wine?' Heloise murmured in Maddy's ear.

Maddy pretended not to hear, determined to blend in with Ruthie's new family, for Ruthie's sake. 'Hey, everyone,' she said cheerfully, as if this wasn't only the second time that they'd all been together and thrusting aside the memory of angst and ill feeling in the past. She introduced Heloise, saw to Lyla's banana milkshake, and reached down the mince pie tin from the top of a cupboard. As either Ffion or Chloe had apparently made hot drinks for themselves and Ruthie, she did then open the fridge for the wine.

'I hope you don't mind us dropping in,' Ffion ventured, after refusing wine, as did Ruthie.

Maddy smiled at the small, pinched-looking woman. 'Of course not. It's Ruthie's house.' She patted Ruthie on the shoulder as she squeezed past for wine glasses, only to realise that Heloise was already waiting expectantly with one in each hand. Maddy half-filled them, and then returned the bottle to the fridge. 'Shall we sit in the front room where there's more space? Perhaps Ruthie's Alexa will play us some carols.'

As everyone else filed out, Chloe putting Lyla down and giving her the mince pies to carry, Ffion giving Ruthie an arm up from the table, Heloise carrying both wine glasses, Maddy hung back to gather plates.

Then Ffion reappeared, gently pushing the door closed behind her. 'Maddy,' she said, 'I'm sorry we hurried off on Monday before you got back. I realised afterwards that we didn't change our beds.'

Maddy smiled. 'Don't worry about that. I was just grateful you could stay with Ruthie.'

Ffion's face lit up. 'It was wonderful. We learnt more about each other in a weekend than we could have done in a year of polite visits. And Chloe was reassured that her new grandmother wasn't about to expire.'

Maddy forced a laugh. 'I hope Ruthie has years and years left. She's great for her age.'

'Of course,' said Ffion looking less certain. 'Anyway, I'm still not sure we should have just dropped in today—'

'You should, if that's what Ruthie wants,' Maddy cut in firmly.

'—but it won't all be one way,' Ffion went on, her face beginning to glow. 'I'll have her for weekends. When I'm recuperating from my op, she can keep me company. I won't be able to drive for a while, though.'

'Right.' This time, Maddy couldn't muster a smile. 'Well, I'm happy to drive her where she wants to go.'

'Oh, dear.' Ffion's smile died. 'I'm not sure if I'm treading on your toes or you're being territorial.'

If only Heloise hadn't gone off with Maddy's wine.

She felt as if she needed a slurp of it now. 'Neither, I hope,' she said mildly. 'If she asks me to drive her to your house then I will, any time.'

Ffion's face cleared. 'I was forgetting that she's your job.'

Heat swept over Maddy from her toes to her hairline. Even the roots of her hair felt angry. 'I would never describe Ruthie as a "job" in a million years. First and foremost, we're family, even if I receive carer's allowance. We share all the household expenses.'

Ffion quirked her eyebrows ruefully, as pale as Maddy felt her own face to be red. 'We should probably begin the conversation again. I feel as if I'm blundering my way through it.'

Realising she'd been unnecessarily short, Maddy summoned a smile. 'Good idea. I'm sorry if I seemed territorial. I might not be doing a good job of it, but I'm actually trying not to overstep my role as niece and carer.'

'And I'm completely new to being Ruthie's daughter. Tell me what I said wrong,' Ffion suggested composedly.

Mollified by such a clear olive branch, Maddy wrinkled her nose. 'It's just . . . Ruthie decides what Ruthie does. She's an intelligent woman with a will of her own so when you said, "I'll have her" or "she can keep me company" it felt like you making her decisions.' Tentatively, she added, 'Also, she might need your arm in an unfamiliar place, because of her eyesight, but she doesn't need it to move from her own kitchen to her own front room.' She wanted to add that using muscles was good for health and independence at any age but felt that might constitute a lecture.

Ffion made that rueful face again. 'Mum – sorry, I mean Sindy.' She flushed. 'She was quite doddery towards

323

the end, so I suppose I was automatically stepping into the role I had with her. Thanks for being OK about it.'

Maddy warmed to her. 'Thank you for being OK, too. It's a new situation. I'd hate to be fighting you over Ruthie.' Then they went together into the front room, though they found everyone had begun the mince pies and dropped crumbs, rendering the plates Maddy carried redundant.

Heloise shoved a glass of wine into her hands. All the furniture seemed to be in use, so they lounged on the floor together, watching Ffion chatting to Ruthie and Chloe listening to Lyla list all the things she'd requested from Santa.

Heloise's voice was barely a whisper at her shoulder. 'OK?'

'Mm.' Maddy took the slug of wine she'd promised herself.

'Conference with Ffion?' Heloise questioned in the same thready voice.

Maddy held her glass before her mouth so her lips couldn't be read. 'I should have realised that there would be things to debate but it just didn't occur that me knowing Ruthie best but Ffion being more closely related has the potential to be a problem. I ought to be dancing with joy that I've sorted most of my Adey problems out, but instead I'm feeling worried about Ruthie.'

'And pissed off about Raff, like I'm pissed off about Harris,' murmured Heloise into her wine, the glass misting with her breath. 'Let's down these drinks. It *is* Christmas.'

Maddy's heart clenched at the reminder that Raff was ghosting her. She'd never have put him down as a ghoster, and, speaking as the ghostee, it sucked. Her laugh was dry. 'Let's.'

Half an hour later, Ffion decided it was time for her

and Chloe to go. While Ruthie and Lyla followed them to the door, Maddy hugged Heloise, who'd also put on her coat to leave. 'Shall I see if I can get Della to come tomorrow evening so we can go out to the Duke of Bronte?'

Heloise grimaced. 'Harris is always at the Duke. How about you come to mine, instead?'

Maddy made her hug apologetic this time. 'Sorry. I didn't think. I'm too wrapped up in my own woes. That would be lovely.'

When they opened the door, they saw the snow had stopped, leaving such a thin covering that Ffion's car looked as if it was wrapped in muslin. It was still like opening a refrigerator door, though. Ruthie and Lyla retreated to the warmth of the front room; Heloise hurried down the path. Chloe dawdled towards the car, but Ffion hung back.

'Maddy, there's just one more thing,' she said hesitantly.

'Oh?' Maddy stepped out into the porch so she could pull the door to, pulling her fleece around her. She hoped it would be a quick 'thing' because supper had been delayed by the visitors and Lyla could get 'hangry'.

In a rush, Ffion said, 'Don't give up on Raff. From the little he told me, it sounds like he's been clumsy. He's trying to do the right thing by leaving you to sort things out with your husband, but I saw him yesterday and he's miserable.'

Surprise shimmered through Maddy, having expected more Ruthie-related comments from Ffion. Raff was unhappy about Maddy? A *whoosh* of relief made her mouth blossom into a smile. 'It's hard not to give up when he's refusing to answer texts.'

Ffion rolled her eyes. 'He thinks he's doing the right

325

thing, and sometimes he curls up in a corner when he has hurt feelings. Try again,' she urged. 'He cares about you and Ruthie's told me that your marriage is definitely over.'

'Definitely,' Maddy confirmed, with feeling.

Ffion smiled. 'Then call him.' She moved a couple of steps down the path, raising her voice sightly to add, 'And I'll remember everything you said about Ruthie having a will of her own.'

At that, Chloe turned back, smiling. 'Oh, have you told her and she's OK about Ruthie's will?'

Dismay and horror flitted over Ffion's face.

Maddy stared from Ffion to Chloe and back again. Shock was an odd thing. It made you hear blood rushing in your ears but turned other voices to distant gurgles. She was aware of Ffion speaking sharply to Chloe and Chloe looking confused, but time slowed so the passage of that short exchange gave Maddy time to think a hundred thoughts and feel a dozen emotions.

Then Ffion's face swam back into her vision, and she was only a step from Maddy again. Maddy said, 'Of course. I suppose she'll change her will in your favour.'

Ffion's forehead was creased in distress. 'Spending all weekend together, we talked about all kinds of things, so it cropped up, but nothing's decided and I certainly haven't presumed. Oh, dear. This conversation should be a long way down the road. Would you like us to come back in to talk it out?' She sounded mortified and her skin was as pale as the snow.

'It's OK.' Maddy seemed to hear her own voice reverberate around her head before it left her lips. She blinked and tried to focus. 'I can quite see—' She pulled herself together with a huge effort, though she felt as if she'd just been punched hard in the heart. 'Only come in if you need to sit down or something. You're looking very white.'

In fact, Ffion looked as if she was about to burst into tears. 'I'm mortified,' she choked. 'You must think I've been scheming.'

Maddy took in a breath. Nelson's Bar was still here on the planet and Lyla and Ruthie were safe indoors. Everything else could be coped with. 'Don't be mortified and I don't think anything of the kind. But I do need to get on with the meal.' Performing ordinary, everyday tasks would let her heart rediscover its usual rhythm. She noticed Chloe had taken out her phone and was stabbing at the screen. Knowing Ruthie's phone had text-to-speech enabled, she said more loudly, 'I'll give Ruthie the opportunity to talk to me if she wants after Lyla's in bed. Would you do me a favour and not tell her about this conversation, meanwhile?'

Chloe's phone hand sagged.

'Oh, gosh,' said Ffion, miserably, as she turned and trailed towards the car.

Maddy passed the rest of the evening in a dream. Lyla had taken the commencement of Christmas seriously and had made paper cones as Christmas hats to wear at dinner. After admiring the colouring in of the wobbly star on the front, Maddy perched hers precariously on her hair. She made bread sauce – Lyla's favourite part of Christmas dinner – even though it was an odd accompaniment to sausage casserole. After she'd washed up, she snuggled with Lyla to look through the paintings she'd brought home, describing them in loving detail to Ruthie. She asked Alexa to play children's Christmas songs and waltzed around the front room with Lyla holding her hands and hop-skipping-and-jumping.

She thought about putting Lyla to bed and then disappearing into her room with the last third of the bottle of wine, but, instead, she read Lyla to sleep and then lay beside her for twenty minutes listening to the sweet, even breathing of her darling daughter. She thought hard about her life, present and future, what was important, what she could or should expect, and how to behave now.

She also thought about parents and children and had to wipe a couple of tears.

Finally, she went downstairs. Ruthie sat in her armchair with everything to hand on her side table, listening to glockenspiel music, slow and sweet with a hint of melancholy. She glanced up with a smile of welcome when she heard Maddy arrive.

Maddy pulled up the footstool and took Ruthie's hand. 'I've been thinking how lovely it is that Ffion found you,' she said. 'Do you think Nigel would have been pleased?'

A smile wavered over Ruthie's lips. 'I was just thinking about him,' she confessed. 'I think he would. Ffion, she's sort of brought a bit of him back to me. And Chloe too, of course. I'm blessed, but I do miss him, dear.'

Maddy's eyes stung for her aunt. Many women – most, even – would have felt bitter and neglected but somehow Ruthie had valued what Nigel could give her, and understood that he'd been incapable of more. 'Ffion and Raff have only good things to say about him.' She swallowed. 'I hope Ffion appreciates that you gave her adoptive parents worth having.' She spared a thought for her own dad who'd been acceptably married to her mother when they'd brought her into the world but who hadn't even sent Maddy a Christmas card this year or last. Her mother's Christmas card was on the mantel and read

Felice Navidad. It had contained money for Maddy to 'get presents for you all'.

It was this woman before her who'd given Maddy what was important in life – love and support.

She cleared her throat. 'You know, Ruthie, when you made me the beneficiary of your will, we didn't know about Ffion. You'll want to change it now.'

Ruthie's head swivelled her way and her hand tightened over Maddy's. 'But, my dear, you and Lyla have been everything to me . . . I can't bear you to be hurt.' She tailed off, face crumpling.

'But you didn't know where Ffion was. Now you do,' Maddy insisted gently. 'She's your daughter and I'm your niece. Of course, she should have your house, just as Lyla would get High Cottage if anything happened to me.' Once Adey had signed it over, anyway. She even tried to joke. 'I have a solicitor's appointment for January, and I don't need it now Adey's turned up. You can have it.'

But Ruthie was crying, not laughing, dragging a piece of kitchen roll from the sleeve of her enormous cardigan. 'You're the best, Maddy, dear. You are just the *best*.'

Later, when Maddy had checked Ruthie had what she needed at bedtime and then that Lyla was sound asleep, she did help herself to the last of the wine. She carried it upstairs to her room, then lay down on her bed and cried. She wasn't crying for being usurped in Ruthie's will. It was true that if she'd left her the house Ruthie would have given Maddy and Lyla lasting security; true that when the time came Maddy would now have to find another way to be a working mum. But it was being usurped in Ruthie's life that made her heart hurt. Ffion and Chloe, intentionally or not, were taking her place.

But Ruthie had taught Maddy how to give uncon-
ditional love.

Now it was Maddy's turn to show it.

She could make the transition easy for Ruthie, or hard.
Easy, she thought. *Ruthie deserves that one thing in her
life comes easy, and I will make it happen.*

Chapter Twenty-Four

In the morning, Maddy suggested to Ruthie that they tramp around the village to see all the cottages lit up for Christmas. 'We'll wrap up warm,' she said. 'There's not much snow but Lyla will enjoy skidding about in it.' Ruthie had been quiet so far this morning and Maddy was sure it was a hangover from their difficult conversation yesterday evening. Getting out into the crisp wintry day might lighten the atmosphere.

Before long, Lyla scraping her feet along the pavement and declaring it 'skiing', Ruthie and Maddy linking arms, they strolled along Jubilee Crescent. 'Number twenty-five has a reindeer on its porch and number twenty-seven has a gorgeous Christmas tree in the window,' Maddy reported, so Ruthie could supplement her blurred vision with imaginings.

Lyla chimed in. 'And nearly all the houses have O's on their doors.'

'Circular Christmas wreaths, like the one we made for our door,' Maddy clarified, in case that was lost in translation.

Lyla undertook telling Ruthie what arrangement of lights hung on each lamppost. 'There's a snowman, a star, a walking stick—'

'Candy cane,' Maddy supplied.

'Santa, a snowflake,' Lyla continued, undaunted, giving a pirouette and almost slipping over.

Maddy was about to steer them up to Droody Road, with the intention of walking a rough circle around the village, when she spied a familiar colourful figure outside a house. 'Look, there's Della. Shall we say hello?'

'Lovely,' said Ruthie.

Della was already waving and calling, 'Hello, everyone. Coming in to try my ginger snaps?'

'Yes, please,' Lyla bawled back, skipping off to be first in the queue.

Maddy was happy to add her voice to the acceptance, remembering, once indoors, that she was to ask Della if she was free to visit Ruthie that evening. Della answered, comfortably, 'Of course,' without pausing in her task of laying out ginger snaps dusted with icing sugar.

While they were eating, their coats hung in a row on hooks on the back of the door, Maddy's attention strayed to the craft items Della had readied for her final fair of the season. Topping one pile was a square Christmas card, bigger than the rest. White, it was decorated with a glittery red heart wrapped in gold ribbon that Della had sewn through the card and tied with a bow. Maddy opened the card to reveal an inner sleeve of thick white paper, and *I wish you only good things this Christmas* lettered in Della's best calligraphy.

It was a heart-warming sentiment, typical of genuine, lovely Della. Impulsively, Maddy asked, 'Is this ordered? Or can I buy it?'

'Have it, have it,' Della cried expansively, wiping sticky hands on an apron with a big poinsettia printed on it.

Then Maddy had to do what she thought of as a reverse haggle, Della not wanting to charge a friend and Maddy reluctant to cheat one. Finally, they agreed on two pounds, which Maddy thought was about half of what she'd charge at a fair. But she had a purpose in mind for the card . . .

Later, when they'd said bye, finished their circuit of the village and returned home, Maddy's phone rang with the number of Emiline, better known in their household as 'Misty's mummy'.

'Hi,' said Emiline, when Maddy answered. 'Would Lyla like to come for lunch and to play this afternoon? Misty's brother's got a friend over and she's moping because they're leaving her out.'

Lyla bounced around to demonstrate how much she very much *would* like to play at Misty's house, so they all got into the car, Ruthie along for the ride, and drove to nearby Thornham to deliver an excitedly chattering Lyla and arrange to pick her up at five.

'Doesn't the car feel quiet now?' Maddy joked, as they drove home.

'Bless her,' Ruthie said fondly. 'But yes.'

They ate lunch, then Ruthie settled down to listen to Radio 4, one of her favourite channels to nod off to.

'Will you be OK if I nip out to deliver a card while you have your nap?' Maddy asked, trying not to go pink.

Ruthie twinkled knowingly. 'That lovely big card? Of course, I'll be fine.'

Maddy settled at the kitchen table with the card open before her, pen in hand. The moment she'd seen it, she'd known it might provide a way of reopening communications with Raff. Letters had worked well enough for Ruthie and Nigel, after all, creating something so lasting that they'd brought Ruthie together with Ffion more than two decades after death had parted her from Nigel.

This wouldn't be exactly a love letter but . . .

Above *I wish you only good things this Christmas* she wrote, *To Raff* and below it – after a hesitation – *love, Maddy x.* Then she stared at the other page, virgin white, empty of words but full of potential.

It took a while to marshal her thoughts, but then she began, trying to express herself honestly without making frightening declarations, at the same time as keeping her writing neat. She wrote quickly, letting her feelings flood onto the page and not overthinking. Then she slipped the card into its envelope and wrote *Raff* on the front.

A peep into the front room told her Ruthie was nodding peacefully, her glasses still on her face, as if they might show her more in her dreams than in real life. Maddy wriggled into her outdoor things and quietly let herself out of the house.

It didn't take long to reach Docking, as the snow petered out almost as she hit the main road. The sky was a glorious winter blue above the hedges and her heart felt lighter than it had since Saturday, when Raff had transformed into a flint-eyed stranger who'd turned on his heel and vanished from her life. In ten minutes, she was turning up the drive to his little home.

'Damn,' she whispered, as she saw that his car wasn't in its usual place. Her imagination had supplied her with a scenario of him being there, answering the door, asking her in, reading her card and – maybe? – pulling her into his arms, like a Christmas movie.

Then she cheered up. This way, he could read without her having to wait self-consciously to see if he wanted what she wanted.

After parking, she hopped out of the car, clutching the card. It was so wide that it would only just fit through the letterbox, which she had to hold open with one hand while sliding the envelope carefully through with the other. When she turned away, she caught sight of a small figure strolling up the drive. 'Hello, Ffion,' she called. 'I don't think Raff's here.'

As it was Ffion who'd suggested she try again with Raff, she was nonplussed to catch the other woman's expression of almost comical dismay. 'Ah,' said Ffion unhappily. 'I've been wondering whether I should phone you.'

They gazed at each other.

When Ffion only gnawed her lip, Maddy prompted her. 'Well, here I am. You might as well just say it.'

Ffion shuffled her feet, shod in sensibly wintry boots. 'When we spoke yesterday, I hadn't realised that one of the cards I hadn't opened was from Raff. He must have posted it through the door.' She hesitated, and Maddy wondered what was coming next. Ffion took a step closer. 'Inside, it said he was going off somewhere. For Christmas week.' Her forehead wrinkled. 'He said not to worry but . . . well, he's with Antonella, apparently. I've tried to ring, but only get voicemail.'

A cold thrill of dismay shivered through Maddy. 'Oh, shit,' she breathed, thinking of the card she'd just slipped through his letterbox.

Ffion clutched her gloved hands together. 'I'm so sorry. When I said what I did about him and you yesterday, I was out of order, evidently.'

'Oh, *shit*,' Maddy said on a groan this time. The card had a heart on it. Tied with a *bow*. Like, 'Here is my heart at Christmas . . .'

'Had you come to see him?' Ffion sounded anxious, but sympathetic.

Maddy ignored her words. All she could think of was that damned soppy Christmas card. Then she grasped that Ffion must be here for a purpose. 'Do you have a key?' she demanded eagerly. 'I . . .' She fought for an explanation. 'I accidentally posted something through the door with a Christmas card.'

But Ffion shook her head and pulled a small envelope from her pocket. 'I'd written his card by the time I saw his note, so I thought I might as well leave it for him to find after Christmas.' She reached around Maddy and posted it through the flap.

Maddy rubbed her forehead, which was unpleasantly tight, probably through both cold and stress. Raff had gone somewhere with his ex-wife? For Christmas? And he'd return to read Maddy's bleating. She screwed up her eyes as she was struck by the full horror of the depths of her humiliation. And it wasn't as if she'd never see him again. He was Ffion's brother. She wanted to drop her face into her palms and wail, *Nooooo* . . .

Then she realised that Ffion was asking if she'd like to go home with her for a cuppa.

'Can't,' she said. Then, realising she'd been ungracious, added, 'But thanks very much.'

Then she hopped back into her car and, reversing it around so fast the engine whined, shot down the drive, aware of Ffion staring after her. She had a plan. Not much of a plan, but the best she could come up with. She knew the whereabouts of the village shop, which she'd passed only minutes before. She drove there right on the speed limit, and parked. Inside, she ran to the rack of Christmas cards and snatched up the first innocuous one she saw – a robin looking chirpy and wearing a Santa hat. The words inside were a simple *Merry Christmas* and she queued to pay for it and hurried inside to the car to scrabble for the pen she kept in the centre console.

A deep, calming breath or so, then, balancing the card awkwardly, she began.

Dear Raff,
This is a message to say I've got the message.
I really hope you'll bin the other card unread. I'm mortified to think I wrote it at all, let alone while you were with Antonella. I have obviously completely misread everything and thought that you were upset that I might be letting Adey back into my life and you minded.

That was too many ands in one sentence but who cared. If she could edit anything in her life, it would be that bloody card she'd left at his house ten minutes ago.

Anyway, she went on, *as our paths are almost sure to cross again, let's not let our misunderstandings get in the way of Ruthie, Ffion and Chloe's growing closeness. It's what we both wanted. I wish you happiness, not just at Christmas but always. Maddy.*

All the *oomph* seemed to go out of her as she sealed the envelope with the card inside. When she'd written his name on the front, she added in block capitals on both front and back: *IMPORTANT! READ ME FIRST!*

She drove back to High Street, praying he hadn't arrived home and had time to read her other card. But his parking space was still empty, and no light showed indoors as the colour began to leave the sky. She shoved the second card through the letter plate as carelessly as she'd been careful with the first, then plumped dispiritedly back into her car and drove home.

Back at The Hollies, she dumped her coat and boots, pausing to examine a delivery that had been left in the hall addressed in familiar handwriting to Miss Lyla Austen. Her eyebrows arched. Adey had sent Lyla a Christmas gift? Somehow, Maddy hadn't expected it. Well, OK. Good. Arrogant shit assuming Lyla had been given his surname, though.

She heard Ruthie's voice float from the front room. 'OK, dear. Keep safe, now.' Then, more loudly, 'Maddy? Is that you? Ffion's just been on the phone.'

Maddy took a breath, then pinned on a smile and entered the room. 'Oh?' she said, sounding lightly interested.

Ruthie was frowning. 'She sounded a bit low. This horrible heart condition. She gets too tired for words, and Christmas can be exhausting for anyone.' The face she turned on her niece was crumpled with anxiety. 'And apparently, Raff's spending Christmas somewhere else.'

Perhaps to ensure that Ruthie would forget about Raff's Christmas, Maddy took only a nanosecond to divine what would make Christmas perfect for her aunt. 'Why don't you invite her and Chloe here for Christmas? That would be one less pressure for Ffion.'

Ruthie's expression transformed. 'Maddy, really?'

Maddy laughed, stooping to give Ruthie a hug. 'Of course. It's your house, after all.' Then she wished she could take that back, in case it had sounded like a pass-agg reference to the house never going to Maddy.

But Ruthie was evidently either too happy or too kind to infer any such thing. 'But it's you who does the cooking,' she protested unconvincingly.

'I'm all about cooking though, aren't I?' Maddy joked, taking comfort from being enveloped in Ruthie's arms. Hugs were the universal medicine. 'Even with Heloise, that's only six of us. Unless Della's coming?'

Ruthie pulled back and lifted her glasses to wipe her eyes. 'Not for dinner, but later, for drinks.'

The more she thought about the Christmas Day arrangement, the more positive Maddy felt about it. It would be an opportunity to get to know Ffion and Chloe better without having to invite Raff, as he'd made other plans. Pain darted through her at the thought of him spending Christmas with Antonella, but she shoved it ruthlessly aside. Ffion and Chloe were part of her big picture. Part of the rest of her life. Raff would be . . . just a connection, through his sister. 'A big gathering will help cheer Heloise up. She's still upset about Harris.'

'I hope he has a horrid Christmas,' Ruthie said vindictively. 'Ratfink.'

Maddy laughed. 'You won't get a disagreement from me. Most importantly, though, you'll spend Christmas with your daughter and granddaughter. Lovely.'

Ruthie gave a sniff. 'You're so sweet to me, Maddy.'

Don't cry, Maddy thought. *I'll just join in. And then I'll have to explain. And I don't want to.* 'Pah, I'm ordinary,' she scoffed. 'Why don't I fetch Lyla from Thornham while you call Ffion back?'

It was a good plan to get Maddy a little alone time while she conquered her emotions. But it went wrong when her own phone rang as she drew up outside Misty's house. The caller ID said *Ffion*.

'Are you really sure about Christmas Day?' Ffion asked hesitantly, when Maddy answered. 'Two extra people can seem like a lot.'

'Not to me,' Maddy answered truthfully. 'I trained as a chef. It'll be good for you to put your feet up. You can host next year, when you've had your heart fixed.'

It proved to be exactly the right thing to say, as Ffion's voice filled with joy. 'I definitely will. I was feeling a bit . . . with Raff having made other arrangements. *Thank* you. Thanks a lot. We really appreciate it. Chloe's thrilled to bits.'

'Perfect,' said Maddy. And realised that, under the circumstances, it was as close to perfect as it could be. Ffion and Chloe had changed Ruthie's life for the better by being in it, which gave Maddy the warmest glow. Maddy's life was better for Adey ceasing to be a threat to her happiness – unless he caused future problems with Lyla.

OK, Maddy's life was worse for Raff not being in it. It was as if a fire had gone out.

But two out of three wasn't bad.

Chapter Twenty-Five

On Christmas Day, Maddy woke even before Lyla, which was *not* fair because it wasn't as if she was excited about Christmas. Oh, she'd enjoy watching Lyla open her gifts and spending time with family and friends, but there was a gaping hole in the celebrations without Raff.

She sighed and turned over. Into her mind floated a rosy daydream of Raff arriving with Ffion and Chloe today, presuming he was invited, declaring that Ffion had been hallucinating when she read his note about spending Christmas with Antonella. Then he'd stay long after everyone else had left or gone to bed and they'd lock the door of the front room and make love before the fire . . . Heat raced through her to gather in all the best places.

She had to focus on the future. The past was over. There was a lot to be done, so she gave up on sleep, squashed the daydream into the back recesses of her mind, rolled out of bed and got on with her Christmas Day.

She'd only had time to get the woodstove going and the kettle boiling before Lyla came flying down the stairs bawling, 'Mummy, it's Christmas! Has Santa been? Can I have my presents?'

Maddy had assembled the gifts beneath the tree last night, after Lyla and Ruthie had gone to bed, before Heloise came round to drink Christmas champagne. Well, cava, because champagne was expensive. It had been fizzy and dry, anyway, and a real Christmas treat when accompanied by a movie called *A Bride for Christmas*, which had made them flick Pringles at the screen when a man – inevitably – turned out to be a dud.

Now Lyla skidded to a halt on the knees of her Christmas pyjamas before the heap of presents, hands reaching greedily for a red stocking with her name embroidered on it – Della's handiwork, of course – and ornamented with jolly green tartan ribbon.

'Whoa,' called Maddy, hurrying to stop her. 'Merry Christmas, but Ruthie's not up.' She planted a kiss on the soft, young cheek.

Lyla groaned and wheedled, 'Pleeeeease? Just my stocking?'

Maddy was unmoved. 'We can have a special breakfast while we wait,' she promised. 'How about pancakes with Nutella?' She'd made the batter last night and she and Heloise had eaten pancakes with the champagne and Pringles.

'Yeah!' Lyla wriggled down and pelted into the kitchen.

As Maddy had expected, the sugary aroma of pancakes brought Ruthie out of her bedroom, blinking through her glasses, wrapped in an enormous blue fluffy dressing gown that made her look like a walking teddy bear.

'Presents!' Lyla squealed, jumping to her feet.

Maddy caught her neatly and swung her back onto her chair. 'As soon as we've eaten our pancakes.'

342

Ruthie laughed. 'Ooh, Mummy's fierce, Lyla. Let's eat up quickly.'

No sooner had the last bite of pancake disappeared than Lyla bounced from her seat and careered into the front room shouting, 'Presents, presents!'

Maddy laughed as she and Ruthie followed. Almost all Lyla's presents were known to Maddy, of course, as she'd bought and wrapped them, either on behalf of herself or Ruthie.

The little girl squealed and cheered as she powered through the small gifts in her stocking, wrapping seeming to fly off on its own: hair slides, a game, a book. 'Dressing gown!' she crowed. 'Jewellery maker! Camera! Backpack! Drinks bottle! And my *scooter!*' In minutes, she was in her new dressing gown, scooting gently on her silver scooter. 'Can we go outside?'

Maddy gave her a hug. 'Later,' she promised. 'We're not dressed.'

The only parcel with unknown contents was the one from Adey. As it was addressed to Lyla directly, Maddy hadn't even removed the outer wrapping. Now Lyla stopped and frowned at the brown paper. Her hair swirled as she swung towards Maddy. 'Is this for me?'

'It says it's for Miss Lyla. Is the writing a bit grown up for you to read?' Maddy asked, glad to avoid the question of Lyla being addressed as Austen instead of Cracey.

Lyla abruptly tired of the subject and ripped at the brown paper. Her eyes grew big and round. 'A chocolate lolly maker and a set of glitter tattoos,' she breathed delightedly.

Maddy smothered a laugh. Adey had probably bought her exactly what he'd like himself, had he been a six-year-old girl. Messy, extravagant, and totally fun. Not for him mixing in useful gifts like a dressing gown. Her gaze caught on a pink envelope. 'There's a card.'

Lyla opened it, frowned, then brought it over to Maddy. 'It's grown-up writing again.'

Probably the only thing about Adey that had ever grown up, Maddy thought, turning the card so she could read it aloud. 'It says, "Happy Christmas, Lyla. Love from Daddy."'

'Daddy?' Lyla looked up at Maddy with Adey's grey eyes. 'He sent me a present?'

Maddy gently gathered her up. 'That was nice of him, wasn't it?'

Lyla nodded, her expression thoughtful. 'Will he send me a present for my birthday, too?'

'Maybe.' Maddy shrugged. 'But that's not till June, so we won't find out for ages.' She made a mental note to give Adey Lyla's date of birth, which gave her a funny, sad feeling inside. She stowed it with all the other sad feelings and began to open her own gifts. She and Ruthie always bought each other things they needed as well as wanted, and Maddy did the shopping for them both. She received a rust-coloured dress that Lyla declared 'orange' and a pair of soft black ankle boots. Ruthie received new cardigans and, from Lyla, underwear.

Lyla burst into a fit of giggles. 'I bought Grauntie Ruthie big knickers.' She'd chosen them herself on a shopping expedition to Hunstanton.

Ruthie grinned imperturbably. 'Good. I've got a big bum.'

Lyla laughed until she sprawled sideways on the floor.

They hardly had time to shower and dress in their Christmas Day finery before Heloise arrived, to be greeted at the door by Lyla shouting, 'Grauntie Ruthie's wearing new knickers.'

'So am I,' Heloise announced amiably, though she declined to show Lyla, making Maddy suspect that Heloise had treated herself to something lacy and wispy rather than the kind of secure upholstery Ruthie favoured.

Heloise had brought Lyla the promised unicorn backpack and a mermaid nightlight, which required some assembly, and Maddy was lying on the floor poring over the instructions when the doorbell rang. Lyla flew to the door as if attached to it by elastic. 'Chloe,' she shouted excitedly, fighting with the deadbolt before flinging the portal wide.

'Lyla!' Chloe called back, sounding just as happy to see Lyla as Lyla was to see her.

Maddy knelt up, grinning as she watched Lyla drag a grinning Chloe over the threshold and Ffion follow more sedately. Before the door closed, she risked a quick squint at the garden path, in case Raff lurked there as in her Christmas morning fantasy. The path was empty – Christmas morning reality.

Chloe wore the biggest hoodie Maddy had ever seen, pink and black striped with a beanie hat to match. 'Here's your prezzie, Lyla.' Chloe held out a squashy gift in silver wrapping and Lyla ripped into it without delay.

When it proved to be a version of Chloe's outfit but in her own size, she breathed, 'I'm going to look like Chloe.'

Chloe wrapped her arms around her. 'That's why I wore this outfit today, so we'd look the same.'

Ffion retrieved the label to show the writing to Lyla. 'It's from me and Raff as well.'

Lyla looked at Maddy. 'Is Raff coming?'

Maddy didn't let her expression shift from its current bland smile. 'He's gone away for Christmas.'

'Aw,' mourned Lyla. Then she leapt up to hover at Ruthie's elbow while Ruthie opened her present from Ffion, Chloe and Raff, which proved to be a deeply carved wooden box.

'Lovely.' Ruthie ran her fingertips over it and located the catch. She plunged a hand inside and felt around, then frowned in puzzlement. 'What's in here? It feels like paper.'

Ffion turned pink. 'I hope you like it. It's a keepsake chest. I've put all your letters to Dad in there, and I thought you might like to add his to you. Keep them together.'

'Oh, my dear,' Ruthie breathed, and had to stop and wipe the corner of her eye. She stroked the carving. 'What a lovely thought. Together.'

With scant regard for privacy, Lyla demanded, 'Can I read your letters, Grauntie Ruthie?'

Ruthie laughed and patted Lyla's shoulder. 'They're all in grown-up writing, I'm afraid, dear.'

'What a thoughtful present. And thank you for my lovely perfume,' Maddy said, unwrapping hers with *Ffion, Chloe and Raff* on the label. It was something she wouldn't buy herself, but about as wishy-washy as the toiletries she'd bought Ffion and Chloe and the pretty silver necklaces she'd bought for them on Ruthie's behalf. Safe, ordinary presents.

Ruthie went into her bedroom and reappeared with the shirt box of Nigel's letters, placing them with gentle reverence into the beautiful keepsake box, and carefully snapping it shut. Maddy made a mental note to suggest Ruthie keep it out of Lyla's reach, just in case some imp

346

of curiosity prompted the little girl to broach the contents and damage something that could never be replaced.

'Right,' she said, jumping up. 'The turkey's been in for a while but it's time I moved things on.'

Ffion came to help with vegetable preparation while Heloise took charge of clearing up wrapping paper, so she and Chloe could transform the front room into a dining space by carrying in the kitchen table and working out how to insert the extra section. Lyla had dressed in her new outfit like Chloe's and now played with her Christmas presents in a corner. Ruthie pottered from kitchen to sitting room, carrying a cloth and cutlery for Heloise and Chloe to add to the table. As they all worked together towards a traditional festive feast, with carols playing and the house filling with delicious aromas, it was, Maddy thought, as Christmassy and loving as it got.

Or so she thought, until, entering the kitchen, Ffion grumbled, 'I'm going to brain my brother when I see him.'

Maddy looked up from squishing together bread, milk and onion for the bread sauce. 'Oh?' What on earth had Raff done to earn such a ferocious frown from his usually placid sister?

Ffion shot her a look over the sprouts she was peeling. 'Apart from the card he left before he went, he's been completely incommunicado. Not even a reply when I sent him a "Merry Christmas" text this morning.'

'Oh, he's ghosted you, too?' Then feeling that was possibly a touch too revealing, Maddy picked up her sharp knife to check whether the potatoes had parboiled.

'Apparently. And he never does that.' Ffion groaned. 'I just want to know he's OK.'

Biting back, 'Maybe not to you,' and forbearing to mention the several silences from Raff's side while Ffion and Chloe had been deciding whether to meet Ruthie, Maddy sighed. It had been bad enough thinking he was off somewhere enjoying himself with his wife. But why wasn't he in contact with Ffion? With her, at least, he'd always seemed so concerned and attentive. The thought brought back the horrible first weeks after Adey left. Or . . . her heart turned over. Was he hurt somewhere?

Apart from that shadow over the day, Christmas went beautifully. Dinner was devoured, and Maddy showered with compliments, which she accepted gracefully. She might not be able to exist without scaring men off, but she knew she could cook.

Della arrived in the middle of the afternoon, with gifts for Ruthie and a delighted Lyla, who ripped into hers as if it was her first all day and was over the moon to find a girl's make-up kit, which Maddy hoped washed out, along with the gravy stains and white sauce currently ornamenting Lyla's new hoodie. A new guest meant fresh food, of course, and Maddy broke out mince pies, cinnamon cookies and chocolate cupcakes, which somehow everyone found room for.

Eventually, Heloise pulled Maddy down on the sofa. 'Sit still and enjoy a glass of wine. I expect you've been on the go all day.'

'I have.' Maddy gladly accepted a frothing glass of pink fizz poured by Heloise's generous hand. Keeping busy had kept her mind off Raff, but now chat and laughter, too much food and a little alcohol would do almost as good a job.

Chloe approached Maddy with a tentative smile. 'Do you watch mushy Christmas movies on Christmas afternoon?'

Maddy gladly passed her the TV remote. 'We have

Netflix because Heloise bought us an extra member slot. You'll be bound to find something.'

And if anyone saw a tiny tear escape the corner of Maddy's eye during the movie, they'd all blame it on *The Family Stone* and Sarah Jessica Parker's character demonstrating how it's possible to feel alone in a crowded house.

Lyla became restive and peeled off her tights to stick glitter tattoos on her bare legs. Then she came over to Maddy, who was sitting on cushions on the floor as the sofa was full of Chloe, Della and Heloise, and Ffion and Ruthie were each snatching forty winks in an armchair.

'Are we going to FaceTime Grandma?' Lyla asked. 'You said we would.'

Christmas Day and birthdays were when they usually spoke, though it seemed to get later in the day each time. Understanding that a movie full of elves and reindeer would have been more Lyla's cup of tea, Maddy climbed to her feet, yawning. 'Thanks for the reminder. Let's go up to my room.'

They lay flat on Maddy's bed while she held the phone above them, and they managed fifteen minutes of chat with Linda, who'd snatched a break from serving in her boyfriend's bar and looked tanned, despite it being winter. She pushed back her hair, a similar brown to Maddy's but worn short and stylish, and asked, 'How's Ruthie? Have you had nice presents?' as if she hardly knew them at all, which was very nearly true.

When they went back down to join the gathering, Maddy said, 'Mum said "hi",' and reflected that having low expectations of her mother at least ensured that she was never disappointed.

Then Lyla ran to the sitting room window. 'It's snowing again! Snow, snow, snowy snow.'

Della stirred. 'Norfolk's due a packet of snow tonight. I think I'll get off home.'

Heloise decided it was time she went, too, and offered to walk with Della. In ten minutes they'd gathered up the gifts they'd received, wrapped themselves snugly, said ten goodbyes and twenty thank yous, and gone out together into a world of fat snowflakes that whirled to earth to settle silently on roofs edged by fairy lights.

Although Ffion gave the snow a dubious look and said, 'We'll have to go soon. I wouldn't want to get stuck,' Chloe had begun teaching Lyla a breakdance move in the hall, where she looked as if her feet were climbing an invisible wall before she flipped and landed on her feet.

Maddy went into the kitchen for a big mug of coffee, alcohol at lunchtime having made her heavy-headed. While she waited for the kettle to boil and wondered whether there would be coffee makers in the January sales, she cleared lunch debris and stacked plates to be washed.

Then she heard footsteps and turned to see Ruthie and Ffion, wearing matching serious expressions.

'What's up?' she asked in sudden alarm.

Ruthie shuffled forward and groped for Maddy's hands. 'Maddy,' she pronounced solemnly. 'You have been wonderful to me. Can I adopt you?'

Although her eyes burned with sudden tears at the accolade, Maddy laughed. 'I don't think you can adopt adults, Ruthie. If you'd asked when I was ten, I would have left Mum for you like a shot.'

Ruthie didn't laugh, but edged closer, as if trying to see Maddy as best she could. 'What I mean,' she said, her voice trembling, 'is that I want to *treat* you like my daughter and leave everything equally between you and

Ffion. Not that I mean to fall off my perch any time soon,' she cautioned with sudden asperity. 'But you've been everything to me, dear, and though I've found my daughter after so long, that doesn't erase what we mean to each other.'

Tears burned in Maddy's eyes and then began to slip down her cheeks. 'Ruthie,' she quavered. 'You don't have to—'

'I don't have to,' Ruthie agreed firmly. 'I want to.'

'I want it too,' Ffion said. 'I only ever had that manky brother of mine, so a pseudo sister will be great.'

A strangled half-laugh, half-sob emerged from Maddy's throat. Wordlessly, she slipped her arms around her aunt and her 'pseudo sister' in a group hug. Family was what you made it, after all. 'You've made my Christmas Day,' she managed to choke.

Except for, you know. No Raff. Maddy had looked under the tree and waited for Santa to return on his sleigh . . . but no sign of Raff at all.

It was late when Raff reached his home in Docking, dizzy from driving through snow, fed up with the world and particularly with the stupidest Christmas he'd ever experienced. He was stiff from sitting in crawling lines of traffic, while snow stuck to the faces of signposts – thank goodness for sat navs – and hid kerbs. It had sent a car into a ditch not far ahead of him. He'd stopped to make sure no one was hurt and for a heart-stopping minute his own car wheels had spun before he got going again. After that, he hadn't dared leave the endless wheel ruts in the snow to stop for fuel, and his gauge had been stuck at zero for at least twenty miles.

He almost fell into his bijou house, comparatively warm

but feeling unlived in and unloved. When he put down his laptop bag and switched on the light, he saw his phone where he'd been hoping for several days it was: sitting on the kitchen island, charging. 'Idiot,' he muttered, picking it up.

The screen alight with red dots denoting messages and missed calls. He groaned. Ffion was going to be so pissed with him for being out of touch.

Should he just go to bed? She'd probably be asleep. Christmas Day was tiring for anybody, let alone someone with a leaky heart valve. He could just send a brief, *I'm home. Sorry to be out of touch. Will explain tomorrow. Exhausted now.* But if she did happen to be awake, she'd immediately call. He needed food, a hot shower and a night's sleep before he talked to anyone in anything but a pissed-off growl.

He put down the phone, wondering what quick meals the freezer held. Amazing how six days away could wipe your memory. Then he noticed a scattering of envelopes on the doormat, unceremoniously trodden over as he came in. It would have been easy to continue to ignore them, but one had scrawled upon it in block capitals, *IMPORTANT. READ ME FIRST.* First? Before what? Intrigued, he scooped up all the mail, tossing all but *READ ME FIRST* on the counter and opened the envelope.

A Christmas card. Oh-kay. Didn't seem that urgent. He opened it and scanned quickly . . . *I've got the message.* What? . . . *bin the other card unread* . . . his eyes flicked to the rest of his mail, wondering if 'the other card' was in it . . . *mortified* . . . *while you were with Antonella.* 'With Antonella?' he said aloud, frowning . . . *thought that you were upset that I might be letting Adey back into my life . . . I wish you happiness, not just at Christmas but always. Maddy.*

Maddy. He reread the line about him *thinking* she'd let Adey back in her life several times, then he snatched up the rest of the envelopes and flipped through for another with his name in the same handwriting.

It was the largest.

Impatiently, he fumbled and ripped at the white envelope until the thick, beautifully embellished card was in his hands. A split second to admire the heart wrapped in ribbon, then he opened the card.

Dear Raff,

I thought about borrowing 'My dearest, darling' from Ruthie and Nigel's letters that spanned so many years, but this is not quite a love letter. It's an I-like-you-very-much-and-miss-you-and-that-night-together-was-very-special letter.

I made a mess of telling you about Adey at the hospital. I was stunned by everything, including the way Gina, Adey's girlfriend, bosses him about. My only feelings for Adey are exasperation and wry amusement because Gina has him exactly where she wants him. I wanted him to meet Lyla for Lyla's sake, though it's too early to know if she'll want contact in the future. I'll give you the whole story when we talk, if you're not too sick of my weird life to hear it.

The important thing is that Adey and I will get divorced next year.

So . . . I really hope that despite your text silence you'll want to see me again to talk, even if you don't feel like taking up where we left off. In fact, I hope you'll come to The Hollies on Christmas Day. That would make it into the best Christmas for years.

But, if not, I hope that you have a fantastic festive season with your family. It's obvious that Ffion and Chloe love you very much.

Merry Christmas.

Maddy xx

He went back to the beginning and read it again. Then he tossed it onto the counter.

Chapter Twenty-Six

The Hollies was silent.

Lyla was asleep, surrounded by Christmas gifts, her mermaid nightlight glowing. Ruthie too was in bed. Probably, her carved box of letters would be close by. That present had been well-judged by Ffion, Maddy thought – putting Ruthie and Nigel's letters together was a message. Ffion accepted that their love had brought her into the world.

Maddy performed her night-time routine, then selected one of the books Heloise had bought her for Christmas and climbed into bed, leaving the lamp on so she could read. Tomorrow, being Boxing Day, she'd produce another feast. Whether Ffion and Chloe made it would depend upon the snow. It had been about three inches thick when she'd last checked. It might not be so bad in Docking but Long Climb being so impossible in bad weather, she thought it likely they'd stay in their own home.

Never mind. Heloise and Della would come again, and everyone would be out playing in the snow, scarves flying, faces laughing, uncaring that Christmas Day had been and gone.

Almost gone, she amended, checking her bedside clock. Not quite midnight yet.

That's when she heard the sound. Loud in the silent darkness, it was exactly like the clap of the letter flap. She waited, listening, wondering. Then something thunked against her bedroom window. When she pulled the curtain aside there was a blob of snow on the diamond pane, as if someone had thrown a snowball. The snowy porch roof blocked her view of the path, but the village looked asleep after a busy Christmas Day, alight in the darkness, because of its mantle of white.

Dragging on her red fleece robe and the white slipper boots that reached almost to her knees, she crept to the top of the stairs. From there, she could see that an envelope lay on the front doormat. Slowly, she padded down the stairs.

As she drew nearer, she saw that printed on the front of the envelope was: *MADDY. READ ME! URGENT!*

With a feeling of unreality, she picked it up, slit it with her thumb then withdrew and unfolded a piece of lined paper covered in blue-inked handwriting.

My dearest, darling Maddy,

Thank you for your cards – or, at least, the first you wrote. It's about the only good thing to happen to me this Christmas.

As for your second card – you'd obviously heard something of my Christmas plans. I have been with Antonella but not 'with' Antonella, if you get my drift. She and her boyfriend organised the whole farce I've been caught up in.

But who cares about that? I care about you. This is an I-like-you-too letter, an I-have-missed-you-like-crazy-and-want-you-like-crazy letter. An I-can't-forget-that-night letter. And definitely a yes-I-want-to-talk letter, and I'm sorry I was a jealous idiot about Adey.

My dearest darling Maddy . . . it is a love letter. Merry Christmas. Love,

Raff xx

PS: I'm standing outside in the snow. Please will you let me in?

Maddy read the missive with ever-widening eyes. She had to read the love letter line at least three times. Then her gaze dropped again to the postscript, and she fumbled to unlock the door and snatch it open.

Under the shelter of the porch Raff waited, snow on his hat and shoulders. The frozen air of the glittering world outside made her gasp, and she reached out and pulled him indoors, uncaring of the snow he brought in on his boots.

Unable to help the huge grin that seemed to take over her whole face, she whispered, 'Ruthie's asleep in there.' She pointed in the direction of Ruthie's door and lifted a finger to her lips.

'Merry Christmas,' he whispered. Silently, slowly, he leant forward and pressed a soft kiss to her cheek. By turning her head, she managed to catch the next one on her lips, hearing a low noise in his throat as their mouths met. Then she stepped into his arms as their kisses deepened. His mouth was hot, but the skin of his face was cold. He smelled of fresh air.

Somehow – still silently – they managed to keep their

mouths on each other as he picked her up and slowly spun her around. Maddy squeaked. Placing her mouth close to his ear, she hissed, 'You're snowy. It's melting into my dressing gown.'

With a grin, he returned her slippered feet gently to the floor and whipped off his hat, coat and boots. 'I walked from Docking,' he whispered. 'My car was almost out of fuel and the roads are treacherous. Google Maps said it would take a couple of hours, but it didn't know about the snow. It was more like two and a half.' Then he turned glittering eyes on her. 'Would we wake anyone if we talked in there?' He nodded in the direction of the front room.

Maddy took his hand. 'Better in my bedroom. Lyla's close by but she sleeps well.'

His grin told her he wasn't about to argue. Together they trod softly up the carpeted stairs until they gained her room, closing the door quietly behind them. Then, once again, he pulled her into his arms and just held her and held her. His warmth filtered through her, despite his snowy trek.

She murmured, 'We might be warmer under the duvet.'

'Shared body heat,' he agreed solemnly and withdrew enough to yank off his sweatshirt and shove down his jeans, until all he wore was his boxers and a thermal top. He glanced at her as if for permission, then gently undid the belt of her robe and pushed the fleece from her shoulders. His eyes smiled when he saw her black, star-spangled pyjamas with a goofy reindeer on the front.

By then, she was glad to throw back the duvet and bundle him beneath it. 'I'm really going to splash out on double glazing for the bedrooms,' she mumbled, burrowing into his arms and pressing her body against his.

Instantly he reacted, not just by tugging her closer but with an erection that headed straight for her. 'I rather like things as they are.' Stroking her hair down her back, his hand wandered on to cup a buttock.

She giggled but wasn't about to wipe out the past week of disappointment and worry because his happiness to be in bed with her was evident. 'Where have you been?'

He dropped a kiss on her head. 'At a writing retreat.' On a sigh, he loosened his embrace so they could see each other's faces. His lashes were dark around his blue eyes. 'My mood was low after I came back from Cornwall. I was in a jealous funk about you bringing Adey back here, and about how happy you'd looked about it. Then I hated myself for driving off and leaving you there, but I just couldn't get over the conviction that you should deal with the Adey situation first and then see where you were.'

'You could have told me that,' she reminded him levelly. 'Silence was rude. And hurtful,' she added.

His gaze never left hers, though he winced, and his arms tightened. 'Sorry. I painted myself into a mental corner. Then I got this email from my editor saying she was leaving, and it felt like the last straw. I wanted to finish the book in the hopes that she'd work on it before she leaves, and decided my Christmas was going to stink anyway, so I'd write through it. Then I got an email from Antonella about this writing retreat her boyfriend had organised.'

'Boyfriend?' she wondered aloud. 'Ffion didn't mention a boyfriend. She said you'd gone to spend Christmas with Antonella.'

He frowned. 'Maybe I wasn't very clear when I scribbled the note. Antonella has just signed a publishing deal of her own and said that the boyfriend, Cezary, didn't observe Christmas, and they had a group of friends who weren't festive either, so he'd hired this big house in the Pennines, and they were going to have an "Un-Christmas". Someone had dropped out and there was a cheap place available, so I said I'd take it. I've read about writing retreats on Facebook. People work all day and get loads done, then it's all writerly chat and too much wine in the evening.' He laughed, dropping a kiss on the end of her nose. 'But this was not like that, except for the work all day part, so at least I've finished my first draft. Cezary organised what he insisted was a "proper retreat", so he had the owner of the house take the Wi-Fi router away. We were halfway up a mountain, and it was terrible weather. I accidentally left my phone here on charge and, anyway, there was no mobile signal. We had to take turns to cook and, as it was Un-Christmas, there was no alcohol. I thought Un-Christmas would suit my mood, but it was terrible.'

He rolled his eyes. 'When Cezary and Antonella had a big row today because she'd bought turkey for lunch, I said I was leaving. She asked for a lift home because she'd driven up with Cezary and now they aren't speaking. Northants isn't exactly en route from the Pennines to Norfolk, but I couldn't leave her in that atmosphere.' He smothered a yawn. 'I feel as if I've been driving forever. Then the snow began. I dragged my arse home wanting nothing more than a shower, food and bed. Till I read your cards. Then decided to accept your invitation to come to The Hollies on Christmas Day,' he wound up, on a kiss. 'Sorry I was late.'

She smiled against his mouth. 'My Christmas was nicer than yours. Ffion and Chloe came.'

He drew back. 'Seriously? How did that come about?'

She told him how she and Ffion had come together on the subject of Ruthie, how joyful Ruthie had been, how Lyla had a girl-crush on her big cousin and that Chloe seemed fond of Lyla, too. She said, 'I felt odd when Ffion first talked about inviting Ruthie to her house for weekends and she accused me of being territorial. But I think it will be a good thing, not just for Ruthie but for me. It will give me and Lyla freedom to do things that Ruthie could never attempt, like hiking through the salt marshes. But, lovely as Christmas Day was, I couldn't enjoy it properly, because I hadn't heard from you. Ffion was worried because you were incommunicado.'

'I'll talk to her first thing,' he said guiltily. Then: 'I'm glad I'm here now. And I like hiking through salt marshes, too.'

She edged closer, so that her breasts pushed against him through their clothes. 'Adey's visit was awful. Lyla didn't take to him, though the door's open for them to see each other in the future, and he sent her a Christmas present.' She told him all about it, including the bust-up between Heloise and Harris.

'I knew Harris fancied you the first time I met him,' he said smugly. Then his hand slipped under her pyjama top at the back and his palm glided over her skin. 'Mm. It's toasty here, under your duvet.'

Mischievously she asked, 'Does that mean you don't want to take the rest of your clothes off?'

His hands reversed course and slipped into the waistband of her pyjama bottoms, smoothly sliding them down over her hips. 'I want to take your clothes off more. Truthfully, to get naked with you, I don't mind if we're rolling around in the snow.'

Maddy burst out laughing. 'Don't you think I've had enough of being the subject of gossip in Nelson's Bar?

I'd much rather roll around naked here.' And she began to slide his boxers down.

At the same moment, he murmured regretfully, 'I don't have a Christmas present for you.'

As he sprang free of the constraining material, she caught him, hot and heavy in her hand. 'I think you do. I've just unwrapped it.'

'Oh, yeah,' he growled happily, pulling at her pyjama top. 'And now I'll unwrap mine.'

Christmas Day slipped into Boxing Day marked by skin on skin, mouths on flesh, stroking, teasing, and loving. Really loving.

Maddy had fallen asleep. Raff could reach her bedside lamp to switch it off, but instead he just looked at her, breathing gently in his arms, her gold-flecked eyes closed. Her mass of dark hair tumbled around her.

She hadn't got back into her PJs and he snuggled the bedclothes around the beautiful white skin of her neck, wondering how she'd look with a tan when summer came to Nelson's Bar, and whether she'd freckle. He intended to be around to see it. He wanted to spend endless time with her. That would mean Lyla and Ruthie, too, but that was fine.

All his insecurities about whether you had to be related by blood to share your life with people had drained away. Love wasn't like that. You fell into it, whether that was romantically or via an adoption certificate. Ffion was his sister and Chloe his niece. But Maddy was his love, so it was a good thing that she was the one to share DNA with them, not him.

Finally, he closed his eyes and slept.

* * *

Boxing Day morning. Maddy woke in a haze of happiness at the discovery of warm male nakedness curled around her – swiftly followed by alarm as she heard Lyla downstairs, chattering, presumably to Ruthie.

A glance at the clock sent panic rippling through her. 'It's nearly nine. Lyla must have been up for ages.'

Raff smiled sleepily. 'Oh.'

'Yes, "oh",' she parroted.

He stretched and reached out to touch her breast. 'How are we going to explain me? Or should I sneak out and slog through the snow back to Docking without her seeing me?'

Maddy eyed him consideringly. 'Was last night a one-off?'

His brows snapped down. 'Not for me.'

Warmth tingled through her. 'Are we together?'

His smile reappeared. 'Yes, please. This Christmas is getting better.'

She ruffled his hair, thick and shiny. 'Then we'd better get dressed and go downstairs for breakfast. Expect a thousand questions from Lyla. But I'm OK to say you're my boyfriend now?'

'My favourite introduction,' he rumbled. 'Got a spare toothbrush?'

Soon they were joining Ruthie and Lyla at the kitchen table. They both sat with empty cereal bowls before them and were eating mince pies. It wasn't safe for Ruthie to cook, but she could feel her way through tipping milk and cereal into bowls. Lyla was wearing a pink heart glitter tattoo in the centre of her forehead. It looked like a big zit.

So that Ruthie wouldn't be alarmed at perceiving an unexpected person entering the room, Maddy announced casually, 'Raff's here.'

'Morning, dear,' said Ruthie composedly. 'Are we having coffee?'

Maddy nudged Raff in the direction of the table. 'Sit down. I'll boil the kettle. Would you like a drink, Lyla?'

Lyla gazed at Raff with interest while she munched her mince pie, a crumb perched on her chin and sugar on the tip of her nose. 'Juice please.' Then she turned her gaze on Maddy. 'If Daddy sent me presents, should I telephone to say thank you?'

Maddy had been about to offer Raff breakfast, but now pride in Lyla thinking of this for herself warred with anxiety. 'That's a good idea.' Perhaps Lyla had grown curious about her father. It was a cautious start, Adey sending a gift and Lyla saying thanks, but it was something to build on if they wanted to.

Lyla thrust out her hand and wiggled her fingers towards Maddy's jeans pocket, where her phone was usually kept. 'Can I do it now?'

'Now?' Maddy glanced at Raff, who had assumed a carefully neutral expression. She could take Lyla upstairs to make the call in privacy. But if Raff was her boyfriend now, as she intended to tell Lyla at an appropriate moment, he was going to have to deal with Adey. Jealous idiot moments couldn't be part of the landscape. 'OK.' She found 'Adey' in her contacts and when she heard the ringtone passed it to Lyla.

Lyla put the phone to her ear. Maddy hovered close and heard Adey answer with a cautious 'Maddy?'

'Um, no, this is Lyla on Mummy's phone,' Lyla said. Then she hesitated, her forehead puckering as she paused for thought.

'Merry Christmas,' came Adey's voice. 'Did you have a lovely time?'

Lyla managed, 'Yes,' before hurrying on. 'Thank you for my chocolate lolly maker and my tattoos. I love them.' Then she added chattily, 'Ffion and Chloe and Heloise came for Christmas. And Della for some of the time. And Raff was in Mummy's bed this morning and now we're having breakfast,' she rounded out. 'Bye then.' And she touched the red button to end the call.

Maddy's eyebrows leapt up into her hair as Lyla returned her phone. Had that just been a six-year-old knowing thanks were due for presents and burbling about whatever else floated to the top of her mind? Or had Lyla just given Adey a 'this is how it is' warning shot? Feebly and belatedly, she said, 'Raff's my boyfriend now.'

She glanced at him to see his eyes dancing and felt a reluctant grin tug at the corner of her mouth.

Ruthie said, 'That's lovely, dear. Really lovely. When he arrived so late last night, I had hopes.'

Maddy flushed to think that Ruthie had heard Raff's arrival, despite them creeping about.

'Is there any bacon in the fridge?' Ruthie went on. 'Raff looks to me like a bacon butty man, and I'm definitely a bacon butty woman.'

'Bacon butties!' cried Lyla. 'I like mine with tomato ketchup, Raff.'

'Me, too,' he said. And he sent Maddy a smile so wide that she knew he felt accepted.

'Ruthie and Lyla wouldn't share their bacon butties with just anyone,' she commented, to cement his feelings. Opening the fridge, she thought she must have sensed this breakfast coming, because when she'd bought the bacon, she'd bought a family pack.

Epilogue

My dearest, darling Maddy,

Our second Christmas together (I'm counting last year, even though I only arrived just before midnight). Love letters brought us together so I'm writing this to tuck in with your Christmas present and tell you how much I love you and being part of what you once referred to as your 'weird life'. I love living in Nelson's Bar with you and Lyla and Ruthie. I'm so lucky. Merry Christmas.

With all my love,
Raff xxxxx

Maddy read the note with tears in her eyes. 'Aw, you softy,' she murmured, planting a kiss on his cheek. It was early on Christmas morning, and they were still in bed. Raff had wanted them to exchange their personal gifts before going downstairs where the family gifts were piled beneath the tree. Maddy had been very happy to agree. They'd be going to Ffion and Chloe's house later. Ffion's surgery had been a great success and though, as she said, she wasn't about to start climbing mountains, she had some of her old energy back and colour in her face. This year, she'd been happy to be the one to host the family dinner.

'Open the present.' Raff nudged the gold-wrapped gift closer to Maddy, who'd put it down to read the note that had lain between the layers of pretty paper.

'OK.' Maddy opened the gold box . . . which contained a smaller box, then a smaller one inside that. The last box was red velvet. When she slowly flipped it open, she saw a ring, sparkling with sapphires. Heart thudding, she jerked up to look at Raff, feeling as if her heart must be in her eyes, surrounded by twinkle lights and shooting stars.

He slid his arm around her. 'Maddy, will you marry me? I want us to spend our lives together. Now the first book's doing well and I'm working on the second, I don't think I'm going to be a pauper.'

'Of course,' she said simply. How could he even think she might refuse? 'And I wouldn't care if you were a pauper.'

Several long, deep, drugging kisses later, Raff emerged almost as dewy-eyed as Maddy.

She slipped on the ring and admired it. 'And I won't be making pastry today, so I won't have to take it off. It's beautiful. Gorgeous. The most wonderful Christmas gift I've ever received. But now yours.'

She turned away to open her bedside drawer and fish out a long, narrow parcel. 'I have another gift for you, after this, but this is the special one. Great minds think alike, because I've written a letter for you, too. But open the parcel first.'

Raff felt it. 'Is it a pen?'

'Guess again.' Maddy sat up to watch him, her hair falling down her back, her eyes still burning with happy tears.

Raff did, frowning at the contents – a long, thin piece of white plastic with a small window at one end. A window that bore two blue lines. Dreamlike, he transferred his attention to the envelope that came with it, withdrawing the card with shaking fingers.

My dearest, darling Raff,
  I'M PREGNANT!
  Merry Christmas!
  All my love, always,
    Maddy xxxxxxxxxx

He looked up, his eyes full of love and joy and wonder. Gently, he pulled her to him. 'I think I'm the happiest man alive.'

'Me, too. Woman, I mean. My weird life is totally wonderful,' she choked, diving into his arms, and into the very best future she could ever have dreamed of.

Then the door burst open, and Lyla flew in, wearing elf ears and one fluffy slipper. 'Can I have my presents? It's Christmas – the best day.' She screeched to a halt, eyes wide in outrage. 'You've begun your presents already, when we haven't even had breakfast. And you won't let *me*.'

Maddy opened her arms to welcome her daughter as she landed on the bed with a bounce that made Raff say, 'Oof.'

'Sorry,' she said, meeting Raff's laughing eyes over Lyla's head. 'You're right. But this *is* the best Christmas ever. We couldn't wait to start.'

Loved

The Christmas Love Letters?

Then why not try one of Sue's
other cosy Christmas stories
or sizzling summer reads?

The perfect way to escape
the everyday.

Curl up with these feel-good
festive romances . . .

More heartwarming stories of love, friendship and Christmas magic!

Grab your sun hat, a cool glass of wine, and escape with these gloriously uplifting summer reads . . .

Dive into the summer holiday
that you'll never want to end . . .